John Lescroart is the author   ous novels
(sixteen *New York Times* bestsellers), including *The 13th Juror*,
Damage, *The Hunter*, and *The Ophelia Cut*. His books have
sold more than 10 million copies and have been translated
into twenty languages in seventy-five countries. He lives in
northern California.

Praise for the novels of John Lescroart:

'No one, attorney or not, can write a trial scene better than
John Lescroart' *New York Journal of Books*

'High-class . . . first-rate' *LA Times*

'*The Fall* is a tantalizing legal thriller' *Star Tribune*

'John Lescroart is one of the best thriller writers to come
down the pike' Larry King

'John Lescroart is a terrific writer' Jonathan Kellerman

'A riveting multi-layered complex legal crime thriller'
judithdcollinsconsulting.com

'Unusual in his ability to combine courthouse scenes, action
sequences and well-drawn characters that come together in
a fast-paced text' *Wall Street Journal*

'One smooth ride, and a fine legal thriller to boot'
Philadelphia Enquirer

'A master' *People* magazine

'   n-Times*

'   iness' *Examiner*

By John Lescroart

JOHN LESCROART
THE FALL

headline

First published in Great Britain in 2015 by
HEADLINE PUBLISHING GROUP

First published in paperback in 2016 by
HEADLINE PUBLISHING GROUP

1

Cataloguing in Publication Data is available from the British Library

ISBN 978 1 4722 3087 4

Typeset in Fairfield LT Std

Printed and bound by
CPI Group (UK) Ltd, Croydon, CR0 4YY

MIX
Paper from
responsible sources
FSC® C104740

Papers used by Headline are from well-managed forests and
other responsible sources.

HEADLINE PUBLISHING GROUP
An Hachette UK Company
Carmelite House
50 Victoria Embankment
London EC4Y 0DZ

www.headline.co.uk
www.hachette.co.uk

As always, to Lisa

A loving person lives in a loving world. A hostile person lives in a hostile world: everyone you meet is your mirror.
– Ken Keyes, Jr.

PART
ONE

1

THE BODY FELL straight out of the sky.

Those were the words in her original statement, and that was exactly how it had appeared to Robyn Owen. No foreshadowing, no warning. She had just turned right out of the Sutter-Stockton garage and was about to enter the tunnel when all at once the body fell out of the sky and landed on the hood of her brand-new Subaru. The head bounced against the windshield, shattering the safety glass into a spiderweb. Robyn had slammed on her brakes as she screamed. She'd been going fast enough to send the body flying, rag-doll fashion, what seemed an impossibly long distance in front of her.

The time was exactly 11:03 P.M. on her dashboard clock. She was leaving the parking garage after a nice dinner at Campton Place – and no, she was not drunk!, as she'd told the police officers about a hundred times, blowing into a breathalyzer twice to prove it.

Before turning, she had checked to her left for oncoming traffic in her lane and noted the car about a block down, coming toward her. This turned out to be the BMW that had tried to stop after Robyn had slammed on her own brakes, but still plowed into her after the impact. Robyn hadn't been speeding. The Beemer had not been speeding, either: It hadn't forced her to super-accelerate out into her lane; it was a normal safe distance from her when she had turned. Robyn did not lay rubber coming out of the garage. She couldn't have stopped or slowed to keep from hitting the woman, because she never saw her, never had even a hint of her existence, until she landed on the Subaru's hood. There hadn't been anything she could have done that would have led to a different outcome.

And who was going to pay for the repair to her car? Did insurance cover bodies that fell out of the sky? She suspected it did not.

2

AT ONE A.M. on what was now Thursday morning, San Francisco's police Homicide chief Devin Juhle rolled over in bed and said to Connie, 'It's no use. I'm not going back to sleep. I might as well go down.'

Connie didn't argue. When her husband felt he had to go to a crime scene, there was no stopping him. Although she wondered why his inspectors lately seemed to feel that they had to contact him as soon as they got a call that someone had been killed. They were the ones doing the initial investigating – Devin's job was mostly administration and coordination. Determining the basic facts of a case wasn't usually up to her husband, so she did not understand his need to be there. Back when he'd been an inspector, he'd tried never to call his lieutenant to a crime scene. It had been a matter of pride.

But the department had changed. The city had changed. Hell, their lives had changed, and her man was dressed now, heading out in the middle of the night to see about a dead person.

3

Two AND A half hours after the incident, traffic in both directions on Stockton Street inside the tunnel remained stopped. Gridlock prevailed downtown to the south and all the way up to North Beach. Devin Juhle knew his way downtown on Bush Street, but it didn't help him; he wound up having to park on the sidewalk all the way back on Leavenworth, six blocks away.

Yellow crime scene tape blocked off Bush above the tunnel, and Juhle held up his ID as he came up to the small knot of uniformed officers standing around. One of them directed him to take the second set of steps, which led down to the northbound side.

Before he started down, Juhle stopped at about the spot where he reasoned the victim must have gone over. Cars clogged the streets in every direction as far as he could see. Horns blared in staccato down below. Juhle looked down over the low parapet. It seemed to be about thirty feet to the asphalt below, maybe a little less. Although the rule of thumb was that you would survive a fall less than three times your height, it was an inexact formula at best. Juhle looked down again. If you were going to kill yourself by jumping, he thought, you should opt for a longer drop. Unless, of course, you wanted to kill yourself and decided to land on a car coming in this direction on the street below.

With the constant cacophony of car horns in his ears, Juhle followed the slick, steep concrete steps, over the old newspaper pages and the glittering glass shards – the remains of beer or liquor bottles – crackling under his feet. Halfway down, the passage widened and Juhle noted the sign high up on the wall, assuring him that for his protection, this area was under constant video surveillance.

Something to keep in mind, he told himself. He hoped it was actually true.

The second flight of steps, around to his right, brought him down to street level, and he took in the klieg-lit scene with a practiced eye. To his right, sixty or seventy feet away, what he presumed to be the body still lay surrounded by techs – measuring, photographing – on the asphalt in the middle of the lane inside the tunnel. In front of him, a late-model Subaru with a shattered windshield sat sideways, blocking both lanes, at a right angle to a BMW with a smashed front end. On the sidewalk inside the tunnel, a small group huddled around a young woman who sat wrapped in a blanket. The driver of the Subaru?

At Juhle's appearance at the bottom of the steps, Eric Waverly, the Homicide inspector who, along with his partner, Ken Yamashiro, had drawn the call, looked over and peeled off from the others. Waverly wore black: shoes, slacks, heavy down ski jacket. A boyish face seemed to belie his prematurely gray hair. He might have been any age up to forty-five – in fact, he was thirty-two, young for the Homicide detail.

As Waverly got close to his lieutenant, down in the tunnel, another car horn blared, prompting others to join in as Juhle nodded in greeting. 'We've got to get some of these cars out of here, Eric. This is insane.'

'I know. But there's no place to put 'em. The tunnel's packed. There's nowhere to turn around. What are you gonna do? At least I hear we've got people backing out the other side now. They're saying it ought to clear in another half hour or so. At least enough to get some tow guys in. But if I was a terrorist and ever wanted to shut down the city, this is where I'd start.'

'Good to know you have a contingency plan,' Juhle said. Shifting gears, he inclined his head up toward the victim. 'So what have we got?'

'Young black woman, probably under twenty-five, maybe younger. No ID.'

'Did she jump?'

'Maybe not. We've got a witness, one of the waiters at the Tunnel' – a restaurant at the corner up on Bush – 'who was cleaning up at one of his front tables. He says he heard a woman's scream, abruptly cut off, right before the squeal of tires down below, and then the sound of the car crash.' Waverly paused. 'If she screamed, she didn't jump.'

Juhle immediately realized this conclusion – that the woman did not jump but was murdered – was the reason Waverly had thought it wise to request his lieutenant's presence at the crime scene early in the process. For the past several months, Juhle's Homicide department, as well as the city's district attorney's office, had been defending themselves – separately and sometimes together – against mounting accusations that the PD was soft-pedaling investigations into, and the DA was mishandling trials of, killers of African-Americans.

In the last eight murders of African-Americans, the police had made no arrests. During the same time period, the district attorney had gone to trial six times to prosecute suspects in the homicides of African-Americans and gotten zero convictions. Logically, there was no connection between these facts – crimes that went to trial had happened years before the eight current murders. But to the public, there seemed to be a pattern.

Juhle did not know the reason for this anomaly, or even if there was one, but the plain fact remained that though the nonwhite-to-white murder rate in the city was nine to one, there had not been one successful murder case involving a black victim in the previous six months. Asian victims, yes;

Hispanic victims, yes; Pacific Islanders, several; whites, yes; but African-Americans, no.

A city supervisor with mayoral ambitions named Liam Goodman was riding this political magic carpet for all it was worth, talking about more than just cutting the Homicide budget. Juhle had heard rumors that the board of stupid-visors, at Goodman's urging, was actually discussing a whole-sale reshuffling of the detail, including Juhle's own job, a complete restructuring of the chain of command.

It was just politics, of course, but with serious implications for Juhle and his Homicide inspectors.

If this woman were a murder victim – and that appeared to be the early interpretation – then bringing her killer to justice would take on a whole new importance.

This would be a high-profile case before they even knew the victim's name.

4

As it turned out, four other witnesses came forward before the night was out. Taken together, they painted a very clear picture of a murder, not a suicide.

Zhang Jun was having a cigarette on the sidewalk during a break from his job in the cashier's office of the Sutter-Stockton garage. He saw Robyn Owen's Subaru make its turn and then heard the scream and the subsequent crash.

Up on Bush Street, Mercedes Johnson and her husband, Deion, were a block down toward Chinatown when they heard male and female voices raised in anger and saw what they said looked to be a fight of some kind at the top of the tunnel, punctuated by that scream. Immediately afterward, a man running down the opposite side of the street had passed them, although it was too dark to make any further identification.

The fourth witness was a homeless man who had settled down for the night on the midway landing of the stairway. The fighting above had woken him up, and after the scream and the crash, he'd gathered his stuff and found a recessed doorway to a convenience store down beyond the garage's Bush Street entrance, which was where the initial officers at the scene found him. This man's identity remained a mystery – he never identified himself, and after he'd told the officers what he'd seen, although instructed to remain there, he had wandered away into the milling crowd of stopped motorists, who were getting restless.

At a little after ten the next morning, Devin Juhle, who had been awake since an hour after midnight, was resting his eyes, his head on his arms. Someone knocked on his door. Straightening up and stifling a yawn, he told whomever it was to come in.

Waverly and Yamashiro, back from the lab where they had taken the young woman's fingerprints, were obviously pumped up from their success – the dead woman's name was Anlya Grace Paulson.

'An-LEE-ah?' Juhle asked. 'Another brand-new name I've never heard.'

'There you go,' Waverly said. 'Keeps you flexible. Anyway, she was seventeen years old, fingerprints in two separate databases – California driver's license and Child Protective Services.'

'CPS? She's a foster kid?' Juhle asked.

'Or was,' Yamashiro replied. 'Either way, we've got a home address. It's someplace to start.'

'It's a good place,' Juhle said. 'Don't let me keep you.'

'We just wanted you to know,' Waverly said. 'You said you particularly wanted to stay in the loop on this one.'

'And I do,' Juhle said. 'I remember.' He brushed some dust off his desk, frustrated with himself. 'Don't mind me. I'm barely awake. But you guys haven't slept, either, have you?'

'Not much,' Yamashiro replied.

'Well,' Juhle said, 'drive carefully.'

When his inspectors had left, closing his office door behind them, Juhle considered putting his head down again but resisted the temptation. Instead, he checked his watch – it should be late enough by now – and picked up his telephone.

'Hey, Treya,' he said to the district attorney's administrative assistant. 'This is Devin. Does his lordship have a minute this morning?'

'Maybe one. I'm expecting him momentarily, and his first meeting's at ten-thirty, so if you hustle on down, you might get lucky.'

'I'm on my way.'

5

Wes Farrell was closing in on four years as district attorney. During that time, he'd come to understand that the duties and responsibilities of the job were serious, and his day-to-day demeanor reflected the change in his worldview. When he'd run for the office, he'd worn his hair over his ears and taken pride in his informality – many days he wouldn't wear a coat or tie. He almost always sported a T-shirt with some wise-ass message, such as *How the heck did I get so sexy?* or *Yeah, you need gum.* He'd reveled in unveiling a new one to colleagues (and reporters) nearly every day.

Though rumor had it that the T-shirts remained in his arsenal, his public act had taken a strong turn toward the grown up. Now, with his Armani suits, Italian shoes, muted silk ties, and conservative coif, he cut an imposing, no-nonsense figure. Further burnishing the non-Bohemian image, he'd gotten married to Samantha Duncan, his longtime live-in girlfriend. He didn't like to admit it, but he'd come to believe that all this shallow, superficial, external stuff mattered, at least to enough people that bowing to the conventions was worth it if he wanted to get reelected to his fascinating and challenging job.

But all the externals in the world couldn't change the essential character of the man. When Treya waved Devin Juhle into Farrell's office this morning, the lieutenant was struck – as he almost always was – by the similarities between Farrell's office and the playrooms in his children's preschools.

Maybe, he thought, Farrell was really making the not so subtle statement that most of the people he entertained here were children.

There was no desk, for example. Farrell eschewed the hierarchy of the desk. He preferred low, comfortable chairs and couches, random seating arrangements (if any), and a wide assortment of games and sports paraphernalia – chess and checkerboards, a Nerf basketball setup, several baseball bats, some footballs, a dartboard. Buster Posey's jersey adorned the right-hand wall. Recently, Farrell had installed a Ping-Pong table to take the place of one of the library tables.

Juhle couldn't hold back a smile. 'I've got to get some of this stuff for my office.'

His suit coat draped next to him, Farrell sat perched on the remaining library table, a Nerf basketball in his hands. 'Beware of possessions,' he said, 'lest they come to possess you.'

Juhle kept his smile on. 'Thanks,' he said, 'I'll try to keep that in mind. But I'm thinking a dartboard, for example, might liven up some of the dull hours.'

'Except if you're not careful, it'll eat up your whole day. My favorite' – he held it up – 'is the classic Nerf ball. One or two shots, bam, the tension's gone. Even if you miss. Plus, if you miss with the Nerf, and you will, you don't have to deal with all those little holes in the wall. About which, trust me, Maintenance will give you hell.' Farrell boosted himself down to the floor, set, and pumped a shot at the basket he'd set up on the bookshelf, missing by a foot. Shrugging, he came out with his own 'what can you do' smile and extended his hand, which Juhle took. 'But I'm thinking that's not why you came to see me today. What's up?'

'Did you hear about the logjam in the tunnel last night?'

'I did. Somebody jumped, was that it?'

'Not exactly. We've got some witnesses now, and the consensus is the girl – a black girl – got pushed or thrown over during a fight. So it's probably a homicide, likely a murder.'

Farrell's eyebrows went up. 'Ah, another opportunity for you guys to drag your feet on your investigation and otherwise deny justice to the African-American community.'

'Pretty much, yeah. Just before you guys get another chance to blow the trial and fail to convict. To avoid all that, I thought you'd want to know about the bare facts tout suite.'

'Well, I appreciate that. But you say it was a fight?'

'Three witnesses say they heard a man and a woman fighting.'

Farrell frowned. 'So probably manslaughter, not murder.'

'I don't know about that. I just bring 'em in. You get to charge 'em.'

'Thanks for reminding me. I'm just saying it would be super-helpful if we could get to murder,' said Farrell with unmistakable irony. 'That would prove our commitment, wouldn't it? Going large on the charge. "Large on the charge" – that should be our motto on this.'

Juhle said, 'I'd settle for being able to charge somebody with something, and not have to write this off as an accident.'

'Anything resembling a suspect?'

'No. We've just now identified her by her prints. Her assailant was male, but that doesn't narrow things down a lot, does it?'

'Slightly less than half of humanity. It's something.' Farrell smiled again and let out a breath. 'Well,' he said, 'forewarned is forearmed.' He scrunched up his face. 'Is that how that saying goes?'

'Something like that, I think. But I know what you mean. Anyway, I've got a good team on it – Waverly and Yamashiro – and they're aware of the urgency, if you want to call it that.'

Farrell took a beat. 'You don't think JaMorris might be a little better?'

Juhle frowned at the suggestion. JaMorris Monroe was an excellent Homicide inspector but no better than the team already working the case; the difference was that JaMorris was black. 'As you know, Wes,' Juhle said, 'inspectors get assigned randomly. Eric and Kenny were on call and drew this one, so it's theirs.'

'Okay,' Farrell said, holding up his hands. 'Just sayin'. It was a thought.'

'I know, and not bad from one perspective, but this whole Liam Goodman crusade lately is bogus, and I'll be damned if I'm going to play that game.'

'You might get hammered for it if you don't.'

'I'll take that chance.'

'For that matter, I'll back you up. But it would be nice for both of us if we get ourselves a suspect identified in the next week or so.'

'Right. Yeah. Of course. But it ought to be the guy who actually did it, don't you think?'

Farrell nodded. 'In a perfect world, that would be preferable, I agree.'

6

A LAWYER NAMED Dismas Hardy slipped into the corner window booth at Boulevard, an upscale restaurant in the Audiffred Building at the corner of Mission and Embarcadero. It was a cool and sunny morning in the first week of May, and he'd walked briskly all the way down from his office on Sutter Street, ten minutes early for his lunch appointment. He settled into the comfortable leather seat and ordered a Hendrick's martini straight up.

Hardy normally didn't drink hard liquor at lunch, although he often had wine, but today was a bit of a special occasion – lunch with one of his former law partners – and he didn't think it would do him any harm. He had to be a little careful with alcohol because he was moonlighting a couple of nights a week at the Little Shamrock, the bar he co-owned out on Lincoln Way. If he had gin at lunch, and a couple of glasses of wine, and then went to the Shamrock and had a pop or two . . . well, it added up.

Back when he was just out of college, Hardy had joined the Marines. He'd gotten out of Vietnam alive, then become a cop in San Francisco while attending law school. After passing the bar, he'd worked for a year as an assistant district attorney. Then came what he called the lost years, spent in a semi-alcoholic haze while bartending at that same Little Shamrock after his first child had died in a crib accident and then – in the wake of that – after his first marriage had broken up. Ages twenty-nine to thirty-seven, gone.

He didn't want to go back there.

But today that didn't seem remotely likely.

Life had changed for Hardy since then in a way that made Wes Farrell's transformation seem comparatively trivial. Hardy had remarried successfully, now going on twenty-six years, to Frannie, whose child, Rebecca – 'The Beck' – was Hardy's adopted daughter. She was also the newest legal associate at his firm.

After The Beck's birth, he'd left bartending behind and gone back to work as a full-time lawyer, this time on the defense side. Frannie and he had a son together, Vincent, who was twenty-three years old and doing something at Facebook that Hardy didn't understand but that paid handsomely.

Hardy had won a lot of cases over the years, some of them nationally prominent. He had helped form a major city law firm – Freeman Farrell Hardy & Roake – and become its managing partner. In the past six years, the firm had shrunk from its all-time high of twenty-two lawyers and changed its name – it was now Hardy & Associates – but they were back up to an even dozen attorneys, and the work seemed to be flowing in.

So the martini wasn't a threat to him or his future. Not today. He took his first sip and almost laughed out loud, it was so outrageously delicious. Roses and cucumbers as botanicals. Who woulda thunk?

He raised his hand in a subdued greeting to one of his business clients across the restaurant by the entrance, then a minute later to one of the city's superior court judges, out with her husband. For a cultured and sophisticated city, San Francisco remained in many ways a small town, one of the things Hardy loved about it. He could not imagine living anywhere else.

He sipped again, closing his eyes to savor the drink, and when he opened them, Wes Farrell was making his way through the press of citizens, shaking hands here and there, heading toward Hardy, greeting him with a 'Yo.'

'Yo, yourself. I would have ordered you a drink if I thought you were going to be this close to on time.'

Farrell checked his watch. 'Am I not two minutes early?'

'My bad.'

'It certainly is. But luckily, here's Steven, just in time to slake my thirst and save you from my wrath.'

The waiter took Farrell's cocktail order, the tasty yet unfortunately named Negroni, and Hardy said, 'If I were a public figure such as yourself, I wouldn't order that drink on general principle. Somebody misinterprets or hears it wrong, and five minutes later, everybody thinks you're a racist.'

'If that happens, I'll just tell 'em I'm not, which, up until this year, my record clearly supports. Meanwhile, I get the drink I feel like drinking. Life's complicated enough. If they gave it another name, that's how I'd order it, but I think for now we're stuck with the one it's got.'

'Maybe we could start a campaign.'

'You go ahead. One campaign is plenty for me. Farrell for DA.' Steven arrived and set Farrell's glass down before him. 'Ah, just in time to drink to my reelection.' The men raised then clinked their glasses – 'Four more years!' – and sipped.

'So you're really going ahead?' Hardy asked.

'I never thought I wouldn't, to tell you the truth. The longer I'm in it, the more obvious it is that this is the job I was born to do. I'm just surprised it took me so long to realize it. Although some days, speaking of the job and racism . . .' Wes launched into a quick recital of the events of the previous night, concluding with Devin Juhle's entirely orthodox decision to leave the murder investigation in the hands of the non-black officers who had caught the case.

'You really think it would make any difference?' Hardy asked.

'You mean in the case itself? Hell, no. But in the perception that we're not putting the most motivated people on it . . .' He shrugged. 'I don't know. As if Waverly and Yamashiro aren't motivated. Christ! It's their job. These are skilled cops, seasoned inspectors, Diz. It's taken them years to make Homicide. Of course they're motivated. You don't think the PD has black inspectors investigating crimes with black victims?'

'I bet it does.'

'Damn straight.' Farrell took a breath, leaned back, and turned sideways in the banquette, his arm out along the top of it. 'What do they want us to do? Juhle needs a solid case before he can arrest anybody, and we need even more before we bring anybody to trial. Imagine the outcry if Homicide just beat the bushes and started bringing in suspects on little or no evidence. The damn thing is, we get accused of that, too. I mean, how do either of us win here? You tell me.'

Hardy cracked a small grin. 'I thought you loved the job.'

Farrell nodded in sheepish acknowledgment. 'I do. I know. I must be an adrenaline junkie, to add to the long list of my failings. But this is just a false crisis. Liam Goodman wants to be mayor. Here's this rich white dude holding himself up as the go-to empathy guy for poor black victims. My heart goes out to the victims, too. Their families, friends, everybody. Really.'

'I believe you.'

'As if I want murderers to get away with it. As if I don't care about black victims.'

'As if,' Hardy said.

Farrell reached for his drink. 'Go ahead,' he said, 'patronize me.'

Hardy kept his grin on. 'Just 'cause it's so much fun. But I do have a suggestion.'

'Shoot.'

'How about you put Abe on this thing?' Abe Glitsky was Hardy's best friend in the world and, after a long career in the SFPD, now an inspector in the DA's Investigations Unit. Glitsky was half-black. 'Make him a plenipotentiary grand poobah or something to oversee these investigations, or at least this one.'

Farrell considered the suggestion. 'Actually, Diz, that's not a completely goofy idea.' It was not unheard of for the DA to assign one of his own investigators to assist the regular police department. 'I get Juhle on board, then we both have ownership of the investigation. At least there'd be no finger-pointing between us about who wasn't doing the job right. It's an important homicide, we put on a united front. Who's going to criticize that?'

'Goodman will find a way,' Hardy said, 'but at least you'll be out in front of it.'

'I'll talk to Devin, get him on board. I'll be damned if I'm going to stab him in the back.'

'Spoken like a man with actual ethics.'

'Now, now,' Farrell said, 'let's not get all carried away.'

7

WAVERLY AND YAMASHIRO wasted some time trying to track down where Anlya lived. The address on her driver's license – apartment 5 in a building south of Geary Street on Divisadero – was no longer current. The resident in 3, an elderly woman who'd resided in the building for fifteen years, told them that Anlya and her brother had moved out a few years before. Anlya's parents had fought a lot and moved somewhere shortly after, she couldn't say where.

Since Anlya's fingerprints were also in the Child Protective Services database, Yamashiro put in a call to that office and left a message on a machine, the bored tones of which did not inspire confidence. Someone, the voice assured him, would be back with him shortly, a term of limited specificity that in this case turned out to be three hours.

So it was early afternoon before they had another couple of addresses – one at Anlya's mother's house down near Daly City, and another at a group foster home on McAllister near Webster, not too far from the address where they'd struck out earlier and in the general area where they still found themselves. The two inspectors knew that the medical examiner's office would be contacting Anlya's mother as next of kin, a task neither of them envied. They decided to start at McAllister Street instead.

The house was a large three-story Victorian, freshly painted in bright colors so that it stood out on the street as a welcoming spot. The two inspectors parked right in front and climbed the twenty-two concrete steps to the covered front porch, then rang the bell.

The woman who opened the door looked to be around fifty. Packing maybe forty extra pounds on her medium frame, she wore a green and yellow cotton dress over blue jeans; she also had an apron tied around her waist. Sporting a graying Afro, she identified herself as Nellie Grange. She exuded a weary serenity, but as soon as the inspectors introduced themselves, what seemed to be a hopeful kindness in her eyes faded to a dull acceptance of what she clearly knew would be bad news.

More bad news.

'Is this about Anlya?'

Waverly nodded. 'I'm afraid it is.'

Nodding, she said, 'She didn't come in last night, which sometime happen, but it always got me thinkin' the worst.'

Waverly came right out with it. 'Anlya's been in an accident. I'm so sorry to have to break it to you, but she's dead.'

Nellie shot a helpless look at both of them, then brought her hands up to her mouth, hung her head, and closed her eyes. 'Oh my Lord.'

Yamashiro asked if they could come in for a minute. She ushered them inside, where the large circular first room on the right was cheerfully bright due to its huge, curved glass windows. Surrounded by an assortment of mismatched chairs, an enormous circular wooden table filled the center of the room.

The inspectors took their seats next to each other, but Nellie remained standing, gripping the back of a chair. 'You mind I ask how it happen?'

'We're not completely sure,' Waverly said. 'She went over the parapet of the Sutter-Stockton tunnel downtown. There is some indication of a struggle.'

'So somebody pushed her? Off a tunnel?'

'We don't know that,' Waverly said. 'That's what we're trying to find out.'

'You're saying somebody killed her.'

'That's not definitely established,' Waverly said, 'but it appears that might be the case.'

Yamashiro took over. 'Do you know who she might have been with last night?'

'No.'

'She didn't have to sign out or anything like that?'

The caretaker shook her head. 'It's not like they're locked up.'

'What about a curfew?'

'None of that. We try to be home to these girls. They don't need no jailers or curfews, no lockup, just a room and a safe place to stay. There's not a single one of them bad.'

'How many girls live here, Ms Grange?' Yamashiro asked.

'We got eighteen . . . well, now seventeen.' The number seemed to catch in her throat. 'But we've been as high as twenty-three.'

'And what's the age range?'

'Nobody really comes here until they're fourteen. When they're eighteen, they're out of the program. So all of them are in that range.'

'Was Anlya close to any particular one of them? Or some of them?'

With a sigh, Nellie pulled out the chair she had been holding and sat on it. 'We all get along most of the time. But, you know, teenage girls . . .'

Yamashiro nodded. 'I've got two of 'em at home myself.'

'So you know. Some days . . . nothing anybody can do. But mostly they all good to each other, more like family.'

'Might Anlya have gone out with another of your girls last night?' Waverly asked.

'I don't know. Like I say, we don't keep track of them. They're free to come and go.'

Waverly kept the questions coming. 'Are any others of them here now?'

'No.'

'Do you know where they are?'

'Not for certain. Probably they're in school. They start getting home any time now.'

'Sometime in the near future we'll want to talk to each of them, if that's all right with you.'

'Fine with me. But I don't decide. You have to ask them one by one.'

Yamashiro asked, 'How long has Anlya been living here?'

'Just about a year and a half.'

'And how'd she wind up here?'

'Same as them all. She got delivered one day. Some trouble at her home, the CPS come and do the evaluation and take the kids, but by the time they get here, mostly I don't ask. Don't tell, neither. The point is, they're here and they're welcome.'

'We heard she has a brother,' Waverly said. 'Can you tell us anything about him?'

'Oh.' A fresh wash of emotion. 'That poor child. Her twin, you know. Max.'

'Do you know where he's staying?'

'With his auntie, I believe. Someplace in the city it must be, but I don't know where.'

'This auntie, she couldn't take Anlya, too?' Waverly asked.

'You mean to live with them? It ain't like it's free, you know, takin' on a child. Even if you getting some money from the foster people, that ain't going to cover it all,' Nellie said. 'His auntie, his actual blood, she took him, and there's a miracle by itself. But Anlya and Max, they still were seeing each other. Another miracle. He's come by here a few times. A good boy.' Running her hands through her hair, she spoke in a strangled voice. 'How does something like this happen? You want to tell me that?'

NELLIE WAS ACCURATE about when the girls would start showing up. The first one – Felicia Rios – came into the house in the next minute or two. After she heard the news, she walked halfway around the table before she shrugged out of her backpack and lowered herself onto a chair. She didn't cry, but the news clearly rocked her. She stared at Nellie, cast quick glances at the two inspectors. 'So,' she said, 'are you saying somebody killed her?'

Yamashiro nodded. 'We don't know. Was she a good friend of yours?'

She shrugged. 'I knew her okay. She was nice. We didn't hang out together much. She was older, you know.'

'How old are you?'

'Sixteen. But she's seventeen and a senior, and smart, way smarter than me. She helped me with homework sometimes. Helped everybody, really, whoever asked.'

'And did that happen frequently?' Waverly asked.

She lifted her shoulders, let them drop. 'If the timing worked. It wasn't like organized or anything, but we all knew we could go to her if we got stuck on stuff.' Suddenly, the enormity of it seemed to strike her. 'I mean, she's really just dead, and that's all? She's gone?'

Yamashiro nodded. 'I'm afraid she is. Did you see her last night, Felicia?'

'No.' The girl turned to Nellie. 'Was she even at dinner?'

Nellie frowned, trying to recall. 'I don't think so. I'm trying to think if she came home. I don't remember seeing her.'

'Honor might know,' Felicia volunteered.

'And Honor is?' Waverly asked.

'Honor Wilson,' Nellie said.

Felicia's expression clouded. 'Her BFF. Or used to be, anyway.'

The front door opened again – more teenage-girl chatter – and Nellie pushed back her chair and stood up with a sigh, on her way out to intercept them and convey the horrible news.

● ● ●

By the time Honor came in at a little past four o'clock, more than half of the places around the table were taken, and through some sort of social osmosis, nearly all of the girls were teary-eyed. The inspectors hadn't learned too much more about Anlya: Everyone seemed to agree that she was nice, smart, a bit of a loner, but always willing to chip in and help with homework or housekeeping. No one knew where she'd gone the previous night, whom she'd met, what she'd been doing downtown. The consensus was that she hadn't been home for dinner.

Honor stood out in the hall and took in the situation at a glance. 'What's going on?'

At the sound of her voice, Yamashiro did a double take, so different did Honor come across. Almost everyone else at the table was recognizably a teenage girl; they mostly reminded him of his own mid-teenage daughters. Honor Wilson, by contrast, was immediately and obviously a woman. He had assumed that the maximum age in the group home was eighteen – this was when people typically left the foster system to go out on their own – but he realized that there must be exceptions to the rule and that Honor must be one of them.

She was made up like a cover girl. Her hair looked as though it had been professionally done. There was no backpack, no sign that she'd just come in from a day in high school. She wore tight designer jeans, a leather jacket, and fashionable low-heeled shoes. Two gold chains encircled her neck. An emerald on one of those chains matched her earrings and plunged into an impressive cleavage.

She repeated her question. 'What's happening? What's going on here?'

As a chorus of sobs broke around the table, Nellie turned to face her. 'It's Anlya.'

'What's Anlya?' She waited impatiently, until all at once her eyes flashed and she slapped the wall next to the door with her palm, an enormous sound in the subdued space.

Adding to that, her voice doubled in volume. 'What the *hell*? What are you saying? Is she dead, is that it? Are you saying she's *dead*?'

Nellie nodded. 'She's dead, Honor.' Then 'This here is the Homicide police.'

Honor's eyes raked the table, maybe hoping for a different, better answer. Not getting one, she went still again, then with a small pained cry, she turned and ran off down the hallway.

A HALF HOUR later, Nellie persuaded Honor to come down and talk to the two Homicide policemen. They were here to investigate what had happened to Anlya, and surely, if Honor had information that might shed any light, she would want to share it with them, wouldn't she? They were here now. This would be the easiest, most convenient time to talk to them.

At last she agreed to come down.

For a little more privacy, Waverly and Yamashiro had moved to the room Nellie used as her office, not much more than a large closet behind the kitchen with one outside window, a wall half-full of cardboard packing boxes doubling as file cabinets, a bare lightbulb hanging from a wire in the ceiling, two wooden chairs on one side of a linoleum-topped kitchen table, and a saggy green love seat facing it on the other.

Honor came in, said hello, and closed the door behind her. Yamashiro was on the love seat and Waverly sat behind the table. She pulled out the only seat left for her, sat, and started right in. 'Anlya was my friend. I still can't believe it. But I don't know anything that could help you find out what happened to her.'

'So you don't know where she went last night?' Waverly asked.

'No.'

'One of the girls said that you two went out together.'

'That's not true. We left the house together. But then she

went wherever she was going, and I went to meet some friends.'

'She didn't say what she was doing?'

'No, but she'd gotten herself dolled up. I think she was going to meet a guy.'

'Do you know who?' Yamashiro asked.

'Not really, no.'

As Yamashiro had expected, Honor was totally unwilling to drop a name to the police. Nevertheless, he kept asking. 'She didn't have a regular boyfriend?'

'Not that I knew.'

'How about guys in her past?'

Honor's head tracked from side to side. 'Not really. I'm sorry.'

'Hey,' Waverly said, 'if you don't know, you don't know. Can you think of anything else you can tell us that might be helpful?'

'About last night?'

'About anything, really. If something had been bothering her. If her behavior had changed. Maybe something at school? Anything you can think of.'

Honor shook her head. 'She was just a normal girl. Somebody else here might know something, but it's all . . .' She shrugged. 'I just don't know anything.'

Waverly said, 'But you were best friends. If you wouldn't know about her, who would?'

Honor just looked at him.

Yamashiro spoke from the love seat. 'You know, Honor,' he began in a conversational tone, 'I've got a couple of daughters near your age at home. They're as different from each other as you can imagine, but if there's one true thing about both of them, it's that they know what's going on with the social lives of their friends. One of them or any of their friends has a boyfriend or gets a new one, it's topic number one. Somebody's having trouble at school, the word goes around. Somebody has a fight, or says something bitchy, or tells a secret they were supposed to keep, everybody knows before the sun goes down.

'I don't imagine things are so different here, which is why it doesn't feel like you're telling us what you know about Anlya. She must have had a life, and if you're her best friend, we've got to believe that you know a little something about it, at least more than you're telling us.'

'Somebody might have killed Anlya last night, Honor. I know that's scary for all of you here. You might even think you have an idea who it could have been, but you're afraid of what he might do to you if you talk to us. Okay, but I'm here to tell you that we can protect you. If you know something about Anlya that might have led to her death, anything at all, you won't necessarily have to give a formal statement about it. Nobody needs to know that you're involved. We're just looking for a place to start on this investigation, and it seems you might know something more that you're not telling us. Are you sure there isn't something? Any little thing?'

As he spoke, Honor's expression hardened until at the end it had completely clamped down, lips tight, brow drawn. 'I'm telling you the truth,' she said. 'We used to be better friends, but we haven't been that close for a year. I'm sorry she's dead, but we haven't really hung out in a while. I don't know what she was doing last night, or last week, or anything. Really. And you can either believe that or don't. Can I go now?'

Waverly nodded. 'Of course. But if you think of anything . . .'

But she was already out of her chair, turning for the door. 'Got it,' she said.

WHILE THE TWO inspectors were at Anlya's home, and since she had her own room, as long as Nellie didn't object, they decided to check it out.

It was not large. The wall across from the door had the room's only window, covered with white lace. Under that window squatted a three-drawer oak dresser with a runner of more white lace. On the lace, Anlya had framed pictures of a smiling young black man and a snapshot of a slightly older – mid-twenties? – white guy on a beach somewhere with the inscription, 'All My Love, G.' Also on the runner were a collection of small colorful beach stones in a jade jar; three votive candles, never lit, on small red plates; and an empty teak box. In lieu of a closet, Anlya had a wardrobe with a mirrored front along the right-hand wall. Her backpack, stuffed with schoolbooks, class binders, tennis shoes, a couple of pairs of plain white underwear, and a light sweater, huddled in the corner.

She had made her bed, pulling up a pale green comforter with the wrinkles patted out and squared off at the corners. The pillow was fluffed, perfectly centered on the bed, and covered with a lacy white case. Three books sat on a bedside table made out of cinder blocks and driftwood. A poster of Nelson Mandela hung on the wall over the bed's pillow; on the remaining wall, she had two other posters, Beyoncé and Obama.

Of the books on the bedside table, two were paperbacks – one of the *Twilight* books and Maya Angelou's *I Know Why the Caged Bird Sings* – and the other, at the bottom of the stack, was a leather-bound hardback. This turned out to be a diary and, from the looks of it, one that she'd written in nearly every day.

May 6, 2014

> *I decided that if I wanted him to really know me, and really love me for who I am, I had to tell G. all about what really happened with L., how far it went. G. needs to know that I'm damaged goods, not so that*

*he can forgive me, since it really wasn't my fault and
there's nothing to forgive, but just so he isn't under
any illusions, thinking I'm all young and don't know
what it's really all about. I mean, the whole thing of
having to be eighteen to be legal shouldn't really apply
to me since everything that could happen already has
happened, and when I was fourteen and fifteen.*

*I'm just still so surprised and happy that I have
these feelings of wanting to get together with G., that
I'm not just sickened and turned off forever by the
idea of sex because of how it was when L. was
hounding me. I feel like I've come out the other side
of this nightmare, that some kind of real life is going
to be possible, that some righteous man might find me
attractive and worthwhile.*

*I'm going to tell him tomorrow. How I really feel.
Not have him need to guess about it anymore. We
have a real date and we'll be alone and I know it
won't scare him off. If he needs to wait until I'm
eighteen, okay, we'll wait, but at least he'll know for
sure where I stand and we can take things from there.*

*Maybe we can even start living together when my
time runs out here.*

Hopes and more hopes.

'I'LL TELL YOU what,' Waverly said as they got into their car
after they'd finished their search, 'I'd like to have a talk with
this guy L., not to mention G.'

8

ABE GLITSKY WAS a lifelong policeman, and even in plain-clothes, all six feet two inches of him looked it. He weighed two hundred and twenty pounds and came across as rock-solid, no-nonsense, more than a bit sardonic. He'd been everything from patrolman to Homicide lieutenant to deputy chief of inspectors, and for the past few months – after a squabble with Vi Lapeer, the chief of police, had led to his resignation – he'd been nominally under Wes Farrell's command as an inspector with the DA's Investigative Division. Abe's father was Jewish, his mother had been African-American, and he split the difference about equally between them, with milk chocolate skin, kinky hair, blue eyes, and a prominent nose. Easily trumping all of his other distinguishing characteristics was the slash of white scar that ran top to bottom through his lips, which he let people believe was the result of a knife fight sometime in his misbegotten youth, although its true source had been a grade school playground accident on the climbing bars.

Glitsky's wife was Wes Farrell's administrative assistant, Treya. At the close of business, Wes came out of his door to find Abe sitting on the edge of Treya's desk.

'You busy?' Wes asked.

'Just putting some moves on this babe here.'

Wes said to Treya, 'If he's harassing you, I can have him arrested.'

'He hasn't crossed the line yet. I'll let you know.'

'Can I borrow him for five?'

'Ten if you want.'

'Hey!' Glitsky said. 'Do I get a vote here?'

Farrell held open his office door. 'I doubt it,' he said. 'Inside. Please.'

IN THE INNER sanctum, the door closed behind them, Glitsky picked up a handy football and tossed it absently hand to hand. 'What up?' he asked.

Farrell got right to it. 'You've heard about the young black woman who got killed last night at the Stockton tunnel?'

'Sure. Thrown off, I understand.'

'Right.' Wes ran down the details and concluded with a little riff on the quality of Juhle's staff, particularly Waverly and Yamashiro, and his confidence in them. By the time he finished, Abe had stopped tossing the football and lowered himself onto the arm of one of the love seats. 'It sounds to me as if they've got everything under control.'

'I'm sure they do.'

'Okay?'

With an embarrassed smile, Farrell said, 'I haven't run this by Juhle yet, but if he's good with the idea, what if I asked you to assist in this investigation?'

Abe frowned. 'You want to tell me why? I mean, it's not like I don't have my own cases. Besides, I used to be the boss of these guys, even Devin. It might be a little awkward. Why would they need a DA investigator? And why, specifically, me?'

'I'll bet you can guess.'

'The obvious strikes me as pretty offensive.'

'That's a good call. But sometimes ugly has a place.'

'And this is one of those times?'

'As a way to deflate Liam Goodman and his ilk? Yes.'

Glitsky made a face. 'Really? And me because I'm half black?'

'Not just that.'

'No? What's the other part, then?'

'You're a good cop. Everybody respects you.'

'Nice try, Wes, but not true. Vi Lapeer, our very own chief of police, hates me and thinks I'm a menace.'

'Okay. Not her. But everybody else. If you join the team, this office is actively aiding Juhle and the PD. So they won't be able to pick us apart as two separate entities.'

'Which we are.'

'Yes, but evidently, we – and by "we," I mean all of law enforcement in the city – don't care about justice for crimes perpetrated against black people. We don't put enough priority on finding and convicting the people who committed them. Finding is the cops. Convicting is us. Not really related, except in the public consciousness somehow, and putting you on the team addresses that issue. In fact, takes the teeth right out of it. We're all in it together, trying to get and convict the bad guys.'

'The idea that we don't care about crimes against black people? That's nonsense.'

'I know it is. But it doesn't stop people from believing it.'

'People believe in Santa Claus, too.'

'True,' Wes said, 'but not as many.'

9

MAX'S AUNTIE JUNEY was, in his opinion, the world's best person. She was a couple of years older than her messed-up sister, Sharla – Max and Anlya's mother. He'd been living with her in her tiny walk-up on Broderick ever since CPS had taken him and his sister from their mother and her boyfriend, who themselves had been embroiled in mind-altering substances and domestic violence as a way of life.

Max had some vestigial good feelings for his mother, but no recollection at all of his birth father, Daniel, and no *good* memories of his common-law stepfather, Leon, who was psychologically unbalanced, a crackhead, an alcoholic bully, and not least by a long shot, a child molester who had several times forced himself sexually on Anlya, threatening to kill her if she told, right under Sharla's nose.

Just over three years ago, Leon and Sharla had broken up, and shortly after that Leon had been arrested for the murder of one of his homies in a bar fight; he had been found mentally incompetent to stand trial. Since then he'd been institutionalized in the state's care at the Napa medical facility, where he would remain until he was found competent to face a trial, which Max thought unlikely because Leon was a complete whack job. Max believed that Leon being in custody made the world a better place. Leon had screwed up not only his and Anlya's life but his mother's as well, with drink and drugs. Sharla might never recover. At least Max had given up on believing she would.

But now he was building a good life with Auntie Juney, and in spite of all the awful stuff he'd endured, he considered himself one of the truly blessed. The only thing he sometimes still felt bad about, even a little guilty, was Juney taking him in and not Anlya. He knew that at first, when CPS had come to Juney as next of kin and asked if she would please consider taking the children for a day or two until they could find a permanent placement, Juney hadn't wanted to take either of them. He couldn't really blame her. After all, a single child-less high school dropout working the perfume counter at Sears didn't exactly bring home huge money. Neither did taking on a foster child – $761 a month wasn't close to what it cost to raise a teenager in San Francisco. Without some serious budgeting, lots of bulk foods, corner-cutting, and plain old doing without, it couldn't be done.

But Juney had taken them both in that first night. Anlya had been far more traumatized than Max. She'd curled in a blanket and cried quietly, silent and withdrawn. Max, wanting nothing more than to protect the twin sister he so loved – the closest person to him in the world – helped Juney prepare the mac and cheese and Oscar Mayer dogs for dinner, brewed tea for Anlya to sip, got her settled on the couch, and took the floor for himself. Before going to sleep, he had sat up talking to Juney for hours, adult to adult – though he'd been only sixteen and she thirty-seven or so – about what they were all going to do, how they would survive.

He hadn't been kissing up to her, trying to get the one possible spot at Juney's one-bedroom apartment – if there was one – for himself. It had never entered his mind that the system would separate twins.

And then on day three, the social workers had located an open room at the McAllister Street home, an all-girls' place not a half mile away. Anlya could move in there and be safe, surrounded by other girls and young women. Though it broke his heart while they were moving her, Max had been able to put a brave face on it, ignore his emotions, pretend that what was best for Anlya would be best for everyone, even if it meant the two of them splitting up.

They'd find a place nearby for him soon. Anlya should go to the new home while it had a room for her.

Back at Juney's apartment, after Anlya was gone, his auntie had come up behind him as he, tough and silent, had stared out the window, arms crossed, at the street down below. She'd put her arms around him and rocked him and told him it was okay, and he'd stood there leaning back against her, already about her size, and let the tears silently roll down his cheeks.

The next day, she called CPS and told them she'd keep him.

Now, a year and a half later, Thursday afternoon, he sat on their front stoop, waiting for his ride downtown.

He had beaten the odds already by getting this far. Who was to say his run of good luck might not continue? Especially now that he had a plan and a smart, dedicated friend to help him execute it. A bit of unbelievable, extraordinary luck.

It was weird, he thought as he waited for Greg Treadway – counting on him, believing in him, considering him a friend. It made no logical sense. Greg was ten years older and as white as Walt Disney. He had degrees from Berkeley and Stanford and now a job with Teach for America at Everett Middle School in the Mission District.

For the past fifteen months, he'd been Max's court-appointed special advocate, or CASA. When they'd first met, Max wasn't inclined to give Greg the time of day. He didn't need another social worker in his life, meddling. He and Auntie Juney had worked out their life together with very little help from anybody else. Why did he need a CASA, whatever the hell that was? Besides, these people, they were just doing their job, going through the motions, padding the résumé. It wasn't like they really cared or got involved emotionally or personally or anything like that.

Max had been spouting off in this vein to Greg when he came by to introduce himself. Why did they need him? Everything was working out all right without him. Max wasn't about to start believing that people like Greg or any of the CASAs really cared about him — it was just a job to them, and most of the time they mucked things up. How much did they pay Greg, anyhow? Maybe they could just give that money directly to him and Auntie, where it would do some good in the real world.

'Actually,' Greg had said, 'it's a volunteer position. I don't get anything for it.'

Which turned out to be true.

A CASA was exactly what the name said it was: a person who helped make sure that foster kids got treated fairly in family court. They were the voice of these kids, who typically couldn't afford and wouldn't get assigned an attorney, unless they had committed a crime. But if some bureaucrat decided, for example, that Auntie Juney's wasn't the right place for Max and he should be in a group home, he could bring his argument to Greg Treadway, who would help him plead his case before the court.

Or if they wanted to move him someplace else;

Or if he felt he didn't need to take his medication;

Or if he did need some;

Or if he was being molested or otherwise abused;

Or if, as was happening today, Max was going to plead for another three years of foster care monthly income for Auntie Juney.

Until recently, that money ended automatically in California on the child's eighteenth birthday. This put largely unskilled, often undereducated children out into the real world — to find a job, rent an apartment — at a time when they were unlikely to make it on their own. But lately, the court had been making more and more exceptions, extending benefits to some applicants until they turned twenty-one.

Still, it was by no means definite policy, and the bottom line was that unless Max (and Greg) could convince the family court that Max's situation merited this extension, they were going to cut off Juney's foster care stipend in three more months, when Max turned eighteen, before he'd even graduated from high school. If this happened, neither Max nor Juney knew how they could make it, continuing as they were.

Max, knowing his friend Greg was on his way, allowed himself to believe that something good could happen.

AND NOW HERE Greg was, pulling up in his powder blue Honda Fit. Max went around to the passenger side, opened the door, and, sliding into the front seat, sighed. 'Dude. Didn't we talk about this car? That it had to go. Wasn't you gettin' new wheels?'

'*Weren't* I getting new wheels, and no, I wasn't. I said I'd try. It didn't work out.' Pulling out into the street, Greg asked, 'How have you been?'

Still rolling with his 'tude, Max huffed, 'Better if we had a better ride.'

'How about no ride at all?'

'That'd be worse, but only just.'

'We're just going to have to bear up.'

'All right. I'll slump in the seat. That way, nobody see me,' Max said with a sly smile.

Greg had his own smile on. 'Nobody *will* see me. It's a good idea to put in all the words so people don't think you're ignorant.'

'Bustin' my chops now.'

'Only when necessary. We don't hang out for a while, and you fall into bad habits.'

'Either that, or I fall into consciously drawing you into an overly didactic response to a superficial touch of street argot, thereby exposing your own regrettable tendency to pontificate.'

Greg gave him an appreciative look. 'Or that,' he said.

Max was grinning broadly.

'Proud of yourself, are you?'

'Gotcha! You can't deny it.'

'I wouldn't even try. Those were some pretty good words.'

They drove in companionable silence for another block. 'So,' Max said, 'how do our chances look today? You have any idea?'

'My sense is that things are good. I can't think of any reason they might turn us down, but I don't want to get our hopes too high.' Greg threw over a sideways glance. 'Not to jinx us even more, but Anlya thinks it's a lock, too.'

'When did you talk to her?'

Greg shot him a quick impatient glance. 'You keeping tabs on my activities now?'

'Simple question, dude.'

Greg's eyes went back to the road. 'You're right. We went out last night. She was going stir-crazy, so she called me and I took her out for Chinese. She figures if you get the extension, she might as well go for it herself, and wanted to talk to me about that, too.'

'She *should* get it.'

'Of course. But she doesn't have a CASA, since Heidi quit on her, and she didn't want the opportunity to go by without applying. So she hit on me.'

'You wish.'

'Figuratively, Max, figuratively.'

'Jeez. Are we a little touchy today or what? I know figuratively, of course. What else would it be? Obvi.'

'Yeah, but some topics aren't great joking material. You hear me?'

'Duh.' After a short silence, Max went on. 'But for the record, I'd eat Chinese, too. Next time it comes up. Just in case you're going to Chinatown with, say, my sister, and you're thinking, "Hey, I wonder if Max would like to come with us." Just sayin' maybe he would.'

'Since we're just sayin', would he be paying for himself at this dinner? Because believe it or not, it costs more to take out two people than one. Besides, I knew I was seeing you today, and sometimes you can get too much of a good thing.'

'You're hurting me here.'

'You'll get over it.'

They stopped at a red light and Max asked, 'So how was she?'

'Not as good as she could be. Basically uptight and distracted. I worry about her, tell you the truth. She needs a CASA of her own instead of borrowing me for these piece-meal things.'

'Did she say what was bothering her?'

'No. As usual, she denied it was anything until I reminded her that she'd called me wanting to get out of her house, which kind of won that debate for me.'

'But she wouldn't say?'

Greg shook his head. 'I'm thinking it's girl stuff. Whatever it was last night, I'm going to put out the word down at the CASA office, try to set her up with one of the new volun-teers.'

'Why not you?'

'Because – and we've already done this today, remember? – I am a guy and she is a girl.'

'Yeah, but nobody's going to think anything funky about you and her. And you know her story. You could help her.'

Greg shook his head. 'I could, maybe. But she needs a female CASA.'

'Was she really in a bad way? Maybe I should call her, see what it was.'

'You can try, but I'd give it a day or two. She's probably all talked out for now.' They were pulling into the parking lot. 'I don't know if you'd get anywhere.'

10

ON A SLOW night at the Little Shamrock, the young man who'd pulled up a stool in front of the beer spigots ordered a black and tan – half Guinness stout and half Bass ale – and Dismas Hardy said, 'It'll take a few minutes, you know.'

'Got to.'

'Yes, it does.' Hardy grabbed and wiped clean an already spotless pint glass, tipped it under the Bass spigot, and carefully filled it to the halfway point. Then, picking up a bar spoon and inverting it over the ale, the 'tan' part, he pulled at the Guinness tap. The darker liquid, the 'black,' ran down over the back of the spoon – slowly, slowly – settling on the surface of the Bass and gradually filling the glass until the perfect creamy foam head hit its lip. The result was textbook: clear Bass underneath, Guinness floating above it.

Hardy gave his work a quick appreciative glance and slid it across the bar. 'Sláinte.'

'Well done,' the man said. 'And back at you.' He toasted, sipped, and said, 'Can I buy you one?'

It was six o'clock. Hardy had been on duty for about an hour. A half dozen other patrons claimed a table here, stools down the bar there. Outside the front window, a late splash of sunlight created long shadows from the cypress trees across the street in Golden Gate Park. The television droned quietly over the back bar behind him. 'I don't see how it could hurt,' he said. 'Thanks.'

Grabbing another pint glass, Hardy began again with the

routine. When he finished with the same results, he took his own sip, put the glass down, and extended his hand over the bar. 'Dismas Hardy.'

'Greg Treadway. Did you say Dismas?'

Hardy nodded. 'The good thief. Saint Dismas.' He spelled it out.

'I'm afraid I'm not familiar with him.'

'You're not alone. He was crucified next to Jesus. Dismas, another thief, and Jesus, the three of them up there on Calvary, all of them having a pretty bad day.'

'I'd say.'

'So the other thief – the bad thief – starts giving Jesus grief, as if things weren't shitty enough, and says if Jesus really is the king of the Jews, which is what it says there on his cross – what he's being punished for – why doesn't he order somebody to get them all down off these damn crosses? But Dismas stands up for Jesus against this other cretin and then asks Jesus to remember him when he comes into his kingdom. So Jesus says to Dismas: "Today you'll be with me in Paradise." ' Hardy drank off some Guinness. 'Anyway, that's the short version. The bottom line is that Dismas, in some traditions, is the first saint, and my parents must have liked the sound of the name.'

'Good story.' Half-turning, Greg scanned the bar. 'I like this place.'

'First time?'

'No. I stopped by with some guys a few weeks ago. But we hung out in the back room throwing darts the whole time. So I thought I'd come back and check out the front. It's cool.'

'It is. Especially given that it's a hundred and twenty years old.'

Greg's brows went up and Hardy filled in some history for him. In fact, the Little Shamrock was one of the oldest continuously operating bars in San Francisco. Some, including Hardy, put the opening date as early as 1893. The clock on the wall behind Greg had stopped during the Great Earthquake of 1906 and had never ticked again. The bar had stayed open during Prohibition by masquerading as a restaurant with a never-ending pot of beans in the front window and a cigar counter inside.

When Hardy finished, Greg said, 'If this bartending thing doesn't work out, you could be a history teacher.'

'I could,' Hardy said, 'but my law associates might run out of work.'

Greg straightened up in obvious surprise. 'You're a lawyer?'

'Most of the time. This hanging out behind the bar is how I try to preserve my humanity, such as it is. How about you? What do you do?'

'I am a teacher. Eighth grade.'

'That's real bravery.'

Greg shrugged. 'Somebody's got to do it. I'm with Teach for America now, so I'll probably only last a couple of years, but it's a good experience. I'm actually liking it most of the time. The kids are great.'

'I remember when my son was in seventh grade, I thought it was the worst time of his whole childhood. My daughter's, too, come to think of it. Seventh grade was hell.'

'Yeah, well, seventh grade is a whole different ball game from eighth. Seventh-graders are sadistic and mean, and then suddenly in eighth they get better, nobody knows why. It's a mystery. So, not to pry, but is it normal being a bartender if you're a lawyer?'

'Probably not, but I own half of this place, so I like to keep my hand in. I stopped worrying about what was normal a while ago.'

'Good idea.' Greg paused. 'I'm supposed to be a mechanical engineer. I got a master's at Stanford. So naturally, I'm teaching elementary math to eighth-graders.'

'There you go. My daughter, Rebecca, majored in English Lit, and now she's a lawyer working with her old man. I'm coming to the conclusion that there is no normal. There's just what you do.' Down the bar, Hardy saw an empty glass, said, 'Excuse me,' and walked over to see if his other customers needed him.

Hardy was turned to reach for a top-shelf bottle of Scotch when the door opened and a young woman came in wearing business clothes – gray skirt, low heels, trench coat. She wore very little makeup and didn't need it. A few freckles bridged her nose, and she wore an expression of upbeat expectation. Glancing up and seeing that Hardy was busy and facing the other way, she ran a hand through her shoulder-length reddish hair and shook it out, then shrugged and moved on.

She passed right behind Greg and continued a few more feet to the end of the bar, where she removed her coat, hanging it on a peg in the wall. Ducking under the bar, she reappeared behind the spigots, nodded at Greg, and pointed at his drink. 'Get you a refill?'

He pushed the glass toward her. 'Sure, thanks. Black and tan?'

'Comin' up.'

After watching her start another glass, he asked, 'Do they let just anybody get behind the bar here, or do you have to be a former English major now working as a lawyer named Rebecca?'

Her eyes narrowed before the answer dawned on her and she broke a sheepish smile. 'Did my daddy give you my birth date, too?'

'Not yet.'

And then her father was next to her, arm around her shoulders, planting a kiss on the top of her head. 'Hey, sweetie. I see you've met Greg.'

'We hadn't gotten to his name yet.' She turned to him. 'Hello, Greg.'

'Hello, Rebecca.'

●   ●   ●

FIVE MINUTES LATER, she was sitting next to him at the bar. She was in a bourbon phase and was sipping a Maker's Mark over a couple of ice cubes. 'It wasn't really anything I planned,' she was saying, 'except that when I graduated and looked at the job market, I realized I didn't have any skills, unless you count that I could read really well, and nobody seemed to care too much about that. So I figured, if nothing else, law school would give me three more years to look around and make up my mind about what I wanted to do.'

'That's pretty much what I'm doing now. Treading water, maybe doing some good for the kids, I don't know. But I'm done next year, and after that . . . real life, I suppose.' He lifted his glass.

'It's pretty funny, don't you think?' she said. 'Here we are, probably the most educated generation in history, and some-where along the line it's like we never figured out what we were supposed to do with all the stuff we know. If they'd told me that it's basically about being able to get a good job, I think I would have said, "That's it? A job? You mean maybe I ought to learn how to do something I can get paid for." Instead, I studied Milton. Milton! What are we supposed to do with Milton out in the real world? Can you tell me?'

'I'm afraid I cannot. Milton doesn't come up much in eighth-grade math.'

'Or anywhere else. Trust me.' Mid-sip, she stopped and put her glass down and focused on the TV. 'Uh-oh.' On the screen was Supervisor Liam Goodman, speaking into a bank of microphones. 'Dad,' she called, and when he turned, she pointed.

He came down and turned up the volume.

Goodman was in fine form, getting prime time, beating the usual drum. 'It's simple if we look back. Since the begin-ning of Wes Farrell's administration as DA, any objective observer would have to conclude that there is, at the very least, a demonstrable lack of prosecutorial zeal when it comes to trying the perpetrators of crimes against African-Americans in this city. Likewise, with the police department under Devin Juhle, we have a young African-American victim of a violent crime, and so far, no indication that there are any suspects, much less any kind of rigorous investigation . . .'

'Yeah,' Hardy said over the audio, 'and if Homicide does start pulling in witnesses and suspects willy-nilly, then watch this idiot come out busting them for profiling black people disproportionately. Isn't it great how this town can spin any set of facts to fit any political agenda? I'd like to get a few minutes alone with Mr Goodman and see if I can—'

Greg slammed his pint glass down. He was captured by the television, which had cut away from Goodman and was airing a photograph of last night's victim.

Rebecca reached over and put her hand on his arm. 'What is it?'

He couldn't tear himself away from the screen, staring as though perhaps trying to understand or memorize what he was seeing, or accept the possibility of it.

'Greg?' Rebecca said, squeezing his arm.

He glanced down at her hand, then brought his eyes up to meet hers.

'Are you all right?' she asked.

'No. I mean, not really,' he said, then added, 'Not even close.'

11

THE BECK TOOK over behind the bar for most of the hour it took Hardy to contact Devin Juhle, then for Juhle to locate Eric Waverly, and finally, for Waverly to appear in the Shamrock's doorway. Greg Treadway had totally rejected Waverly's suggestion that he go down to the Hall of Justice to give his statement. Greg was tired and very upset, and while he wanted to help, if they wanted to talk to him tonight, they would have to come to him. And Waverly had agreed. The priority was to do the interview promptly, and if that meant it was going to be sans Yamashiro, sometimes that was how it had to go.

The bar had filled up. Patrons filled every stool at the rail and crowded around the tables. Zac Brown was singing with his toes in the water, ass in the sand, and noise from the first round of darts was filtering in from the back room.

Hardy remained behind the bar. He had told Juhle he'd recognize Waverly on sight – he was confident that at the very least he'd know a Homicide cop when he saw one. This turned out to be true. And apparently, the recognition was mutual, as Waverly raised a hand and nodded to Hardy, who directed him by another nod toward the back, where Rebecca and Greg had repaired to a relatively quiet seating area near the restrooms – three low-slung easy chairs and an antique couch surrounded a stained and pitted coffee table, the whole small area dimly lit by a pair of Tiffany lamps.

Waverly wore jeans and a heavy sweater. Running shoes.

His hair was unkempt, eyes heavy and dolorous. He all but flopped into his chair.

Two minutes later, they'd done the introductions and Waverly had taken out his tape recorder, explaining that this was SOP. They taped everything in a murder investigation. He hoped Greg was okay with that.

'Sure,' Greg said. 'I called you, remember.'

'And we appreciate it.' Waverly set the device down on the table between them and reached over as if to turn it on.

Rebecca interrupted him. 'You really need the tape?' she asked. 'As Greg says, he called you. He's not a suspect, is he?'

Greg said, 'Of course I'm not a suspect.'

'I'm just asking,' Rebecca said.

Waverly sat back. 'We don't have any suspects yet. But if you don't mind, what is your relationship? The two of you?'

'I'm a lawyer, but I'm not his lawyer. He didn't hire me. In fact, we just met not much longer than an hour ago. He was having a drink at the bar, and we saw the picture of the dead girl on the news. When it came out that he'd had dinner with her last night, my dad insisted that he call you guys and tell you about it. Maybe Greg knows something that would be helpful. So he agreed, and my dad called your lieutenant and set this up.'

'Got it,' Waverly said. 'And we're glad you did. But we still need to tape.' He frowned and brought his right hand up, squeezing his temples.

'Are you hurting?' Rebecca asked. 'You don't look too good.'

Waverly managed a wan smile. 'Thirty-six hours without sleep can slow a guy down.'

Rebecca asked, 'Can I get you some coffee? Anything?'

'A gallon of Diet Coke?'

She hopped up. 'Give me a sec.'

The men, each worn down for his own reasons, followed her movements as she slipped under the bar rail and filled a glass with ice, then gave it a long shot from the bar gun. She walked farther down the bar to have a few words with her father. After the short discussion, she ducked under the rail again and was back with them. 'Here you go. On the house.'

Waverly thanked her, took a drink, and set the glass down. 'I have to say, Ms Hardy,' he began, 'if you're not Mr Treadway's lawyer, then he and I need to have this discussion together, just the two of us.'

Rebecca telegraphed some resignation. 'My dad told me you were going to say that.'

'No flies on him. But it really is the way we do it. And if you're not his lawyer . . .'

'All right. I get it.' She turned to Greg, 'I'll just be hanging up front. Good?'

Greg nodded, and Rebecca headed back toward the bar. 'I don't know what help I'm going to be to you,' Greg said to Waverly, 'but whatever I can do . . .'

'Let's just start with the basics,' Waverly said, reaching over to turn on the tape recorder. After his standard introduction – date and location of the interview, identification of his subject, his badge number, and so on – he began by asking how long Greg had known Anlya.

'A couple of years. My real connection to her is through her brother, Max.' Greg spent the next couple of minutes outlining the relationship that he'd developed with the twins, his involvement with Max as a CASA volunteer, the occasional field trip he got permission to take with both of them to ball games or museums, parks, wetlands, movies, films. 'They're great kids,' he said. 'I mean, were . . . I mean . . .' He hung his head.

'So what happened last night?' Waverly asked.

'She called me. She said she was going crazy at her home and needed to talk to somebody who wasn't a teenage girl. I hadn't taken her out alone in a few months – we used to have what we called date nights – and I didn't have any other plans, so I told her if she wanted, I could take her out to dinner in Chinatown. She loved Chinese. So I picked her up around the corner from her place . . .'

'Why was that?'

'Why was what?'

'Why you didn't pick her up where she lived?'

'The other girls would give her grief if they saw me picking her up – you know, an old white man and all – so I met her around the corner at our spot – we called it our secret spot – which was just the bus stop, but far enough away that nobody saw us together.'

'And where did you go to eat?'

'The Imperial Palace. Cheap and good.'

'Did she say what was bothering her?'

'No. I wish. I've been trying to think of what it might have been ever since I saw . . . saw her on the television. She did say she was going stir-crazy, but it seemed to me that something more, something else, was bothering her. Almost like she was afraid of something, but I couldn't get it out of her. She was the kind of girl where, you push her too hard, she shuts down. You kind of have to sneak up on her if you want to find things out, and I guess last night I didn't.'

Waverly lifted his soda. 'Do you remember what time you picked her up?'

'Five-thirty, quarter to six. It was still light out when we got to the restaurant.'

'And you stayed how long?'

'We were done by eight, I'm sure.'

'And then what?'

'Then we said good-bye.'

'You didn't drive her home?'

'No.'

'Was that unusual?'

'A little bit. I thought I was going to – I usually dropped her off at home on date nights – but she wanted to stay out awhile.'

'And do what?'

'She said shop. We were in Chinatown, and one of the girls in the house was evidently having a birthday, and she thought she'd find a present down there.'

'Did you offer to go with her?'

'No.'

'Why not?'

'Well, first, she didn't ask. We'd just spent a couple of hours talking, and I was somewhat frustrated that she wasn't telling me what was bothering her. She was getting snippy with me that I was pushing her a little. So the idea of us sitting in my car together for another half hour while I drove her home wasn't exactly appealing to either of us, I think. In any event, I had lesson plans to prepare and hadn't counted on making it a late night anyway.'

'So what did you do then? After you decided you weren't driving her home?'

The question seemed to stump Greg for a moment. Finally, he shrugged. 'Nothing. I mean, we said goodbye, gave each other a hug, and then I went and got my car and drove home.'

Waverly waited for a beat, then sat back and crossed an ankle over his knee. 'Did she give you any idea, while you were having this dinner, why she called you in the first place?'

'Well, yes, but it wasn't that. I mean, we settled that part early on.'

'And what part was that?'

Greg launched into a recounting of the foster exten-sion-of-benefits program, from eighteen to twenty-one, that he'd argued for Max just that very afternoon. Anlya had been hoping to return to her mother's home up until only a couple of months ago, hoping that Sharla had made strides in her battle with alcoholism.

Greg explained that the state's foster program liked to give formerly abusive or incompetent parents eighteen months to get rehabbed or otherwise straighten up their act, after which they could be reunited in their home with their children. Max was happy with Auntie Juney and didn't want to go back to Sharla's dysfunctional life, but Anlya had wanted to give her mother another try – she could move back in and the two of them could make it. Sharla would stay sober and Anlya would get a job or go to college, maybe both.

But when CPS had arrived to do the evaluation on Sharla, they found that she'd fallen off the wagon in a bad way (if indeed she'd ever been on it), so Anlya's dream of moving back in with her mother had been shattered. Psychologically, Greg said, this was probably bad enough, but 'worse, now she's turning eighteen in three months, and without an extension for her at her group home, she's out on her own with no high school diploma, no job, no place to live – although then she'd be eighteen, and if she wanted to, she could go back to her mom. But that would have been a disaster from the get-go. Sharla's not getting sober any time soon. So the clock was ticking, and it was a real mess.'

'And she wanted you to argue her case in family court?'

'Essentially, yes. I knew the basics because of Max. Her group home on McAllister is fairly well run, I gather. They could just extend her payments for another three years. At the very least, the extension would give her some time and a place to live. So I told her I'd get on it if they let me – for obvious reasons, they usually don't want a male CASA like me with a female juvenile – or I'd try to hook her up with a female CASA who could get it done.' Greg realized that he'd been talking for a while. 'In any event, that's what she'd called me about originally, but we covered all that in about the first fifteen minutes. After that, she just got more uptight.'

'And you don't have any clue what that might have been about?'

'No. I sensed she wasn't giving me the whole story about when she'd gone to see her mother. Pretty obviously, something else seemed to be going on, but she wouldn't say what it was.'

'What'd you make of that? After you'd already been talking, she just clammed up?'

'Well, as I've said, it kind of frustrated me, but when you deal with these social service kids and their problems, that's not unusual at all. They're always throwing something at you that you don't expect. So you either go with the flow or it burns you out. I figured she'd get around to telling me about it if it was important enough. I wish it had been. Or maybe it was and she just didn't see it. Or I asked the wrong questions.'

Changing tacks, Waverly asked, 'Was she carrying a purse when you picked her up?'

'I think so. I'm pretty sure. Why?'

'Because she didn't have an ID when we found her.'

'So,' Greg said, 'it could have been a mugging or a purse snatching gone bad. She fought back, they struggled, the guy threw her over the tunnel? Or something like that?'

'Not impossible,' Waverly said. 'It fits the facts as well as anything.'

12

HONOR WILSON SAT with her boyfriend, Royce Utlee, at the tiny table farthest away from both the cashier and the front door at Starbucks. She tried to keep her hands from shaking, but every time she picked up her coffee, the surface of the liquid betrayed her. She hadn't managed much more than a sip in the ten minutes they'd been sitting there, and when she put the cup down again, untouched, Royce moved up out of his slump on the tall stool and put his elbows on either side of his own cup. 'Damn, girl, what is it bothering you?'

'Nothing.'

'Nothing? You shaking so much, you like to spill coffee all over yourself.'

'I'm just cold.'

'First nothing. Then you cold.'

She just looked at him, flat-eyed, low affect.

'What?' he asked.

'Okay. Like I already told you. The police.'

'What about them?'

'Asking around, that's what. "Weren't you and Anlya best friends? How long you been best friends? You her best friend, how come you don't know nothing about her?"'

'That's making you shake?'

'No.' She picked up her cup and sipped. 'Just what I do know.'

'And what's that? That she try to break up our business?'

'Some of that, yeah. It's not like it was a secret at the house.'

'Nobody's gonna say anything. How's it help them if they do?'

'They find out who's trickin', they let 'em go on that if they tell something about Anlya.'

'They not lookin' at who's trickin', Hon.' He pronounced it to rhyme with John. 'Why they even gonna look for that when they tryin' to get who killed her?'

'They not gonna be lookin' at our business, Royce. They don't have to be lookin' for anything special. That's what I'm saying. Somebody's gonna get nervous, the po-po snooping around. "What you know about Anlya? What you know about Anlya and Honor? Who's this Royce dog we keep hearing about?" '

'Why they be hearing about me?'

She wanted to tell him to get real – there was no possibility that he didn't understand what she was saying – but that was the kind of response that made him lose his temper. She didn't want that. She didn't want him to take it out on her. Not that he had ever really mistreated her – he'd only hit her once before, when she'd asked for it. But she was afraid and knew she had to take care with what came out of her mouth, because he could go off at any time, without warning. She took a deep calming breath. 'Because,' she said, 'it's no secret in the house about you and me. Even the girls not working with us . . .'

'They better not be talking.'

'What I'm saying is we want to get out in front on that.'

'What do you mean?'

'I mean, I can tell 'em, get the word out, don't nobody be talking. We all just hang in there and say nothing, and pretty soon it all blows over and we get back in business.'

'You're saying for now we close up shop? That ain't happening, girl. It does, what do we do for scratch?'

'Couple of weeks is all, I'm thinking. We'd get by.'

'You'd get by, maybe. Me? What am I supposed to live on?'

'You get by, darlin'. What I'm sayin' is the main thing, we don't want no police thinking we had troubles with Anlya. They start thinking that . . .' She shrugged. 'It wouldn't be good. They start lookin' at you, they see maybe you got a reason, you already on strike one . . .'

'So they ask, we tell 'em we was together the whole night.'

'Which, you know, we weren't. What if that comes out?'

'How's it do that?'

She shrugged. 'All I'm sayin' is layin' low awhile can't hurt. We don't even want 'em lookin' this way. You know we don't.'

'So what about the girls? If they go out on they own, they never come back to me, then what?'

'That won't happen. I see to that. Plus, you take care of them, and they know it.' She reached over and put her hand over his. 'It's just better nobody's lookin'.'

AFTER DEVIN JUHLE had gotten the call from Dismas Hardy at the Shamrock and located Eric Waverly, he'd told his inspector to report back to him that night if it turned out that the new witness had anything important to say. Or even not so important. Foolish though it might seem, Juhle wanted to make sure that this investigation, wherever it led, was going to proceed with a greater than usual sense of urgency.

Whatever that meant.

As if there weren't always a sense of urgency about trying to identify and apprehend a suspect in a murder case. But Juhle wanted something he could point out in his defense if the criticism came up. No, *when* the criticism came up. He and his inspectors would be working around the clock if need be.

So when he finished the interview with Greg Treadway, Waverly called Juhle, as instructed. He did have something provocative to report. He hadn't been positive until he'd gotten back to his car and dug out the framed photograph of the guy on the beach from Anlya's room, but after he'd checked it, he was certain. 'G.,' the man who'd signed his picture with the inscription 'All my love,' was Greg Treadway. So there was undoubtedly a personal relationship between him and the victim.

When Waverly arrived at the lieutenant's house, his partner was already down in Juhle's finished basement, a comfortable low-ceilinged room with a pool table, a television, sagging shelves of paperback books, a coffee table, a leather couch, and upholstered chairs that had seen better days. Earlier, Juhle had tried to contact both partners, but Yamashiro hadn't been reachable on his cell phone – it turned out that one of his daughters was in the school play. But now here he was.

Urgent, indeed.

Connie Juhle made sure the men were happy with their coffees, and after she closed the door behind her, Waverly started right in. 'I don't know if there's too much real information to analyze. Okay, he knew the woman, but he never pretended he didn't. I didn't pick up any sense that the guy – Treadway – was hiding anything. If anything, he seemed like he really had just found out about it. In shock, almost. And he called us, remember? He came forward on his own.'

'And yet,' Yamashiro spoke up, 'Devin says he was accompanied by his lawyer.'

'A lawyer, but not his lawyer. She told me they'd just met, but I got the impression maybe she wouldn't mind being his girlfriend. Dismas Hardy's daughter.'

'Nevertheless,' Juhle said, 'a lawyer. He calls us and we show up and he's next to a lawyer.'

'I was there, guys,' Waverly said. 'I wouldn't make too much of it.'

Juhle nodded. 'Good enough. We'll try not to rush to judgment. Maybe you want to play the tape?'

'Sure.'

For most of the next hour, they finished their coffee and listened without comment. After the interview ended and Waverly had shut off the tape recorder, Juhle drew in a breath and said, 'So, it wasn't clear to me. What was Treadway's relationship to Anlya?'

'He's the CASA for her twin brother. So they got to know each other over the last couple of years.'

'Platonically?'

Waverly made a face. 'Unknown.'

'Really?' Juhle looked over to Yamashiro. 'Ken? You hear anything different?'

'When they went out, they called it a date night. They had their secret spot where they met up. He signed the picture of him "All my love." '

'Figures of speech,' Waverly said. 'He wouldn't have used those terms if he was trying to hide anything. He was very matter-of-fact about it.'

'But the fact remains,' Juhle said, 'he took this seventeen-year-old girl out for a dinner alone, just the two of them. The same one who, according to her diary, was going to tell him that she loved him. And then, as far as we know, he's the last person to have seen her alive.'

Showing some frustration at this direction, Waverly shook his head. 'Dev. That was like three hours before she went over the tunnel.'

'How do we know that?'

'What do you mean?'

'I mean, how do we know he wasn't with her until she went over?'

'His statement is that when they finished, he left her to go shopping.'

Yamashiro asked, 'He just left her in Chinatown on her own?'

'She was seventeen and wanted to go shopping. Why not?'

'Not saying it didn't happen,' Juhle said, 'but do we know what he did when he left her off?'

'He says he went home.'

Juhle prodded, 'Anybody see him? Does he have a room-mate?'

Waverly shook his head. 'You heard everything I got, Lieutenant. He doesn't have an alibi. Do I have to say again that this was a cooperating voluntary witness?'

'No, I got that, but I'm not sure we're looking at what we know the same way. You want to hear my equally plausible explanation of the facts as we know them? Probably not, but here goes: We've got a young male in a relationship with an even younger female, taking her out on what he calls a date night. They meet at their special spot, and he takes her out to a nice sit-down dinner in Chinatown. The very second the girl's death makes the television, he happens to be with a defense lawyer – hell, two defense lawyers.'

Waverly said, 'Who let him sit in the back with me and say whatever he wanted.'

Juhle held up his hand, acknowledging the valid point: Most experienced defense attorneys were reluctant to let their clients talk much during interviews with the police. But he wasn't finished. 'Finally, for all we know, Mr Treadway was the last person to see the victim alive. My point isn't that I think this guy's a slam-dunk suspect. It's more that there are a few real reasons to think he's simply a good citizen trying to help us out. He wouldn't be the first guy to try that head fake. And given our time frame here, it would really piss me off if we fell for it and lost a couple of days without looking any further at Mr Treadway. If in fact he was our guy.'

'I'm sorry, Lieutenant,' Waverly said. 'I don't believe I've heard anything about a specific time frame. So you're saying we've got one?'

'Essentially, yes,' Juhle said.

'What is it?' Yamashiro asked.

'Fast,' Juhle said.

A KNOCK ON Max's door.

It had to be his auntie. She was the only one in the apartment with him. But he had come into his room because he didn't think he could deal with anybody, even Juney.

How would he deal with anybody or anything ever again?

He still didn't know what to do, didn't know what, if anything, he was supposed to do, or feel, or think, or imagine.

Anlya was dead.

It had been only a couple of hours since they'd found out, but he didn't feel anything like the same person he'd been up until they'd gotten the news, Sharla calling Juney in hysterics right in the middle of supper. He'd sat there, getting the gist from Juney's side of the conversation, the meat loaf and gravy congealing on his plate, tears just flowing, then stopping, then flowing again, without any sound, with no passage of time. He didn't know he was crying, or when he stopped, or when he started again.

He looked up. Juney had gone off somewhere. She knew him enough to let him be. Nothing she could say would make any difference, and she knew that, so said nothing.

After a block of empty time, he somehow made his way the few steps from the kitchen to his bedroom and closed the door behind him. Over on his desk, there was Anlya's school picture in the frame he'd bought for it only a few weeks ago, she wearing that big heart-warming smile. Turning the picture facedown, he crossed back over the room, turned out the light, sat on his bed, and pulled the blankets up over his shoulders.

When the knock came, he was lying down, the comforter pulled up over him, so he must have gotten that way somehow, but he had no memory of it.

Another knock. 'Max.' She turned the knob and let in a sliver of the hallway's light.

He heard Greg's voice, a whisper. 'It's all right, Juney. I'll come back later.'

Max sat up. 'No,' he said, 'it's all right. Just a second.' He stood up and walked out into the hall.

Greg stood in the doorway to the kitchen, arms at his sides, his face drawn and slack. His head moved back and forth almost imperceptibly. Like Juney, Greg knew enough not to try to say anything when there was nothing to be said.

Max walked up and put his arms around his advocate. In Greg's tight embrace, for the first time since he'd gotten the news, he let a sob escape.

13

AT A LITTLE after ten A.M., Yamashiro and Waverly started where Bush Street met Grant Avenue, a couple of blocks from the murder scene, an intersection that, due to the ornate Gate of Chinatown archway over Grant, marked the more or less official southern boundary of Chinatown. At that time of the morning, business was getting into full swing, and most of the shop doors were open.

The inspectors had a picture of Anlya from her CPS file, and her school photo, which they'd gotten from Nellie Grange at the McAllister Street home. They had shown these to the workers in every place they walked into, and no one could say for sure whether the girl in the photographs, or any other black girl, had been in their shop on Wednesday night.

But when they got to the Imperial Palace, Fred Liu remembered the mixed-race couple perfectly. Fred was the maître d' for the restaurant's most busy time, which was the breakfast/brunch they were coming out of right now.

'Nights,' he said, 'it's just me and the chef, and I'm on tables. We're all about the dim sum here, which is morning. Nights are cheap Chinese food for the tourists – Kung Pao shrimp, hot and sour soup, General Tso's chicken, chop suey – and we are so slow, usually, it's almost not worth keeping the place open. But we're not open, we make no money at all, right?'

'You remember this couple?' Waverly asked.

'Hard to miss 'em,' Liu said. 'They were about the only customers. Plus, especially at the end, they were squabbling something fierce.'

'Squabbling?' Yamashiro asked.

Liu nodded. 'Fighting. Quietly, you know, intense. But you could tell. They were not happy. At the end, she was crying, then threw down her napkin and got up so fast she knocked her chair over and left it.'

The inspectors looked at each other. 'You mean left the chair on the floor?' Waverly asked.

'Yes. I came and set it back up.'

'Did she come back?'

'What do you mean?'

'I mean, back to the table.'

'No. The man, he paid and said he was sorry about the scene. His girlfriend was upset.'

'He called her his girlfriend?' Yamashiro asked.

'Yeah.'

'You're sure of that?'

Fred Liu looked at Waverly, squinted as though thinking hard, remembering. 'Maybe he just said, "She was upset." And I said something like "Girlfriends," and he said, "Yeah." '

'But,' Yamashiro asked, 'you had the impression that they were a couple? A romantic couple?'

Liu shrugged. 'Well, they were holding hands, at least before they started fighting.'

'And she never came back after she knocked over the chair?' Waverly asked.

'No.'

'For sure?'

'This time for sure. He paid the check, cash, and then left on his own.'

'Thank you,' Yamashiro said. 'You've been a big help.' He

turned and let Waverly fall in beside him. He held up his tape recorder, which, with Mr Liu's permission, had captured the entire interview. 'Got him,' he said.

AT 1:07 BY his desk clock, the intercom buzzed on Dismas Hardy's desk.

The only person who ever used the intercom was his secretary/receptionist, Phyllis. Hardy always purposefully paused for a second or two before he punched the 'reply' button; this afternoon he asked himself for the millionth time why he even had a receptionist. Surely he could pick up his own telephone when it rang, or open his office door when a client arrived. But the role of Phyllis and her place in the organization's culture had been set in stone long before by David Freeman, the firm's progenitor. That crucial role was controlling access to the managing partner, in this case Hardy, either by telephone or in person.

Fully nine times out of ten, perhaps more often, Hardy replied by saying, 'Yo.' He could tell from Phyllis's exasperated tone, *every single* time, that she hated this – it was not the serious tone one expected from a managing partner. And Hardy was just immature enough to keep on saying 'Yo' forever, so long as he got that response.

But this afternoon, he pushed the button and said on a wild hair, 'Yes, Phyllis, how can I help you?'

Her flustered pause while she dredged up an answer was its own reward. 'Um, it's – I mean, your daughter would like to see you if you have a moment.'

'My daughter, Rebecca? That one?'

'Yes, sir.'

As if Hardy had two or nine daughters. 'Well, as it happens, I do have a moment. But Phyllis?'

'Yes, sir.'

'I believe I've mentioned that when The Beck wants to come in and see me, except if I'm with somebody else, she gets to knock directly on my door and come on in.'

'I told her that, sir, and she said she wanted to make sure she wasn't interrupting you.'

'Some would call the intercom itself an interruption.'

'I'm sure they would. Should I send her in?'

'That would be nice, thank you.'

Even after all that, The Beck knocked twice quickly before she opened the door.

'Come in, for God's sake,' Hardy all but bellowed. When the door opened, he said, 'People have an easier time dropping in on Obama, I bet. Am I that terrifying a personage?'

Rebecca sat herself in one of the nicer chairs at the formal seating area in front of his desk. 'People who use the word "personage" instead of "person" when referring to themselves sometimes project an aura of authority that can make them appear frightening.'

Hardy broke a grin. 'Well stated. It's nice to know all that law school money wasn't wasted. So what's up?'

'Greg Treadway.'

'Ah, I had a feeling . . .'

The Beck was shaking her head. 'Not that.'

'It sure seemed there was some of that.'

Now she shrugged. 'The spark kind of went out the night when he learned about Anlya.'

'As well it should have.' But. 'He didn't ask for your number?'

'No. But I gave him my business card, and maybe a good thing I did, too. He was on my voicemail when I got back from lunch. Inspector Waverly and his partner wanted to come by and ask him some more questions.'

'After his taped interview last night? What about?'

'Evidently, stuff Waverly had forgotten to ask.'

Hardy's hackles went up at the ominous portent.

'What?' his daughter asked.

'Maybe nothing, but Waverly didn't get to Homicide by forgetting to ask things.'   .

'You're saying he thinks Greg might be, what, a person of interest here?'

Hardy shrugged.

'But that's not possible.' Rebecca's voice carried an edge of concern. 'He was devastated by the whole thing.'

'Could he have been faking that?'

'Daddy, Jesus!'

'No, then?'

'Not a chance in the world. How can you even think that?'

'We're in the criminal law business, Beck. If you don't think that, you're not doing your job. And he called you as a lawyer, I gather. Didn't you say that?'

'For advice, anyway.'

'That's as a lawyer, don't kid yourself. So what did Homicide want? Did the inspectors get to come by to see him?'

'I don't know. He just left me the message, and nobody answered when I called him back. Maybe I should put my cell number on my business card if people need to reach me outside of hours.'

'You could do that if you want, of course, but I believe you'd wind up working every waking minute every day for the rest of your life, not counting when clients woke you up in the middle of the night.'

She laughed. 'I already work all the time.'

'Yes, but you'd work even more. Maybe better to just write your cell number on your card once you've decided the potential client won't abuse it and call you every fifteen minutes, which some of them will, believe me.'

'You mean physically write it down in ink?'

'Ink, pencil, Magic Marker. Whatever.'

'Daddy, you are so old-fashioned.' Her laugh tinkled again. 'Ink? As if.'

BACK IN HER office, Rebecca called Greg's number again. 'I should have said this on my first message,' she said to his voicemail, 'but you might want to think about if you really want me there if these inspectors come to interview you again, if they haven't already. Last night I wasn't your lawyer. I was just another person you knew from the bar who happened to be an attorney. If I come to be with you, even to hold your hand next time, that's going to be a more difficult sell.

'The basic rule is the same: If you're being questioned about your involvement in a crime, even if you didn't have any part in it, you generally don't want to talk to the police without a lawyer in the room. Of course, I'm a lawyer. That's my perspective, and I would say that. But the plain fact is that the police agenda is almost never going to be the same as yours, and it's smarter to cover your bases. The foregoing advice,' she added in a lighter tone, 'is given gratis and should in no way be construed as an advertisement for my legal services. If you'd like to talk more before you make any decisions, I'm here.'

Hanging up, she pulled over the hard copy of the motion she was working on, booted up her computer, and was about to get back to her daily work – to be filed today by four o'clock! – when her telephone rang. She gave it a ring, then two, unsure whether she should pick up or let it go to voicemail so she could actually do something billable. God! the pressure! 'Shit,' she said matter-of-factly, and grabbed at the receiver. 'Rebecca Hardy.'

'Hey. This is Greg Treadway. Thanks for getting back to me. I'm on my afternoon break at school and just now got your messages.'

'So did you talk to Waverly again?'

'No. I told them I was at work. We made an appointment for after school.'

'At school?'

'Sure. We've got a conference room. It's private.'

'Did they say what it was about?'

'No. They just had a few more questions. Whatever it is,

it doesn't matter. Maybe I know something more than I'm aware of. If it'll help them find who killed Anlya . . .'

This was pure naïveté on the hoof, Rebecca thought. 'Have you thought of anything that you didn't mention last night?'

'Not really. But maybe something new will come up and prove to be important.'

Or maybe, she thought, you'll tell them something that will hang you. 'So, not to be aggressive, but what I said on my message, it's the truth. We know from Liam Goodman's little speech on TV yesterday that they're looking for a suspect—'

'They can't think that I'm—'

'They absolutely could, Greg. That's what I'm saying. My father just brought up the same point ten minutes ago in his office. If nothing else, they can use you as a placeholder until they focus on the real guy, but in the meantime, in the eyes of the public, you're the real guy. You will not enjoy that experience, I promise you.'

He hesitated. 'You're telling me I shouldn't talk to the inspectors?'

'Not necessarily. Then you're not being cooperative, and why would that be if you have nothing to hide?'

'So what am I supposed to do? What do you suggest?'

'I suggest,' she said, 'that you get yourself a lawyer and have him or her there with you.'

'How about "her" as in "you"?'

'I'm not pushing for the job here, Greg. I'm swamped with my regular work, though I appreciate your confidence in me. I could recommend—'

'But to whoever that is, I'd be a bona fide suspect, wouldn't I? I mean, a regular client who probably did it.'

This, Rebecca knew, was the unvarnished truth.

'I don't think I'd like to start off on that foot,' he said.

She sighed and said, 'You'd really want me?'

'You might not have been trying, but you sold me. How expensive are you, by the way?'

'Too. Meaning too expensive, not two hundred an hour. But I'd cut you a deal just to be a presence, at least until they decide they're going to leave you alone and move on. Say a hundred for this first interview, maybe two-fifty an hour if it goes any further.'

'Two-fifty an hour. I can't do two-fifty for an hour.'

'Don't worry, it'll probably only be the first hundred, assuming you don't get arrested. I can bring a standard retainer contract with me and make it official.'

'What if I — it sounds ridiculous even to say it — what if I . . . if they do arrest me? Could that really be possible?'

'Let's not worry about that now. All we want now is to be cooperative without saying anything that would incriminate you. Do you have an alibi, by the way, for Wednesday night around eleven o'clock?'

'An alibi?'

'You know. Where you were. If you were with somebody else, or in a public place where people could have seen you?'

'That's ridiculous. Eleven o'clock on a school night, I was home.'

'Can you prove it? Did you make any phone calls? Lend a neighbor some sugar, anything like that?'

'Rebecca. Repeat to yourself: "Eleven o'clock on a school night." I promise I was in bed. Alone, more's the pity. And I live by myself.'

'So "no" would be the alibi answer?'

'I guess so. And I've got to say, you're worrying me here.'

'I don't mean to. We just don't want to get surprised. What school are you at again?'

'Everett Middle. It's down in the Mission.'

'I'll find it. What time does school get out?'

'Three.'

'Okay, if they get there first — they probably won't, but

if – tell them you've brought me aboard, and then don't say a word until I get there. Not one word, even to be polite, 'cause they'll try to keep you talking, and you're not allowed to talk, lawyer's orders. You think you can do that?'

'It'll be a little weird, don't you think? "Hi, guys, come on in, but we can't talk." '

'Exactly.'

'Won't that make them even more suspicious, especially if they already are?'

'We don't care how it makes them feel. How they feel doesn't matter. I really need you to get this, Greg. It's serious.'

'I'm picking that up,' he said.

'Good. Don't drop it.'

'I DIDN'T KNOW what else to do. It just kind of happened.' Rebecca was standing in front of her father's desk, her eyes close to overflowing with tears. 'But I can't call him back now and get myself unhired. He's back in class and wouldn't get the message until Waverly is already there, and then he really would be screwed. Meanwhile, I've got this motion due at four o'clock, and now there's no chance I can even work on the rest of it, much less get it done, and I just—'

Hardy held up one hand. 'Shh . . . shh . . . easy now.' He came up out of his chair, around the desk, and took his daughter in his arms. 'It's all right. It's really all right.' He kissed the top of her head.

'I'm so sorry,' she went on. 'I just wasn't thinking, or thinking clearly, anyway. And now Amy's going to kill me, either that or never assign me work again . . .'

'I'll talk to Amy. She'll put another associate on it. It'll be fine.'

'But if I wasn't your daughter . . . and by *four o'clock* . . .'

'Well, luckily, you are my daughter. And we'll get an extension. Or not. Either way, it's not the end of the world. These things happen. You got involved in a client's real problem, and it has to be dealt with right now. So you do what you have to do. Welcome to criminal law.'

'I should have gotten Amy's permission first. I never should have just said I'd be there.'

'But you did say that. And now you're committed, and you'd better get moving if you don't want to be late. Here, why don't you give me your motion? Maybe I'll take a crack at it myself, see if I've still got the chops. And hey, look at the bright side – you're bringing aboard your first client.' He added, 'I hope he can afford you.'

'Well,' she said, 'that's another thing.' And told him about their salary negotiations.

'A hundred bucks?' Hardy asked with a stern glance. 'We're talking three hours, maybe four hours, for a hundred dollars total? Twenty-five an hour? Not finishing your motion is one thing, but charging below your billing rate, now we're talking problematic.'

'I didn't know what else to do. I didn't ever think he really wanted me there. But I knew somebody needed to be, so I—'

'Beck. Beck.' He raised her chin and kissed her forehead. 'I'm kidding, the old man trying to lighten things up. Really. But no joke. Your instincts are completely right. Get him on retainer to protect him. The guy needs help, and he wants you. So go help him, and we'll worry about all the other stuff later.'

'But—'

'No buts,' he said, pointing at the door. 'Go!'

14

THE INSPECTORS AND the lawyer were the first ones into the conference room, and they took their places on opposite sides of the table, which mostly filled the space. The Beck started out introducing herself to Yamashiro, adding a courteous enough greeting to Waverly, asking if he'd had a chance to catch up on his sleep. But the sense of low-key camaraderie with the inspector that she'd imagined from their previous night's interaction wasn't much in evidence today.

The inspectors couldn't hide their displeasure over the fact that Greg Treadway had lawyered up, though of course they didn't say anything about it. The object was to get him talking and then keep him talking, and Rebecca knew that. She was already on her guard.

Greg had struck her as a pretty trusting guy last night – almost dangerously so on the phone earlier – and she knew that the inspectors were under a great deal of pressure to come up with a plausible suspect in Anlya's murder. Put those two facts together and Greg's need for a lawyer was all but absolute, even if the evidence hadn't changed.

Except that the inspectors wanting to talk to him again meant that *something* had changed.

She was willing to see how this would go, but it was her job to keep her client on a short leash.

Greg opened the door. He entered with a smile, extending a hand for Waverly to shake. 'Hey, Inspector, how are you? Sorry I couldn't meet you earlier, but if I miss my classes, they fire me. Not really, but still.' He turned to Yamashiro, again with his hand out. 'How you doin'? I'm Greg Treadway.'

A friendly nod and a polite shake. 'Ken Yamashiro.'

'So I gather,' Greg said, including Rebecca while he cluelessly played host, 'you've all met one another.' He turned to her. 'Okay, what else do you need to know?'

Rebecca wondered if he could really be so unattuned to the basic reality he was facing. If not, it was a damn convincing display of disingenuousness. After an awkward moment of silence, Greg's gaze went around the room, his smile cooling by degrees, awareness dawning. But then, his inner jokester resurfacing, he came back to Rebecca with a sly personal look. 'So should I be talking to these guys?'

She realized with an almost physical start that he'd saved her not just from embarrassment but possibly from legal malpractice, and that this was the right answer. She didn't want him talking at all to these guys, not under these conditions, period. She hadn't even asked him about any of the details he'd disclosed in his taped interview the night before.

'Now that you mention it, maybe we should confer further before you make any other statements.' Turning to the inspectors, she said, 'Gentlemen, sorry to waste your trip out here, but I'll need time to talk to my client before he speaks with you. Meanwhile, let's remember that he initiated this communication with you. He's been nothing if not a cooperative witness, sharing whatever information he knows, and I anticipate that once we've had a chance to confer, he'll be happy to supply any further information that you may need.'

'And we appreciate that,' Waverly said. 'But we had just one or two quick questions come up that we thought he'd be able to clarify for us now.'

'All right,' Rebecca said. 'Let's try one.'

Waverly looked over at his partner, and Yamashiro nodded. 'Last night you said you left the Imperial Palace with Anlya at around eight o'clock. You gave her a hug and went and got your car. Thinking back on those moments now, is there anything you'd like to add?'

A lightning bolt of concern creased Greg's brow. It cleared as quickly as it had appeared, but it was all Rebecca needed to see to convince her that something about his story wasn't completely as he'd recounted it, and that the inspectors had come upon some new information. She spoke up, cutting off whatever might have been Greg's reply. 'You've got his statement from last night, Inspector. Have you talked to someone who's contradicted him?'

Waverly brushed her inquiry aside. 'Do you think you forgot something last night?'

Greg started to say something. 'Well, I—'

Rebecca held up a hand, stopping him. 'Uh-uh-uh. That's enough.'

'But—'

'No buts.' She turned to the inspectors. 'I'm afraid that my client will not be able to answer any more questions today.'

Again, Greg saying, 'But—'

'I'm sorry, Inspectors, but that's all he's going to say.'

'I know what you're doing,' Waverly tried to schmooze Rebecca, 'and I'm sure you believe it's in Mr Treadway's interest, but really, it's not.' He turned his attention to the client. 'We're all already out here together, sir. You can answer one or two simple questions and help us catch the person who killed Anlya, and then we'll be out of your hair, and that'll be the end of it. I'm sure that's what you want, to catch her killer. How could you not want that?'

Rebecca moved between Greg and Waverly. 'It is his choice to talk to you or not, and he's made it. Now, unless you're prepared to arrest him . . .'

Yamashiro groaned. 'We're talking a little clarification, that's all. We know he's cooperative. We just want to get the story right.'

'I'm sure you do, Inspector. But right now the right story and the only story is on tape, and it's the one he told last night. We're leaving it at that.'

Yamashiro appealed directly to Greg. 'Sir? Are you okay with this? This is not helping your situation.'

Rebecca whirled on him. 'That's really completely enough. I am not joking even a little here. My client isn't talking. End of story.'

For a few seconds, nobody spoke. Finally, Waverly shook his head in disgust and turned to grab the doorknob. Yamashiro followed his lead and straightened up. Leaving a flat hostile gaze in his wake, he said, 'Big mistake,' then turned and walked out on the heels of his partner.

EXUDING FRUSTRATION, REBECCA sat with her hands clasped on the table in front of her. Her client was directly across, his chair pushed away from the table, one leg crossed over the other, his back flat against the chair, as far away from her as he could get in the little, enclosed room.

'You were with me last night,' he was saying, 'when they showed Anlya on TV. You think I knew she was dead before that? You think I had any clue? You think that was an act? I don't know anything about what she did after she left me, which was like three hours before whatever happened. And by that time, I was home sleeping.'

Rebecca could hear blood flowing in her ears. She knew that her complexion was flushed. She felt light-headed, maybe near fainting, and the unexpected physical reaction frightened her. Fighting to keep her tone level, she said, 'But you didn't tell them the truth last night, did you? Did you think they wouldn't check out what you said?'

'I didn't—'

She cut him off. 'Never mind. Why don't we start with you telling me what you said last night and then where it deviates from the truth. No, first tell me why you'd agree to talk to the cops and then lie about anything having to do with a murder.'

He gave her the short version – the argument in the restaurant, Anlya knocking her chair over as she pushed away from the table. By the time he'd finished, he was completely deflated. 'The basics were all true,' he concluded. 'We were out from five to eight. I didn't see her after that. I wasn't anywhere near where she got killed when it happened. What else matters?'

'Well, clearly, something seemed to matter enough that you lied about it.'

He stared into the middle distance between them. 'We were holding hands over the table. I didn't think that would be particularly useful to the inspector.'

'So what was your relationship?' she asked. 'Was it intimate?'

He nearly jumped. 'No. Christ. She was a mixed-up kid, and she was only seventeen. I'm not getting involved with a teenager.'

'But you were holding hands?'

He dredged up a frustrated sigh. 'I was telling her how I'd try to get her foster extension, either myself or another CASA. But I'd really try to go to bat for her if I could, which was my plan. And she reached out and put her hand on top of mine. So what am I going to do, freak out and pull it away? No, I just decide to let it stay there, and next thing you know, she picks up my hand and kisses it and tells me she's in love with me.'

'So why didn't you tell the inspector that last night?'

'Because I didn't want to confuse things with stuff that didn't matter.'

'You've already said that. It didn't matter.'

'I'll say it again if you want. It didn't matter. That was the truth. And by the way, if you remember, it wasn't exactly my idea to call up Homicide and tell them I needed to talk to them. But when your dad was so adamant about it, what was I supposed to say: I don't want to be involved? Of course I wanted to be involved. If I could help . . . I don't know . . . somehow . . . it seemed like a reasonable idea.

'And if I said no to your dad, how weird would that look? I'm innocent but I don't want to say anything about it? I didn't want to tell the cops what I knew about Anlya's last night? Why not? So I went along with the basic idea.'

'Greg, you don't get to decide what matters. Any time you lie, even tell a half-truth, to the police in a murder investigation, it matters a lot. And you didn't tell the whole truth.'

He shrugged. 'I didn't want the guy thinking there was something personal between me and Anlya when, A, there wasn't, and, B, even if there was, it had nothing to do with her death.'

'How do you know that?'

'Because it didn't. It couldn't have.'

Rebecca's knuckles were white. She unclasped her hands, met her client's eyes. 'I wish,' she said, 'that you'd mentioned this last night. So what was the fight about?'

'It wasn't really a fight.'

'Okay, whatever you call it. You just told me she was upset enough to bolt out of the place, is that right?'

'When I didn't come right back and tell her I loved her, too . . . Hell, I told her she was special, you know, and a great person, but I didn't have those kinds of feelings for her, and I don't, didn't . . .' He scratched at the wooden tabletop.

'What?'

'Well, you know, so here's this high-strung, very pretty seventeen-year-old girl who's been abused as a child by her mother's boyfriend . . .'

'I hadn't heard about that.'

'It wasn't something she bragged about, but there's no doubt it happened, though the asshole never got charged, or even investigated, I don't think, which happens when the mother is a complete loser and . . .' He let a breath escape. 'Anyway, old familiar story. The point is, she felt worthless and rejected, and especially when the rejection is personal, it tends to hit her pretty hard, and she lashes out.'

'And she lashed out at you?'

Nodding, he said, 'She got a little crazy about how I'd been leading her on . . . I mean, why else have our date nights? And why did I sign my picture to her "All my love?"'

'Wait. You did what?'

He shrugged. 'She signed one of her for me. I signed back one of me for her. But it was make-believe.'

Rebecca closed her eyes and shook her head.

'Anyway,' he went on, 'she asked me why was I doing all this stuff to help her if I didn't love her.' He brought his hands to his face and dragged them down over his cheeks. 'She got herself into a tizzy. I was a liar and unfair and a horrible human being because I didn't want to be with her. It was a bad night all around.'

'It was worse for her, I promise,' Rebecca said. 'Way worse.'

MAX COULDN'T FACE the day at school. He'd only gotten to sleep around dawn. When he forced himself to roll out of bed after eleven, Juney had already gone off to work, so he rattled around in the apartment for an hour or so, scrambled up some eggs, took a shower.

Cried some more.

Without ever making the conscious decision to go there, he found himself down in his mother's neighborhood near the Daly City border.

Sharla's place was a yellowing stucco duplex in a depressing row of similar places – bars on the windows, metal over the doors. The unkempt or nonexistent lawns gave the entire block a deserted feel. The few cars at the curbs were almost uniformly decrepit, older models with bashed fenders, duct-taped windows, and faded paint jobs. A feeble early-afternoon sun shone, and the wind was up, blowing debris like tumbleweeds across the landscape.

Max stood at the corner, his jacket zipped, collar up, and had no idea why he'd come out here. He tried to remember living on this block and couldn't dredge up any kind of good feeling for the place. The whole time, they'd lived in fear and confusion – his mama drinking or partying, Leon looming, an unpredictable and terrifying presence to Max and worse for Anlya, a fact she could never bring herself to talk about until after everything terrifying that they'd feared – her own sexual molestation; she and Max separated, relocated; Mama broken down, addicted – had already come to pass.

The wind at his back seemed to prod him to move forward. He stood for a minute or two on the sidewalk right in front of the duplex, then walked up the cracked concrete path to the front door and rang the bell. He was about to ring again when he heard footsteps. 'Who is it?'

'It's Max, Mama.'

The inner door opened, then the metal outer one. Her eyes betrayed drink or lack of sleep or both, but she clearly was surprised and moved by his appearance here on her stoop. 'Oh, my baby.' Stepping forward, Sharla brought her arms up around him. He hugged her back and they stood, holding each other. After a moment, she started to cry and he patted her back until she pulled away enough to focus and see him. She brought a hand up to his face. 'How we gonna get through this now?'

15

Dismas Hardy stood in his daughter's office and said, 'I feel guilty about this, to tell you the truth. I shouldn't have meddled and stuck in my two cents. And just possibly, I shouldn't have been so pushy about him getting in touch with the police.'

'Of course you should have,' Rebecca said. 'Since he didn't believe anybody could ever think he killed her, he never thought he'd be a suspect. But your call, Dad, was absolutely the right thing to do. If Greg hadn't agreed, or you hadn't called Juhle, when they eventually tracked him down, that would have really rung bells, wouldn't it? And there's no way he wasn't completely stunned when he saw her picture on the tube. You were there, you saw him. He was in pure shock. He had no idea she was dead, much less murdered.'

'I thought so, too. And so why, again, did he feel like he had to lie to Waverly?'

Rebecca shook her head. 'I know. So stupid. People who haven't ever dealt with the cops don't get how serious it gets, and how fast, do they? And Greg could be the poster child for that. Everything he lied about was three hours before Anlya was killed, and he was in bed sleeping when that happened, so why did the details of their dinner matter? And he's right. They don't matter.'

'But what does matter is lying,' Hardy said. 'Now they think he's a liar, and therefore, no matter what he says, it's suspect. "What upsets me is not that you lied to me, but that from now on I can no longer believe you." Nietzsche said that.'

'Of course he did,' The Beck replied. 'Everybody knows that. I was going to say it next, and you beat me to it.'

Hardy grinned at her. 'I can't help it if I remember things.'

'I know. It's cute. But the fact remains, they don't believe him anymore.'

'Being his brilliant lawyer, you didn't let him put any lies on the record, correct?'

'Correct.'

'So you did the right thing, too.'

'Then why do I feel so terrible?'

Hardy knew that answer. 'Because you let him down. You made a rookie mistake. Right at the beginning, last night before Waverly even got there, you should have, if nothing else, impressed on him that he shouldn't lie to the cops.'

'It never occurred to me that he would.'

'No. I know. But you were assuming that he was innocent.'

'I still am.'

'Fine. Even so, as a lawyer, you've got to give him the advice he needs that will protect him if he's not. That's the job.'

'So what should I do now? What's the strategy? Just keep stonewalling the inspectors?'

Hardy almost broke a grin. He loved his daughter, and loved this legal give-and-take with her. She was going to be a monster talent one day. 'I know what I'd do, but it's going to be your decision. But before we go there, can I tell you a little story?'

'As long as it's billable?' Obviously teasing him. 'Sure.'

'It's about Graham.' This was Graham Russo, one of the firm's shareholders, whom Rebecca knew very well. 'I know you've heard the story about how we met, Graham and I. He was charged with killing his father, Sal.'

'Mercy killing, right? His father had Alzheimer's.'

'Right, but still completely illegal if he'd done it, which of course he hadn't. But nobody knew that when they arrested him. So while he's becoming the big-time suspect, what does he do but get involved with Sarah Evans, the female inspector working the case, who is now his wife of many years.

'And the whole time I'm telling him what you've been telling Greg, which is shut up around the cops. Don't answer any questions. Don't give them any ideas. Let your lawyer do all the talking or you can get yourself in some deep and unnecessary shit. Of course, he completely ignored my every word and got himself into the aforementioned deep and unnecessary shit.

'My point is that his talking to Sarah against my expert advice is not only what saved his ass at the trial but also what hooked him up with the love of his life. Like your friend Greg, he didn't get that somebody really thought he could have killed anybody. That was just off his radar. And that's probably the main reason why I decided to stick with him after he got arrested. He simply didn't do it. It was obvious to me. He was already a lawyer himself and knew the rules, but he decided that he needed to break them.'

'So he talked to Sarah, okay. But did he lie to her?'

'Only about a hundred times. In fact, the greatest moment in the trial was when Sarah got called for the prosecution, and they ran down a litany of all the lies Graham had told during the investigation. Then David Freeman – God bless his soul – took her on cross and asked only one question: Did she think Graham was trustworthy? Without any hesitation, she said yes. The courtroom went berserk. It was beautiful.'

'The judge let that in?'

'It happened so fast, it was over before anybody thought to object. They objected afterward, of course, and even got sustained, but by then it didn't matter. The jury had heard it. It turned the whole trial.'

'So the moral is lie to the cops and ignore your lawyer's instructions?'

'No. The moral is that truly innocent people get caught up in this stuff before they understand what's going on, and until they get their feet a little wet, they're going to make strategic mistakes, which it probably behooves you to forgive or ignore or both. We're not talking moral turpitude here. We're talking a white lie to save everybody some needless grief and confusion.'

'Okay, so what do I do now?'

'As I say, anything you're comfortable with. Drop Greg as a client. Bail out of the whole situation. Find him another lawyer. I'll tell you what I'd do. I'd get the inspectors back on the line ASAP and tell them your client is through talking to them, but if there's any information they want, you'll pass the question on to Mr Treadway and get back to them.'

'Then what I tell them will be hearsay, and they can't use it.'

'Good about the hearsay part. But not quite correct about if they can use it.'

'No judge would—'

Hardy stopped her. 'I'm not talking about what might happen at trial. I'm talking about their theory of the case. They can simply wind up believing what you tell them. It wouldn't be admissible in court, but there's nothing stopping you – that's you, Rebecca, not Greg – from going back to them and answering their questions in full, including the reason for the inconsistencies with last night's story.'

'Admit that he lied?'

'Right. You know why? Because they won't care if he lied. They're looking for the person who killed Anlya, for real evidence. Anything else, so what? Greg's reasons for not telling the whole truth are plausible. If the inspectors believe you, he falls off the list as a person of interest, which frees them up to move ahead with a better suspect.'

'You think that could really happen?'

'Short answer, yes, although that means nothing, since the

variety of things that could really happen on any case is just about infinite. But my gut says go for it. Oh, and by the way . . .'

'Yes?'

'Your motion? I got it filed by four on the dot, and Amy said it was superb. Best she's ever read.'

'The best. I'm sure.'

'That's what she said.'

'Yeah, well, you're her boss, and she is such a kiss-ass.'

NELLIE GRANGE INVITED Max in and poured him a tall glass of iced tea while he sat in a rigid posture at the big round table in the circular living room. He drank off most of it in one long pull, then put the glass down precisely over the condensation ring that it had left on the wood.

Nellie pulled out a chair a couple of spaces away. 'Anything I can do to help you out, all you got to do is ask.'

'Thank you. I don't know what I want. I don't know why I'm here.' He spun the glass on the table. 'I've just come from visiting our mama.'

'How's she holding up?'

He shrugged. 'She's somehow the victim here. Again. She knows Anlya's gone, all right. It's broken her heart, she says, and I'm sure it has. But it's still all about her. How's she going to go on? Maybe I could move back in with her and help her?'

'Maybe you could—'

He held up a hand, stopping her. 'That's not going to happen, because she's not ever going to change. Sorry. Not to burden you with it.'

'Hey. I asked.'

He raised his eyes, met her gaze. 'There is one other thing.'

'What's that?'

'My mama told me Anlya talked to her about some problems here. Maybe something to do with a girl named Honor? Do you know anything about that?'

Though Nellie's reaction – he'd clearly hit on some tender point – was immediate and obvious, she forced an apologetic smile. 'I don't like to get in the girls' faces when they're mixin' it up with themselves. They never got to no actual fighting, so I just stayed out.'

'So you don't know about anything that might have been going on between them?'

'They used to be better friends. I know that. Hang out all the time together. But Honor, lately, she . . . Well, she's eighteen in June and movin' out, making some changes.'

'Bringing some of the other girls with her?'

Nellie sighed. 'Five or six. But all of 'em, they go out the house any day, they free to do what they want. We're not a jail here. Girls come and go.'

'And those five or six. They're tricking?'

'Not my place to ask. But they're all grown up now, out in the world. Honor says she'll take care of 'em, her man take care of 'em, everybody makes some money, gets protected. I don't blame nobody.'

'Honor and Anlya, they argued about this?'

Nellie let out a long breath. 'The two of 'em were the smart ones. Honor, she does all right, sportin' her fine clothes, her hair, the jewels and doodads. The other girls, they see that and want it, too. Hook up with Honor, maybe, her man's got his friends, some of that good stuff rub off on them.'

'Anlya tried to talk them out of it?'

Nellie hesitated, then nodded. 'She don't like to see her little sisters go into the life. She kept trying to get 'em to see what else there is.'

'And Honor didn't like that?'

'Honor say Anlya tryin' to be stealin' from her.'

'Do you think Honor would want to punish her for that?'

Nellie shook her head. 'I can't see—'

Max interrupted her. 'Or her man. Do you know his name?'

'No. He don't never come in. I never seen him.'

16

Up in Juhle's office, end of the day, his two inspectors had no objection to the addition of Glitsky to the investigative team. In fact, they welcomed him back to Homicide almost as though he were the prodigal son. Wes Farrell had laid out the situation clearly to Juhle, and the lieutenant had welcomed the idea, because to a large extent it took the heat off both him and his inspectors.

Surely, the fact that he was willing to accept an African-American (well, half African-American) DA investigator underscored Juhle's own sensitivity to the reservations and concerns of the black community. Because of Glitsky's reputation and – Juhle couldn't deny it – his skin color, they had at least one card to counter the argument that the police and the DA's office weren't committed to finding and convicting the person who'd murdered Anlya Paulson.

It wouldn't stop Liam Goodman, but it certainly didn't help him.

The decision was both political and cynical; it pandered to the lowest common denominator of the populace and all in all was not very pretty, but it gave the police and the DA's office a little breathing room.

Not that they all hadn't felt that they were hot on the scent of Greg Treadway. Or were, at least until Waverly started telling them about the call he'd taken fifteen minutes ago from Mr Treadway's attorney, admitting that her client had been less than truthful and forthcoming during his statement last night, and purporting to explain why. And in all, it was a perfectly plausible explanation, not that any of the inspectors were remotely tempted to believe it.

'But this wasn't Treadway telling you himself that he lied?' Yamashiro asked.

'No. Specifically not. It was his attorney. She pointed out that since we'd seen them at Everett, Mr Treadway had told her the whole truth and now, out of her love for justice and the goodness of her heart, she was telling us the real story. That makes it hearsay, which she also took pains to point out. But our knowing the real truth will help keep us from error, and we won't have to waste any more of our time suspecting or investigating her client.'

'That is so thoughtful of her,' Juhle said.

'I know,' Waverly said. 'I was profuse in my thanks.'

'The bottom line,' Glitsky said, 'is we're not getting anything more from him.'

'That's what it looks like.'

'How do you want us to handle this, Dev?' Glitsky asked. Then, to the two inspectors, 'Do we have anything else that resembles a lead?'

Yamashiro spoke up. 'Something may have been going on in the foster home she lived in. Eric and I talked to some of the girls there, and evidently, Anlya had some kind of falling-out with one of them. Her best friend, Honor.'

'Honor?' Glitsky asked.

'Her name, the friend's name,' Yamashiro said. 'Honor Wilson. The two of them left the house together that night, the same night Treadway picked her up. Then they split up.'

'Basically,' Waverly added, 'Honor didn't want to talk about any of it. Nothing had happened. They just said goodbye, and that was the last time she saw Anlya. But in the absence of Mr Treadway, we're going to want to talk to her again.'

'Which leaves the witnesses from the original scene,' Juhle said.

'How many?' Glitsky asked.

Juhle looked to his inspectors. 'Guys?'

'Five,' Waverly said, 'but maybe only four we can contact again, since one of them was a homeless guy who walked away before anybody thought to get his name. But the patrolman who talked to him said he might recognize him if he saw him again. Not that he'd necessarily be able to provide much in the way of reliable evidence, but you never know. The other four didn't have too much to say beyond the basics – somebody was arguing, a girl screamed – but they'd probably talk to us some more.'

'That's heartening,' Glitsky said. 'Anything else?'

Juhle shrugged. 'In theory, the tunnel's got surveillance video twenty-four/seven. I don't know that anybody's taken a look at that yet, or if it was even working.'

'It was,' Waverly said. 'I called in first thing yesterday and got them to hold it for us. I wouldn't get my hopes up. The camera is down in the inside stairway, so it couldn't pick up anything on the streets above or below, or we would have been all over it.'

'Still,' Glitsky said, 'someplace to look.'

'Absolutely,' Juhle said. 'Let's not lose sight of what still seems to me like the best bet. Lawyered up or not, I'm reluctant to let go of Mr Treadway.'

'Yeah, but he won't be talking to us anymore,' Waverly said. 'Ms Hardy was clear about that.'

Glitsky straightened up in his chair. 'Ms Hardy? Rebecca Hardy? Is that his lawyer?'

'That's her. Why? You know her?'

Glitsky nodded grimly. 'Only since she was born. She calls me Uncle Abe. Her dad's one of my pals, Dismas Hardy.'

After a moment of silence, Yamashiro said, 'So I guess we don't want to have her killed.'

'Probably not,' Glitsky said. 'It would be awkward over Sunday dinner and at family gatherings.'

'Is her involvement a problem for you, Abe?' Juhle asked.

'Shouldn't be,' Glitsky said. 'Her dad and I have managed being on opposite sides about a hundred times and only rarely came to blows. I didn't know The Beck was taking clients of her own, but I guess it's got to start sometime.'

'The Beck?' Yamashiro asked.

'Her nickname,' Glitsky said.

The Homicide inspectors shared a skeptical glance.

'It won't be a problem,' Glitsky said. 'I promise.'

'I ask,' Juhle said, 'because I had a thought about how to keep Mr Treadway on his toes, which, if it works, might lead him to make a mistake. And I'm predicting Ms Hardy isn't going to be too happy if I go ahead.'

'And do what?' Glitsky asked.

'Out him as a person of interest. I don't care what his lawyer says, the bottom line is he lied giving his statement. Most people will admit that lying raises questions about a person's basic innocence. Even if Ms Hardy tries to explain the lies away, lying is something guilty people do. So yeah, evidence or not, he's a person of interest. He gets his defenses up, who knows what he might do. Or her, if she's inexperienced. And it also, perhaps, gets Liam Goodman off our ass, at least for the weekend. No objection, Abe?'

Glitsky shrugged. 'Sounds like a plan to me. The goal's still to get the bad guy, right? If The Beck is going into defense work, she has to get used to defending guilty people, and now's as good a time as any. So' – he clapped his hands – 'how are we going to divide this thing up?'

GLITSKY HAD DINNER with his family – Treya, eight-year-old Rachel, and five-year-old Zachary – and by eight o'clock he was back at the Hall of Justice, sitting in front of a computer monitor. The camera angle for the surveillance video in the bowels of the tunnel was from high above and captured the steps leading from Bush Street to the landing halfway down, then followed the steps in the opposite direction the rest of the way down to the sidewalk inside the tunnel.

The panoramic lens captured both the up and the down sets of steps and most of the landing, although the homeless man sleeping against the wall wasn't really visible – and then only his back – until he stood up, gathered his stuff, and walked back up to Bush. Since there was no message to the contrary from the department that had pulled the CD from the camera, Glitsky assumed that the time signature in the screen's lower right corner was correct.

Glitsky moved the image to begin at ten-thirty and watched for five full minutes before he went back to fast-forwarding because of the lack of activity. In the hour's worth of video that he watched, only seven people – including the homeless guy, at about the halfway point – used the steps, all of them except the homeless man coming down from Bush Street.

Besides the residence-challenged individual – whom Glitsky assumed was the as-yet-unnamed witness – the first two people coming down from Bush were women. The first one was Asian and appeared to be middle-aged or older, in a long dark coat. The second one, four minutes later, at 10:41, was a white female in her twenties, in jeans and a black jacket. Hands in her pockets, she hesitated slightly as she approached the landing, probably noticing the sleeping homeless man. Then she continued down. To Glitsky, it was probable that Anlya was still alive at this moment, and possibly hadn't even started the argument that would end in her death, just above and out of the camera's range.

At 11:04, a white man in a trench coat over what looked to be a suit – he was wearing a tie – descended the stairs in a hurry, almost at a run. He slowed to a full stop at the turnaround, perhaps surprised by the presence of the homeless man there, and Glitsky imagined that this was probably seconds or at most a minute or two after Anlya had hit the street below. This might, he thought, be her killer, coming down to make sure she was dead.

Glitsky stopped the playback and went frame by frame, trying to get a good glimpse of the man's face. But as he descended, he kept his gaze lowered, eyes on the steps, then down at the homeless guy.

Try as he might, Glitsky couldn't make out any particular features. The man had a full head of dark hair that he wore fashionably long, just over his ears. He was the approximate height and build of Greg Treadway. Beyond that, he could have been anybody.

Almost immediately after, at 11:05, the homeless man stood up and appeared at the bottom of the picture, although since he trudged up the stairs and therefore away from the camera, his face was never visible, either. At 11:11, a couple – two of the witnesses who'd talked to the police that night? – also in a hurry, as though coming down to look at something specific, entered and then exited the picture. Four minutes later – an eternity! – the next pedestrian appeared on the stairway, a heavyset black man in a kind of a peacoat. He came halfway down, got to the landing, then stopped and seemed to examine the stairway ahead before continuing the rest of the way down.

Finally, at 11:15, a San Francisco patrolman in uniform showed up on the screen. He, too, paused at the landing before heading down the rest of the way.

Much to his frustration, Glitsky was all but certain that he had been watching what was happening during the exact minutes when Anlya and her assailant argued and she was thrown to her death. That reality was *right here*, just outside the vision of the camera. With the exception of the couple who may have been the ones who stayed around to answer police questions about what they'd seen and heard, Glitsky knew that getting a positive identification of any of these people would probably be an impossible task, since all of them had appeared only briefly, turned the corner, then walked down facing away from the camera. None of them had appeared startled, or looked up, or given any indication they were aware that anything unusual had just happened.

THE BECK WAS spending that same Friday night out with her client. They were sitting across the table from each other in a booth at a pizza place on Clement, and she had assured him that there would be no bill for her time or services. Because she knew that her father – no joke – would surely disapprove of her decision, she felt uncomfortable about this.

But she also felt like it might be her best chance to get to know more, not just about her client but about some of the background of the general situation. Greg had been filling her in for the past ten minutes on the basic story of Max and Anlya when another name came up and she interrupted him. 'Who, again,' she asked, 'is Leon?'

'I don't know if I've mentioned him yet,' Greg said. 'Leon Copes. Anlya's mother's live-in boyfriend for a while. A truly bad guy, nothing but trouble, especially for Anlya. He raped her while he was living with them.'

'Are you kidding me?'

'No. She was like fourteen at the time, or the first time.'

'There was more than one time? And he was still living with them?'

'I know. It was bad. Eventually, Sharla threw him out, but he scared everybody enough that they never pressed charges. They were just relieved to have him gone.'

'There's a lovely story. So where is he now?'

'Last I heard, Napa State Hospital.'

This was an unexpected answer. Though it was filled with people who'd been arrested, Napa wasn't a jail but a secure holding institution for people who'd been found incompetent to face trial.

'What did he do to get in there?' Rebecca asked.

'Got in a bar fight and killed a guy, then got found incompetent.'

Sometimes confused by laymen with a ruling of insanity, legal incompetence was an entirely different concept: It applied when a defendant could not participate in a trial because of a mental disorder or developmental disability, as a result of which the defendant was not able to understand the nature of the criminal proceedings or assist counsel in the conduct of a defense.

'And when was this?'

Greg chewed pizza. 'After he moved out but while the kids were still with Sharla, maybe a year and a half before they were removed from her custody.'

'So – what? – three years ago?'

'That sounds about right. Why?'

'I'd have to check to make sure of the law on this, but I think there's a maximum of three years you can be held if you're Thirteen Sixty-eight.'

'Thirteen Sixty-eight?'

'Sorry. Legalese. That's the penal code section when you're incompetent to stand trial.'

'After three years, then what?'

'They either let you go or, if you're a complete batshit loonball and you meet certain criteria, you can be institutionalized longer, under what I think they call a Murphy Conservatorship, but don't quote me on it. Two years out of law school and the details are already fuzzy. It's one of the reasons I don't feel right charging you for tonight. But once I get back up to speed and know most of these answers for sure, watch out.'

'I'll consider myself warned. But I still don't get your point about Leon.'

'Well, if it's been three years, my question is whether he's still at Napa, if maybe they've let him out.'

'Could they let him out and not bring him to trial? I

mean, he was charged with killing somebody. They wouldn't just declare him competent and then not have a trial, would they?'

She put her beer glass down. 'Good point. You're right. He'd either be Murphy'd or found fit for trial. Either way he's still in custody somewhere.'

'And that matters because . . . ?'

She brushed a lock of hair back off her forehead. 'Only that if he were out, he would definitely be a threat to Anlya, wouldn't he? If she accused him of raping her . . . Except that's moot if he's still in custody and charged with murder.' She picked up her beer glass and drank. 'Are you good if we keep going a little more?'

'Sure, but I do have a question.'

'Hit me.'

'If you believe I'm innocent, and I am, why do we need to keep going over any of this?'

Rebecca put her glass down and straightened up. 'It's not a question of whether I think you're innocent. You're my client, and my job is to protect you. That doesn't mean I think you're guilty.'

His expression went decidedly cold. 'Well, thanks all the hell for that.'

She shook off his objection. 'Hey! Listen up, Greg. Until I'm convinced that you're no longer on Homicide's radar, I feel obligated to know as much as I can about all of this stuff, okay? Anlya, her family, the other players in her life. And you're right – all of that might not matter. None of it might matter. But what if it turned out that part of it did, and I just wasn't aware or missed it? Or didn't think to ask about it?'

'But I'm not—'

Holding up her hand, she stopped him. 'The other thing is that I screwed up with you last night. I had lots of time before Waverly showed up to give you a primer on what to do when you're innocent and you talk to the police, the main thing being tell the whole truth, no matter what. Because if you tell them up front, the worse they do is go, "Hm, that's a little weird, but he knew it was, too, and even though it made him come across as squirrelly, he told us." But I didn't do that. And now you're paying for it, and that's my fault.'

'You're being a little hard on yourself. You weren't my lawyer at the time.'

'It doesn't matter. I screwed up, and you're still not in the clear here, don't kid yourself.'

He shook his head. 'I'm not worried.'

'Good for you. You don't have to be. I do. Until they get themselves another suspect, anyway. You still might not see it, but this is all dead serious, and until it goes away, I'm the only one standing between you and at least a very bad few months. Really.'

'Okay. I give up. You're right, and I should take this more seriously. Thank you.'

'You're welcome.' She blew out some of her pent-up adrenaline. 'How did they wind up in foster care in the first place? I mean the actual event that got CPS involved?'

'Long story short is that Sharla had a new boyfriend – after Leon – who'd gotten hold of some ecstasy, and they were partying loud enough that somebody called the police. By the time the cops arrived, the partying had turned into a fight. Anlya and Max had locked themselves in their mom's bedroom to be out of harm's way, and when the cops found them there, they called CPS.'

'Is that boyfriend still in the picture?'

'No. But there's probably another new one in the wings. You hate to say it about anybody, but Sharla's pretty much a lost cause. Max won't even go see her anymore.'

'What about him? Max?'

Greg shrugged. 'What do you want me to say? He's a great kid. Smart and somehow motivated in spite of everything

he's been through. Ripped up over this, though. I was planning to hang with him tomorrow, not that I'll be able to do
much, if anything. I mean, twins, you know. Together from
birth.'

'They were close?'

'Very.'

'Was she like him?'

'In what way?'

'Motivated and smart?'

'Not exactly.' He rotated his beer mug. 'She was intelligent
enough but much more idealistic and dreamy than Max,
who's got some good street smarts. She wasn't that way –
maybe, ironically, because of the bad stuff she'd been through.
She just wasn't going to let that defeat her. Everything was
going to work out all right for her. Her grades were good.
She was going to get into college. All of that.' He let out a
sigh. 'Except not, as it turns out.'

'But,' Rebecca pushed, 'she was having some other problem
in her life. Something was bothering her. I mean, besides
the unrequited crush on you.'

Greg's face closed down tight. 'I wish to hell people would
stop talking about that. There wasn't anything to it. It was
a stupid teenage thing, and it makes me look like I was part
of it. Which I wasn't.'

'You don't feel like you led her on?'

He leveled his gaze at her. 'To be honest, that question
really pisses me off. Are you trying to get a rise out of me?
You just did it.'

Rebecca, startled at the vehemence, pushed herself all
the way back in her chair.

The angry moment gave way. 'I'm sorry, it's just . . .' He
blew out heavily. 'All our jokes about date nights and secret
places where we'd meet up, our places. They weren't really
anything, although in retrospect, I can see I screwed up.'
Another sigh. 'I'm sorry, I didn't mean to snap at you.'

Rebecca swallowed, grabbed at her own breath. 'So what else, besides you, might have been bothering her?'

He shook his head. 'If I had to guess, I'd say it's something going on in the home. Estrogen overload. There was a crisis going on with somebody there every week or so. I can't imagine anything so serious that it might have played a role in her death. You want to know what I think happened?'

'I'd love to hear that.'

'I don't think it was personal. Somebody saw a woman walking alone late at night, an easy target. He mugged her, grabbed her purse, she fought back, he threw her over.' He waited.

'Well.' Rebecca sipped at her beer. 'If only you hadn't left out some of the details in what you told Waverly last night, that might be the working theory of the case.'

'But now it's not?'

'I'd be lying if I said I thought it was.'

17

Rebecca Hardy stood over the sink in her Laguna Street apartment and tipped up the orange juice, drinking it straight from the mouth of the carton.

Delicious.

She'd just finished her run, nearly four miles, along the track by the bay and out to the end of Crissy Field, almost all the way to the Golden Gate Bridge. A solid workout and another reason to love the weekend.

It wasn't by any stretch a warm day, and though the bright orange shorts and green nylon T-shirt she wore hadn't given her much thermal relief, the running had kept her cozy enough. Dying of thirst but cozy. She lifted the carton again.

Her roommate, Allie Jensen, appeared in the room's doorway. She was two years older than Rebecca, three inches taller, and thirty pounds heavier; they'd been roommates their 3L year and graduated from Hastings College of the Law at the same time. 'My mom would kill me if she ever caught me drinking right out of the carton.'

'My mom hates it, too, but she can't kill me because my dad does it all the time, and then she'd have to kill him, too. Anyway.' Rebecca raised the carton again and let it pour.

'Good run?'

'Excellent.' Rebecca looked over and picked up on something. 'Is everything okay?'

Allie was still in her pajamas. She stood with one foot on top of the other one, leaning against the door jamb. 'Not great.'

Rebecca put down the OJ. 'Why don't you tell me?'

Letting out a breath, Allie said, 'You want to sit down?'

'It's sit-down bad?'

Allie shrugged and turned to take a chair at the table in what they called their breakfast nook, though it was more like a walk-in closet.

Rebecca followed and sat. Somewhat surprised to see that her roommate had tears piling up in her eyes, she reached over and patted her knee. 'What?'

Allie couldn't answer right away. She looked up, stared and then blinked at the ceiling. Wiping away the streak of a tear that had fallen onto her cheek, she took a breath and essayed a weak smile. 'I think I'm going to have to give up.'

'What do you mean?' Although Rebecca thought she might know.

'I got my last two rejections from this round yesterday.'

Rebecca sighed in sympathy. 'I'm so sorry. And I know that's hard, but it's just another round.'

'It's, like, the tenth, Beck. Somewhere in there. I don't think I'm hirable. Nobody wants a law student who can't pass the bar. Twice.'

'You'll get it this time. You'll see.'

'Yeah, but in the meantime . . . I talked to my mom last night and told her. And she was real nice about it, but . . . The bottom line is they said they can't help do the rent anymore. I'm welcome to come home and live with them until I get something, but they've given me a ride as long as they can, and it has to stop. I don't blame them. I'd feel the same way. I mean, how long do you carry somebody who can't make it on her own?'

The question didn't call for an answer. Instead, Rebecca asked her, 'You'd consider going back to Carbondale?'

Allie was shaking her head miserably. 'I don't know what choice I have.'

'You've always got choices. For starters, you could go for a non-law job.'

'After all my parents spent on law school? That doesn't seem right.'

'At least it would pay the rent, Al.'

'If I could even get a job that paid enough for that.'

'There's got to be something that could pay you more. Maybe my dad could bring you on part-time. I could ask him.'

'Then that would be him giving me charity instead of my parents. I don't want any more charity. I want to work.'

Rebecca chortled. 'Oh, he'll make you work, believe me. And when you pass the bar, you'll have the inside track on getting hired full-time.'

'If I pass the bar.'

'You will. I know you will.' Rebecca reached out and put her hand over Allie's. 'I really don't want you to move out, Al. Just selfishly. We're great roommates, aren't we? Can you at least give it another month or two? I could lend you—'

'No. I don't want that.'

'Why not? You can pay me back when you start getting paid. No interest.'

Allie sighed. 'You'd really do that?'

'Come on. What are friends for? Give it two more months, and if nothing's happening still, then okay, nobody can say you didn't try. Meanwhile, I'll talk to my dad and see what he can do, or one of his friends. Something will come up. We'll make it happen.'

Allie sniffed. 'You're the best.'

'Okay, I think we'll all agree to that.' Rebecca got to her feet. 'Hug?'

Allie stood up and the two women embraced.

'Better?' Rebecca asked when they'd separated.

'Much. Thank you.'

Rebecca gave her a slight nod. 'As my dad says, "I live to serve." '

'Do you think he'd really take me on?'

'I don't know, but it's worth asking. I'm going over to see them for lunch today. If you want to get dressed in the next half hour, you could come with me, and we could call it an interview and ask him flat out.'

'Just like that?'

'Just like that. Why not?'

'It just never occurred to me that . . . Oh!'

'What?'

'I forgot. I mean, I just remembered. You got a phone call on the landline when you were out running. Your uncle, he said. Abe?'

'Uncle Abe called here? Did he say what he wanted?'

'Just that he needed to talk to you as soon as you got back. I'm sorry I forgot to tell you till now.'

Biting back her frustration at the already lost time, Rebecca managed to conjure up a smile. 'Don't worry about it. I'll give him a call. Meanwhile, you go get some clothes on, and I'll take a shower, and we'll be ready to go.'

'Got it.' Allie disappeared down the hallway.

Rebecca followed her out the kitchen door but turned the other way, jogging to her own room, where she picked up the cell phone she'd left charging on her desk.

He picked up on the second ring. 'Glitsky.'

'Uncle Abe? Hi. It's The Beck. What's up? Is everybody okay?'

'Sure. Everybody's fine. Actually, the reason I'm calling? I'm afraid it's business.'

'Business?' she asked, as if it were a foreign concept. 'Okay.'

'I understand that you're representing Gregory Treadway. The Anlya Paulson homicide.'

Rebecca felt her head go light. This was her father's best friend in the world, her wonderful uncle Abe, who'd bounced her on his knee when she was a baby, whose children she'd babysat. On the other hand, this was the daunting and powerful Lieutenant Abraham Glitsky, former head of Homicide and now an investigator with the district attorney's office. If this call was business, as he'd just admitted, he was calling her in the latter capacity, and even the mere possibility of that scared the living shit out of her. 'Yes, I . . . I am,' she stammered. 'Is Greg all right?'

'I assume so. I was calling you because we've had a development in that case, Beck, and Eric Waverly told me you were the person we should contact if we wanted to talk to him.'

'Okay?' She took a breath, tried to gather her thoughts. 'That's true. It's what I told him yesterday so they wouldn't keep trying to hassle him. But why was he telling you about that? Are you back in Homicide?'

'Short-term only. Wes Farrell assigned me to assist on this case. I'm calling you now as a courtesy because we need to take a DNA sample from him. Your client.'

Rebecca found herself shivering from head to foot. She lowered herself into the chair at her desk. 'What do you need the DNA for? What's going on?'

'I really can't say, Beck. As I did say, this call is more of a courtesy. We would like you to bring your client down and have him provide a sample.'

'So you found something to compare his DNA with. What kind of sample was it? What have you got?'

'I've got a chance for him to prove that the DNA is *not* his. You know, it doesn't take a minute for a swab. But I figured that if you didn't want anybody to talk to him without you being present, you wouldn't be too keen on the idea of the swab without you there, either.'

'Not too, no, I don't suppose.' She ransacked her brain for the appropriate words. 'I'm sorry, Uncle Abe.' Should she be calling him Uncle, or even Abe? 'You're saying . . . what, exactly?'

'I'm saying exactly what I said. We want a DNA sample from your client. We'd like you to bring him down. I thought the easiest way would be if I just asked.'

'I don't see why not, but I've got to ask him first.'

'Sure. If it's not his DNA, you know this can only help him.'

'I see that,' she said. 'I get it. Let me talk to him, and I'll get back to you. Would that be okay?'

'Perfect. Although sooner would be better.'

'Of course. As soon as I can reach him, I'll call you back one way or the other.'

'I knew you would. Talk to you soon?'

'I'm sure you will. Bye, Uncle Abe.'

'Bye, Beck. Take care.'

THE FOG HAD burned off and the temperature topped seventy, which in San Francisco happened about twenty times a year. Frannie and Dismas decided to take advantage of the weather by turning their lunch into a picnic on the grounds of the Palace of the Legion of Honor, which was a few hundred very uphill yards from the Hardys' home on Thirty-Fourth Avenue.

Since both of them had known Allie for the past three years, the job 'interview' lasted about five minutes and was over before they even left the house. She should start at Hardy & Associates the following Monday, if she could accept the wage of twenty dollars an hour. She would be doing paralegal work, which the firm billed out at eighty-five dollars per hour. She would be evaluated after three months and either kept on as a full-time employee or let go. If she passed the bar and had been retained to that point, she would be offered a job as an associate, beginning at ninety thousand dollars a year, with full benefits. If she didn't pass the bar, she could continue on as a paralegal, as long as her evaluations were positive.

When Allie began to express her gratitude, Hardy cut her

off. 'I can't believe that between the two of you, you didn't come to me sooner.'

'I didn't think it would be fair,' Allie said, 'since you'd already taken Beck. I wouldn't even let her ask you.'

'But you said you applied to every other firm in the city.'

'Most of them twice,' Allie said.

'Okay, so why would you decide to deprive us of your skills and talents when everybody else in town was getting a fair shot at them?'

'I wasn't thinking of it that way. Since I didn't pass the bar—'

Hardy stopped her. 'Allie, you graduated from one of the top law schools in the country. You are going to pass the bar, I guarantee it. Do you know my associate Amy Wu? She's a genius, but the bar freaked her out, and it took her four tries to pass it. Four! And she's probably done more to keep the firm afloat than any other single employee. So let's put all this "I haven't passed the bar" nonsense behind you and start fresh Monday morning. Deal?'

'Deal.'

'All right, then. You're hired. Let's go have some lunch.'

The four of them were sitting on a blanket among the cypress trees, eating roasted chicken, sourdough bread, and potato salad, and drinking rosé wine (all except Rebecca, who was hoping to have a more or less imminent interview with her client). From this prime vantage, they could look straight north past the towers of the Golden Gate Bridge, across the sailboat-studded bay, and all the way up beyond the green hills of Marin County.

For the third time, Rebecca got up, moved out to the edge of the cliff that fell off precipitously from their picnic spot, and made a phone call. Evidently, yet again, to no avail. When she got back to the blanket, she said, 'Why do people have cell phones if they're not going to turn them on or take them along?'

Frannie said, 'If you'd just left one message, I'm sure he'd call you back.'

'But not as fast as if he got three messages.'

Frannie shrugged. 'Well, that remains to be seen.'

'What's so urgent?' Hardy asked.

The Beck sighed. 'I don't know if it really is, although it would be great to get Homicide off Greg's case, and what I've got to talk to him about would move things along in that direction. At least that's what Uncle Abe seemed to think, and I agree with him.'

Hardy finished his sip of wine and slowly lowered his glass. 'You talked to Abe?'

A nod. 'He called me this morning, letting me know as a courtesy that they wanted to ask Greg for a DNA sample. We talked an hour ago. Why? Does that bother you?'

'Not really.'

'Not really, but really yes? For the record, it looks like it bothers you.'

'Okay, it's of some slight concern, yes.'

'How come?'

'First off, it means that Abe is formally part of the investigation.'

'Is that bad?' Beck asked.

'On the face of it, maybe not. After all, bringing him on was at least half my idea.'

This made Frannie sit up. 'It was? How did that happen?'

He gave everybody the short version: his lunch with Farrell, the strategic political decision to convince Juhle to bring Abe aboard on the investigation.

'But then why would that be a problem?' Beck asked. 'I always thought Uncle Abe was one of the good guys.'

'Of course. Personally, no question, he's a great guy. But it would be bad luck to confuse that with thinking he's got some sort of a soft spot for the defense. Even if he was just brought on to balance the ticket, so to speak. If he's working a homicide, don't kid yourself, whatever else he's up to, his main commitment is getting a suspect behind bars. If he's interested enough in Greg Treadway to call you about him, then I'm willing to bet that your boy is still very much a live suspect. It's also disconcerting that he called you first and not me.'

'He should call me, shouldn't he? I'm Greg's lawyer, not you.'

'No. I know that. And going by the book, he shouldn't call anybody. He should just show up and ask for a sample. That's the correct protocol.'

'But . . .' Beck didn't like the way this was going.

'But more important, you've been dealing with Waverly all this time, haven't you? Why would Abe be calling you instead of the guy you've been talking to?'

'He's on the case now. Maybe they divided it up some way.'

'Maybe,' Hardy replied. 'Entirely possible. But also maybe, because you've got a long history and you love each other, and because – no offense – you're inexperienced, he's trying to avoid embarrassing you by pulling your client off the street and taking a swab without notice. But it comes out the same way. If they've got probable cause, they can get a warrant and take a sample. If they don't, there's no way you should let Greg provide one. So you call your dear uncle and tell him if he gets a warrant, you'd be happy to bring your client down, but if they can't get a warrant, you still hope he has a nice day.'

'Warrant or not, why not let him give a sample if he's innocent? I mean, how can it hurt if Greg didn't do it?'

'A better question would be, how can it help Greg in any way?'

'If the DNA doesn't match . . .'

'Then it's not his DNA. So what? You don't even know what sample they're comparing it to. What does that have to do with her getting killed? Did the person who left the DNA necessarily have anything to do with that? No. If Greg takes the DNA test and there's no match, does that take him off the hook for the murder? Not necessarily. Can it possibly do him any good at all? You tell me.'

'I didn't think of it that way. I saw it as trying to be cooperative after not answering any of Homicide's questions yesterday.'

'Getting back in their good graces, especially Abe's?'

'Something like that, yes.'

'On the other hand, ask yourself what happens if they didn't have probable cause for a warrant, but you get Greg to provide his DNA and they get a match. Suddenly it's a whole new ball game. It could be a lot worse than one more tiny little lie he told about the night he went out with her. Depending on what they're trying to match, or what sample they're comparing his to, it could change everything.'

The Beck's shoulders settled in disappointment. 'But then they'll say we're not cooperating, which must be because he's guilty, right? Otherwise, why wouldn't he volunteer to give them the swab if it could prove he didn't do it?'

'Think about it. It doesn't prove he didn't do it. Whatever the result, Beck, only two things can happen. If it isn't a match, it doesn't mean he didn't kill her; and if it is, it increases the chances that he did. Either way, it's at best a no-win and at worst a dead loss for you and Greg, so why would you even consider it?'

Chagrined, Rebecca said, 'Because Uncle Abe asked me, and it sounded so reasonable.'

'Right.'

'I can't believe he would try to play me like that. It makes me feel like such an idiot. I mean, if I hadn't talked to you about this . . . I think I'm really mad at Uncle Abe.'

'That'll happen. I've wanted to murder him several times. And maybe he was just trying to do you a solid. Maybe he knows he can get a warrant and take the swab, but you can't count on that. Even if he was trying to pull something, you can't take it personally. As it turns out, this was a good lesson with no real harm done. You'll have your chance to get back at him.'

'It's not really that I want to do that.'

'Get back at him? Yeah, it is. You'll see.'

'So meanwhile, what about Greg?'

'What about him? What's changed? Have they found anything that proves him guilty?'

'Of course not.'

'Okay, then. Until they do, he's innocent. Don't forget it.'

18

JUHLE WAS ON the telephone that Saturday afternoon with Wes Farrell. 'So now he's a liar who also refused to give us a swab until we got our warrant. All things being equal, and all politics aside, I'd say this makes him at least a true person of interest. And when the lab tells us his DNA matches the semen on Anlya's underwear, he's a hell of a lot more than that.'

'Well, fine,' Farrell said, 'he's a person of interest. But really, what we've got here, Devin, is a lot of nothing. You've got a twenty-seven-year-old lying about having a sexual relationship with a seventeen-year-old. Lying about sex doesn't make somebody a murderer. There are a whole lot of reasons he could have told those lies about Anlya that have nothing to do with killing her. What you need to find is something positive, actual real live evidence. You know this. I'm not just making it up. This is how we do it.'

'This is exactly the kind of thing that keeps us from arresting guilty people, Wes. You and I both know it, and it sucks.'

'Look, Dev, I appreciate your passion. I might even believe that this guy's our guy. But it doesn't do either of us any good to build a case against him that'll fall apart at the first big push. And there's no way in hell I'm going public with calling him a person of interest. The only purpose for doing that would be to smear a kid we can't charge, and I won't sink to that level.'

'But if I do nothing, the way Goodman's talking—'

'To hell with Goodman. You're not doing nothing. You're trying to find a viable suspect. Sometimes that takes a couple of days, sometimes a week, and as you know, sometimes it never happens. If you're worried about your job, you know what I'd do, no kidding?'

'Tell me.'

'I'd call Her Eminence Vi Lapeer. Yes, Vi the Chief. Tell her what you've been up to and get her to make a statement about Mr Goodman and his irresponsible call for haste. She may have a bone to pick with Abe, but she'll have to stand behind you for trying to do the job right. Because any criticism of you and your guys is also a criticism of her and the way she runs the department. Treat her as one of your allies, and she'll have no choice but to become one.'

'Unless she thinks Goodman's going to be mayor and won't call him on his bullshit.'

'That's not going to happen. Mainly because Goodman isn't ever going to be mayor, but also because it would make Chief Lapeer look terrible as a leader and administrator. Nobody expects anybody to solve a bona fide murder mystery in a day or even a week. If it came out that that was her expectation, she'd be a laughing stock in the whole law enforcement community. I'd really call her, Dev. Give her a report and bring her up-to-date on the investigation. And speaking of that, is there anybody else your guys are talking to?'

WAVERLY AND YAMASHIRO were planning to have interviews with all of the residents at the McAllister Street home, and they wouldn't need Glitsky's help for that.

This left Abe with nothing to do until Monday morning, a prospect he found intolerable, so he sat at his desk reading the exceedingly slim case file on Anlya's murder. Looking it over, he was struck anew by the paucity of relevant material, and by the almost total lack of information about Anlya's life and general situation. Waverly and Yamashiro were partially addressing that problem today by talking to her housemates, but with the exception of Greg Treadway, there was so far no other person – no name – connected to Anlya as even a remote person of interest.

This made Abe somewhat nervous. It was always better to have more than one potential suspect whom the police had interviewed, if only to combat the eventual defense attorney's accusation that the investigation hadn't been rigorous enough, that the police had decided on one suspect early and hadn't followed up on any other promising leads.

The way the file read today, three days after Anlya's death, was that Greg Treadway was their quarry and they were going to pursue him until they brought him to ground.

Maybe the inspectors would make some progress today, he thought. But he knew that the lack of alternative suspects was not a deal breaker, especially when the prime suspect was, like Treadway, a proven liar who wouldn't even cooperate in supplying a DNA swab without forcing the police to get a warrant for it.

Still, if they were building a case against Treadway, and the case file made it clear that they were, they needed a lot more than they'd gathered to date.

To that end, he suddenly had an idea.

Twenty-five minutes later, he stood at the southern opening to the Stockton tunnel, where Anlya had gone over, cars whizzing by him every few seconds. Stepping just inside the tunnel proper, he turned right, into the stairwell, and walked up to the midway landing. Above his head, in the corner, the surveillance camera kept its silent vigil. Turning left, he continued up the stairs until they let him out on Bush.

For the next hour, he circumnavigated the neighborhood, stopping to chat with every homeless man he ran across. On this atypically warm Saturday afternoon, they were even thicker on the ground than usual, and usual in this zip code was about three or four per block. Out of the twenty-six people he spoke to, none was particularly happy to talk to him when he identified himself as an inspector, but neither was anyone actively hostile. He knew that, in general, the homeless in the city were a blight on the landscape, but a nonviolent one, unless one of their own tried to take over a prime begging site – several times in the past few years, that situation had turned bloody, twice resulting in death.

After his first complete circle of the surrounding five-block area, Glitsky wanted to bludgeon the uniformed officer who had talked to the homeless witness inside the tunnel the previous Thursday morning and neglected to get so much as a name, to say nothing of any contact information (though that might not have been a possibility). Back at the top of the tunnel, he considered taking another round in the opposite quadrant, this time up through Chinatown, but in the end decided that he could come back tomorrow, and he should really get home and see his family.

So he started down the steps again, and right there in front of him, on the landing under the surveillance camera, a husky black man was arranging his bag full of stuff and getting settled on his sleeping bag. Abe stopped a few steps up; he didn't want to barge down and spook the guy. But a few seconds later he heard footsteps and laughter coming from the tunnel below and moved to one side as a gay couple came around the landing, dropped some coins in the man's hat, and continued past. The homeless man barely noticed.

Abe pulled out his wallet and badge and walked down the last few steps, introducing himself and getting right to it. 'By any chance were you here on this landing when all the trouble was going on last Wednesday night?'

The man was a mountain of hair – over his shoulders, drifting into a waterfall of a beard. He squinted into the light coming in where Glitsky had come down, then brought his clear gaze back to Abe. 'Sure was. I've been staying here forever. Couple of weeks, at least.'

'So. Wednesday?'

'Got to be a regular madhouse, didn't it? I don't think the place cleared up till morning. Anyways, I had to lay down someplace else.'

'Down Bush, was it?'

'I can't really say. Other places are pretty much all the same. Except here. This place is pretty good. Out of the wind, usually. Warmer.'

'You mind if I ask you some questions?'

'What you been doing up till now?'

Glitsky had to smile. The man was right. 'You mind if I see some identification?'

'Some what?'

'An ID.'

The man chuckled. 'Tell me where to find one, and I'll be happy to show it to you.'

Glitsky cocked his head. The city had dozens if not hundreds of social service nonprofits and other similar organizations – food banks, free clinics, various shelters and other overnight accommodations – and the homeless population was supposed to provide identification at these places so the organizations could keep track of whom they were serving.

But, evidently, not always.

Glitsky tried again. 'What's your name?'

'What do you need my name for?'

'Don't do me like that. I just want to call you something. I'm Abe. Who are you?'

The homeless man considered a moment before answering. 'Malibu.'

'Got it. Like the city.'

'No, man. Like the car.'

'Like the car,' Glitsky repeated. 'Got it.'

'That's my street name.'

'Sure,' Glitsky said. 'Malibu, the car.'

'Just so you know. 'Cause they got me down as Omar

Abdullah over at Glide. But I don't mostly go by that no more.'

He was referring, Glitsky understood, to the soup kitchen at Glide Cathedral, where Malibu was apparently registered under the other name.

'I got it,' Glitsky said. He reached in and turned on the recorder in his shirt pocket. 'So anyway, Malibu, when did you arrive on this landing last Wednesday night?'

'Just about this time, I suppose. Seemed like, somewhere in there. What is it now?'

Glitsky checked his watch. 'Quarter to five.'

'Yeah. About this time.'

'And how long did you stay?'

'Until just after all the noise. When I could tell everything was going to get crazy.'

'What was the noise about?'

'Well, first somebody was having an argument up the stairs there.'

'You mean the steps behind me that lead up to Bush Street?'

'Yeah.'

'You heard people arguing?'

'Yelling, more like.'

'How many voices?'

'Two. A man and a woman.'

'And what did you do?'

'Nothing. I was just waking up. The yelling turned into what sounded like they were struggling with each other. And then the woman screamed and the scream got cut off and there was all kinds of screeching tires and crashing cars down in the tunnel. So I'm like, "Jesus." '

'And what happened next?'

Malibu scratched at his scalp, moved down to his beard. 'You know, this is pretty much what I told the other cop when he got to me that night. If you want something new, I don't think I got it for you.'

'That's all right,' Glitsky said. 'There wasn't any record of what you said last time. Plus, I think I've got something new for you in a minute here. Meanwhile, you heard the scream and the crash . . . Then what did you do?'

'I sat up. Now I'm wide-awake. And decide it would be a good idea to get out of there.'

'Did you go downstairs to see what was going on?'

'Are you kidding me? I don't run toward trouble. I was going up and out of here.'

'Okay, Malibu. This is the new part I was telling you about. Before you went up the stairs, did anybody else come down from Bush Street?' Glitsky knew the answer because he'd seen the surveillance footage. When he'd been brooding in his office earlier, it had occurred to him that the homeless man on the landing – Malibu – had undoubtedly been sitting right there as the man who perhaps killed Anlya came barreling down the stairs to see what had transpired below, if he had to make sure she was dead.

Malibu scratched at his beard, then nodded. 'Yeah,' he said. 'Now that you mention it. A young white guy, a business guy . . . in a raincoat or some kind of overcoat.'

'Why do you think he was a business guy?'

'He had a necktie on.'

'Did you get a good look at him?'

Malibu paused, considering. 'Pretty damn good, I'd say. He came down the steps and stopped when he saw me sitting here, and looked right at me, then shook his head like he couldn't believe I was there, and kept moving around and down.'

'You saw his face?'

'I just said, we looked right at each other.'

'And how was the lighting down here?' Glitsky indicated the spot above, where a bulb behind a wire mesh covering was dark, either turned off or broken. 'Does that thing work?'

'Yeah. It was on,' Malibu said. 'You watch. It'll light up in a couple of hours. It's always on after dark, automatic or something.' He pointed up to the corner. 'They need it for the camera. It's the problem with sleeping here. You gotta cover your head up completely.'

'Do you think you could identify him again, this guy?'

'I don't know. Young white guy, you know. He looked like a lot of people.'

Before he'd left the Hall of Justice, Glitsky had put together a 'six-pack,' printing out the picture of Greg Treadway from his California driver's license and inserting it into a six-pocket plastic sleeve with CDL pictures of five other young white males who were neither balding nor bearded. Glitsky took the six-pack from his pants pocket and read Malibu the admonition on the back that said, among other things, that he was not obliged to identify anyone, he was not to assume the suspect's photo was there, and that it was just as important to free innocent people from suspicion as to identify guilty ones. Then he handed the six-pack to Malibu. 'Can you see these faces? Would you rather go up on the street?'

'No. It's good here.'

'So what do you think? Could any one of those pictures be of the man you saw here on this landing just after you heard the woman scream and the cars crash on last Wednesday night?'

Malibu didn't take long, and when he looked up, he spoke with finality. 'It's this guy on the lower left, no doubt. I mean, absolutely, that's the guy. Couldn't be anybody else.'

Glitsky had Malibu sign and date the six-pack and circle the person he'd identified.

Greg Treadway.

PART
TWO

19

ALLIE JENSEN KNOCKED at their bathroom door. 'Beck? How are you feeling?'

'I think I'm going to throw up.'

'I've got some tea brewing, and I've made some dry toast. When you come out.'

'I don't know if that will help, but thanks. I'm not sick. It's nerves. I've just got to get myself together.'

'You'll do it, don't worry.'

'I am worried. That's the problem. What if I get into court and this is still going on? "Excuse me, Your Honor, let's put the trial off for a while until I get so I can be here and represent my client without barfing." How much time do I have?'

'You're fine. It's only seven-thirty. You've got all the time in the world. The tea's waiting.'

'I'll be out in a minute. I hope.'

'DIZ,' FRANNIE ASKED through their bathroom door, 'are you all right?'

'Not perfect, no. I feel like I'm going to be sick again. Except that I've already been sick enough for one day. This is worse than my own first day in court.'

'I doubt that. If memory serves, you sometimes get a little uptight when you're about to start a trial. Even after all the ones you've done.'

'But not physically. Not like this.'

'True. You actually get the real flu or whatever else is floating around in the ether.'

'It's a stressful business.'

'Over time, I've figured that out.'

The toilet flushed and the door opened. Hardy had splashed his face and was drying it with a towel. 'I don't know how she's going to do this. Should I call her?'

'Maybe not now, first thing in the morning. Give her a chance to wake up.' Frannie took the towel and touched it to his face in a few places. 'Besides, I think the four calls last night might be enough to give her a general idea of what she can expect.'

'A general idea isn't going to do it.'

'I bet it will. It doesn't get specific until it starts. I remember you telling me your legs went out on you just before your first opening statement.'

'They did.'

'But then there you were, standing on them, and they came back, didn't they?'

'Don't try to confuse me with facts.' Hardy checked himself in the mirror. 'I'm pale as a ghost, and all of my blood is in my face. How can that be?'

'Magic?'

'You're not taking this seriously.'

'Actually, I'm taking it just seriously enough. This isn't your trial. It's Beck's. You'll be there in case she starts to fly off the rails, which she will not do. She's smart and well prepared. She'll be fine.'

'So's Phil Braden. Smart and well prepared, I mean, which is why Wes assigned the case to him. Plus, he's experienced. You know how many cases our assistant district attorney has done in his first two years in Homicide?'

'Unless he did another one since Friday, when you mentioned it last, that would still be six. Right?'

'Six wins. No losses.'

Frannie clicked her tongue. 'Imagine that. Good for him. Sounds like somebody I know on the defense side. It's too bad they didn't give him any of the African-American victims' cases before. Maybe Wes wouldn't have been in so much of a hurry to get this one to trial. Which, you've said yourself, ought to be to Beck's advantage.'

'Slightly. Though she never should have caved in to Treadway's refusal to waive time.' Not waiving time meant that the client had demanded a trial within sixty days of his arraignment on the indictment, which presented all kinds of logistical problems for both sides, although maybe fewer – marginally – for the defense.

'Maybe not,' Frannie said, 'but the same thing's happened to you, and more than once. Innocent people don't want to stay in jail for a year, waiting for their trial. And you always say it's to the DA's disadvantage, having to hurry. Plus, as you also admit, the case against Greg, evidence-wise, is pretty weak, isn't that true?'

'As far as it goes. Still . . .'

'Still, Diz, really.' She touched his face. 'She's your daughter. Have faith in her.'

'I do.'

'Okay, then I've got one last little bit of advice for you.'

'What's that?'

'Have more.'

THE BECK WORE a conservative dark business suit, a white blouse, low heels. She'd had her hair cut back to shoulder-length over the weekend. At nine o'clock, she entered Department 24 of the Hall of Justice, Judge Karl Bakhtiari presiding. The door was open, the lights were on, and some of the other courtroom personnel were present, because the judge had a number of other smaller matters to handle before jury selection in Rebecca's case was scheduled to begin at nine-thirty.

Walking up through the fifteen rows of seats in the gallery, she carried a thick briefcase – a gift from her parents when she'd passed the bar – that now, filled with her notes, binders of discovery material, legal pads, laptop, and other paraphernalia, weighed close to twenty pounds. The room felt surreal to her, the prosaic setting at first hard to reconcile with the roiling emotions she'd experienced back at her apartment. Viewing it objectively, Rebecca was struck by its institutional character. She had been inside the hall and its courtrooms many times, but today everything about it felt different.

She hesitated for half a second before pushing open the gate and stepping into the bullpen. She was now 'before the bar' in a murder case, and the realization hit her that all of her law school training, all of the hours and hours of studying, then working at her father's firm, had finally led her to this. Setting her briefcase down beside her, she drew in a sharp breath and placed her hand on her stomach, hoping she wasn't going to get sick again. Another minute passed; apparently, she wasn't. She took a few long, deep breaths to relax. The crisis passed, and she lifted her briefcase and moved over to the right to the defense table, positioned farthest from the jury.

After a couple of minutes during which Rebecca arranged the contents of her briefcase on the table, the door behind the judge's bench opened, and a middle-aged woman came in. Rebecca came forward and introduced herself to the court reporter, Theresa Shepard. 'Hi. I've got the trial here,' she said. 'Sometimes I talk a little fast, but I take direction. If I'm going too quickly, just give me the high sign and I'll slow down.'

The woman smiled.

'May I ask you a question?' Rebecca asked.

'Sure.' Ms Shepard was setting up her own workstation, just in front of the judge's desk. 'What's on your mind?'

'Is there any chance my client is already back in the

hallway?' Rebecca was referring to the small holding cell behind each department where defendants were kept before a bailiff came to escort them into the courtroom. 'It's his first time dressing out, and I want to make sure his clothes fit and he's presentable.'

'I didn't notice, but there's no rule against looking, I think, as long as you can get a bailiff to let you in.' She pointed to the table. 'I'll keep an eye on your stuff. And welcome to the show.'

'Thanks.'

IN THEIR VERY first telephone conversation, Greg had told her there was no way he could afford her regular hourly rate. Now, for every day Rebecca was at trial, she would be billing him at twice that, nearly five hundred dollars for every hour spent in the courtroom. And her father, Dismas, in hard-ass mode, had argued that was too low for a murder trial.

Nevertheless, that was the number they'd come to, and once Greg found himself arrested and charged, he had called his parents, Barry and Donna. After they'd gotten over the shock and disbelief of not only the basic fact of Greg's position, but what it would cost them to pay for his defense, they'd taken a second mortgage on their Lake Tahoe cabin and written the first check – seventy-five thousand. And that was basically a placeholder until the real bills started to come in.

Another expense was for three conservative business suits, something Greg hadn't had much need of before. His classroom attire ran to corduroy slacks, four or five ties, and a couple of sport coats that he alternated between daily.

But, as with nearly everything else that occurred in the courtroom environment, there was a precise strategy involved in what the defendant wore at court. By now it was a well-established fact that a defendant showing up at trial in a jail jumpsuit was prejudicial: Jurors tended to equate the jail garb with guilt. So defendants were allowed, if not mandated, to 'dress out' in civilian clothes. Different defense attorneys took different approaches to sartorial style, but the norm was a decent, although probably not extravagant, business suit. (Off the clock, Rebecca had gone with Donna to a sale at Jos. A. Bank with Greg's measurements, and they'd picked up three suits for the price of one.)

The first bailiff she saw in the hallway – J. Finian, by his name tag – told her that they'd dropped off the first string of defendants only a few minutes ago. (Shackled together in chains, they came from one of the two jails attached to the Hall of Justice – across the building from one or downstairs from the other.) Finian said he would be happy to escort Rebecca down to see if Greg was one of the ones who'd already been dropped off and deposited in his five-by-seven-foot locked cage.

He was.

It was decidedly chilly in the hallway, and Greg had the suit coat draped over his shoulders, his hands cuffed in front of him. He sat on the cement bench that provided the only seating in the holding cell. Sitting hunched over, his tie hanging between his legs (in leg irons), his elbows resting on his knees, he was the very picture of despair. Rebecca had been visiting him in jail, and after the first few times, she had grown accustomed to the orange jumpsuit. Now, seeing him in regular clothes but handcuffed and shackled was nearly as great a shock as it had been the first time she'd seen him in jail.

Finian put his key in the lock, and Greg looked up at the noise, then pulled himself to his feet. He made an effort to smile in greeting, but it didn't take.

'Hey, sailor,' she said. 'Nice threads. How's the jacket fit?'

'I won't know until I can get my hands in the sleeves.'

'It'll work. Your mom was careful about getting your exact

sizes.' She stepped forward and adjusted the knot in his tie. Backing away, she gave him another quick up-and-down. 'Pretty good,' she said. 'The tie's not too tight?'

'The tie is fine. If it's time to go in, maybe they could take these chains off?'

'We're still a little early yet. It'll happen soon enough.'

'No, it won't.'

She gave him a sympathetic look. 'You're right. I'm sorry.' And she was sorry. She shouldn't have come back here early and allowed him to think they'd be unshackling him right away. He had at least another half hour before J. Finian or another bailiff would set loose his hands and his feet. She tried to imagine herself in handcuffs, her ankles bound in iron, a heavy chain between them. It was a terrifying thought. 'I just wanted to stop by and make sure you were all right, see if you needed anything. Any last-minute questions about what to do out there?'

'I've got a pretty good idea. I sit still. I pay attention. I take it seriously, which, believe me, I do. I'm never going to tell another lie in my whole life.'

'Probably a good idea. I also wanted to remind you that their case isn't strong, Greg. There's no real evidence tying you to her murder. That's the bottom line, so I'm not really worried. And that's no lie.'

But in reality, she knew it was.

DISMAS HARDY HAD remained edgy throughout his entire drive downtown. Taking his wife's counsel, he had refrained from calling The Beck with some last-minute advice that she didn't need.

Expecting to see her in the courtroom, he felt his stomach tighten when he didn't. This was playing a little fast and loose with her time, in his opinion. He knew that his daughter was somewhere in the building, because her briefcase was open on the defense table. Wherever she was, her old dad was thinking that she had better make sure she was back in the courtroom in the next fifteen minutes, when they would call the court to order and Judge Bakhtiari would ascend to his raised platform. It would be bad form, to say the least, if she were not in her chair when the judge sat down in his.

Of course, this was not even close to The Beck's first appearance in a courtroom. In her twenty months of practice, aside from a smattering of corporate litigation, she'd more than dipped her toe in the criminal side of the law, defending any number of DUIs, a couple of shoplifting cases, some small-time drug dealers, and an aggravated assault charge stemming from a fight after a Warriors game. But none of these, Hardy knew, held a candle to the inherent gravity of a murder case.

Now he stood at the bar rail. *Where was Rebecca?*

'Mr Hardy?'

Shaken from his reverie, Hardy turned to see a man in his early thirties – dark blue suit, white shirt, red tie. He had a thin, angular face, inset with piercing green eyes, under a handsome head of thick dark hair.

'Guilty,' Hardy said.

'I just wanted to introduce myself. I'm Phil Braden.'

'Ah, Mr Braden.'

The two men shook hands.

'I heard the talk you gave at the Commonwealth Club last year and thought it was terrific,' Braden said. 'I'll confess I also slipped in to watch one of your crosses a couple of years ago. The forensic accountant?'

'Oh yeah.' Hardy broke a grin. 'Michael Jacob Schermer.'

'You remember his name?'

'It's a curse,' Hardy said. 'I remember everything. If I recall, and I do, I more or less ate his lunch that day.'

'That's my recollection as well. Anyway, as you probably know, I'm doing this Treadway case. And his counsel is, I presume, your daughter.'

'Rebecca, yes.'

'Well, I just wanted to say hello from a fan.'

'That's very nice of you. I'd say good luck, but . . .'

'No problem,' Braden said. 'I get it.' He hesitated. 'So, are you sitting second chair to Rebecca?' Trying to sound casual and not entirely succeeding.

Hardy took the question as a compliment of sorts. Clearly, Braden didn't want him as an adversary. There were some elements about Hardy's role that were none of Braden's business, though if he knew about them, they might set his mind somewhat at ease. For one, Hardy wasn't getting paid to sit second chair, that role being a victim of the financial negotiations among Rebecca, himself, and the Treadway parents.

In fact, he had no official role in Treadway's defense other than that of concerned and interested father. So he kept his answer simple. 'Only informally.' He was here today to wave the flag for his daughter on her first day of jury selection. He probably wouldn't be in the courtroom again until the opening statements, which might be as much as a week away or even longer. 'I doubt if I'll have a speaking role.'

Braden clucked. 'That's a shame,' he said, but Hardy didn't believe he was being sincere.

THIS, THE FIRST scheduled trial day of what was going to be a very high-profile case, would be taken up with relatively routine motions. Nevertheless, there was a good crowd in the gallery – several reporters, the usual trial groupies, Supervisor Liam Goodman, and apparently, his entire staff.

To Hardy's practiced eye, the contingent of about two dozen African-American spectators looked a lot more like professional agitators than family or friends of Anlya. It was clear to him that their presence in the gallery had been orchestrated by Goodman as a constant and visible manifestation of the black community's support for the victim, Anlya Paulson – and this even though there was only the faintest, if that, hint of a racial overtone to the crime. True, Treadway was white and Anlya was black, but any objective reading of the bare facts revealed that it was, if anything, a crime of passion, not of racial prejudice. Not that the facts mattered to Goodman, who was riding a wave of publicity and popularity. Because apart from Greg Treadway's arrest – in the wake of which Goodman had lauded Devin Juhle and his inspectors for their dogged and even brilliant police work, identifying a suspect in under a week – there had already been a constant stream of drama that had kept the case in the public eye.

The first trickle in that stream was Goodman's cynical but effective bifurcation (in the public eye) of the police and the DA's office. Again. The police, Goodman spewed to anyone who would listen, had done their job admirably. But that was only half the equation. Identifying a suspect was all to the good but a long way from securing a conviction. That next step was up to Wes Farrell, and his terrible record prosecuting those who preyed on the African-American community spoke for itself. For all intents and purposes, the police had identified Greg Treadway as a suspect on Saturday night, and still it had taken Farrell three weeks to get around to indicting him. Why was he dragging his feet?

Wes and his team seethed under this patently ridiculous criticism. First of all, by indicting Treadway, the DA had eliminated at least a year's wait for a preliminary hearing. And second, to assemble a grand jury and get all the witnesses and evidence together in only three weeks was rocketlike speed in the typically glacial world of the judicial system.

That, too, was not enough for Goodman. Even after an indictment, it often took over a year for either side to prepare a murder case. There were motions, evidence issues, discovery delays, more motions, a hearing or two, and regular and expert witnesses to subpoena and schedule – plenty of work to keep both sides busy for months and months. After

Treadway had refused to waive time for his trial, which meant it had to begin within sixty days, Goodman had kept up the press. Even that amount of time, which everyone in the law business knew to be stupidly short, wasn't fast enough. 'Okay, fine, they've charged Mr Treadway,' Goodman had said. 'Now let's see if they're really going to try to convict him.'

The other hugely significant change was the charge. The prosecution had chosen to allege 'lying in wait,' which essentially meant that Greg had bided his time, waiting for the moment to strike. This enhancement, called a special circumstance, meant that he faced life in prison without the possibility of parole, or potentially the death penalty.

Farrell had drawn the line and elected not to ask for death. Like every district attorney in San Francisco over the last twenty years, he had pledged during his election campaign never to ask for the death penalty. With breathtaking hypocrisy, Goodman had pointed to this as another sign that Farrell lacked prosecutorial fervor, in spite of the fact that Goodman himself had denounced the death penalty as racist and unfair. Naturally, Rebecca had challenged the special circumstance, arguing that there wasn't a shred of evidence to support it, but her motions had been denied.

The judge, perhaps sensitive to the political nature of the case, had said there was enough to go to the jury. 'After all,' he had said, rendering his verdict at the preliminary hearing to bind Greg over for trial, 'one fair reading of the evidence might be that Greg Treadway spent the entire evening with Anlya after their argument at the Imperial Palace. They had sex somewhere. Then, with Treadway threatened by her exposure of him as her lover – or whatever else they'd been fighting about – he walked with her to the tunnel. Instead of knocking her over the edge in a fit of rage, he had planned on that destination, seen the cars approaching the tunnel on the street below, and chosen his exact moment to throw her over.'

• • •

REBECCA MADE IT back into the courtroom with five minutes to spare. Her father pulled out the chair for her at the defense table and whispered in her ear, 'Are you all right?'

'Good,' she said. 'I was just in the back there, talking to Greg.'

'How is he?'

'Nervous. Scared. I think he's still having a hard time believing this is happening to him, since he just flatly didn't do it.'

Hardy cast her a sideways glance. 'I hope you didn't ask him.'

'No. He volunteered it. Again. Which he does about every other time I see him.'

'Well, if he testifies, he'll get to tell that to the jury.'

'What do you mean, if he testifies? He's got to testify.'

He reached over and patted her hand. 'Maybe. Wait and see what develops. You don't have to make a decision for a while now.'

Rebecca half-turned toward him. 'You don't believe him?'

Hardy hesitated. He loved his daughter. But he'd been through the naïve idealism of any number of young attorneys getting their feet wet. Very few wanted to believe that their client had done the probably heinous thing they were charged with. Or if they did do it, something truly extraordinary, which they had no control over, had made them do it.

He remembered his own baptism in these waters. His first client. Of course, it had been a little bit different for Diz because he'd been to Vietnam, then worked as a San Francisco policeman, and finally had become an assistant DA, so his vision of humanity was already far more skewed to believing in the basic evil nature of man than, God willing, his daughter's might ever be.

Still, the twenty-seven-year-old man he'd been dealing with back then, Jason Railey, had been charged with sexual assault of an eight-year-old girl named Sally Freed. Railey was one of the most personable guys Hardy had ever met, and while they had been waiting for a meeting with the investigating officers, they had cooled their heels in an interview room and, to pass the time, started talking about the Giants. Both were big fans. Then Hardy glanced at the case file and noticed not only that Railey's birthday was the same as his, October 19, but that the two of them were also born in the same year.

They chatted some more, and Railey finally, without any prompting, came right out and denied the accusations against him. The girl was the child of one of his friends, and she had serious problems, always looking for attention. Her dad was going nuts with her. And now this. He flat out didn't do it. Hardy would see. And meanwhile, she'd ruined his life.

Hardy's heart went out to the guy. He knew these things happened, false accusations. It was heartbreaking, was what it was. No way had this Giants fan born on the same day as Hardy molested an eight-year-old. Hardy believed him absolutely.

And then the cops showed up at the meeting, and they played him the tape of the pretextural phone call the girl had made to Jason, in which he had told her that he'd not only fuck the shit out of her again but kill her afterward if she didn't drop the charges she'd leveled against him.

So much for believing in your clients.

'Dad?'

'Sorry,' he said. 'I zoned out. What did you say?'

'I asked if you believed him. Greg.'

'I believe he's been very good at lying about some things, Beck. Which, I grant you, doesn't mean he lies about everything, including what went on with Anlya at the tunnel. So I don't know if I believe him about that. I know I want to.'

'But he wasn't even at the tunnel. One crazy homeless guy picks him out of a six-pack and they—'

'Is there any proof that Mr Abdullah is crazy?'

'No, but—'

'Then I wouldn't say it. I don't know if I'd even think it, lest it come out when you don't want it to. He's an eye-witness, sweetie. And eyewitness testimony, especially from somebody who's got nothing to gain, carries a certain weight, you must admit.'

'I realize that. But this time, he got it wrong. It was just another white guy with a tie.'

Hardy looked around enough to get a glimpse of Goodman and his African-American troops seated in the gallery. He lowered his voice. 'Not to overload you with advice, but I would not go there, either. Mr Abdullah may be wrong in his ID of Greg, but no matter what, I would not play the race card. It just will not fly.'

She let out a small sigh. 'Okay, deal.'

The door behind the judge's bench opened and J. Finian came in, stepping to one side. The bailiff intoned, 'Please rise. Department Twenty-four of the Superior Court of the State of California, Judge Karl Bakhtiari presiding, is now in session.'

And with that, it began.

20

HARDY MAY HAVE planned to leave his daughter to her own devices, but he found himself incapable of doing so. He knew that he was setting a bad example both for The Beck and for the firm's other associates, sitting there at the defense table as though he were part of the paid team, which he emphatically was not. But he didn't care. He wasn't about to let his daughter go through her first murder jury selection without availing herself of the benefit of his experience if she felt she needed it. If nothing else, she'd have someone besides the client to bounce ideas off.

Picking the jury took three and a half days. The fireworks presaged by the presence of Mr Goodman and his activists never went off, to the extent that by Tuesday afternoon, the gallery was all but empty except for the remainder of the jury pool. When the last juror was seated at eleven o'clock that morning, Judge Bakhtiari announced an early lunch recess and told the principals that they should be ready to go promptly at one o'clock.

Word had gotten out that the trial proper was going to get under way, so the gallery was packed again, and not just with Goodman and his hand-picked team of rabble-rousers but with Sharla Paulson and, Hardy presumed, some of the girls who'd lived in the home with Anlya. Also on the prosecution side, Wes Farrell had come down and now sat in the front row, accompanied by several of his acolytes. He and

Hardy exchanged an infinitesimal nod but otherwise pretended they didn't know each other.

Greg Treadway had his own supporters and believers sitting behind his table. His mother and father sat in the first row; they introduced Hardy and Rebecca to two of Greg's brothers and a sister, as well as one of his uncles. Additionally, several of Greg's teaching colleagues from Everett sat with a small posse of younger people he evidently knew from Teach for America or when he'd been in school at Berkeley and Stanford.

As the wall clock clicked the hour, Phil Braden stood up at his table and walked to the podium. 'Ladies and gentlemen of the jury,' he began. 'Good afternoon. Before I begin my opening statement, I'd like to thank you for your patience during the jury selection process. Now I'd like to take just a few more minutes of your time before I begin calling the witnesses who will testify in this case and who together will prove the charges that have been brought against the defendant. But before I begin that process, I want to give you an outline of what that evidence will show. Hopefully, this will give you some insight and understanding into the questions that you'll be hearing and help you to organize the information that we'll be presenting to you.

'On the night of Wednesday, May seventh, the defendant, who is twenty-seven years old, picked up a seventeen-year-old young woman named Anlya Paulson for what he called their date night.' In his first sentence, Braden served a bit of strategic notice: He wasn't going to give Gregory Treadway the dignity of a name. Throughout the trial, at every mention, Braden would call him simply 'the defendant,' while in contrast The Beck would try to humanize him to the jury as much as possible, and hopefully by the end make him 'Greg' in their eyes, a person.

Braden continued, 'At this time, the defendant was working as a court-appointed special advocate, or CASA, helping to

represent children in foster care in their administrative deal-
ings with the courts. In this role, he was assigned to Anlya's
twin brother, Max. This is how he met Anlya, as the advocate
for her brother; in other words, he was in a position of trust.
The evidence will show that he betrayed that trust in the
most vile manner possible.

'The defendant met her for their date night at a bus stop
that he called their "secret spot," around the corner from
where Anlya lived at a young women's group home adminis-
tered under California's foster care program. If this sounds
like a sexual liaison to you, it was. DNA later confirmed that
sperm from this twenty-seven-year-old adult was present on
the underpants of his seventeen-year-old victim.'

Early on in the jury selection process, Hardy had moved
Greg from the center of their defense table to the end seat
closest to the jury, with Rebecca in the middle and himself
at the far end. Immediately, he was glad he'd done that,
though it had been more instinctive than anything else. He
had felt that it would be better if he were near enough to
touch her, to silently signal her at various times. Such as this
one. At Braden's characterization of the relationship of trust
between Greg and the Paulson children, he felt his daughter
tense up next to him, as though to push her chair back and
stand up with an objection.

This would have been not a disaster, only a little mistake.
But in a murder trial, every mistake counted, even the small
ones. An unwritten rule of the courtroom was that you didn't
object to opening statements unless your counterpart went
egregiously outside the lines prohibiting argument, conjecture,
or hearsay. The Beck could object, but Braden had artfully
walked the line between a permissible recitation of fact and
impermissible argument. The judge would overrule The Beck's
objection, and she would succeed only in annoying the jury
members, at this point concentrating on getting the basic story
of the case, not appreciating too many picayune interruptions.

Keeping his face blank, Hardy moved his left hand over a couple of inches and pushed down on Rebecca's wrist, delivering the message: Stay cool, there will be time.

Braden was going on. 'The defendant took Anlya to a Chinatown restaurant called the Imperial Palace, where they sat at their own table and ordered dinner. Sometime during that meal, a man named Fred Liu, the manager there, had noticed that the defendant and Anlya went from holding hands at their table to arguing. Suddenly, the argument became heated enough that, with a cry, Anlya jumped up, knocking over her chair and rushing out of the restaurant, while the defendant stayed behind and paid the check.

'What happened next?

'The defendant gave a version of events to police. He told a story about the dinner with Anlya, conveniently leaving out the argument. He told officers that they had parted amicably so that he could drive home alone and she could go shopping in Chinatown. He denied ever having a sexual relationship with the young woman. It was a lie. Every bit of it was a lie.

'Instead, DNA evidence proves sexual activity after their dinner.

'Finally, at around eleven P.M., five witnesses heard the sounds of argument and struggle between a man and a woman on Bush Street where it crosses over the Stockton tunnel. They heard Anlya scream. The defendant threw her over the low parapet and into the oncoming traffic coming by below. She suffered five broken ribs and three separate skull fractures. Both her arms were broken. Her left leg was broken. She died horribly on the street.

'How do we know that it was the defendant and not some other random person who threw Anlya Paulson to her death? No sooner had he let her go than he wanted to make sure that his attempt at a gruesome killing had been successful. There are steps leading inside the tunnel from Bush Street down to Stockton, which was where Anlya's body had fallen and been thrown nearly a hundred feet by an approaching car. Fortunately, this staircase is under constant surveillance by video camera, and this camera unmistakably shows the defendant coming down the stairs within seconds of Anlya's death.

'How do we know that the figure we see is the defendant?'

'First, the body build, size, and hairstyle matched the defendant's. But much better, an eyewitness happened to be in the stairway to the tunnel at this very same time and positively identified the defendant. In the tunnel. Within minutes if not seconds of Anlya's death.'

Braden, apparently overwhelmed with the drama and poignancy of his recital, went silent, making eye contact with as many jurors as he could. Finally, after half turning to cast a scornful and judgmental eye on the reviled Mr Treadway, he took a deep breath and found that he was able to go on.

'Why?' he asked. 'Why would the defendant resort to this ultimate and violent end for a young woman with whom he shared an intimate relationship? We may never know for sure, but we do know that the revelation of an intimate relationship, and of the bare fact of statutory rape between the defendant and Anlya, would certainly result in the defendant's dismissal from his job as a schoolteacher, as well as his position as a court-appointed special advocate. Additionally, Anlya Paulson kept a personal diary that sheds a glaring bright light on this question. I am not here today to share with you all of the evidence you'll be hearing in the coming days. If I did that, it would take as long as the trial itself.

'But I am here to tell you that the evidence clearly proves on May seventh, the defendant and his victim quarreled, made up, then quarreled again. At some point that night, the defendant realized that Anlya threatened his livelihood and his future and that he could not control her actions. So he decided to kill her.

'Ladies and gentlemen of the jury. This was not a thoughtless, spur-of-the-moment decision. The defendant may not have conceived of this murder in the weeks, days, or hours leading up to it. But when he did decide, he led Anlya to Bush Street above the Stockton tunnel. Then, with cars passing by underneath, he made the conscious decision to end her life. And he acted on this decision. These are circumstances that the law defines as murder. After you've heard the court's instructions and evaluated all the evidence, that is the verdict I will ask for and the verdict your oaths will compel you to return. Thank you.'

IN CALIFORNIA, DEFENSE attorneys have an option regarding their opening statement. They are allowed to deliver their opening immediately after the prosecution's, or they may elect to wait until they are ready to present their defense case in chief, after all of the prosecution's witnesses have testified.

Rebecca had agonized over this decision almost from the moment she knew that Greg Treadway was going to trial. Her father, who very much believed in an instinct-based, freewheeling approach to trial strategy, had counseled her to wait until she'd heard what Braden had to say before she made up her mind. Now she'd heard it, and the answer still wasn't clear.

True, Braden had hewed to a consistent line that, if he could prove any of it, might cast Greg in a bad light. But the issue of proof, especially proof that relied on physical evidence, was questionable, to say the least. Did Rebecca want to point that out right away, or might she be wiser to let Braden present all of his so-called evidence and then – much closer to the time when the jury would begin deliberating – pick it apart piece by piece?

Next to her, Hardy ventured no opinion. And in the end, she played it as he would have, with her gut.

Braden went back to his table, and Bakhtiari turned his gaze on her. 'Ms Hardy?'

Rebecca stood up. 'Your Honor, the defense reserves the right to present its statement after the prosecution rests.'

Bakhtiari intoned his thank-you and went back to the prosecutor. 'Mr Braden. Are you ready to call your first witness?'

'I am, Your Honor. The prosecution would like to call San Francisco's medical examiner, John Strout.'

Closing in on eighty years old, Strout was by a good stretch the oldest man in the courtroom. The doctor probably should have retired years before, possibly could have been forced to, but it wasn't really anyone's job to prod him out, and no one particularly wanted to see him go, so he stayed, mostly laying low at the morgue, a widely respected and more or less beloved fixture down at the Hall, plus an experienced witness in the courtroom.

He came to the witness stand today, thin as a pencil, in an all but threadbare blue suit, badly scuffed brown shoes, mismatched black and brown socks, and a narrow yellow tie. He sported a full head of snow-white hair, a prominent Adam's apple, and sunken blue eyes that, in spite of his immersion in the intricacies of death, seemed to hold a permanent twinkle.

Braden had called Strout as his first witness under the well-trodden theory that if you were trying someone for murder, it was wise to establish that a death had, in fact, taken place.

'Dr Strout,' Braden began after he'd established Strout's credentials and entered the autopsy photos and the death certificate as exhibits for the prosecution, 'can you please tell the jury what killed Anlya Paulson.'

'She suffered massive trauma and internal injuries to the head and body. Two sets of injuries, actually.'

Although there was little if anything in terms of controversial evidence or prosecutorial value, Braden nevertheless walked Strout through the autopsy photos, outlining the

various injuries she'd incurred, not only from the first contact
with the windshield of Robyn Owen's Subaru but then the
further injuries from landing on the street after she was
thrown in front of that car. Rebecca had objected to all the
autopsy photos, arguing that the cause of death wasn't in
dispute; these photos would simply inflame the jury.

Braden, on the other hand, had argued that he required
thirty of the more than one hundred eight-by-ten color photos
that substantiated Strout's testimony. Ultimately, the judge had
allowed him to use eight. Distasteful, even gut-wrenching though
these photographs might be, prosecutors felt, and appellate
courts agreed, that it was important for members of the jury
to get a visceral feeling for the violence and finality of death
that, unspoken but implicitly, the defendant had caused.

But out of arrogance, laziness, or overconfidence at facing
a rookie in Rebecca Hardy, Braden was all but phoning in
his questions, and as this largely meaningless testimony was
going on, she realized that he was giving her an opportunity.
It was going to be her first cross-examination, and she'd try
to make it one that, though short, people might remember.

'Dr Strout,' she said, 'you have testified at some length
here as to the cause of death of the victim in this case, Anlya
Paulson.'

'That's right.'

'And these photos document your autopsy, do they not?'

'They do.'

'So you performed the autopsy yourself?'

'Yes, I did.'

'All right, then, Doctor.' She moved over to the table that
held the exhibits. 'What in your autopsy precludes a finding
that Anlya killed herself?'

'Well, nothing. Nothing about my examination says how
or why she came to go over that parapet.'

'What about an accident? What about your examination
precludes the possibility that she fell by accident?'

'Same answer, counsel. Nothing.'

A rippling undertone of comment made its way across the gallery, enough so that Judge Bakhtiari picked up his gavel, although he did not have to use it.

Rebecca went on. 'Are you saying, Doctor, that as far as your examination goes, Anlya's death could have been a suicide?'

'Yes. It could have been. I found nothing inconsistent with suicide.'

'Or an accident.'

'No. Nothing inconsistent with an accident.'

Rebecca stood for a moment, shocked by a sense of exhilaration so strong that she nearly forgot where she was. In all of her time preparing for this trial, no one had ever talked about the idea that Anlya had committed suicide, and now here it was, front and center, a glaring flaw in Braden's case almost before they'd begun. Out of nowhere, one of her law school lessons kicked in: When you've made your point, sit down and shut up. 'Thank you, Doctor,' she said.

The judge turned to Braden. 'Redirect?'

Rebecca hadn't gotten back to her seat before a visibly shaken Braden was back on his feet. 'Doctor, your findings are also perfectly consistent with someone throwing her off that bridge, are they not?'

'Yes.'

'So there was no evidence of any kind that this was other than murder, isn't that true?'

'That's correct,' Strout repeated patiently. 'I can't say anything about how she came to fall, only that the fall killed her. From her injuries alone, those that caused her death, she might have jumped, or she might have fallen.'

'The jury will have to determine from other evidence how she went off the bridge. Correct?'

Rebecca, still in an almost surreal state, found herself rising from her chair, objecting to the question as argumentative, and Bakhtiari sustained her.

Braden cast her a fast, appraising look, as if really noticing her for the first time. He came back to the witness. 'Nothing inconsistent with murder. Is that correct, Doctor?'

'Correct.'

'Thank you. No further questions.'

21

THE HARDYS' TWO-STORY house was the only stand-alone residence on a block of mostly four-story apartment buildings, although the occasional duplex slightly broke up the monotonous elevations. Distinctively, a true white picket fence ran along the sidewalk, preserving the Hardys' as the only house with a lawn, albeit a tiny one bisected by a crushed stone path. Until it had been gutted by a fire about a decade before, it had been a one-story railroad-style Victorian – a long hallway ran down the left side from the front door to the kitchen, and both the living and dining rooms opened off that hallway to the right.

The kitchen was large and, artificially, well lit. The three windows to the outdoors were over the sink, but they didn't let in much light. The view – fifteen feet away, the towering side of the neighbors' apartment house – left a little something to be desired. Nevertheless, the kitchen tended to be the gathering place when they had company, as they did tonight.

The Glitskys were the last of the Hardys' generation of friends to have young children living at home. (Several of their friends had grown children who'd moved back in after high school, college, or grad school, but that was an entirely different situation.) Abe and Treya had the sensitivity and intelligence not to include the youngsters in every single adult meal or event to which they were invited.

Tonight, for example, Glitsky was explaining, they'd left both the kids in a pickle barrel in their living room.

'I don't remember seeing a pickle barrel there last time I came by,' Frannie said.

Treya corrected her. 'Two pickle barrels. They're new, and you can't fit both kids their size in one pickle barrel, Frannie. They each get their own. You know, Abe's been working on his whole new pickle-barrel theory of how to raise children, and I must say, it's working out better than I expected.'

'So this is kind of permanent?' Hardy asked.

'We figure only until they're eighteen. Before that, we just feed 'em through the bunghole, and when they're done, we let 'em out and send them off to college.'

'I like it,' Hardy said. 'Though of course we'll miss them in the interim.'

'Oh,' Abe said, 'you can say hi to them whenever you come by. It's not like they won't have a life.'

'That'll be nice,' Frannie said. 'Kids should definitely have a life, I think.'

'That's what we're going for,' Treya said. 'Quality of life for all of us, with just a slight emphasis on the "us" part, meaning me and Abe.'

'But seriously,' Frannie said, 'you do know they're always welcome for dinner over here.'

'We do, and thank you for that, but we thought it wouldn't be the worst thing in the world to have the four of us grown-ups hanging out together.'

'Who are you calling a grown-up?' Hardy asked.

'Well, relatively,' Treya replied. 'Not in the sense of old or anything.'

'Okay, then,' Hardy said. 'In that case, does anybody else want a relatively grown-up beverage?'

THEY ATE FROM a large paella pan that Frannie placed on a hot pad in the middle of the dining room table: shrimp, clams, mussels, halibut, chorizo, chicken wings, peas, pimento, saffron, and rice. It was one of Frannie's signature meals and had been the Glitskys' request when she'd asked them what they'd like for dinner.

After the first couple of bites, with appropriate exclamations of delight, Abe drew a breath, drank some iced tea, and then asked, 'So, is trial talk off limits? Maybe I should ask you, Fran.'

She put her fork down. 'I have no objection.' Then, to Hardy, 'Counselor?'

'Good by me. But any slander regarding my daughter will be dealt with severely.'

'No slander,' Abe said. 'The word is that The Beck drew first blood today. Braden kicked a chair so hard in his office that he hurt himself. He never saw it coming.'

'Yeah,' Hardy said. 'It was a good moment. But to be honest, I don't know if even I would have picked up on it.'

'I'm betting you might have,' Frannie said.

'Maybe, but it didn't enter my mind today until The Beck did it. And you know, once the jury gets over the grisly pictures, Strout has been known to put people to sleep.'

'That's a kind spin, Diz,' Treya said. 'But let me just say that you didn't want to see Wes when he got back to the office.'

'Unhappy, was he?' Hardy was grinning. 'That's what you get when you go too fast. No offense, Abe.'

'No. Of course not. It wasn't me who went too fast. I just happened to find our eyewitness. Since then I've been mostly out of it.' He forked another bite of paella. 'Are you guys really giving any thought to going with suicide?'

Hardy shrugged. 'Can't prove it wasn't. Although I don't see The Beck making a major point of it. But after today, it's in the jury's mind, I guarantee that. And every little bit helps.'

THE MEN SAT in the living room, Hardy in his wing chair with a snifter of Laphroaig, Glitsky on the love seat with more iced tea.

Hardy savored a sip of Scotch. 'You're still a witness, though, right?'

'I'm on the list,' Abe said. 'I can't imagine they wouldn't call me, since I'm the one who talked first to Mr Abdullah, but that's about as far as that ought to go. Other than that, I'm pretty much not involved with Mr Treadway anymore, and haven't been since the arrest. I couldn't even tell you the names of the outlying players, if they ever found any. And I can't say it breaks my heart.'

'You don't like the case against him?'

Abe leveled a gaze at him. 'Let's say I'd be more comfortable if we'd found a little more before we charged him.'

'You found your eyewitness.'

'Yes, I did. And I believe him. But a little corroboration from another source or two wouldn't have hurt before the grand jury got ahold of him. Just in terms of convictability. Not saying that I have any doubts at all.'

'No. God forbid you should. If it makes you feel any better, in my darker moments I think Braden's story sings pretty well. If I'm on the jury, I'm damn close to buying it.'

'We'll see.'

Hardy sipped again, then sat back, feet on his ottoman. 'So what's going on in the office?'

'Nothing to do with your case. But some pretty interesting stuff. A couple of weeks ago, we got this call from a DA in Minnesota, where they were holding a guy, Ricardo Salazar, for a murder he committed there. The problem was, they dialed him up out there in Fargo-land, and their records indicated that he was in custody in Napa.'

'What do you mean?'

'I mean, he's supposed to be locked up here, but he's physically present in Minnesota.'

'How'd he do that?'

'I know. It's a good question.'

'No record of his release? Nothing?'

'Well, listen.' Abe drank some tea. 'Mr Salazar, it turns out, was arrested here a little over three years ago, but he got declared incompetent to stand trial, so they sent him to Napa to see if he could get to competence over the next three years. So I call there – Napa – and sure enough, they knew he was gone, but they thought he was still where they released him after the three years were up.'

'And where was that?'

Glitsky's lips turned up a fraction of an inch, for him a broad smile. 'Here,' he said.

'What do you mean, here?'

'I mean San Francisco, superior court. From where he disappeared, after he got declared incompetent again. In any event, he got sent to a halfway house, instead of held here in jail for murder or returned to Napa.'

'They released him to a halfway house? A guy in for murder?'

'A couple of murders. So they should have been keeping him on some sort of—'

'Murphy Conservatorship,' Hardy said. 'But that means he stays locked up. He gets sent back to the hospital.'

'True, in theory. But somebody here didn't get the memo. Instead of checking the box for a Murphy, they checked the box for gravely disabled and shipped him out to this halfway house, still on the books as imprisoned, and next thing you know he's killing somebody in Minnesota.'

'Yah,' Hardy said in his best Norwegian accent. 'Killing somebody in Minnesota.'

'You want to hear the weird thing?'

'Yah, shure.'

'Stop. Apparently, in the last year or so, there was a rash of this kind of thing in our very own city. Mr Salazar, and no doubt a few other gentlemen who were legally incompetent and in custody for violent crimes, got sent to a halfway house as disabled instead of back to Napa, and nobody seemed to worry about it at all. And since he was in a halfway house, he decided to walk away. And since he was disabled, nobody bothered to report it back to the court. They just say he eloped—'

'Eloped?'

'That's the word. Eloped. These guys walk away, and basically, they forget about them. Unless he shows up around another crime someplace like Minnesota. And we get the call in San Francisco, which is where I come in.'

'Where is that, exactly?'

'This is a bigger problem than you'd think. Wes has us looking at records of the Thirteen Sixty-eights over the past ten years in San Francisco to see if we can find where these people are now, how many of them are there, and whether they were found competent and had their trial, or if not, then where they were. I've got two of my guys, Villanova and Schwartz, working on this pretty much full-time. Depending on how many of these bozos there are, the whole unit might have to get involved.'

'And after they get these elopers, then what?'

'I don't know if that's completely clear yet. First we need something like a census on them, to find out how many of them there are. If these guys are supposed to be in jail but they're not, Wes wants to know about it, at least be aware of the numbers we might be dealing with. Put out a net of some kind to drag 'em in.'

'And how, again, did they get out of jail without anybody noticing?' Hardy asked. 'Did I miss that part?'

'I know,' Glitsky said. 'It blows the mind.'

AT ABOUT THE same time her father and Abe were calling it a night, Rebecca hadn't yet gotten home. After her long day in court, she'd gone back to the office and spent some more time with her discovery folders, which she'd already all but memorized. She subscribed to the same theory her father did – that it never hurt to go through them again. She'd ordered a sandwich delivered, and at around nine o'clock, she'd made a phone call.

Now she was sitting across the desk from Hardy's go-to private investigator, Wyatt Hunt, in his office at the Audiffred Building over Boulevard restaurant. Hunt was in his early forties and newly married to his longtime assistant, Tamara Dade. Rebecca had always considered him distractingly hand-some and was kind of glad he was married so she didn't have to think about it anymore. Tonight Hunt was wearing jeans and a western-style shirt with pearl buttons. He was nearly horizontal, slumped in his chair, cowboy boots up on his desk. He clasped his hands behind his head, the picture of lanky relaxation. 'I thought you and your dad had ruled out that whole third-party thing.'

'We have.'

Hunt was referring to a defense tactic that Hardy had used to good effect several times; quite often it found its way into jury trials, because when it worked, it was a very effective way to introduce reasonable doubt into the proceed-ings. This was the so-called SODDIT defense: 'some other dude did it.' Formally, it was known as 'third-party culpability.'

The big problem with it was that over the past couple of years, several upper-court rulings had limited the admissibility of evidence related to that other dude. It was no longer enough, as it once was, to produce an alternative suspect with a motive, even if he had a terrific motive. It still wasn't enough if the defense attorney added the other dude's oppor-tunity to have committed the crime. No. Besides both motive and opportunity, they had to show direct or circumstantial evidence linking the third party to the actual perpetration of the crime.

In Hardy's last big trial, he'd taken three shots at three different other dudes, all of them plausible, all with great motives and opportunities, and the judge hadn't allowed one

word of it. There had been no evidence, direct or circumstantial, tying the dudes to the actual crime, so the jury
wasn't going to hear about any of them. End of story.

This time around, Hardy and Rebecca had discussed
putting Wyatt Hunt on a search for other potential suspects
and had ruled it out because there was no evidence of any
kind tied to Anlya's death. Even if they found someone who
might have wanted her dead, they wouldn't be able to get it
past the admissibility issue.

'So if we're not going SODDIT,' Hunt asked, 'what would
you want me to do?'

'You're going to laugh.'

'I promise I won't.'

'Well, cutting to the chase, I want you to find out who
actually killed Anlya.'

After a few seconds, Hunt said, 'That wasn't technically
a laugh. It was more a chortle.'

'I don't really blame you. But I'm not kidding.'

'So I'm guessing you're thinking your boy didn't do it.'

'He didn't.'

'You sound pretty certain.'

'There's just no way, Wyatt. If you met him, you'd think
the same thing.'

'Maybe not. What's your father think?'

Rebecca made a face. 'He's so cynical. He doesn't believe
anybody anymore, except Mom, and even her only most of
the time. He says I'm going to get to be the same way when
I get a little more experience in the criminal law business;
I should just wait. I reminded him that he'd had innocent
clients. It happens. Especially when they move so fast with
making the arrest.'

'Which I'm sure you're going to argue about.'

She nodded. 'I am. But I've got to admit, it's not a great
argument. The judge will just say if they don't have what
they need to convict, the jury in its wisdom will find Greg

not guilty. If anything, he'll say, the rush to arrest is a positive for the defense.'

'Okay?'

'Okay. So . . . if Greg is in fact innocent . . .'

'Now it's "if." '

'No. He is. And that means someone else killed her.'

'Maybe.' Hunt broke a small grin. 'How about the suicide angle, by the way? That sounded like a sweet moment.'

Rebecca allowed her own tiny smile. 'You heard about that, huh?'

'I was talking to your proud father on another matter. But might she just have jumped?'

'Possible, barely, but no way does the jury buy it. Not with all the witnesses hearing the struggle and the scream.'

'How about the random mugger?'

'Again, possible. But that's where the eyewitness hurts us.'

'While we're on that, what's your boy's story?'

'It wasn't him. He wasn't there. He was home sleeping.'

'I heard they had him on the video.'

She shook her head. 'Any white guy wearing a tie.'

'Really?'

'You can check it for yourself. Believe me, without Mr Abdullah, there's no ID.'

'The logical move, then, I suppose, would be to kill him. Abdullah, I mean.'

'It would be, I know. But it just seems a little wrong.'

'Picky, picky.' Hunt waved off her objection, then brought his boots down off the desk, straightening up. 'So we've still got the question: What about the mugger?'

'If it was a mugger, and it might have been, then Greg's in trouble. Unless the mugger shows up with her purse.'

'Her purse? What about her purse?'

'She had her purse with her, and it hasn't turned up.'

Hunt shrugged. 'That's easy. She dropped it in the struggle.

Somebody picked it up, took what they wanted, if anything, and threw it away.'

'Probably. And once they got on Greg's trail, nobody looked. Which is the problem all along here. Once Greg got on their radar, with all the pressure to identify a suspect, the inspectors didn't look at any other possibilities. I was looking through some discovery documents earlier tonight, and that's when it hit me: There are at least a couple of unexplored leads that they just dropped after they glommed on to Greg.'

'Like?'

'Like something was going on at the home she lived in. There was some kind of drama with another one of the girls, but after the first interviews, nobody followed up. Then there's something about her mother and her old boyfriend, a guy named Leon. You can read the transcript of Sharla's interview. Apparently, he sexually abused her—'

'The mother?'

'No. Anlya. When she was younger, thirteen or fourteen. In any event, the mom, Sharla, is damned evasive when she ought to be bending over to help the inspectors find Anlya's killer, wouldn't you think?'

'Unless she just hates cops.'

'Okay, maybe that, but still. Somebody should talk to her again and try to find out.'

Hunt cocked his head. 'Is that it?'

'Not completely, no. Last is that nobody's talked to the person closest to her. Her twin brother. Max.'

'You're saying he's a suspect?'

'No. I can't see that. But they never talked to Max to see if he could give them some idea of what else might have been going on in her life. They never even asked.'

Hunt lifted and dropped his shoulders, resigned. 'That's what happens when you identify your main guy, Beck.'

'Yes, but it sure does leave a lot of unanswered questions, and I believe that one of them is going to lead to her murderer.'

'And you want me to ask them?'

She nodded. 'I think you'll turn up something.'

'Then what? They confess?'

Now she broke a real smile. 'That would be ideal, though I'm not counting on it. I was thinking more you get something real and pass it along to Devin Juhle. You guys are buds, right?'

'Reasonably. But that doesn't mean he's going to jump on evidence I turn up.'

'Yes, he will. With all this Liam Goodman stuff in the background, if it looks like something that truly might threaten Greg's conviction, he'll want to know all about it, if only to cover his own ass.'

Hunt chewed the side of his cheek for a moment. 'I don't want to seem unenthusiastic, and I could use the work, but you realize it is overwhelmingly likely that I won't find anything and it all might get us nothing?'

'I don't think that. I think there's something out there that nobody's looked at, and that's why Anlya died.' She reached down and opened her briefcase, extracting a thick folder and reaching over to place it on Hunt's desk. 'Something's in there,' she said. 'Give it a look. See what you think. What do you say?'

'I say I'll do what I can. I'll read all that tonight.'

'Great. Thank you.'

'Always a pleasure.' He stood up, and they shook hands over the desk. 'By the way,' he said, 'do you want to hear a coincidence?'

'Always.'

'You know that third-party culpability we were talking about earlier? At your dad's last trial, when he had three of them lined up – you want to guess who one of them was?'

'Mr Abdullah?'

'Beck. Come on. Seriously.'

'I am serious. You said it was a coincidence.'

'And it is.'

'Okay. I give up.'

'Liam Goodman.'

Rebecca reeled, almost as though she'd been slapped. 'Really?' Then, considering it further, 'As a suspect in a murder case?'

Hunt nodded. 'Your dad knows all about it. I went and talked to Goodman. You'll love this. Somebody was blackmailing him. His blackmailer wound up dead. But no evidence tied him to the actual perpetration of the crime, so the judge never let us get him on the stand.'

'Wow,' Rebecca said. 'That is interesting.' She took another beat, thinking. 'Do you have any idea what, if anything, it means in the context of this trial?'

'No clue,' Hunt said. 'Or if it has any meaning at all. It might be just one of those things.'

'Wow,' Rebecca said again. 'Small town.'

IN HER NIGHTGOWN, Frannie came into the bedroom from the adjoining bathroom, and Hardy closed his hardback copy of Karen Joy Fowler's *We Are All Completely Beside Ourselves* and put it on the bedside table. 'Are you going to read this when I'm done?' he asked.

'I'm planning to. I love her stuff. Is this one good?'

'No. It's great. But I want to warn you, whatever you do, don't read the jacket. They ought to have a banner ribbon around the damn thing saying, "Spoiler Alert." Why don't they just tell me the whole story so I don't need to read the actual book? Except that I *want* to read the book without knowing what happens next. Is that so hard?'

'Apparently so. And I am now forewarned. Why don't we just throw the jacket away so I'm not tempted? Here, give it to me. I'm not kidding.'

He grabbed the book, took off its cover, and handed it across. 'Don't even glance at it! You might pick it up by osmosis.'

'I'll be careful.' Frannie crushed the paper in her hands and went to throw it in the bathroom's wastebasket.

Also next to Hardy's bed, the phone rang. Hardy checked his watch: 11:20. 'Got to be The Beck.' He reached over to pick it up. 'Isn't it slightly late?' he said by way of greeting.

It was, in fact, the Beck. 'I don't know . . . Oh. I'm sorry. I didn't realize . . .'

'It's okay, sweetie. What's up?'

Frannie reappeared from the bathroom. 'Is she all right?' she whispered.

'Are you all right?' Hardy repeated, nodding at his wife, then spoke into the phone. 'Are you still at the office?'

'No. I'm home now. Were you asleep? I'm sorry. I'll let you go.'

'No. That's all right. We're night owls tonight. Uncle Abe and Treya came by and we ate your mom's paella and it ran late. What can I do for you?'

'I wanted to let you know that I've gone ahead and put Wyatt on something with Greg.' In a few sentences, she laid out her idea. 'I just thought you'd want to know.'

'Well,' Hardy said, 'that's why we have a private investigator. If you think it might do some good, it's probably worthwhile. If anybody can get results, it's Wyatt. But maybe you want to think now about hitting the sack, since if I'm not mistaken, you've got another day in court tomorrow.'

'I don't see how I'm going to get any sleep. I'm too wound up.'

Hardy took a deliberate breath, slowing himself down. 'Sleep is part of the gig, Beck. You've got to give it a try. Are you still in your work clothes?'

'Yes.'

'Maybe get them off, put on some pajamas, and lie down. That might be a start.'

'Good idea. I'll do that.'

'All right. Sleep tight. I'll see you tomorrow. I love you.'

'Love you, too. Say hi to Mom.'

'Hi, Mom. Now you, Beck, go to bed.'

'Okay. I will. Promise. Bye.'

Hardy hung up, let out a deep breath. 'Have I told you how glad I am that this is The Beck's trial and not mine? Not that I wish the insomnia on her.'

'And not that you ever had it yourself. Or still don't sleep too well when you're at trial.'

'Which is why I'm glad I'm not.' He shook his head. 'She hired Wyatt Hunt.'

'To do what?'

'To find out who killed Anlya.'

Frannie sighed. 'Well, I hope he does.'

'Me, too,' Hardy said. 'Notice, though, I'm not holding my breath.'

22

OF COURSE, REBECCA'S lucky break on the suicide question with Dr Strout was by no means where the first day of testimony had ended. They'd been back from the lunch recess only twenty-five or so minutes by the time Strout was done, and Braden hadn't wasted any time trying to get away from that fiasco by calling Eric Waverly and walking him through the visit to Anlya's apartment, finding the photo, and the interview with Greg Treadway. It had been a slow process, almost as long in the telling as it was in the living, and the court had adjourned for the evening just after Waverly's description of visiting Anlya's group home on the day after her death.

And now here it was, day two of the trial proper. Hardy and a bleary-eyed and somewhat spacy Rebecca were getting set up at their table, the client in the holding cell behind the courtroom, when Hardy nudged her, directing her attention to the prosecutor, who was limping up the center aisle in the gallery. As he was pushing open the gate, letting himself into the bullpen, Braden kept his eyes straight ahead, all business. He wore a portable cast on his right foot.

Hardy, suddenly on the verge of the kind of hysterical laughter that could only bloom in an inappropriate and restricted setting, had to cover his mouth and look down at the grain of the desktop in front of him.

Rebecca turned to him. 'What?' Then 'What happened to Braden's foot?'

Hardy kept his hand over his mouth, leaned forward on

his elbow, and looked to his right, away from the prosecution table. His shoulders shook with his silent laughter. 'Oh God,' he said, wiping tears from his eyes.

'What?' Rebecca asked again. 'What's so funny?'

At last Hardy got his breathing under control and risked a glance across to where Braden was arranging his props – legal pads, pens and pencils, briefcase. 'Last night Abe told me that Phil was so mad about the suicide thing when he got back to his office that he kicked a chair and broke it. I thought he meant he broke the chair. But I guess not.'

She looked over at Braden, made a face of commiseration, came back to her father. 'That is so not funny, Dad,' she whispered.

'No. You're right.' But he couldn't do anything about his reaction as he turned away, giggling, his eyes tearing up again. It was exactly like the time during a super-serious lecture in the strictest teacher's class in his all-boys' high school when the guy behind him had passed a note that said, 'Smile if you're wearing a bra,' and Hardy had just lost it. Laughed so hard he cried, got sent to the office, pulled a week of JUG – Judgment Under God. And totally worth it to laugh that hard.

'Not funny,' he now said, nearly recovered. 'My bad. Not funny at all.'

'IF YOU CAN stand it, one last last-minute tip.' Hardy was leaning over, whispering to Rebecca, still before Greg had entered the courtroom. 'This just occurred to me as I've been sitting here, so I might be wrong and you can overrule me, but you're going to have a lot of opportunities to talk about the actual crime, the scene of the crime, the night of the crime, the gravamen of the crime, and so on.'

'Okay?'

'Okay, you might want to think about convincing yourself not to call it "the crime." '

'What do I call it, then?'

'Anything else. The incident. The accident. The death. The street location. Anything but crime. You might even try potential suicide. And so let's say Braden objects. Regardless of whether the judge sustains or overrules, the jury gets to hear again that this was a possible suicide. And if he doesn't object, then you've got the jury halfway to believing it might have been an accident of some kind, not a murder. Either way, you win. You might just consider it.'

Rebecca knew that her dad had years of experience, but sometimes, she thought, he got carried away with esoteric minutiae. 'You really think one word like that matters?'

'Guilty. Not guilty. One-word difference,' he said. 'Just give it some thought. That's all I'm saying.'

BRADEN FINISHED UP with Waverly in the first hour. With no break for a recess, Judge Bakhtiari turned to Rebecca and said, 'Ms Hardy. Cross-examination?'

Without quite realizing how she'd gotten there, Rebecca was standing facing the judge and the witness. 'Inspector Waverly,' she said. 'To begin at the beginning, you have testified that shortly after midnight, when you arrived at the scene of the accident' – she tensed for an objection, but none came – 'you called your supervisor, Lieutenant Devin Juhle, the chief of Homicide, and requested that he come down and join you and your partner there, is that correct?'

This was not Waverly's first rodeo. 'Do you mean the scene of the homicide?' he asked innocently. 'Yes, I did.'

'Is that your normal procedure when you've been called to an accident scene in the middle of the night?'

'It varies.'

'So sometimes you do not call your lieutenant and ask him to come down?'

'That's correct, yes.'

'More often than not, do you call him or not call him?'

'As I said, it varies.'

'In the past two years, Inspector, how many times have you been called to the scene of an incident in the middle of the night?'

'I don't know, exactly.'

Rebecca, who had discussed with Hardy their suspicion that this would be the way to introduce the super-expedited handling of this case to the jury, had done her research and did know the exact answer. 'Would it surprise you to know that you've had thirteen such calls?'

'No. It wouldn't surprise me. That sounds about right.'

'Knowing that number, would you hazard a guess as to how often you asked your lieutenant to come down?'

Braden objected. 'Irrelevant.'

'Bias of the witness, Your Honor,' Rebecca said. 'They didn't treat this case remotely like any other, and the jury is entitled to know why.'

The judge couldn't suppress a small smile of appreciation at the adroitness of Rebecca's tactic. Not only was she getting the line of questioning she wanted, she had gotten to explain to the jury the point she was driving at. 'Overruled,' he said.

Rebecca repeated the question. 'How often have you asked your lieutenant to come down?'

'I haven't really thought about that. When there's a compelling reason, my partner and I decide whether we think we'd benefit from the lieutenant's presence.'

'And you have no idea how often this has happened in the past two years?'

'No, I don't.'

Though the cross-examination had just begun, Rebecca found herself riding a wave of adrenaline. She was vaguely aware that it would take a while, and at the same time realized that she'd have to temper her inclination to get to everything at once.

There was, as her father had counseled her a million times,

such a thing as a rhythm, and you had to be aware of it and sensitive to its presence. Like so much else she had been told over the past three or four years, the advice had sounded like so much mumbo-jumbo. But now, facing the apparently benign Eric Waverly, she found the rest of the courtroom, indeed the world, receding.

It was just her and him.

She was subliminally aware that she had to slow down if she didn't want to skip past an important item. One small question after another, leading inexorably to her point. It was a long cave she'd entered, and she was just inside, blackness all around and a light at the end.

'Inspector Waverly,' she said, 'do you remember any other time in the past two years when you have called Lieutenant Juhle or his predecessor, Lieutenant Glitsky, to come to a scene in the middle of the night?'

'Not specifically, no.'

'So calling him was an unusual situation, was it not? Not your normal procedure?'

Waverly shot a quick 'What can you do?' glance at Braden's table. 'I suppose that's right. Yes.'

'Was there one particular thing that made it unusual?'

'It wasn't so much unusual as . . .' He paused.

'Inspector Waverly, you have just testified that calling Lieutenant Juhle was out of the ordinary. Would you like the court recorder to read back your reply?'

'No. That's all right. It was a situation we'd talked about in the event that it happened, so when it did, I made the call.'

'And what was that situation?'

'Well, in the event that we had an African-American victim, and in this case we did.'

A loud buzz of comment cut through the gallery, enough so the judge felt compelled to tap his gavel twice in quick succession. 'I would ask those of you in the gallery to refrain from further outbursts. Ms Hardy, please continue.'

Rebecca nodded. 'Inspector Waverly, what was the special significance of an African-American victim in this case?'

Waverly, obviously uncomfortable, pulled at the knot of his tie. Behind her, Rebecca heard the scraping of a chair – Braden standing up to object, doubling down on a counterproductive move. 'Your Honor, relevance? There is nothing sinister or strange about Inspector Waverly calling his superior to the scene of a homicide. This happens all the time.'

Bakhtiari nodded. 'Ms Hardy?'

'Inspector Waverly has just told us that this was unusual, Your Honor.'

'Perhaps for Inspector Waverly,' Braden replied, 'but other Homicide inspectors do it all the time. It's well documented.'

Bakhtiari said, 'Let's hear why Inspector Waverly thought it was unusual this time. Objection overruled. Ms Hardy, go ahead. Inspector, answer the question.'

Rebecca repeated it – what was the special significance of an African-America victim in this case?

'Well,' Waverly said, 'over the past few months before this killing, the Homicide detail had been heavily criticized in the media for failing to identify suspects in homicides involving African-American victims.'

Someone yelled out in the gallery. 'Damn straight!' And another round of interruption ensued, with Bakhtiari gaveling the gallery into a tense silence again: 'Any more of this kind of behavior, and I'll have the courtroom cleared and the individuals responsible charged with contempt. This is not a theater but a court of law.'

Thinking, So much for rhythm, Rebecca finally got to ask her next question. 'Because of this criticism, Inspector – that your department had not been successful in identifying suspects in the deaths of African-American victims – you decided that you needed to call your superior, Lieutenant Juhle, is that correct?'

'Yes.'

'This was to underscore a sense of urgency to solve the crime, if in fact it was a crime, is that correct?'

'Something like that, yes.'

'You were under pressure to find a suspect immediately, were you not?'

'We're always under pressure to find a suspect in a homicide case.'

'But this one was, as you say, unusual, because of the race of the victim. Didn't Lieutenant Juhle tell you that you needed to identify a suspect as quickly as you could?'

Braden tried another objection.

Bakhtiari looked down on Rebecca from his bench. 'Is that the thrust of your questioning here, Ms Hardy? To imply that the investigation was mishandled because there was an urgency to identify a suspect?'

'An *unusual* urgency, Your Honor, that led to a less than rigorous investigation.'

The judge was shaking his head. 'You've made your point. The objection is sustained. Let's move on.'

Rebecca, who had let herself believe that she was scoring a few important early points, realized that she'd been kidding herself. In spite of the haste with which Waverly et al. had settled on Greg, Homicide had built a very strong circumstantial case that had sold the grand jury. Rebecca might have hired Wyatt Hunt to pursue suspects perhaps not adequately examined by Waverly and Yamashiro, but here in the courtroom, there was one suspect, and it was her client. The police had investigated him. Bona fide solid evidence tied him to the victim. Based on that, the grand jury had indicted. The DA had charged him. He was a plausible suspect, and the jury might believe that he was a guilty one.

She had been planning to question Waverly and Yamashiro at length about the other potential scenarios that they'd failed to investigate – the girls at Anlya's home, for example; or Sharla and Leon; or what Max may have known. Now she couldn't go further down that road, and that left her feeling hollowed out and lost. She'd figured she'd have another half hour, at least, bringing the jury around to her belief that the cops hadn't done a thorough or even marginally competent job, but the judge had cut her off before she'd really begun, telling her to move on, and that was what she would have to do.

She turned, walked back to her desk, forced a smile for Greg and her father. Taking a sip of water, she glanced at her yellow legal pad. In her near-panicked state, she saw nothing helpful. She went back to her place in front of the witness.

She cleared her throat and began again. 'Inspector Waverly, you've testified that you first met Greg Treadway on the day after the incident, after he arranged through an intermediary for the two of you to meet, is that right?'

'Yes.'

'And you tape-recorded the interview you had with him, did you not?'

'Yes, I did.'

'During that interview, did he volunteer the information that he had spent part of the previous night, the night she died, with Anlya Paulson?'

'Yes, he did.'

'He told you that he and Anlya ate dinner at a restaurant called the Imperial Palace in Chinatown, is that right?'

'Yes.'

'In other words, he told you the exact location where you could go to verify his movements on the night of the accident. Is that right?'

'Yes.'

Rebecca ground to a stop. She took a breath, hoping she wasn't giving away too much of her frustration. After her rush-to-judgment strategy had fallen apart, she had precious little to criticize or call into question about how Waverly had conducted the investigation. He was an affable, good-looking professional who'd wasted no time identifying a suspect, collecting a persuasive array of evidence, and making a righteous arrest.

She might continue with her cross-examination, but it would be at her own peril, so she decided to cut her losses. 'Thank you,' she said. 'I have no further questions for this witness.' And she returned to the defense table.

23

AT ONE O'CLOCK, Wyatt Hunt had knocked on the door of 3B. He'd called and made his pitch for an interview earlier, and though Max Paulson hadn't been too enthusiastic about it, he'd agreed to an hour. He had a job in a hardware store and he had to be there at three.

Now they'd said hello and Max had shown him in. They were sitting across from each other at a Formica table in Auntie Juney's tiny but clean kitchen. Wyatt blew on a cup of tea that Max had poured for him. Outside the window, the late-June fog wasn't going anyplace fast, and up here on the third floor, the feeling of isolation was palpable.

As was Max's pure suspicion.

'Okay, I said I'd talk to you,' Max said. 'But I really don't know what you've got in mind. I'm not inclined to go out of my way to help Greg Treadway.'

'You think he killed your sister?'

'I don't know. Probably. They wouldn't have him on trial if they didn't believe he did. Whether he killed her or not, he was having sex with my sister. He betrayed me. And her, too. Both of us. So I don't really care how the trial comes out on the murder charge. Or what happens to him. I just don't want to see him again.'

'But you did see him pretty regularly before he got arrested?'

'Once a week or so, sometimes twice.'

'And on these visits, was Anlya included?'

Max threw a look toward the ceiling, his eyes suddenly

brimming at the mention of Anlya's name. 'Sometimes. Usually not during the work-week, though. We'd invite her along when we were doing what we called field trips.'

'And what were those?'

'You know. Greg would pick someplace he thought was cool or educational or whatever – a concert or a movie or maybe a museum. And the three of us would make a day of it.'

'This happened frequently? With the three of you?'

Max took in a breath, closed his eyes. 'Once or twice a month. Like I said, usually on a weekend.'

Hunt took a sip of his tea. 'On these trips, did you notice any particular closeness between Greg and your sister? Any inappropriate behavior?'

Max brought his gaze down and leveled it at Hunt, who could almost feel the rage coming off the young man. 'It doesn't really matter what I saw between them, does it?' he asked. 'There's only one way she gets his DNA where they found it, isn't there?'

'I guess his lawyers are hoping that the DNA evidence isn't conclusive. Maybe somebody screwed up at the lab. Or they can make the jury believe that. If that happens, then it would be helpful to know if anyone else saw them acting like they were together. Or rather, if no one else did.'

'You mean me?'

Hunt gave him a nod. 'You'd be a good place to start. Did you ever have reason to believe, from the way they were with each other, that they were romantically involved?'

Max shook his head and said, 'But they were. Everybody knows they were by now. If you're trying to get him off on that, you're pretty much wasting your time. And mine.' Abruptly, he pushed his chair back and stood up, crossed to the window, looking out at the fog. After another few seconds, he turned around. 'Sorry to be so uncooperative. I don't mean to bust your chops. You're just doing your job, but I don't see how there can be any doubt.'

'About their relationship, maybe not. But do you have any doubt that he killed her?'

Something went out of Max's shoulders. 'I've tried to imagine that. I've got to say I can't. I mean, he loved her. Loved us both, I would have said. Took care of us. He was always such a good guy.' This time tears broke from his eyes and coursed down his cheeks. 'But if he could . . . fuck her, you know. It's so weird because he talked about CASAs like him not being assigned clients of the opposite sex, how he understood it was a smart policy. If he could do what he did after being hyper-aware of all that, I guess I really didn't know him. He just fooled everybody.'

Hunt kept his eyes off Max's face, leaned back in his chair, crossed one leg over the other, let the shimmering emotion of the moment subside. 'Let's be hypothetical for a minute,' he began in a different tone. 'Let's admit that taking unfair advantage of your sister was something he did. It's bad, but it's a very different thing from murdering her. And you've just been telling me that you can't imagine he could have killed her or anybody else. Can't imagine it, right?'

Max sighed, came back to the table and sat down in his chair. 'Pretty much no. I can't.'

'Well then, let's also assume for the sake of discussion that it wasn't some random mugger, because if it was, we'll likely never know. So we're pretending it's not Greg and not a mugger. And while we're eliminating possibilities, what do you think are the odds that she just jumped?'

'Zero. She loved life. She never would have killed herself.'

'All right. So who does that leave, assuming she was murdered by someone she knew?'

Now Max leaned back in his chair, pensive. 'I really hadn't thought of it that way. You're saying . . . what?'

'I'm saying if it wasn't Greg, and you yourself seem to have ruled him out, and it wasn't a mugger – why would a purse snatcher take the huge and unnecessary risk of killing her? and let's face it, that parapet was too high for her to go over by accident – then it was probably somebody she knew and, by extension, somebody you might know about. Was she having troubles in other areas of her life? Did she have enemies? Did she talk to you about people from school, for example, or her home, or anything like that?'

'Not too much. A little. Most of the time we were together, we had fun, joked with each other. She wasn't like all-emo all the time. Besides, wouldn't any of that stuff . . . Isn't that in her diary?'

'Evidently nobody serious enough for the cops to pursue, except Mr Treadway.'

'Nothing about Honor Wilson?'

Hunt came forward. 'There we go, Max. What's the deal with Honor Wilson?'

'Well, it's complicated, but . . .' He gave Hunt a truncated version of his understanding of what went on at the group home with the entrepreneurial young woman who'd recruited several of the other girls into a life of prostitution. As a foster child himself, and then a worker with Child Protective Services before becoming a private investigator, Hunt thought he'd seen it all, but when Max was done with the recitation, Hunt found himself all but unable to speak.

Picking up on Hunt's reaction, Max said, 'That's the way I felt when Anlya told me about this. Pretty appalling, isn't it?'

'Was your sister involved in this, too?'

'Oh God, no. She was the one who tried to talk the other girls into *not* going out. That was the conflict with Honor.'

'But the other girls, they went out on the theory that this was a good life?'

Max shrugged. 'They're most of them going on eighteen and leaving the program and the home as soon as the birthday comes along. Few of them have jobs, and if they do, they're minimum wage at best. So what's the option? Not saying I believe that, but obviously, a lot of them do. And Honor didn't exactly put them out on the street. She ran it more like an escort service. Or runs it. It's probably still going on, maybe more now that Anlya's gone.'

His mind reeling with this basic reality that had been completely off his radar – and apparently off Rebecca's – Hunt grabbed for his mug and took a sip. 'Does the woman who runs the house know about this?'

'Nellie? She might, but she's not saying anything. Honor will be gone in a few months and most of her gang with her, and then it'll probably stop. Unless somebody else steps up and moves into her spot. But if it's not going on *in* the house, Nellie doesn't want to know about it.'

'And she, Honor, came to this by herself?'

'No. I don't think so. Anlya said she used to be like her, smart and kind of motivated. Or at least enough like her that they were friends. Then maybe a year ago she got a boyfriend, and the two of them hit on this idea where they could make some pretty good money just by being organized.'

'So the two of them take a cut from what the girls make?'

'I think so. Same as it works everywhere, I gather, except these girls aren't on the street. The clientele, if you want to call it that, is all by referral. Even Anlya admitted it was pretty well managed, and so far it didn't seem like anybody was getting hurt.'

'Maybe not yet,' Hunt said, 'but just wait a few years.'

'I hear you. But obviously, they're not thinking that far ahead. To them, it's better than being a manicurist or a grocery bagger. And who knows, for some of them it might be.'

Hunt drew a breath and shook his head in sadness at the stark reality. 'So this guy,' he said. 'Honor's boyfriend, what do we know about him?'

'I know his first name is Royce, but that's about it. I think Anlya said he might have come over from Oakland.'

'And he's a full-time pimp? With Honor? Does he have a criminal record?'

'I don't know any of that.'

'But you do know that Anlya was interfering with the girls working for them?'

'She was like the unofficial homework tutor and counselor to the younger girls, and I think she tried to convince them that going out with Honor wasn't the smartest way to get ready for the grown-up world.'

'So she was trying to take business away from Honor and Royce?'

'I don't think it was a full-time job or anything like that, but anybody who'd listen, she'd give them an earful. She got at least a couple of them to, let's say, rethink their position. It was a little tense around the house.'

'Do you know if anything happened between Anlya and Honor in the last couple of days before she died?'

'No. Or I never heard of anything. She – Anlya – was all focused on getting the extension of benefits that I was going for.'

'Yeah, but didn't she tell Greg – at least this is his story – that she was really uptight the night they went out, her last night? Something was bothering her, but she wouldn't talk about it. Do you think that could have had something to do with Honor and her boyfriend?'

'It's possible, I suppose. But let's not forget one major thing,' Max said.

'What's that?'

'Greg's a liar.'

'All right,' Hunt said. 'I'll keep that in mind as we move ahead here. And you should keep in mind that just because he's a liar doesn't mean he's a killer.'

As though suddenly struck with overwhelming fatigue, Max hung his head for a moment. He sighed, then raised his eyes and checked the wall clock hanging by the stove.

'What more do you want to talk about?' he asked wearily. 'I really do have to go to work in a few minutes.'

'If you've got another five minutes, I'd like to ask you a couple of questions about your mother. Sharla, right?'

'What about her? Besides that she's a mess.'

'Okay, but didn't Anlya think she'd straightened out, enough so that she went and talked to her about moving back in when she turned eighteen?'

'That must have been wishful thinking. Sharla never straightened up that I saw. Or if she did, it didn't last long. When CPS came to check her out – and she knew they were coming, so she easily could have gotten herself together for one day – she was clearly on something, the house was a pigsty. For her, it was pretty much the usual.'

'But Anlya had been seeing her, hadn't she? She must have thought your mom was on the road to something better.'

'Maybe she thought she was. Maybe Sharla thought so, too. But then some other guy comes around . . . it was always some guy. Probably not as bad as Leon, because who could be? Whoever it would be, once they hooked up, everything revolved around him, period. And she made the worst choices in the world around men, let me tell you.'

'So who's Leon?'

'Leon Copes. The worst of the worst. He lived with us for five awful years. Beat the shit out of Sharla, raped Anlya before Sharla finally threw him out . . . just an absolute monster.'

'Where is he now?'

'I don't know. I heard he eventually killed somebody in a fight. Which was no big surprise. When I think about how he was, I'm kind of amazed he didn't kill one of us first.'

'So you think your mom got hooked up with another guy like Leon, and that's why she screwed up her chances with Anlya again?'

'That was the general pattern, yeah. She'd get in some

loser's orbit where, whatever he says, goes. Whatever he wants her to do, she does. Even if it screws up her kids' lives. It's like she has no sense for who she is herself. Without her guy, she's nothing. And then you throw in a guy like Leon or one of his clones . . .' He shook his head. 'Hopeless.' But a thought struck him. 'You don't think my mom could have had anything to do with Anlya getting killed, do you?'

'I doubt it. I'm just trying to identify areas of conflict in her life, and your mother was definitely one of them. I'm thinking if Anlya tried to get between Sharla and her latest . . . maybe he'd see her as a threat to his lifestyle. He'd want to get rid of her. I don't know. It's admittedly a long shot. Is Sharla with somebody now?'

'As far as I know.'

'Same guy as when Anlya was coming around?'

'That's my guess, but I'm not sure. You might ask her, if she'll talk to you.'

'I intend to. But why wouldn't she talk to me?'

'Because she'll see you as a cop. She hates cops, since they're always a threat to her men.'

'I'll see what shakes out. Meanwhile' – Hunt gestured around the kitchen – 'it looks like you landed in a pretty good place here.'

Max nodded. 'My Auntie Juney. Sharla's sister. They're complete opposites. I've been super-lucky.' He let out a breath. 'You know, I can't believe all this has gone on. I just keep thinking if only Greg hadn't had sex with her. I mean, how could he not stop himself? Even if she . . . And I thought after Leon, she wouldn't want anything to do with . . .' The words stopped coming. He sighed a last time, looked across at Hunt. 'I don't want to toss you out, but I've really got to get ready for work.'

24

YAMASHIRO HAD FOLLOWED Waverly with essentially the same testimony, just enough variation that Rebecca could not object to the evidence as cumulative – their identification of the victim, the call from Greg Treadway at the Little Shamrock, the meeting at Everett Middle School, and so on. Rebecca had halfheartedly tried to get into the perceived shortcuts of the investigation, as she had with Waverly; not unexpectedly, Bakhtiari cut her off after a brief foray. She decided not to push it.

Now, after a short afternoon recess, Fred Liu raised his right hand and swore to tell the truth, the whole truth, and nothing but the truth. Phil Braden, the walking cast on his right leg, gave Liu a few seconds to get comfortable in the witness chair, to look at the courtroom and get his bearings, to glance at the jury and the gallery and the defense table, where Rebecca sat with her father and her client.

Neatly dressed in a tie and sport coat, Liu faced Braden head-on with an air of happy expectation, almost as though it were he who'd be doing the questioning. Braden gave him a welcoming smile and started in. 'Mr Liu, what is your profession?'

'I'm the maître d' at the Imperial Palace, a restaurant in Chinatown.'

'And were you at that job on the evening of May seventh, earlier this year?'

'I was. I worked the whole day. Dim sum in the morning and then dinner at night.'

'On that night, did you see anyone in the restaurant whom you see in court today?'

'Yes, I did.'

'Would you tell us please where he is in the courtroom and what he's wearing?'

Without any hesitation, Liu pointed directly at Treadway. 'He's the man at that table in the blue suit, seated next to the lady.'

'May the record reflect that he has identified the defendant, Your Honor,' Braden said.

'So ordered.'

'Where was the defendant when you first saw him that night?'

'He was seated at table number nine in the corner with an African-American girl.' Liu then identified a photo of Anlya as the defendant's companion that night.

'Was there a reason why you remembered this couple particularly?'

'Several reasons. First, it was not a crowded night. We only had eight, maybe ten, parties at the other tables. They requested to sit back in a corner off by themselves. But mostly, I became aware of them after they'd been there a while, since they appeared to be having an argument. I went to pour water at their table a few times, hoping it would slow down the escalation, but that didn't work.'

'How do you mean?'

'Well, it was clear they were having a serious argument.'

Rebecca considered objecting to the word 'serious' as a conclusion, if for no other reason than to throw off the rhythm of the interrogation. Fred Liu was far too comfortable up there for her taste. She knew she'd be overruled and decided to let it go.

Liu went on, 'They just waved me away as I approached.

And then at the end, the woman made an angry noise and stood up so abruptly that she knocked her chair over and rushed out of the restaurant.'

'She rushed out on her own?'

'Yes. The man stayed behind to get the check.'

'And did you give the check to him?'

'Yes.'

'So you interacted with him close up?'

'Yes.'

'And did you later identify him from a group of photos shown to you by inspectors?' The six-pack signed by Liu was duly marked and admitted into evidence.

'Mr Liu, is there any doubt in your mind that you saw this defendant and the woman whose photo you identified, arguing in your restaurant the night of May seventh?'

'No. No doubt at all.'

So far, the testimony didn't present much of a problem for Rebecca. After all, Greg had always admitted that he'd gone to the Imperial Palace with Anlya and they'd had dinner there. But she knew that the most disturbing stuff was just ahead.

'Mr Liu,' Braden continued, 'before the fighting escalated and before the young woman left the restaurant, did this couple appear to you to have a romantic relationship?'

So quickly that she surprised herself, Rebecca was on her feet, objecting. 'Mr Liu's characterization of what their relationship might have been is pure speculation, Your Honor.'

Braden, knowing he'd turned the tables on Rebecca by drawing an objection that would only focus the jury's attention on an area he considered important, could not completely suppress a smile.

'Overruled,' Bakhtiari said. 'You can go into that on cross, counsel.'

Braden barely hesitated. 'Did you witness these two people holding hands during their dinner?'

'I did.'

'Did you notice any other display of affection?'

'Yes.'

'And what was that?'

'The woman leaned over and kissed him.'

'I take it this was before the argument?'

'Yes. They were at dinner for about forty-five minutes, and the argument started maybe two-thirds of the way through.'

Satisfied with Fred Liu's performance, Braden gave his witness a small nod. 'Thank you. I have no further questions.'

FROM REBECCA'S PERSPECTIVE, it was pure mercy that the judge, as soon as Braden had finished up with Fred Liu, asked if she'd mind holding her cross-examination until the next day, then adjourned court. She already felt as though she'd been defeated and then capitulated on the first major plank of her defense, which had been the hurried and therefore slipshod investigation. Without that, she found herself empty-handed after Yamashiro's testimony, and she hadn't been able to muster even the most perfunctory of cross-examinations.

But it wasn't until Braden was halfway through Liu's direct that she started to realize the dimension of her miscalculations. Because here today had been Mr Liu, clearly describing Greg and Anlya as a romantic couple out on a date on the fatal night, and Rebecca had no idea how she could refute any part of what he'd said. She had been thinking that she could at least call into question Liu's identification of Greg, or Greg and Anlya together, but the plain fact was that he had admitted to being there with Anlya. That was not in dispute. And she knew that with the DNA evidence coming up, there was no point in trying to deny the carnal reality of the relationship.

It was a few minutes after five, and Allie Jensen sat in

one of the client chairs in Rebecca's small office, listening to her roommate's litany of despair.

'The jury would laugh at me,' Rebecca said. 'If they hadn't already decided that I was extraneous baggage sitting in the courtroom anyway.'

'You're not doing nothing,' Allie said, 'there's just not much to refute so far. It'll be different when you bring out your own case in chief. You already zinged Braden on the suicide thing, and you've got a compelling alternative story once you start to tell it.'

'I do? Remind me what it is.'

'Come on. Look at Greg. His job, his volunteer stuff, two college degrees, for God's sake. Plus, he's got no criminal record of any kind. He comes across, and will when he testifies, as the nicest guy on the planet. You're telling me that this guy decides out of nowhere that he'll have to kill this woman whom, okay, he shouldn't be having sex with, but even that's only illegal by about three months.'

Rebecca didn't want to rain on Allie's parade, but she knew that nothing could be further from the truth. Sex between an adult and a seventeen-year-old was unlawful intercourse, the California equivalent of statutory rape. If convicted of even a misdemeanor, Greg would never work for any educational institution or youth group, even as a supervised volunteer, again. He would never get a security clearance. In the age of Google, he probably wouldn't get any sort of responsible job for years. And if Anlya had so much as suggested that her relationship with a twenty-seven-year-old white male who had power over her brother was for even a moment slightly less than one hundred percent consensual . . . The sex crimes inspectors had a saying: 'Seventeen will get you twenty.' It was not meant as a wisecrack.

Greg Treadway could have had every reason to kill Anlya.

'Well, yes,' Rebecca replied evenly. 'Except that somebody actually saw him.'

'No, they did not! Nobody saw anybody push or throw Anlya over that parapet. You can't forget that, Beck. That's the bottom line. After that, it was bad luck that someone who looks a little like Greg happened to be coming down those steps when he did. But Mr Abdullah never even hinted that he saw Greg up on Bush. Nobody says they saw Greg up there, fighting with Anlya or anybody else. That's the moment. The only moment. And nobody saw it. This was all very clear to you a couple of weeks ago, when you pitched it to me.'

'I know,' Rebecca said. 'I know. But my vision back then was that I'd be fighting the good fight all the way along, cross-examining everybody on everything. Instead I just sit there like a bump on a log, letting Braden pile it on. I swear to God, if the judge hadn't adjourned when he did today, I was dead. I've still got nothing to ask Fred Liu about. Everything he said was the gospel truth. How am I supposed to attack that?'

'Just leave it. You'll get your turn. Especially when Greg testifies and you get to make an argument. It's mostly circumstantial against him. And you know this town. It doesn't like to convict.'

'Maybe not, but you remember what they told us about circumstantial evidence in school. Sometimes it can be very convincing,' Rebecca said. 'Like a trout in the milk.'

HER FATHER SAT behind his desk, which had papers spread out all over it. He'd been doing some of his own billable work, which had taken a hit over the past week while he'd been attending the trial.

But when Rebecca poked her head in, he put down his pen and listened to her concerns: that she was failing, that the trial was already lost, that she was unprepared and didn't know what she was doing, that the jury thought she was an idiot.

Hardy listened to it all, and when she finished, he gave her a nod and said, 'It's always this way at the beginning. They trot out the case piece by piece, and you come to realize that if they didn't have something pretty compelling, it never would have gotten to trial. So you wait it out. Some of the evidence is good and some is weak, and once in a while you get lucky with a small point, like your "maybe it was suicide" moment. But this is the time when Braden gets his licks in, and you've to got to expect it to hurt a little. Or a lot.'

'I can take hurt. But I feel like I'm sitting in the middle of the road and he's steamrolling me. I mean, take Fred Liu today. The whole time he's testifying, I'm thinking that I'm going to get up on cross, pick apart his testimony, and generally kick his ass. But when he's done, I freeze up and realize I don't have anything to say. I'm sure everything happened just like he described it, and that's what the jury believes, too. Thank God the judge adjourned us or I would have been a stammering fool.'

'Hardly that. You don't have to cross-examine everybody. Only when you think you can draw blood. Oh, by the way, did you wind up getting any sleep last night?'

She gave him a weary smile. 'I think I finally dozed off around four.'

'So today you were going on, what, two hours?'

'Maybe three.'

'And you were – I'm just guessing – planning to stay up again tonight and take notes and prepare for tomorrow.'

'Pretty much, yeah.'

'Call me a radical thinker, but you might consider forgetting about that for tonight. Get a nice dinner someplace, then go home and go to bed.'

'Dad! I can't do that. You never did that!'

'Actually, I did, quite often, and so can you. You've already got all the facts. Now what you need, mostly, is to be sharp and pay attention. Do you really want to talk about Mr Liu, for example? You start out with him tomorrow, right? You're sure you don't want to cross him?'

Rebecca straightened in her chair and cocked her head with interest. 'On what? He didn't say anything that paints Greg in a worse light than he's already in.'

'No? Really? What was the gravamen of his testimony?'

'If I had to say anything, it would be that Greg and Anlya were romantically involved.'

Hardy nodded. 'Good. And what if they weren't?'

'The DNA evidence is going to clear that right up, don't you think?'

'What DNA evidence? Has the jury heard any DNA evidence yet?'

'No, they haven't, but when they do—'

Hardy raised a hand, stopping her. 'We're not there yet, are we? Right now the jury is still trying to figure out the relationship between Greg and Anlya. Mr Liu says they were romantically involved, but how does he know that?'

'Well, they were holding hands.'

'They were? Were their fingers interlocked? Whose hand was on top? Is it possible Greg was holding his hand over hers to calm her down because he was delivering bad news about her foster extension? Did Mr Liu hear any romantic or intimate language between the two of them? Any words of endearment? Actually, Liu's testimony is that he was under the impression that they were fighting, wasn't it? Was he waiting on other people? How much attention was he paying to Greg and Anlya? So his entire conclusion that they were romantically involved is based on his observation that their hands were touching?'

'You're a little scary, Dad.'

Hardy grinned. 'I like to think so. But I'm also well rested and logical, half of which at the moment you are, too.'

'Okay, then what about the kiss?'

'What about it? Did Mr Liu see them share more than

one kiss? Who kissed whom? Was Greg surprised? Was Liu paying attention at the exact moment of the kiss? Was it on the lips? If it wasn't, if it was on Greg's cheek, has Mr Liu ever had someone – a child or a parent or an acquaintance, for example – with whom he was not romantically involved kiss him on the cheek? What was the difference between the kiss that he saw and the one Greg received? How could he tell, therefore, that this was a romantic kiss? Might it, for example, have been a quick thank-you kiss because Greg told her something that relieved her or made her happy? You've been known to give me a buss on the cheek to thank me for something, or even if you're just glad to see me. Are you and I therefore romantically involved?'

'What if the kiss was on the lips, though? Isn't it the rule in court never to ask a question for which you don't know the answer?'

'Yes it is. And luckily, in this specific case, we do know the answer.'

'We do? What is it?'

'You've seen it. It's in your file.'

'No way. I've read that whole file through a million times. Where is it?'

'Liu's statement, just after he tells about seeing them kiss, and Yamashiro follows up and asks what kind of kiss it was, and Liu says something like "She leaned over and kissed him on the cheek." Braden, wisely, left that out in his direct. But it makes a huge difference. In fact, it makes all the difference. And if he says something different than he told the inspectors, it's even better. If he decides now that Greg leaned over and kissed her, or that the kiss was on the lips, confront him with what he told the police. The jury will decide he either doesn't remember what happened or never really saw it in the first place, which is good for you. Because if they don't believe he has the story about the kiss right, how can they believe him about the argument?'

Rebecca brought both of her hands up and pushed on her forehead. She looked across at her father. 'I'm never going to be good at this, am I?'

'Of course you will. You're a whiz kid. This is your first murder trial, and my letting you deal with the burden of a murder trial within two years of finishing law school is probably criminally negligent on my part. But this case really chose you, and I know you can do it. You'll get it all, you'll see. Meantime, you've got to learn to walk that thin line between getting enough rest to stay sharp and beating yourself up every waking minute by constantly reevaluating everything and not sleeping so that you can't focus on anything. When do you hear, by the way, from Wyatt Hunt?'

'He's going to check in at six-thirty.'

Hardy glanced at his watch. 'So. Half an hour. Clear your desk. Take his call. Get something to eat and go home and hit the sack. And then tomorrow, start off by cross-examining the living shit out of Fred Liu. Politely and respectfully, because he's honest and the jury likes him. But kick his ass. Does that sound like a good time or what?'

25

GLITSKY AND TREYA, Wes Farrell, and his wife, Sam, had four adjoining seats in the club level on the first-base side of AT&T Park. The Giants had begun the year by running away with the National League West, but after a slew of injuries, the season had degenerated into a nail-biting funk. Still, any time the Dodgers were in town, the vibe was intense and interest was high. Tonight the temperature at game time had been 61 degrees, and now, in the bottom of the fifth inning, a bank of fog was starting to swirl in from left field and it was getting decidedly chilly. The four of them put on the coats they'd brought just in case.

The Giants were ahead 4 to 2, but regardless of the eventual outcome of the game, Farrell and Sam, both of whom loved Buster Posey – Sam had given him the poster that hung in his office – would go home happy, since the catcher had homered in his first two at-bats, accounting for all of the home team's runs.

With the cold, the women had gone inside together for hot chocolate. The game was plodding along, and Glitsky cleared his throat. 'Would it ruin your night if I brought up work?' he asked.

'Nothing's going to ruin my night,' Farrell said. 'I'm thinking Buster might hit four. He's got two more shots, at least. If you give me odds, I'd bet you on it.'

'What kind of odds?'

Farrell pondered for a second or two. 'Say a hundred to one?'

Glitsky threw Farrell a sideways glance. 'Please. I wouldn't give a hundred to one that the world isn't going to end in the next ten minutes.'

'You are such a cheery guy.'

'I know. I work on it.'

'Okay, thirty to one. Ten bucks.'

'So I win, I get ten. You win, you get three hundred. How is this a good deal for me?'

'He likely won't do it, that's how. Those odds are probably way in your favor.'

'Why don't you give me odds that he will?'

'C'mon, Abe. Because the overwhelming odds are that he won't.' Posey was coming to the plate. 'Twenty bucks,' Farrell said. 'Ten to one. I'm essentially giving you twenty bucks for nothing.'

Glitsky pulled his leather flight jacket closed. 'I appreciate it. If you want, you can give me the twenty without a bet. I'd take that.'

'Look at this weather blowing in from left. He'd have to hit it into that. Are you kidding me?' Farrell gave him a nudge. 'Okay, five to one. Twenty bucks. You can't *not* take that bet.'

'Five to one?' Glitsky gave it a moment. 'Okay. Let's make it fifty bucks, though. Make the risk worth my while.'

'Risk, ha!'

The two men shook.

'But you wanted to talk about work?' Farrell asked.

Posey stepped into the batter's box and Glitsky said, 'It can wait an at-bat.'

The at-bat didn't last long, as Posey slammed the first pitch about twenty rows deep into the left-field bleachers.

'It's a good thing I don't use profanity,' Glitsky said as Posey touched home plate, 'or I'd be sorely tempted right now.'

'Save it for when he hits the next one,' Farrell said. 'But really, now, what about work?'

'Well, that Thirteen Sixty-eight assignment? The good news is that Villanova and Schwartz have tracked down the basic problem. The bad news is that it's potentially fairly significant.'

'Like how significant?'

'Twelve people.'

Farrell turned in his seat. 'I know you don't like swearing, but you are shitting me.'

'I wish I were.'

'You're saying that we've turned loose twelve crazy violent felons who ought to be in the state hospital? They just walked away from the jail?'

'Not the jail, really. They get down here from Napa in custody, but one of the clerks who was handling these cases after the hearing – Maricel Santos is her name – evidently wasn't too clear on the concept of which box to check on the form for their next placement.'

'Next placement after what?'

'After they're found still incompetent, with a violent felony pending, and after they've already done their first three-year stint. The judge orders a Murphy Conservatorship, so they're supposed to be sent back to Napa. At which point Ms Santos checks the box for "gravely disabled," meaning unable to care for themselves. So they go to a halfway house. And when a disabled person walks away from a halfway house, there's no particular urgency to tell the court or find them. They just wait for them to be picked up on the street, wandering around.'

'So you're telling me this woman checked the wrong box on a Murphy form twelve times?'

'That I've found so far. Maybe she wasn't well supervised. It also appears her training was somewhat inadequate. In any event, she seems to have gotten more of the hang of it in the past six months or so.'

'But until then, did all of these twelve people just walk away?'

'There's more good news there. A few were so clueless – we're talking some truly space-case people here – that they didn't really get it that they could take a walk away from their halfway house and not come back. As of today, our guys have found six of these people hanging out at the homes where they were delivered. And they're back in jail, pending commitment to more secure facilities.'

'That's some kind of good news, but it still leaves six . . .'

'Right,' Glitsky said. 'Who have eloped. That's including Ricardo Salazar, our Minnesota murderer, so it's really only five. But – bad news time – four of those five were brought in originally on homicides, and they're now wherever they are, maybe alternating between glimpses of sanity and pure delusion. In any case, probably not much enriching the lives of the people they're interacting with.'

'Five of them.'

'Only four who have probably killed people.'

'There's a heartening thought.'

'I know. Isn't it?'

26

LIFE WITH ROYCE was not working out the way Honor Wilson had planned.

When she'd turned eighteen in early June, she had already all but moved out of McAllister and into the place they'd rented together on Turk in the lower Fillmore District. She was starting to think that the quality of her living quarters should have been her first warning – it was a tired, run-down one-bedroom apartment – kitchen, living room, bedroom, one bath – on the first floor of an ugly six-unit building. The previous tenants had painted the walls dark purple. The wall-to-wall carpet was ancient, stained, and smelly. The showerhead was broken; an apparently permanent rusty ring encircled both the bathtub and the inside of the toilet. Two windows in the living room faced the street and provided feeble natural light, but the rest of the place seemed perennially in deep shade, even with the lights turned on. The windowless bedroom was like a cave carved into the back corner of the building. The entryway to the building had gathered unto itself an impressive pile of debris – newspapers, fast-food wrappers, take-out menus, various containers that once held alcohol. Royce had argued that they take the place furnished, so everything they used, from the furniture to the cookware to the utensils, was old, sagging, broken, depressing.

But it was going to be their place at last, their very own, and with all its problems it was still a huge improvement over the truly filthy crowded apartment (and bedroom) Royce had been sharing with his five lowlife criminal friends. They'd fix it all up. They'd be making good money, and even with the exorbitant twelve-hundred-dollars rent, Honor figured they'd be able to buy some new stuff and get the place cleaned up and livable in no time.

But now it was six weeks later, and Honor had to admit that the situation with the apartment – not good to begin with – had, if anything, deteriorated. The first thing that went wrong was that once she had left McAllister Street, her control over the girls began to evaporate. She was no longer on the premises to arrange assignments and follow up on payments, and almost immediately, two of them decided they could make their own arrangements, hooking up with other customers. Another one decided she didn't really like the work and would rather concentrate on school and try to get a real job when she got out.

So the income was falling. About a month ago, Royce had gone so far as to suggest that Honor take on a few customers of her own to make up for the shortfall. That had been a bad night. Honor considered herself a businesswoman who had discovered a lucrative trade that she could exploit, that was all. She was not about to sell her body to some guy for money. She loved Royce, which was why she was with him. They were building a life together. She couldn't believe that he could even consider her like one of her girls. She was a cut above, smarter, different. She was his partner, not just his main source of income. They were equals.

He'd hit her again that night, hard, and more than once. He had told her what she needed to do, and she was going to do it, goddammit. Afterward he'd made up with her, or tried to, saying he was sorry. She was right. She shouldn't ever have to turn tricks. And it wasn't like she was going to leave him. Where would she go, after all?

But it changed things for her.

And then – hard to believe all these changes happened

in a matter of weeks – came the drugs. Royce had always dealt a little weed to augment his spending money, but he'd given that up once Honor had gotten her string of girls steadily producing. With that cash flow slowing down, he had looked up some of his old connections and decided that he could do better than weed by dealing cocaine, for which there always seemed to be a ready market. Since cocaine was available to him, he had started taking the occasional snort or more.

By far the worst of the changes, she thought as she sat in their dirty apartment at eleven-thirty on this Thursday night, was his stepping out on her with a bitch named Lilianne Downs, whom he'd known from his old 'hood and had run into when picking up some powdered product a couple of days ago. Lilianne had called him on his cell three times in the past two days, as if Honor couldn't figure out who it was. Honor also knew that he'd called her back only this evening, just before he remembered needing to go meet a guy about a thing; he'd left the apartment a little after seven, telling Honor he'd be back soon.

She didn't define four hours as soon.

At last, the click of the lock turning.

She started at the sound, immediately and completely awake, and sat up. The built-in clock on the stove read 11:43, and the juice glass in front of her, from which she'd been drinking her wine, was empty.

That son of a bitch.

She got to her feet and made it to the door just as he was starting to push it open. She kicked at it, and it slammed closed with the power to shudder the walls.

On the other side of the door, Royce exploded in a tirade of profanity. He turned the knob again, and she threw her whole body against the door, slamming it again.

'Goddammit, Honor! Open up! Let me in.'

'You're done here, you motherfucker,' she screamed. 'Go on back to your whore! You're not getting in.' She had her foot pressed against the bottom of the door, but when he came at it next time with all of his might, he pushed that wedged foot back a couple of inches, then threw his arm into the crack he'd forced open. She had no time to reset herself before he slammed his whole body against the door again, opening it another two or three inches. He shoved more of his arm in.

Leaning up against the inside of the door, Honor threw a backhanded fist into his forearm, then threw her body back against him.

He screamed in pain and pulled his arm out but didn't give back one inch of what he'd gained, holding the door open with the strength of his body, leaning up against it. He kicked the bottom of the door, got his foot through the breach he'd opened, and once more body-slammed it. And again. Another inch. And another.

Finally, he pulled away and charged, knocking her backward and off the door. Unsteady from her drinking, she screamed, stumbled, and went down, and even though she kicked at him and connected two or three times, he was all the way inside the apartment and hovering over her, kicking at her ribs and then pouncing nearly full length onto her body, holding her down, his knees on her arms up around her shoulders, snapping her head to the left with his right hand, to the right with his left, every breath a swear word as the blows rained down left and right, left and right, left and right . . .

WAS SHE DEAD?

What had happened? Where was she?

In some sort of bed, but not her own bed in her apartment. She could tell, even in her near-unconscious state, that it was too clean, too tightly blanketed, for that.

And her eyes. She didn't have to try opening her eyes to tell that she couldn't. They felt like something heavy was weighing on them, pressing them into her skull. Her arms seemed to be tied to her sides. She had no sense of her face. It was all numb. Maybe she was drugged. That's right, she was drinking wine, she thought. Something also felt wrong in her jaw. She couldn't define it, but it was different. Her mouth, too, the inside of her mouth. Were some teeth gone? She couldn't move her tongue to check.

She was sinking, going under again.

A WOMAN'S GENTLE voice. 'Can you tell me your name?'

'Hunh.' It came out sounding wrong. She tried again. 'Honor.' Her mouth seemed to be wired shut.

'Honor?'

She couldn't nod, couldn't blink, couldn't tell the woman she'd gotten it right. Her eyes let in no light. And the weight on them . . . 'Yes. Honor Wilson.' It still didn't sound like her name.

But the woman repeated it, got it close enough. 'Honor Illsun. Is that your name?'

'Yes.'

'Honor,' she asked, 'who did this to you?'

Did what? she wanted to say. Everything seemed to be broken. She realized she couldn't feel her feet. The whole world was black.

All of a sudden, it came back to her. Royce trying to let himself in. The struggle at the door to her apartment, getting pinned down, his knees on her arms. The fists coming at her one after another until . . .

Until she woke up here, wherever she was.

What had happened? How did she get here?

It was Royce, the fucker. Royce, the man she'd loved. Who'd cheated on her, betrayed her. And now she knew with all her soul that he had killed her. She was going to die.

That's why she had no body anymore. No feeling. She would sink again into blackness and never come up out of it.

The voice spoke again, whispering, gentle. 'Honor, who did this to you?'

'Royce.'

'Rice?'

'No.' She tried to breathe in, get more air behind what she said. 'Royce. Royce Utlee.'

'Rice Sully?'

'No. Ut-lee.' Her tongue could make the T sound. Good. That would be close enough. Rice Utlee. They could identify him from that, and once they started looking, they'd know who had done this to her.

And she would get her revenge for what he'd done. The fists came back to her, the pounding on her. He must have done more after she lost consciousness – her arms and legs, her eyes.

Where had they found her?

Where was Royce?

She was going to take him down. At the very least, ruin the rest of his life. She heard the woman saying something from far away, as though talking to somebody else. Honor forced herself to make a guttural moan.

'It's all right.' The voice was soothing. 'What is it, Honor? Do you want to say something?'

'Yes.' She could say 'yes' clearly, and she repeated it. 'Yes.'

'I'm right here. Talk to me.'

'Royce Utlee,' she managed, with all the enunciation she could muster.

The voice repeated it almost exactly; she had it now. 'Something else about Royce Utlee?'

She drew a breath. 'Yes.'

'What is it?'

'Also killed Anlya Paulson.'

'Also killed who?'

'Anlya Paulson. Tunnel girl.'

'Anlya Paulson.' She got it right on the first try. 'The tunnel . . . Oh my God! You're saying "the tunnel girl"?'

'Yes.'

Honor didn't know if she smiled. She couldn't feel her face. Her heart was glad, though. The woman understood what she'd said. Honor would get back at Royce and give him another murder to explain while he was about it.

Because Honor had long since decided that Royce had killed Anlya to get her out of their business. Back then, that hadn't been her concern, what he'd done with Anlya. But now it was. Now it would be another bullet in the weapon that would take that motherfucker down.

It was already dark. Her eyes could not open. She let out a breath. It went all the way out to where there was nothing left to exhale. She felt warm and suddenly at peace as she went to grab the next breath, but she found no purchase there as the air ran out and the darkness swelled and settled around her and took her all the way down.

OFFICER JANINE MCDOUGAL was twenty-eight years old, and for three of those years she had been a uniformed patrol cop in San Francisco. At about one-fifteen A.M., with her partner, Don Cortes, she had been patrolling a godforsaken bit of turf in the Western Addition when Dispatch had alerted them to the 911 on Turk and Webster – an unidentified young woman, perhaps a victim of a hit-and-run, lying in the street. Janine and Don beat the ambulance there, and Janine rode with the victim out to General Hospital, while Don followed in their cruiser.

Janine didn't know if there was a distinctive pattern of injuries consistent with hit-and-run victims, but in her time on the force, she had gained an unenviable familiarity with the injuries seen in cases of domestic violence. After a good preliminary look at this woman, she felt pretty sure she was viewing a very serious beating that the victim had suffered, probably at the hands of her mate, spouse, boyfriend, whatever. Once the EMT crew had arrived, and even with all of her experience in these situations, she was appalled to hear the medical techs say that regardless of whether the woman had been beaten, they would bet she'd also been run over by a car, probably to kill her for sure and keep her from identifying her assailant.

The victim was obviously tougher than that. By the time they got her to General Hospital, where her condition was pronounced critical by the ER, Janine felt certain that this would turn out to be a homicide.

But it wasn't yet. And she was a cop, and she was here. And she had her tape recorder.

She couldn't call Homicide until the woman was dead. Well, she could, but because of the late hour, it would not be appreciated. The first time she had called for a victim who was still alive, the Operations sergeant had told her drily that the Homicide protocol was for completely dead people, not almostees. So she told Don she was going to stick around, if he could spare her, and try to talk to this victim if she regained consciousness.

At 4:51, against all predictions, that's exactly what the victim did.

Now, forty-one minutes later, Honor was dead and Janine was talking by phone to Devin Juhle. She felt as nervous as she had at her first prom – her career goal was Homicide inspector – and this was her first dance. 'I told Operations this was a homicide. They said they would send the on-call inspectors, but because of what the victim told me before she died, I thought you might want to know right away, so I had them call you and give you my number in case you wanted to talk to me right now. I hope I'm not wasting your time.'

Juhle, sounding like the soul of patience, finally got a

word in. 'It sounds like you handled everything perfectly, Officer. So start from the beginning. What did she say?'

'She said her name was Honor. She said it two or three times. Honor, as in honor thy father and thy mother, last name Wilson. I'm pretty sure that's it, or sounds a lot like it. As I say, I've got it on tape, and I figured we could run her driver's license and see if we got lucky, find out where she lived, and so on.'

'Excellent. But that's not why you called me. What else did she say?'

'Well, when she came to, I told her it didn't look good, that she might not make it, and this was her chance to say what happened. I asked her if she could tell me who had beaten her.'

'That was good thinking.'

'Thank you. Again, between the drugs and the condition of her mouth, the name didn't come out crystal-clear, but she really seemed to want us to know who had done this to her, so she came back to it a couple of times, and eventually, I think we got it. A Royce Utlee.'

'Her killer's name from her deathbed? It doesn't get better than that, Officer. Good work. And though I don't want to sound impatient, that's great stuff for the inspectors, but again, why are you calling me?'

'There was more, and I think it's important.'

'What's that?'

'She said this Royce Utlee also killed Anlya Paulson, the tunnel girl.' After fifteen or twenty seconds, Janine said, 'Lieutenant, did you copy that? I said—'

'No, I heard you. She said he killed Anlya Paulson. Did she give any further details about that second murder?'

'No, sir. Just the bare fact of it.'

'How did she know about it?'

'She didn't say. She just came out and volunteered the information.'

She heard Juhle sigh at the other end of the line. 'Anlya Paulson,' he repeated.

'Isn't that trial going on right now, sir?'

'I believe it is, yes.'

'Is the suspect Utlee? Is he out on bail? Wouldn't that be odd in a murder case? I mean, could he have . . . ?'

'The suspect isn't Royce Utlee. It's Greg Treadway.' Juhle sighed again. 'Okay, after she gave you Anlya's name as somebody else Utlee killed, what happened next?'

'She flatlined, sir. And they weren't able to bring her back.'

27

AT WHAT WES Farrell considered the truly obscene time of 6:50 on Friday morning, he spotted Devin Juhle at one of the back tables near the corner at the Irving Street Café, which was about midway between their two houses. He wound his way through the crowd and took a chair across from the red-eyed, heavy-lidded Homicide chief.

Farrell's face registered pure disgust. 'Well, ain't this a fine kettle of fish?' he asked. Sitting back in his chair, he let the waitress fill his coffee cup, then thanked her and said to Juhle, 'Have you gotten anything else since we talked?'

'Actually, quite a bit, although I can't guarantee you're going to like it.'

'What a surprise. Hit me.'

'The girl's name is, in fact, Honor Wilson. Both Waverly and Yamashiro knew all about her. She lives in Anlya's group home, at least that's the address on her DL, although there seems to be some question if she was still there.'

'What about this Utlee guy?'

'We don't have much of a handle on him yet. This will shock you, but he's not at the address on his DL, which is suspended anyway. He's got a one-strike sheet with a Two-eleven as an adult, but I'm betting it's got more than that robbery charge if you count juvie time. They've pulled a warrant on him based on Honor's deathbed ID, but for the moment, he's nowhere to be found, although my guys are heading out to Anlya's house even as we speak and hope to talk to some of the other girls about what, if anything, was going on there. But last time, with Anlya's death, nobody knew nothing. The usual.'

'Shit.'

'That's what I thought. More important, what are we going to do about the Anlya Paulson thing?'

Farrell drank some coffee, made a face, dropped a couple of sugar cubes into his cup, and stirred. 'First off,' he said after a more acceptable sip, 'you can set your mind at ease about Anlya, because it's hearsay and it's not admissible. It's just this Wilson girl's statement.'

'Deathbed statement, though. A dying declaration.'

Farrell shook his head. 'Nope. A dying declaration has to be about the cause and circumstances surrounding the death. So Utlee killed me, admissible. He killed somebody else, inadmissible. And not to quibble, there's also no foundation. We have no idea why she thinks this Royce Utlee killed the tunnel girl. We don't know if he confessed to her, if she saw it, or if her dead cat came to her in a dream and told her. We can't prove she has personal knowledge. It's not admissible. Maybe when you find this guy, you can sweat him and get a confession or something else you can use, but unless you do, the girl's statement is worthless.'

'Okay,' Juhle said, 'that's the legal answer. But that's not really my question.'

The waitress came by and interrupted to take their orders – eggs over easy, bacon, the best hash browns in the city, English muffins, and orange juice for both of them – then promptly disappeared again.

'So,' Juhle tried again, 'Greg Treadway?'

'Yeah, I know. It's an issue.'

'How about, since you say it's absolutely inadmissible, we just don't mention it?'

Farrell grinned at that one. 'I love the way you think, Dev. But it would take a fairly tortured interpretation to conclude that this doesn't have shit-all to do with the

Treadway prosecution. Beyond that, speaking of legal, if we don't tell the defense, that would be the prosecution hiding evidence that could exonerate the defendant, which would be about the clearest *Brady* violation I could imagine. They'd automatically win on appeal. And by the way, every lawyer involved could lose their ticket to practice law. The short answer is we've got to tell them.'

'And then what? Mistrial? We can't just let Treadway go.'

'Wouldn't Liam Goodman love that? Another suspect we couldn't convict. Will it ever end? But no, we're not just letting Treadway go. I promise you that. I think we have to prepare ourselves, though, to have this officer who took Honor Wilson's statement show up on the defense witness list. And I predict that will not be a pretty moment for the home team. So far, I don't think the jury is going to hear the statement, but the judge could change that in a New York minute. Meanwhile, it might be helpful if your guys could get their hands on this Utlee character.'

REBECCA HAD TAKEN her father's advice the previous night, and when the telephone rang in her kitchen at seven-forty-five, she was already wide-awake, having slept nearly ten hours. She felt terrific. 'Hello,' she all but sang into the receiver.

'Good morning, and it is a very good morning,' her father said. 'I just got a call from Wes Farrell, who, sadly, is not having as good a day as you and I are by a long shot. You're not going to believe this.'

'What? Tell me.'

Hardy told her. By the time he'd finished, Rebecca had boosted herself up onto her kitchen counter. It seemed to her as though a large weight had been lifted from her chest. 'God,' she said, 'that is such fantastic news. To say nothing of the fact that it proves Greg didn't do it after all.'

'Hadn't you always believed that?'

'Most of the time, although I had my moments. But now . . .'

'Not to dim your enthusiasm, Beck, but it doesn't prove anything about Greg one way or the other.'

'Maybe more than you know.'

'What do you mean?'

'You remember last night I was going to hear from Wyatt? He told me he had talked to Anlya's brother, Max, who had a whole story about Honor Wilson and Royce Utlee and why they might have wanted to get Anlya out of the way.'

'Did he say anything that puts this Utlee guy physically close to her the night she died?'

'I don't know, but at least we're going to have a strong alternative theory of the case for the jury to hear.'

'Maybe not quite that.'

'Of course that. What do you mean?'

'I mean, it would be strong if we can get it in.'

'How can we not get it in? The judge couldn't decide to leave it out. It's obviously relevant. In fact, it's major. It's a whole new prime suspect for the same crime.'

'It's also inadmissible hearsay, for starters.'

The Beck didn't speak for a moment. Then, 'If using it against Utlee would be admissible, this is damn close to the same situation.'

'That's your argument for the judge, but I'd prepare myself that he might not go for it.'

'Jesus. That would be so not fair.'

Hardy chuckled. 'If anything, it's too fair. Somebody says somebody else did something. How credible is that?'

'But a dying declaration? An explicit exception to the hearsay rule?'

'True. Maybe as to Utlee. But as to Treadway, don't count your chickens. It's not detailed enough to show she was doing anything more than repeating a rumor. After all, she never said how she knew what she knew. What proof did she offer?'

'Okay, but why would she finger him if she didn't know he did it?'

'Wrong question, Beck. The question is: Did she have personal knowledge, or was she repeating something she heard? I can think of some reasons why she might just make it up. And so can the judge, I'm betting.'

Rebecca drew a breath, let it out. 'For a minute there, you almost had me happy.'

'You should be happy. This is a huge deal. For your client and how you feel about him, if nothing else. And maybe they'll get ahold of Utlee soon and he'll confess, or they'll find Anlya's purse at his house or in his car or something. Then you'd really be talking.'

'I'm not seeing how, if they won't let it in.'

'Something will shake out, you watch.'

Devin Juhle and Wyatt Hunt, high school baseball teammates and best friends, had reconnected about ten years ago, when Hunt was working with Child Protective Services and Juhle was a uniformed cop. Just before Juhle had taken the job as Homicide chief, Hunt had offered him employment as a private investigator and equity sharer in his firm the Hunt Club, but Juhle had turned him down.

Nevertheless, the two saw each other at various gatherings at least twice a month, and met for lunch at Lou the Greek's somewhat more often than that. Juhle had been best man at Hunt's wedding seven months ago, and his kids called Hunt Uncle Wyatt.

So, though they often found themselves on different sides in criminal cases, including Greg Treadway's, it was nowhere near unheard of for them to share information, so long as it did not jeopardize either investigation. And especially in a case like the one this morning, when Hunt could actively help out Juhle's inspectors and they in turn might uncover something that could prove pivotal in the defense of Greg Treadway.

Now Hunt sat at a folding chair across the desk from his old pal on the fourth floor of the Hall of Justice. One of the quirks of Juhle's office, inherited from Abe Glitsky's tenure on the job, was the magically never-ending stash of peanuts in the top right-hand drawer, and Juhle had shoved a small pile of them over in front of Hunt, who cracked and ate them in a thorough, methodical fashion.

'What was it that you had to see me about?' Juhle asked.

'Really? You can't guess? Does the name Honor Wilson ring a bell? Or Royce Utlee?'

Juhle liked to pretend that nothing surprised him, and he almost pulled it off except for a quick squint of his tired eyes. 'That was fast,' he said. 'You're working with Hardy's team?'

Hunt grinned. 'As far as I know, I *am* Hardy's team,' he said. 'I had an interview with Anlya Paulson's brother yesterday, and he mentioned both Honor and Royce. Imagine my surprise when The Beck – that's Ms Hardy to you – called me this morning and told me what had happened to Honor and what she told your guys.'

'Not my guys,' Juhle corrected him. 'A patrol officer who happened to be there. But she got it pretty right.'

'I understand that Honor named Utlee as her killer and said he'd also killed Anlya.'

'That's apparently what she said.'

'You haven't been able to locate Utlee yet?'

Juhle shrugged. 'It's been a matter of hours, Wyatt. We'll find him soon enough.'

'I'm sure you will. Maybe more quickly if I throw you a bone or two.'

Juhle sat back, breaking a smile. 'Are you going to make me beg?'

'It's tempting, but maybe you can just owe me.'

'All right. For what?'

'After I saw Max yesterday, I went over to the McAllister Street home where Anlya lived. And Honor. Do you know anything about what was going on there with her? With either of them?'

'We're working on that, too.'

'I'm sure you are, but to save you a little time . . .' Hunt cracked a peanut and began outlining what he had discovered. 'So the bottom line,' he concluded, 'is that these two, Honor and Royce, they put together an escort service with some of the girls there, pretty darn lucrative, and Anlya evidently was getting in the way of their business development, and at some point it looks like Utlee decided she had to go.'

'Did he tell anybody that?'

'Not that I've heard, no. Although right after Anlya got killed, Honor was furious for a while, and the general opinion was because Royce hadn't had to do that. He'd put himself in jeopardy for no reason.'

'He really did kill Anlya?'

'Well, she thought he did, at least. Which is what you've got, right?'

'Right. But Wes Farrell tells me that's hearsay and you guys can't use it.'

'That's what I hear, too, though The Beck's going to argue against that. Meanwhile, you need to find Utlee, and I'd like to have him in custody to talk to, and the word is you don't have an address on him.'

'How do you know that?'

'Spies everywhere. But don't worry about that. The good news is that one of the girls at McAllister Street yesterday gave me an address where Honor and Royce had moved in together. And if they drop by, your guys might find some evidence of, say, a fight or a meeting or a hookup or something he might have had with Anlya Paulson on the night she got killed. You might even find Utlee himself crashed out there, and wouldn't that be nice for both of us?'

Hunt pushed a piece of paper with an address written on it across the desk. Juhle reached for his telephone.

28

As soon as she'd gotten off the phone with her father that morning, Rebecca had assigned Allie to start working on a motion to admit the deathbed statement of Honor Wilson in this case. As a backup, since she had to consider that the motion might be denied, Rebecca got her laptop out on the kitchen table and started her own motion for a mistrial and dismissal of all charges against her client.

She knew absolutely, with the new evidence, that the judge would have to give her time to investigate the possibility that Royce Utlee had killed Anlya Paulson. Failure to do so would be virtually an automatic reversal on appeal. But she was more than a little concerned about how Greg would handle the idea of sitting in jail for six months, only to begin the trial again.

He would flatly not accept it.

Even the suggestion that they needed to waive time at the beginning of the trial to give her the opportunity to prepare had met with resistance and some surprising, even startling, displays of real anger from her client.

'No fucking way! No way!'

'Greg, just wait. Let me—'

'I'm not waiting. I'm not listening. There's nothing you can say that will convince me. I'm not staying in this hellhole one second longer than I need to, and now you're trying to tell me you'll need at least a few months. Months! Are you fucking kidding me? Do you know what it's like in here?'

'Yes, but if we're not prepared—'

'Well, get prepared. What the hell am I paying you for?'

Eventually, she had allowed him to persuade her that going forward quickly would be more of a disadvantage to the prosecution than to the defense, but it had been damned ugly.

She was afraid the argument about a mistrial would be worse. She knew that the choice ultimately was hers, as his attorney, and given this break in the case, she did not see how she could fail to ask for a mistrial, whether he wanted her to or not.

ALLIE WASN'T DONE with her motion by the time court got called into session, but Rebecca immediately told the judge about the new evidence and the motions that were coming. Bakhtiari wasn't going to keep witnesses waiting, so he decided to start the morning where they'd left off yesterday, her cross-examination of Fred Liu.

After Hardy's brief tutorial in his office, as well as the full night's sleep that had restored her confidence and her spirits, Rebecca actually looked forward to the cross-examination and, by the end of it, felt that she'd succeeded in casting doubt on whether Greg and Anlya had a romantic relationship.

Of course, the DNA evidence was coming up, and that would be challenging to refute, to say the least, but as her father had pointed out, that was another day.

Meanwhile, since both Officer McDougal and Allie (with her motion) had arrived in the courtroom during Liu's cross, no sooner had Rebecca dismissed him and returned to the defense table than Bakhtiari excused the jury. When they had all filed out, the judge kept things moving along. 'The first thing let's do is find out what we're talking about here. Counsel,' he said to Rebecca, 'what's your motion?'

Rebecca handed Allie's papers to the judge. 'Your Honor,'

she said, 'the defense wants to call Officer Janine McDougal and play a tape recording she made of a woman named Honor Wilson as she lay on her deathbed last night. On that tape, she identifies a person named Royce Utlee as the killer of Anlya Paulson. Clearly, this deathbed statement is strong if not incontrovertible evidence that Royce Utlee committed the murder for which my client stands accused.'

One of the Liam Goodman contingent in the gallery called out, 'Here we go!' and it took almost a full minute for the uproar to subside. Bakhtiari looked down from the bench. 'I will tolerate no more outbursts of this kind from the members of the gallery. If there is another demonstration of this type, I will clear the courtroom.' Still glaring, he directed his attention to the prosecutor. 'Mr Braden? I believe you were about to respond to defense counsel's statement.'

'Your Honor,' Braden said. 'The People object. The evidence that Ms Hardy wants to elicit from this officer is inadmissible as hearsay and lacks foundation that the witness spoke from personal knowledge. We have no idea why Ms Wilson thought that Royce Utlee committed this crime, or even if she thought it at all. Her accusation of this Royce Utlee would serve to do nothing but confuse the jury and ask them to indulge in baseless speculation.'

'Your Honor,' Rebecca said, 'it is a critical dying declaration that the jury needs to hear.'

Bakhtiari came back to Braden. 'A dying declaration is admissible as an exception to the hearsay rule in murder cases, Mr Braden.'

'Yes, Your Honor, but a dying declaration has to be about the cause and circumstances surrounding the death. What Ms Wilson said about her own homicide might be admissible, but what she said about the death of Anlya Paulson is not. Plus, Your Honor, it lacks foundation. We have no way of knowing if Ms Wilson spoke from personal knowledge. Even if she were alive, Ms Wilson's testimony would not be admissible until she could tell the jury how she knew what she claimed to know.'

Rebecca had an answer to that. 'Your Honor, in *Chambers* v. *Mississippi*, the United States Supreme Court said that technical rules of evidence could not be used to prevent a defendant from presenting clearly exculpatory evidence to a jury. Nothing could be more exculpatory in this case than a dying statement that someone else committed this murder.'

Bakhtiari glanced down at the papers in his hand. 'I'm going to call a short recess while I consider this motion in my chambers.'

He started to rise, but Rebecca spoke up again. 'Your Honor, if I may.'

'Yes?'

She turned and strode back to the table where Allie sat next to Greg. Dismas had a morning meeting with the client he'd been working on last night and hadn't made it to the courtroom today. Though she appreciated his help and support, Rebecca thought that this was just as well. It was time she took control and made this case her own.

Not trusting herself to give her client even the most cursory glance, she gathered the pages she'd prepared and brought them back up to the bench. 'Your Honor, in the event that you rule Officer McDougal's evidence inadmissible, I've prepared another motion requesting a mistrial.'

'Your Honor!' Braden's exasperation overflowed. 'This is why there is an evidence code. Officer McDougal's evidence is clearly inadmissible on the face of it, and your ruling on it as such can't provide any grounds for a mistrial.'

Bakhtiari frowned down at Braden. 'I think, counsel, you've totally missed the point. Even if I rule the present statement inadmissible, I don't see how I can deny Ms Hardy a mistrial to give her additional time to explore the possibility that they can find evidence that this Royce Utlee might actually be the killer. Meanwhile' – he tapped his gavel – 'court is in recess for twenty minutes. We will reconvene at eleven o'clock.'

'I THOUGHT I'D *made it clear we weren't taking a mistrial, no matter what. I'm not staying here another six months so we can start this all over again, and that's what you're talking about, isn't it? Starting over.'*

'*Yes, but with new evidence that might—*'

'*No! Do you hear me? No!*'

'*Greg. Please keep your voice down.*'

'*The hell with my voice, Rebecca. The jury's not around to hear it.*'

'*That's not the point. Just calm down.*'

'*I'm not calming down. We're not doing a mistrial.*'

'*Greg. Beck. Shh. Both of you.*' At the defense table, Allie had one hand on Greg's near arm, the other reaching over him to Rebecca. '*Easy. We're not even there yet. Let's wait until the judge rules on the tape's admissibility first. The whole mistrial issue might not even come up.*'

'*It better fucking not.*'

'*Greg. Shh. Please.*'

COURT DID NOT reconvene at eleven o'clock.

Because of the unusual nature of this case, the judge had decided early on that there would be no off-the-record conversations. He didn't want to hear later about secret discussions and backroom deals. Every communication among or between all parties, whether it be in open court, at sidebar, or in the judge's chambers, would be taken down and made part of the formal transcript. This was why Rebecca and Braden, who had gathered in Judge Bakhtiari's chambers behind Department 24, were now sitting in a tense silence, waiting for Theresa Shepard, the court recorder, to get her equipment set up so that she could memorialize every word.

Rebecca couldn't help but notice that the judge, in

contrast to his generally affable demeanor in the court, seemed impatient and out of sorts, perhaps because of these unexpected delays, or maybe the gallery outburst. He sat frowning in his robes behind a huge cherrywood desk, his eyes on the papers in front of him. Occasionally he turned a page, although she had the strong impression that he wasn't reading anymore.

Finally, Ms Shepard cleared her throat – clearly a signal, as Bakhtiari looked over at her and then straightened in his chair. 'I've made a decision,' he began without any preamble or fanfare. 'I'm going to defer my ruling on the defense motion to admit Honor Wilson's taped statement and also defer declaring a mistrial until the close of the prosecution's case. I take it, Ms Hardy, that if I rule in your favor and admit the tape, you will not at that point ask for a mistrial or more time to investigate. Correct?'

This was not unexpected, and yet Rebecca's head went light and she closed her eyes against an acute sense of vertigo. She drew on all of her willpower to calm herself down.

But still. After an acrimonious discussion that morning with her father, who'd told her she could be accused of incompetence if she didn't ask for a mistrial, and the much worse session she'd just had with her client, she had decided to go forward without demanding a mistrial if the judge ruled that the jury could hear the tape. 'That's correct, Your Honor,' she said. 'If the tape is admitted, the defense is prepared to proceed.'

'All right.' That should have been it. He could have made these rulings out in the courtroom after the recess, but instead had called opposing counsel to his chambers. Now Bakhtiari should dismiss the attorneys back to the courtroom, and they'd get on with the trial proper. Though he'd rendered his decisions, the judge didn't appear to be finished.

In fact, he wasn't.

'All of that being said,' he began, 'I am not unmindful of

the earlier arguments Ms Hardy made regarding the extraordinary time pressure that Homicide inspectors were under to identify and arrest a suspect in this case. To say nothing of the unusual haste the DA's office displayed in scheduling this trial. Let me be clear. I am not calling into question the validity of the grand jury's decision to indict Mr Treadway. Nevertheless, I have to comment that Officer McDougal's testimony struck me as discordant somehow, if only because there were evidently, as a matter of simple fact, elements of the victim's personal life that might appear to have a bearing on her death, and yet they don't appear in the People's narrative at all.

'I don't think it is impossible,' the judge went on, 'that if we were still at the grand jury phase, and a more complete investigation had occurred, the prosecution might have declined to indict Mr Treadway until more work could be done strengthening the People's case. But as Ms Hardy pointed out in her motion, not letting the jury hear this statement smacks of injustice, and as a purely personal matter, as a private citizen, I find that I do not completely disagree with her. And we're not in the business of injustice here. Mr Braden, let me remind you that your sworn duty as a prosecutor is not to win cases but to pursue justice wherever it may lead you.'

Braden, in a cold fury, spoke with quiet vehemence. 'That pursuit – of justice – led the People directly to Mr Treadway, Your Honor. The fact that someone else may have had personal or business issues with Anlya Paulson, or even hated Anlya Paulson, does not mean Mr Treadway did not have his own compelling motive. His own reasons to kill her. As the evidence will prove.'

'All right, then,' Bakhtiari said, 'I will make my rulings when the People rest, and I've given my two cents, for what they're worth, so let's get back to the business at hand, shall we? Court will reconvene in fifteen minutes.'

29

GLITSKY SHOWED UP with Jewish deli sandwiches and celery sodas at the cubby where Jeff Elliott worked in the basement of the Chronicle Building at Fifth Street and Mission. With a full, thick gray beard and hair down to his shoulders, Elliott had struggled with multiple sclerosis for many years and now was all but confined to his wheelchair in his tiny and cluttered office. If you wanted to see him in person, you came to him. He wrote a popular column, *CityTalk*, which appeared on page two every day but Sunday, and he'd invited Abe down to talk because it sounded like the 'cloped' criminals story was a good one, and 'only in San Francisco,' Abe was saying.

'Apparently not only here, though,' Jeff said. 'And that doesn't mean it's not worth some column space, but check this out.' He picked up the morning's paper and handed it across. 'This stuff's happening all over the place. It's almost an epidemic. You're looking at a guy in Fresno just yesterday.'

Glitsky scanned the story, and sure enough, there were similarities. In the Fresno case, there was no issue of competence to stand trial. The inmate who'd walked out of the jail had done so after the jury had found him not guilty of burglary charges. Or rather, after the foreperson, confused, had signed a 'not guilty' verdict form. Actually, the jury had been unable to reach a verdict. Four had voted not guilty. Eight had voted guilty. But there was no verdict form that said the jury was hung. They had only two forms to sign – one said 'guilty,' the other 'not guilty.' So the foreperson, thinking that a hung jury was the same as not guilty, had signed the form, effectively freeing the defendant. He had to be released.

The foreperson basically had checked the wrong box.

What made that story newsworthy and ultimately tragic was the fact that the Fresno man was out of jail for only about an hour and a half before he showed up at his sister's house and, over an entirely unrelated matter, was stabbed to death by his brother-in-law.

Glitsky finished the article, clucked in commiseration, and handed the paper back. 'I thought it could only happen here,' he said. 'Something in the air.'

'It's everywhere,' Elliott said. 'The ignorant abound. Is that the way it happened here?'

'Not exactly, but close enough.'

'And how many of these people who've "eloped" have you got?'

'Five. But that's only in the last year or so. There could be a lot more.'

'Just to be clear, we're talking murderers here, are we not? The ones still out?'

'Four murder suspects, arrested but never tried, because guess what?'

'They were found incompetent to stand trial.'

'You've been paying attention.'

'At all times.' Elliott straightened up in his wheelchair, folded his hands in his lap. After another minute, he nodded to himself as if making a decision. 'Do you have names and mug shots?'

'Not on me, but you can call Villanova at the office, who's taken point on it. He's got 'em all.'

'Of course he does.'

'In all humility, you are dealing with professionals,' Glitsky said. From the lunch package, he pulled out a manila envelope and handed it over. 'And if you're thinking what I think you're thinking, here's a mug shot of Mr Salazar, our murderer from Minnesota.'

'Normally, I don't run a lot of art with my column, but I think in this case the public would like to see a face. The story is pretty unbelievable, so it would be nice to have some show-and-tell to lend it credibility.'

'That was my thought, too.'

'Okay,' Jeff said, 'so much for business. If I have to sit here hungry and endure the smell of that pastrami for another second, I'll have to rip it from your hands.'

'No need.' Glitsky pulled out the sandwiches and sodas. 'Don't tell Treya. Pastrami is definitely not on my no-fat, no-taste diet.'

'No, it's all right,' Jeff said. 'Pastrami is its own entirely separate food group, healthy under all circumstances. Many cultures actually use it as medicine. They've done studies.'

'I'll tell her.'

They both dug in and were eating in companionable silence when Jeff said, 'Hey, did you see the game last night? How about that Posey? Four long flies, can you believe it? Was that awesome or what?'

30

BACK IN THE courtroom, waiting patiently as Rebecca stood up for her cross-examination of the testimony he'd just given for Braden, the crime scene supervisor Sergeant Lennard Faro sat in the witness box projecting an aura of understated confidence. By far the best-dressed man in the room, he cultivated a tasteful soul patch beneath his bottom lip and presented himself more as a fashion model than a cop. Nevertheless, as a policeman, he had been in his position for over a decade and had testified in court hundreds of times, his testimony critical in establishing the chain of evidence.

'Sergeant Faro,' Rebecca began. 'Was it difficult to get to the scene of the accident on the night that Anlya Paulson died?' She was consciously sticking with her father's idea to use alternate words, such as 'accident,' even though Braden hadn't risen to the bait to call attention to it.

Faro wasn't going to fall for it any more than Waverly had. 'The scene of the homicide, you mean? Yes, it was. Traffic was stopped in all directions from downtown to North Beach and east-west as well. I parked nearly a mile away, below Market.'

'Could you estimate how long it took you to get to the scene after you got called to it?'

'At least an hour. Maybe a little longer.'

'And during all that time, Anlya Paulson's body was lying on the asphalt inside the tunnel, is that correct?'

'Yes.'

'And after you got there, when the crime scene investigators had finished their work, approximately how long did it take to get the coroner's van inside the tunnel so that her body could be removed?'

'Quite a long time. I know that it was light out when we finally could get the van into the tunnel. Say six-thirty, quarter to seven.'

'So the victim's body lay there in the street for close to eight hours?'

'Roughly. I'd say that's about right.'

'And the body was then delivered to Dr Strout's morgue, correct?'

'Yes.'

At this, Braden stood up, objecting. 'Your Honor, relevance?'

The judge looked a question at Rebecca, who was ready with her reply. 'Deterioration of DNA evidence is a function of time, Your Honor, and this line of questioning is foundational for the testimony of the People's DNA expert.'

Bakhtiari nodded. 'All right. I'll allow it. Objection overruled.'

Of course, Rebecca knew all about DNA. She was aware that her questions were, frankly, spurious. But anything she could do to get the jurors to doubt the DNA evidence in general could only help. She came right back to her question. 'So from the time of the accident until the body arrived at the morgue was nine or ten hours, is that right, Sergeant?'

'Yes.'

'And did you accompany the body in the van to the morgue?'

'I did.'

'Was the van heated during this trip?'

Faro's eyes narrowed, his lips went tight, and for the first time he showed a bit of hesitation. 'I don't really know. I don't remember it being abnormally warm or cold.'

'But it was a cool morning, was it not?'

'Normal, I'd say, for May. Probably mid-fifties.'

'Would it surprise you to learn, Sergeant, that the temperature at sunrise that morning was forty-four degrees?'

'It may have been. As I say, I don't remember exactly.'

'Do you remember if the heater was on in the van?'

'Not specifically, no.'

'At forty-four degrees outside, it must have been, wouldn't you say?'

'Objection! Relevance.'

'Sustained. Move it along, Ms Hardy.'

This wasn't very sexy stuff, Rebecca knew, but again, she figured that anything serving to undermine Faro's authority or credibility was to the good. 'All right,' she continued. 'After you arrived at the morgue, what happened to the body?'

'They brought it inside.'

'On the gurney, yes?'

'Of course.'

'Did you accompany the body the whole time?'

'Yes.'

'Once you got it inside, did Dr Strout immediately begin an autopsy?'

Faro shot what seemed to be an apologetic look at the jury. Rebecca was happy for him to show his impatience. 'No, he did not,' he replied with some crispness. 'He had another autopsy he was performing.'

'What then happened with Anlya Paulson's body?'

'They wheeled her into the morgue and prepped her for autopsy.'

'And how is that procedure handled?'

Again, Faro glanced at the jury, as though the nature of his testimony would be graphic and distasteful. 'Well, first they remove her from the body bag—'

'Excuse me, Sergeant. When was she placed in this body bag?'

'At the scene. In the tunnel.'

'And when her body was placed in it, was this body bag then completely enclosed?'

'Yes. It zips up.'

'All right, then, back at the morgue, they removed her body from this body bag and began preparing her for the autopsy, is that right?'

'Yes.'

'Do they remove her clothing?'

'Yes.'

'Do they save that clothing for forensic analysis?'

'Yes, they do.'

'Do they separate the items of clothing? Underwear, shoes, brassiere, skirt, blouse, et cetera?'

'Yes.'

'And where do they put these separated items?'

'A variety of containers, depending on size and volume.'

'And were you present when the morgue attendants did this preparation?'

'No.'

'No? You did not personally witness the removal of the body's clothes or its storage?'

'No, I did not. As per procedure, I returned to my office, knowing that I would be called when it was time to come down for the actual autopsy. If you want to ask the attendants what they did, I'm sure they would be happy to tell you. They have prepped hundreds of bodies hundreds of times, and they knew the drill.'

'The drill. That is, the normal procedure?'

'Yes.'

Perhaps it was only to break up her rhythm, but behind her, she heard again the scrape of a chair and Braden's voice, objecting to further questioning on that line. 'If counsel wants to ask what the morgue attendants did, Your Honor, she should be asking them.'

Rebecca spoke right to the judge. 'Again, Your Honor, the passage of time is one critical component affecting the reliability of DNA evidence. It's critical that the jury understands both the elapsed time and the storage conditions of the victim's clothing from which that evidence was taken.'

Braden said, 'That's ridiculous, Your Honor. When DNA deteriorates, you don't get a false match. You get no results. Anyway, as Ms Hardy knows from our previous hearings, this witness isn't the person to ask about the handling of these exhibits.'

Bakhtiari frowned. 'Enough of the speaking objections, you two. The objection to lack of personal knowledge as to this witness and the handling of the body after he left it is sustained. Move on, please. In fact, Ms Hardy, we're getting toward lunchtime. Would you like to stop this cross-examination for now and continue after lunch, or try to finish up before?'

Rebecca looked up at the wall clock. It was 11.50. 'It shouldn't be too much longer, Your Honor.' She took a stab at levity, hoping the jury would see what a nice and reasonable person she was. 'I'm sure Sergeant Faro would prefer to finish up before lunch as well, and leave his afternoon free.'

In reality, bolstered by Honor Wilson's deathbed declaration, whether or not it would be ruled admissible, Rebecca was riding her own wave of adrenaline and wanted to keep going while she was so much in the zone. 'Sergeant Faro,' she said, coming back to the witness, 'you were not with the attendants when they prepared Ms Paulson's body for autopsy, is that right?'

'Yes. That's right. As I've said.'

'Yes, you did. But just to be clear, you did not see them place any of the articles of Ms Paulson's clothing into their respective receptacles, did you?'

'No.'

'Did you see that clothing in those receptacles when you delivered it to the laboratory for analysis?'

'Yes, I did. I checked it and signed it in.'

'Did you happen to notice the receptacle that held Ms Paulson's underwear?'

'Yes. It was a quart-size Ziploc bag.'

'A plastic bag, in fact. Isn't that correct?'

'Yes.'

Rebecca took a little break, giving a short stick-with-me half-smile to the jury. None of them might know what she was getting at – although she knew that would become clear when she cross-examined the DNA expert – but all of them were following this questioning with rapt attention.

Coming back to the witness, she asked, 'Sergeant Faro, did it concern you to see Ms Paulson's underwear in a plastic container?'

'Not at that time, no.'

'And yet isn't it standard procedure to transport potential DNA evidence in a paper container?'

'Yes, that's true.'

'That wasn't done in this case, was it?'

'No.'

'Why not?'

Rebecca had the feeling that this was a line of questioning that the prosecution simply did not expect, and the thought galvanized her anew. 'Sergeant?' she prodded. 'Why was a paper container not used to transport potential DNA-bearing evidence?'

Faro shot a disgusted glance at Braden. 'Probably because I did not specify it to the attendants.'

'You mean when they were prepping the body?'

'Yes.'

'When you were with them, sometime around seven-thirty or eight o'clock in the morning, is that right?'

'Yes.'

'But once they had removed Ms Paulson's clothing and placed it in its receptacles, including the plastic bag for her underwear, did you then immediately deliver this evidence to the lab for analysis?'

'It depends on what you mean by "immediately." I delivered it immediately after the autopsy.'

'Again, Sergeant, why did you wait?'

'Because I was there to observe the autopsy. We don't stop in the middle and bring some items of evidence to the lab. We wait until it's done and bring it all at once. Also, the evidence was air-conditioned in the morgue, and I thought Dr Strout might find something else during the autopsy that might have to go to the lab, so I figured I'd save myself a trip.'

'So you stayed in the vicinity until the medical examiner had performed the autopsy on Ms Paulson, is that correct?'

'Yes.'

'And when he'd finished, you then took the evidence stored in plastic and drove it down to the police lab in Hunters Point, is that right?'

'Yes.'

Rebecca retreated a few steps to the defense table, where Allie, sitting next to Greg, opened a folder and handed her a sheet of paper. She brought it up to the recorder and had it entered as Defense Exhibit C, then returned to her witness and held it out for him. 'Sergeant Faro, do you recognize the form you are now holding, Defense C?'

'I do. It's a copy of the sign-in form for the evidence I submitted to the lab on the night after Anlya Paulson's death.'

'According to this document, Sergeant, what was the time of this sign-in?'

'Seven-sixteen P.M.'

'Seven-sixteen. Or roughly twelve hours after this evidence was placed in a plastic bag, is that right?'

'It looks like it, yes.'

'After you signed it in at the lab, did you request that it then be repackaged in a paper container until such time as the contents could be analyzed?'

'No, I didn't. I thought they'd get right to it.'

'But they didn't, did they?'

'I don't know about that. I just know I delivered it.'

'Thank you, Sergeant,' she said. 'No further questions.'

31

REBECCA, ALLIE, AND Greg were locked in an attorney visiting room in the jail. They were sharing Chinese food from take-out cartons, chopsticks and plastic forks, and bottled water. 'Why haven't we been doing this all along?' Greg asked. 'This is almost like being out of jail. Not exactly, mind you, but close enough. How'd you get this room?'

'I told the judge that after this morning's events, we needed the time to talk strategy,' Rebecca said.

'If that's all it takes, we should do it every day.'

'Okay, Greg, as long as you don't try to take us hostage and break out of here, we might get a shot at it.'

'I'll try to restrain myself. Although that would be more the action of someone who actually did violent stuff, wouldn't it? As opposed to me, who never has.'

'You're right,' Rebecca said. 'I apologize for the implication.'

'Apology accepted. And while we're at it, I'm sorry, too. About out there. I don't know what happened to me. I'm really sorry, Beck. I just lost it.'

'So I'm not fired after all?'

Allie reached over the pitted desk where they all sat and grabbed a carton of lo mein. 'I'm glad you guys can joke about it.'

'We'd better be able to,' Rebecca said. 'It's a little tense out there.'

'Especially for them. Especially after what you did to Faro,' Greg said.

'And what was that?' Rebecca asked.

'Killed him. I was watching the jury, and you could see the doubt creeping up on them about the integrity of the DNA. As I've always said.'

'I wasn't really talking about that part of the morning,' Allie said. 'I'm talking about the motions. Honor Wilson's stuff. What is this "under submission" bullshit? How could Bakhtiari even consider not letting the jury hear that?'

Rebecca shook her head, resigned. 'We always knew it would be a tough sell.'

'That is just so wrong, though.' Allie turned to Greg. 'I mean, is there anybody out there – I'm talking Bakhtiari or even Braden – who's heard about Honor saying it was her boyfriend and, in his heart, doesn't believe you're innocent? Innocent as in you just didn't do it.'

'I'd like to hope so,' Greg said, 'since I am. I think my parents are pretty relieved, for example.'

Allie objected. 'But they never really thought—'

Greg stopped her. 'Maybe they didn't want to think it, Al, but I promise you the idea was somewhere in the back of their minds. You don't get arrested and go all the way to trial if there isn't—'

'But we know they manufactured that,' Allie protested, her eyes taking on a shine of emotion. 'That ought to be pretty obvious by now, don't you think? All that stupid Liam Goodman stuff, needing to charge somebody before they had all the facts. The judge wouldn't let that in, either. It's like this horrible travesty happening in slow motion right in front of our eyes, and nobody can do anything about it.' A single tear overflowed and ran down her cheek.

'Hey. Hey.' Greg stood up, came around the desk, and draped an arm over Allie's shoulder, leaning down and giving her a hug. 'It's okay. I'm the one they've got in here, and I'm holding up reasonably well. And look at what Rebecca's doing, taking their case apart. It's going to be all right. I really believe that.'

'At least if he keeps out the tape,' Allie said, 'we know we'll get a mistrial. We'll get a chance to prove it was really Royce Utlee.'

Rebecca shot her a warning look, but not in time.

Greg pushed himself back from the table and slapped a flat palm down hard, the noise reverberating in the tiny room. His voice was unyielding. 'There's not going to be any goddamn mistrial.'

'Right, right, we've covered that.' Rebecca put her hand on her client's arm, calming him. 'We don't need to go over it again. Really. No mistrial. I get it.'

'I don't mean to be a hard-ass,' Greg said, 'but that option is just not on the table. *Claro?*'

'Clear,' Rebecca said. 'Crystal-clear.'

Greg looked from one woman to the other, his anger evaporating as quickly as it had come on. 'You guys are the best,' he said. 'I am so lucky.'

32

AT A LITTLE after one o'clock, and armed with the address supplied by Wyatt Hunt, Waverly and Yamashiro rang the bell on the outside door of the Utlee/Wilson apartment on Turk Street. When nobody answered, Waverly rang the other five bells, and in twenty seconds they got buzzed inside. The first door on the left was partially ajar, and they knocked, waited, knocked again, then pushed the door completely open and took a step inside, identifying themselves as police, turning on the dim overhead light.

Directly in front of them, the rug bore fresh blackened stains and splotches of what could only be blood. Yamashiro put in a call to the CSI unit – this was certainly a crime scene and in all probability a murder scene.

Meanwhile, Waverly walked back outside, through the pile of crap they'd negotiated on the front porch, and around the corner where, because it had been the only spot on the block, he'd illegally parked their car by a fire hydrant. Opening the trunk, he grabbed a roll of yellow crime scene tape for the apartment's front door; realizing he'd probably be there for a while, he decided to go around to the driver's side and put one of his business cards on the dash, on the off chance that a parking enforcement cop would see it and refrain from giving the car a ticket.

Straightening up, closing and locking the car door, he cricked his back, by habit looking up and down the street. The day was cool with a gusty breeze and high cloud cover.

A junk heap of a car took the corner he'd just come around, and its young-looking African-American driver gave Waverly a hostile glare before continuing down the street, perhaps looking – like the rest of San Francisco – for a place to park.

Waverly shrugged off the bad vibe. A middle-aged white guy in a coat and tie in this neighborhood was probably a cop, automatically suspect, and in any event not usually welcome. But by the time he'd gotten back to the apartment's cluttered entryway, thirty seconds later, some instinct slowed him down and he looked again at the street. This time he saw nothing suspicious. In fact, nothing moving. Nevertheless, when he got back inside, he said, 'What's the word with CSI?'

'On their way.'

He held up the crime scene tape. 'Let's wait on this.' He turned left toward the street-facing windows and said, 'I'm going to hang out up here for a minute, keep an eye on the street.'

'You see something?'

'I don't know. More felt it.'

The tone of his voice stopped Yamashiro's sure-to-be-witty reply in its tracks. They'd been cops and partners long enough to trust the sixth sense when it kicked in. Avoiding the blood-stains on the floor as best he could, Yamashiro came up and stood next to his partner, who'd opened the blinds a fraction of an inch.

After perhaps two minutes, a woman emerged from her duplex directly across the street. She descended the steps and crossed the sidewalk. Pointing her keys at a beat-up brown Ford Taurus, she stepped up to it, opened its door, and slid in behind the wheel, then started the engine and pulled away.

'What?' Yamashiro said.

'Nothing.' Waverly pulled down a bit farther on the blinds in front of his eyes. Then he squinted down. 'Here you go.' The car with the angry black driver pulled up in front of the open space and began to back in. Waverly nodded once, as if to himself. 'Let's go!' Turning on his heel, he headed for the front door, knowing he didn't have to ask Yamashiro twice.

Out in the street in front of the apartment, the two men split up, with Waverly coming around the front of the parked car and Yamashiro the back.

His wallet out to show his badge, Waverly got to the driver's door just as the man opened it and, seeing the badge, checking the rearview mirror, and seeing Yamashiro back there, just as quickly slammed it shut again. The locks all clicked shut, and when he hit the ignition, the engine sprang to life.

Waverly reached over and tapped the windshield hard with his shield.

The car didn't budge.

Yamashiro came up around the passenger side. He reached inside his coat and took his Glock out of his shoulder holster, leaning over so that the driver could get a good look at it, pointed directly at his face.

For an eternity or twenty seconds, whichever came first, nobody moved. Finally, the driver reached forward and killed the engine. The locks clicked again, came up in the window wells. Waverly took the opportunity to grab at the driver's door handle, yanking it open. 'Hands on the steering wheel,' he said. 'Right now. Leave 'em there till I say you can move them. Right there. Ten and two.'

The man gave him an out-from-under gaze. 'Hey, man. Whatchu hassling me for? I ain't done nothing.'

Waverly smoothly dropped his wallet into his back pocket and, with the same hand, came up and inside his jacket to his shoulder holster, from which he extracted his own gun. 'I show you my badge,' he asked, 'you lock up and start your engine?'

The man shrugged. He sported a do-rag over his Afro, an

assortment of chains around his neck, a black T-shirt under a worn black leather jacket.

'What's your name?' Waverly asked.

'Royce.'

'Royce Utlee?'

He shrugged again. 'Might be.'

Waverly nodded at Yamashiro, who, still on the passenger side of the car, came a step closer to the front. 'Make the call,' Waverly said, and both of them knew what he meant. They wanted backup here and right now. Yamashiro reholstered his weapon and unclipped his cell phone from his belt, started punching some numbers.

'All right, Royce Might Be Utlee. You're under arrest for the murder of Honor Wilson. Get out of the car. Hands still up. Slow.'

Utlee went to move, then sat back with a disdainful grin. 'Yo, man,' he said. 'Seat belt.'

'All right,' Waverly said. 'Slow.'

Lowering his right hand, Utlee reached down behind him, unfastened the seat belt with a click. And then his hand was up in front of him, crossing over, and it held a gun that Waverly never saw as Utlee fired twice in quick succession, the first shot hitting Waverly in the shoulder, spinning him backward, his own gun flying off onto the sidewalk behind him.

The second shot was a complete miss. But Utlee didn't wait around to find out. Instead, he broke from the front seat, half-turned, taking another shot at Yamashiro, missing again in his haste, and started running.

Yamashiro, his phone at his ear when the three-second sequence began, immediately dropped it to the ground and reached for his gun. He jumped forward to rest his shooting hand on the roof of the car and squeezed three shots off at the fleeing murderer, who stumbled and then got to the corner and rounded it, disappearing.

'Shit shit shit! Eric!' Yamashiro yelled. 'Eric!'

'I'm all right.' His partner lay on his side, kicking at the pavement to get back to his gun. 'Get him get him get him!'

'I hit him, I think,' Yamashiro said. 'But he's gone.'

'Get him!'

Yamashiro broke into a run, his gun in his hand. Getting to where Utlee had turned, he stopped, breathing hard, taking cover from the corner building, looking around up the street. No sign of Utlee, of anybody. On the sidewalk in front of him, he saw several large drops of blood, but to go up the street after him all alone would be suicide.

Turning back, he saw his partner lying flat on the sidewalk, and he knew where he had to be and headed back there.

33

AFTER LUNCH WITH his client, Hardy had called Glitsky and asked him what he was doing with this Friday afternoon yawning emptily ahead of him.

'I'm contemplating the unfairness of life.'

'Always a fruitful endeavor. What brought this about?'

'You know about Posey last night, right? Of course you do, and if you say it was awesome, I'll kill you.'

'It was sure at least pretty good. When's the last time that happened, four homers in one game?'

'Josh Hamilton, 2012, with the Rangers. I looked it up.'

'Good for you, and now I know it, too. I bet I could win money with a fact like that. But how does Buster Posey figure into your thoughts on the unfairness of life?'

'I bet against him.'

'What? When? Last night?'

'At the game with Wes. When he only had two.'

'Only two's a good start.'

'Yeah, but still a long way to go to get four.'

'And why would you bet Wes on this?'

'He was giving five to one. How could I miss? I mean, had Posey ever done it before? No. What were the odds? So I took the bet.'

'For how much?'

'Fifty.'

Hardy whistled. 'If I were you, I'd be contemplating

the unfairness of life. That and where I was going to get the extra two-fifty that I'd lost.'

'It wasn't a stupid bet. It was, in fact, a smart bet. It just didn't come up.'

'Yep,' Hardy said. 'That sure is unfair. I feel bad for you.'

'I feel bad for myself. It's all I've been thinking about all day. How these things happen to me.'

'What do you mean, these things? What things?'

'You know. Bad stuff. Here's Buster Posey, whom I would normally love to see hit four home runs in one game, and the night he does it, I happen to be sitting next to Wes, and he happens to want to bet on it, and get this, *I make the smart bet,* and I still lose. So ask me if I'm happy about Posey's four homers.'

'I already know the answer.'

'Well, there you go. It's like I'm cursed somehow. I'm not kidding. Truly cursed. Voodoo. Maybe Santería. Actually, literally, cursed.'

'Don't get too wound up over it, Abe. You might have another heart attack.'

'See? That's what I mean. I'm in basically good health, and next thing you know, I get a heart attack.'

'Six or seven years ago, let's remember.'

'What's your point? It doesn't count?'

'Dude, *you didn't die.* Some people would call that lucky, not cursed.'

'They'd be wrong. Or getting shot, how about that? And all the complications from that. Plus – and while I'm on this, I've got to tell you – I pull up to the tollbooth on the bridge . . .'

'What bridge?'

'Any bridge, it doesn't matter. My point is that every time I get behind the guy who doesn't have the right change or stalls his car. I mean it, this is an automatic.'

'You ought to bet that it happens.'

'No, because then it wouldn't. And let's not even talk about cell phones cutting out in the middle of every call.'

'I wish this one would.'

'Stick with me. It'll happen.' After a beat or two of silence, Glitsky spoke in a different tone. 'Okay, that's out of my system. What'd you call me about?'

'Damned if I remember. Oh yeah, I suddenly had the afternoon free and thought we could do something fun.'

'I thought you were at the trial.'

'Not today. I had some actual billable hours with a client, so I let one of my paralegals go in my place.'

'Okay, what's your fun idea?'

'I think you'll like it,' Hardy said.

LIAM GOODMAN HAD led his two dozen shock troops into the courtroom for the beginning of the trial, but once he'd established his own place in that firmament, he went back to his day job. All eleven of the city's supervisors, as well as the mayor, worked out of their offices in City Hall, which was about as far removed from the rough-and-tumble ambience and architecture of the Bryant Street Hall of Justice as was possible to imagine.

The beaux arts City Hall was a magnificent structure, inside and out. Its exterior was done in Madera County granite; its dome, modeled on Mansart's baroque dome of Les Invalides in Paris, was the fifth largest in the world, forty-two feet taller than the dome of the U.S. Capitol. The enormous rotunda, its walls faced with Indiana sandstone and finished with marble from Alabama, Colorado, Vermont, and Italy, was a favorite setting for weddings; hundreds of couples a year tied the knot there. Joe DiMaggio and Marilyn Monroe were married in the rotunda.

Hardy and Glitsky, largely immune to the building's charms, climbed the grand staircase and found themselves outside Liam Goodman's office. Hardy had called for an appointment to make sure Goodman would be in, before he called Abe, before he decided that Abe's presence as a member of the DA's Investigations Unit would add a certain gravitas to the proceedings. As they got to the door, Hardy was explaining to Glitsky that he may have inadvertently conveyed the impression to Goodman's secretary that he was thinking about making a political donation.

Glitsky broke what he probably thought was a smile, a tiny uptick at the corner of his scar-slashed mouth. 'When he finds out you're not giving him anything, he's going to kick us right out.'

'I'm betting he won't.'

'Don't say "bet," ' Glitsky snapped. 'Betting is off-limits today.'

They opened the door and passed a small outer office where three well-dressed interns, who might have been in their teens, sat doing what looked like massive amounts of paperwork around a small conference table. A short hallway beyond that office brought them to the receptionist's station, where an attractive black woman – Diane, according to the carved knickknack on her desk – sat behind a computer terminal at an uncluttered desk with empty 'in' and 'out' basket. 'Can I help you?' she asked.

Hardy gave her a nod and a smile. 'Dismas Hardy to see Mr Goodman. I believe he's expecting me.' He didn't introduce Glitsky, whose unusual and distinctive name as well as his professional background would have been familiar to the supervisor.

The omission didn't seem to bother Diane, who got up from her desk, turned, and walked a few steps back to another door, where she tapped gently, then stuck her head in. They heard Goodman's voice, nearly booming from inside. 'Send him in, send him in.'

Goodman was standing in front of an empire desk that matched the rest of the general high-toned decor of the room – bookshelves with law books and hardbacks, a large globe, dark wood, and burgundy leather couches and seats. 'Dismas Hardy,' he said by way of greeting, shaking hands. 'The famous lawyer. I thought I recognized the name. I confess I Googled you after Diane made this appointment.'

Hardy knew that this was complete bullshit. When Hardy had subpoenaed Goodman to appear at the murder trial a little over a year before, he had responded to Hardy – albeit through his lawyer – that he would come to court but under no circumstances would he testify about anything. Hardy never got to call him, but he'd been there in the courtroom, as he'd been with Treadway. So he unquestionably knew who Hardy was, though he might not guess what he wanted today. For the moment, he wasn't giving anything away. 'Didn't I see you at the Treadway trial yesterday? That's still going on, isn't it?'

'As far as I know. It's my daughter's case, and as a courtesy, she was letting me sit in on opening day.'

'I'm hoping that she doesn't prevail in getting Mr Treadway off, though I don't suppose there's much chance of that. Still, I'm a lawyer myself, and I must say I greatly admire defense attorneys like your daughter and yourself, who take on these hopeless cases. The best defense the law allows, and all that. Isn't that right? Everyone deserves that. People don't always realize it, but if I had to say one thing that makes our country great, that would be it, the unassailable right to an attorney. I'm sure you'd agree.'

'It's what I do for a living,' Hardy said.

'A noble calling. Sometimes thankless, I'm sure, but noble. I'm not kidding you.' After his politician's prologue, he turned to Glitsky, a silent question in his eyes. 'I'm sorry, where are my manners? Sometimes I get caught up talking philosophy and get carried away.' He reached out his hand to shake Abe's. 'Liam Goodman.'

'Abe Glitsky. Nice to meet you.'

Hardy noticed a flicker of concern, perhaps of recognition, in the supervisor's face. Goodman's brow creased for an instant, then went smooth again, accompanied by a smile that struck Hardy as slightly uncertain. 'So. What can I do for you gentlemen? Do you want to take a seat? Can I offer you some coffee? Tea? Something stronger?'

'I think we're good,' Hardy said. 'Abe?'

'I wouldn't mind a cup of tea,' Glitsky said. 'Plain, no sugar or milk.'

'Have a seat. I'll get Diane right on it.' Goodman strode over to the door, made the request, then came back inside, crossed around his desk, and sat at it. 'To what do I owe the pleasure?' he asked.

'Well,' Hardy said, 'it's a little sensitive.'

'I can do sensitive,' Goodman replied.

'Good.' Hardy came forward in his chair. 'This is really about what I believe you used to refer to as "the Army Business." '

It was as though a small electric current shot through Goodman's face. His lips twitched and his eyes closed a fraction, although he maintained a neutral, interested posture, his hands clasped on the desk in front of him.

Hardy didn't want to give him a chance to respond right away. He had a lot more to say. 'About a year ago,' he said, 'you may remember getting subpoenaed in one of my cases after having a conversation with a private investigator named Wyatt Hunt, who was trying to get a handle on rumors he'd heard of you being blackmailed by your chief of staff, Rick Jessup. Who'd been murdered.'

'Of course I remember that. It was a horrible time. I don't think the office is quite over it yet. Rick was a wonderful person. The idea that he would even think about blackmailing me or anyone else is totally ludicrous. Which is what I believe your Mr Hunt found.'

'Well, no, not exactly,' Hardy said. 'What he found was a conspiracy between you and Rick Jessup to defraud the U.S. government to the tune of several million dollars.'

It had been a slick and lucrative scheme, hatched in the first years of the Afghanistan campaign. Women in the service would return from the war theater pregnant and nearing the end of their term. Here in the U.S., they would have their baby and then, still under enlistment, would have six months postpartum when they would not be deployed back to the war zone. Concurrently, the army had a policy not to send pregnant women to active theaters of war. So if they could just get pregnant again during those six months, they would remain safe.

At the same time, Rick Jessup and Liam Goodman had found an opportunity to make connections with childless wealthy couples looking for a surrogate mother to carry their baby. For a fee of one hundred thousand dollars, Goodman put together these carefully vetted people – servicewomen and wealthy couples. He kept eighty thousand of that money, paid Jessup a finder's fee of three grand, and gave the remaining twenty thousand to the surrogate mother. Hunt found evidence that in all, over a three-year period, Goodman had brokered no fewer than thirty-two of these deals.

What made the scam a federal crime was the fact that the army was not only paying the active-duty female soldier the whole time but also covering all of her pregnancy-related medical expenses.

Hardy had known about the arrangement for well over a year – as far as he knew, since Jessup was dead, he and Wyatt Hunt and now Glitsky were the only people besides Goodman who did know – but until this morning, when the idea randomly occurred to him, he had seen no advantage to be gained from revealing this knowledge.

That had changed.

'All right,' Goodman said.

'All right? You admit it?'

'I have no idea what you're talking about,' Goodman said.

'This is bullshit, and you can't prove any of it.' He did not, however, tell them to get out.

'And yet,' Hardy said, 'here we are, having this discussion.'

'Fine, but so what? Those records are gone. And without them, you have no proof of anything you're talking about,' Goodman said.

'Oh, I'm sure you got rid of the records. But actually,' Hardy said, 'there's plenty of proof readily available in the persons of thirty or thirty-five kids walking around all over the city. I think if Wyatt Hunt, say, went to talk to the parents of these children, in exchange for immunity for their parts in the conspiracy, several of them might be willing to talk about your role in their children's birth.'

Goodman glared at him with reptilian coldness. 'You're an asshole,' he said.

'Maybe, but that won't put me in jail. Whereas you, as a hypocrite who's defrauded the government, are looking at some serious prison time, I would predict. If someone decides to start telling this story to a federal grand jury. Oh, and I might add, that would be pretty much the end of your political career.'

Goodman's gaze traveled to the side. 'Glitsky,' he said, 'you're with the DA.'

'Not today,' Glitsky said. 'Apparently.'

'What's your part in this?'

Glitsky thought for a long moment. 'Today I'm an overworked public servant who wouldn't dream of thinking up more work to do. Unless my close friend Dismas Hardy were to present me with evidence of a crime that I could not ignore.' He cocked his head. 'Sorry,' he said with unmistakable irony.

'Fuck you, too.'

Glitsky shrugged. 'Creative,' he said.

'Yeah, well, fuck you again.' To Hardy, Goodman said, 'What do you want? Money?'

'That would be blackmail,' Hardy said, 'and that would be illegal.'

'So? What?'

'What I'd really like, Liam, is a fair trial for Rebecca's client Greg Treadway. You could argue that as a rookie defense attorney, she should embrace the shenanigans you're orchestrating in the courtroom and chalk it up to experience. Shit happens at trials, and she's got to learn how to deal with all of it. Maybe I should just let it all play out, but that's the other thing – I find it pretty offensive as well, the way you've got your team of rabble-rousers in the courtroom, poisoning the atmosphere. If Treadway goes down, I know Rebecca could base an appeal on their presence in the gallery, but that could take years, and she wouldn't want her client to lose all that time out of his life.

'In the here and now, the jury feels there's going to be a riot or something very much like it if they don't come back with a guilty verdict, so they'll be twice as reluctant to let him go, since if they do that, the whole city might explode. Which is probably what you've been hoping all the while, so you can get more media face time.

'So what I'd like, call it a demand if you want, is for all those people to get out of the gallery, now if not sooner, and for the rest of the trial. Beyond that, I don't want to hear another word out of you about how this city doesn't arrest and doesn't convict on black homicides. It's hard enough getting justice done without stacking the deck against it with all this political posturing so you can get your stupid votes.'

Goodman waited, but nothing else was coming. At last he said, 'Is that it? That's all you want?'

'That's it. Call it your lucky day. Let's go, Abe.'

The two men got up. Hardy opened the door and held it for Glitsky, then closed it on Goodman just as Diane was returning with Glitsky's tea. 'Oh, I'm sorry,' she said. 'Are you all done already in there? If I'd known . . .'

Glitsky took the mug from her, blew on it and sipped, then handed it back. 'Excellent,' he said. 'Thank you.'

On their way down the Grand Stairway, Hardy said, 'Told you that was going to be fun.'

'Oh, yeah. A laugh riot.'

'You didn't like it? I thought he was going to keel over and croak there for a minute.'

'More than a minute. But you could have gotten a lot more out of him.'

'Like what?'

'Quit politics entirely. Join a monastery. A million bucks. Almost anything.'

'I didn't want to be greedy. I just wanted his goons out of the courtroom, and I suddenly realized I had a way to do it.'

Glitsky clucked. 'Wasted opportunity.'

'Home run.'

'I wish you wouldn't use those words.'

34

THE DNA EVIDENCE was crucial for the prosecution for no other reason than if Greg and Anlya were having sex, it helped fill in the three hours between the end of their dinner at the Imperial Palace and the time of the murder. Beyond that, it firmly established the true nature of the couple's relationship – at least for that one night, they had been lovers.

From Rebecca's point of view, the most frustrating thing about the DNA was Greg's adamant denial, even in the face of this apparently irrefutable evidence, that he and Anlya had ever had sex of any kind. As to the presence of his DNA on her underwear, he had no explanation except that the test must have been flawed.

But that was between lawyer and client.

Rebecca had already failed in her earlier motion to exclude the DNA testimony on the theory that the preservation of evidence and the testing were so flawed as to be unreliable. Besides, the DNA evidence did not place Greg at the scene of the crime. Indeed, the sexual encounter could have taken place at any time after they'd met that day. Or, not impossibly, on an earlier day. Bakhtiari had ruled, to no one's surprise, that because Treadway had denied a sexual relationship, the DNA evidence was both reliable and relevant to prove motive, and that he would admit it.

Now, in the courtroom, Braden had brought it in with over two hours of tediously detailed testimony. The lab analyst and forensics expert was a woman named Nancy Sciavo, about forty-five years old and dry as toast.

Rebecca had about an hour before they adjourned for the day, but she was still pumped about what she considered her success with Sergeant Faro, and she knew just where she would begin. She didn't think it was going to take longer than fifteen or twenty minutes.

'Ms Sciavo,' she began. 'We have heard you describe the tests you ran on the DNA present on Anlya Paulson's underwear, and the conclusions you drew from those results. Let me ask you, were you called in especially to run these tests?'

'I'm not sure I understand. It's part of my regular job. So no, I guess. It was just a normal day's workload.'

'And you work during the day shift, do you not?'

'Uh, yes.'

'What time do you get in to work?'

'Eight o'clock in the morning.'

'But we have heard Sergeant Faro's testimony that this evidence was delivered to the lab at seven-sixteen P.M. on Thursday, May eighth. Did you have an opportunity to inspect this evidence or supervise its storage that night?'

'No. I had already gone home for the day.'

'When did you first come into contact with the DNA evidence that you've just testified about in this case?'

'I guess the next morning.'

'You guess? You're not sure?'

'Well, it had to be the next morning, because I logged on to the computer for the analysis at eleven o'clock. So it was before then.'

'It wasn't first thing in the morning, then.'

'It must not have been, but not too much after that, probably. If I had the sample ready by eleven.'

'And how about the storage of the sample? Was it kept refrigerated?'

'Yes. That's standard procedure.'

'After you got it to your workstation, while you were getting ready to work on it, did you happen to notice the packaging of the clothing evidence?'

'Not particularly. There was nothing strange or unusual about it. It was all labeled correctly with the case number and so on.'

'Were all the articles of clothing separately wrapped?'

'Yes.'

'And all in plastic Ziploc-type bags?'

'Yes.'

'Thank you,' Rebecca said. 'No further questions.'

Rebecca was setting up an argument, however feeble, that the difference between a paper and a plastic wrapping was an issue – just one more thing for a juror to hang his hat on.

THEY WERE IN recess, and the jury had been excused while Braden gathered his next witnesses, who had been kept out of the courtroom until it was their time to testify. Rebecca and Allie flanked Greg at the defense table, and they were conversing in muted tones. 'Don't get me wrong,' Greg was saying. 'I thought that was great. I'm just not sure that the jury is going to make the connection between the long storage in plastic and the deterioration of the DNA.'

'You're right,' Rebecca said. 'If we stop now, some of them might miss it, but fortunately, we've got Hiram Kincaid as our expert witness on DNA evidence for when we get to our case in chief. His job is to connect the dots, and I think so far we've made those dots pretty obvious. He'll get it done, don't worry.'

'I'm trying, but it's a little hard not to worry.' He looked at Allie on the other side of him and gave her a tight smile.

She put her hand over his. 'I know I'm the new kid, but I thought The Beck made it pretty obvious. Even without the expert witness to explain it, it seemed clear to me how the evidence got tainted.'

'If, in fact, it is. At least it's a theory,' Rebecca said.

Allie reacted as if she'd been poked. 'Beck! What are you saying? Of course it is.'

'I didn't mean it isn't. I was just saying we want to avoid getting into the plain fact of whether it's tainted or untainted. That's not going to be Hiram's testimony, in any case.'

'So what's he going to be doing?' Greg asked.

'He's going to be talking about the likelihood of deterioration given the storage time in plastic. And that's all we need. Not the deterioration itself, which we can't prove. We're just trying to sow some confusion here. The point is, it doesn't matter.'

'It matters to me, Beck.' Greg spoke with some of his too-familiar heat. 'Listen. We know that something clearly went wrong somewhere with this evidence, because I guarantee you that sample is not my DNA. If it is, they got it from someplace in my apartment when they did their searches there.'

'That's a definite idea,' Allie said. 'Is there any way we can check if they did that?'

Rebecca was shaking her head. 'Not at this stage of the game, Al.'

'But, I mean, really,' Greg said. 'Don't we all know, doesn't everybody know, that the lab cheats all the time? Especially with the hurry they were in with me. They shouldn't have gotten to my stuff for a couple of months at least, right? And you're telling me they get a match the next day? Give me a break.'

They all knew what he was talking about. Within recent memory, the San Francisco police lab had been the subject of a huge scandal involving both the skimming of drugs from samples in narcotics cases and, more pointedly, outright mistakes and sample switching on DNA analysis in rape and homicide cases. In theory, these problems had been dealt with, but given the culture at the lab, no one believed they couldn't reappear.

'I completely hear you,' Rebecca whispered. She'd had enough of this pointless conversation. 'That's a different can of worms and a hill we probably don't want to die on. Unless we've something specific to accuse somebody of, and we don't.'

Greg shook his head in disgust. He turned back to Allie. 'If this weren't so goddamn tragic, it would be farcical. Isn't it obvious to both of you, especially after what Honor said? I didn't kill Anlya. I never had sex with her. How can the judge let this keep going on?'

'I know,' Rebecca said. 'Do you think this isn't eating me up as well? The only thing I can say is we have to be patient and keep to the game plan.'

Greg drew in a breath, closed his eyes, and breathed all the way out before opening them again. He looked to each of the women in turn. 'Patience,' he said. 'Patience. Jesus.'

Allie squeezed his hand, which Rebecca noticed she'd never let go of during the whole impassioned discussion. 'The Beck's right, Greg,' she said. 'You can do this. We can do it together.'

Suddenly, something broke in Greg. His shoulders shook. He extricated his hand from Allie's and pounded at the table, firmly but quietly, with both fists. 'I didn't do this,' he said. 'Why can't they see that? I'm not that kind of person. I just couldn't do it.'

On her side, Allie put an arm around him and pulled him to her, her hand over his again. 'It's all right,' she whispered. 'Shh.' As though he were a baby. 'It's all right.'

She looked up when she heard the harsh male voice – one of the bailiffs, who'd come up to their table. 'Is everything under control over here?'

'Fine,' Rebecca said. 'We're all fine.'

Greg regained his composure as the jurors and spectators began to file back into the courtroom. But no sooner had everyone taken their place than there was another commotion.

Most everyone's attention got diverted to the gallery, where there was a mass exodus of the thirty- or forty-member African-American caucus that had been simmering inside the courtroom since the opening of the proceedings. They arose almost as one with the same type of nearly paramilitary discipline they'd been exhibiting since they arrived, when it had seemed that they were waiting for a call to action. Apparently, it was not going to come.

By the time Rebecca heard something behind her and was turning around to look, six of the rows behind Braden's desk were already empty and a queue had formed by the back door, nearly half the gallery waiting to file out.

THE BULLET FROM Yamashiro's Glock went through Royce Utlee's left side, just a little above his hips. There was a hole in his front and one in his back, and blood was all over the side of his shirt and jacket and seeping down his pants and into his shoes. He was finding it hard to breathe.

He'd made it around the corner after being hit and then down four entryways on the right side of the street. He'd gone down to one knee, wheezing, as he ducked into another filthy entryway that looked exactly like his own, around the corner – six metal mail holders with doorbell buttons under them, two doors leading inside to the right and the left. Here, out of the street's line of sight, he turned back, stuck his head barely out, and saw the cop get to the corner and look this way and not see him. If he'd started down this way, Utlee had no doubt or hesitation, he would have waited until the cop was close and then shot him dead.

Instead, the cop had turned back.

That had been about two hours ago. Utlee's original plan had been to keep going up the street, around a few more corners, where he'd wait and pull somebody out of his car – alive or dead, it didn't matter. And then he'd get to his mama's place. Somehow.

But he found standing up from his kneeling position almost impossible. And severe pain was kicking in on his side. So he leaned back against the mailboxes, bleeding and thinking, his gun hanging down in his right hand. He'd fired three times, he was pretty sure. So the gun ought to have six bullets.

He had heard sirens.

Shit.

He pushed all six of the doorbell buttons and waited.

Nothing.

He had to move. Get out of here, onto another block.

When he tried to walk, his left leg went numb on him. Still, he forced himself to break out of the entryway onto the sidewalk. He made it to the next building's recessed entrance but had to stop again and get his breathing under control.

This was a bigger apartment building, with twelve units and twelve doorbells. He pushed all of them.

Up at the corner to his right, the opposite corner from where he'd come, a black-and-white cop car, its lights flashing, stopped in the middle of the intersection.

So that way was blocked. There was only going back the way he'd come. Or go through the building and out the back, if there were an alley or some connected backyards. Through them and out.

He looked out to his left. A cop car had parked in that intersection, too.

He'd backed all the way into the recess when the door to his right buzzed. He pushed at it and the thing opened.

Now he had barged his way into the lower-left-hand apartment, facing the street. There was no getting out the back way, even if there were one. He hadn't been able to make it much farther than the front door to this place. Through the drawn curtains, he could see a semicircle of cop cars closed in up and down the street, having somehow figured out – maybe from the track of blood – where he must be. He could also see three snipers who had set themselves up on the roofs across the street, and somebody else was trying to talk to him through a bullhorn, but he knew if he stuck his head out to answer, one of the snipers would take him out. Or one of the guys huddled behind the cars in the middle of the street.

Somebody, anyway.

But so what? Everything felt pretty vague. The earlier pain had settled into a numbness that felt like it was spreading. He was probably going to die anyway.

The guy outside was saying that they knew he was hit, and if he just came out to the doorway, they'd get him to a hospital and he'd get a fair trial.

Really? he thought. He doubted it.

He wished he hadn't done all that coke with Lilianne Downs, because face it, that was why he'd gone so off on Honor. He was a different person on coke. He wished he hadn't killed Honor. She'd take care of him if she was here. Get him washed up, bandaged. She could talk to the po-po, make everything work out somehow.

A good woman, that's for sure.

He'd been laying back in a chair and now pushed himself up. They weren't going to give him no fair trial. He'd shot a cop. He knew what happened to brothers who shot cops. He could throw his gun out the front door and into the street and come out with his hands up – if he could even raise his hands, which he didn't think he could – and somebody would still find a way to think he was carrying something and blow him away.

Or he could just sit here and bleed out.

He heard something outside. Not the bullhorn. Movement, somebody coming up on the building, maybe into the recess by the front doors. Charging.

He could get himself to his feet.

He could, though it took him three tries.

He looked to the apartment's door – locked and dead-bolted, but they could shoot that out without a problem.

There wasn't anything else left to do. Dragging his left foot, he got to the drawn curtains by the front window.

He stood a minute, listening to the guys breaking in the front door, thinking he never should've gotten hooked up with Lilianne.

They were at the front door.

He reached up and threw the curtains back.

Raised the gun.

The window exploded in a hail of gunfire.

THEY WERE IN the Solarium, the large circular greenhouse that the firm used as a conference room. The associates and, occasionally, the partners often gathered here at the end of the working day and spent a more or less convivial half hour, sometimes with wine or spirits, sometimes not. By way of celebration after learning that his nonmonetary blackmail of Liam Goodman had apparently worked, and also because his daughter had survived her first full week of her first murder trial, tonight Hardy had broken out a pinot noir called Cherry Pie from Hundred Acre vineyard. He had been thinking lately that this was the finest wine made on the continent, if not in the world.

But Rebecca didn't care about the wine. She'd just heard about her father and Liam Goodman. 'You're kidding me,' she said. 'Is that what really happened? You did that?'

'He really did,' Amy Wu said. 'Abe vouched for it, and Abe would never lie.'

Hardy took a sip, sloshed it around to get all the tastes, and swallowed. 'Even though Abe thinks I should have tried to shake him down a little harder. I've been thinking maybe he was right. It's possible I could've convinced the guy to retire, and wouldn't that have been beautiful? But I just wanted those people out of the courtroom.'

'Believe me,' Rebecca said, 'they left all at once, and it was amazing, like all of a sudden you could breathe in there. Everybody felt it.'

'Well,' Hardy said, 'let's hope at least one juror doesn't feel so intimidated anymore. Aren't either of you going to have some of this wine? It's really pretty adequate.'

Neither of them got to answer, because just at that moment Allie pushed open the Solarium door, surprise and shock writ large on her face. 'Sorry to butt in,' she said. 'You've got to turn on the TV in here. You're never going to believe what just happened.'

35

SATURDAY MORNING BROKE fair, and Rebecca, caught up on her sleep, was out of bed by six-thirty and back from her run through Crissy Field an hour later. In the course of that hour, her brain went over every minute of the trial so far and ping-ponged between hope and despair, elation and gloom. She was winning; she was losing. Greg had actually done it; Greg couldn't have done it. The DNA evidence was tainted; it was solid and incontrovertible.

When she got back to her building, she picked up the morning *Chronicle* on the stoop. Seconds later, when she entered her apartment, she was somewhat surprised to see Allie, not normally an early riser, dressed and apparently ready to go somewhere.

'Where are you off to so early?' Rebecca asked.

Allie, unexpectedly defensive, replied, 'It's not that early.'

'Okay. It's not that early. So you're not going out?'

'No, I am. I don't want you to be mad at me.'

'I won't be. I promise.'

'I thought I'd go down and visit Greg at the jail.'

To buy herself some time, Rebecca put the newspaper down on the kitchen counter. When she turned back around, she said, 'You know when I just said I wouldn't be mad at you? I lied.'

'I told you.'

'Yes, you did. But why in the world are you going to see Greg?'

'I think after this Royce Utlee thing, he needs a friend.'

'He's got friends. His friends come to the courtroom and have been known to visit him in jail. He's got more friends than I do. And what about the Royce Utlee thing?'

'You know, killed before he could confess to killing Anlya. I've been thinking about that all night. If they'd just gotten to talk to him, even for a minute. Utlee, I mean. The trial could be over.'

'If he did confess, and if he actually killed Anlya . . .'

'Come on, Beck, we know he did.'

'We don't, really. We think we do, but it's not a hundred percent certain.'

'That's not what you thought yesterday.'

'Okay. But still, so what? I think your going to see Greg alone is a really bad idea. Weren't you even going to tell me?'

'I am telling you.'

'Why do I think, though, that if I hadn't happened to come home right now, you would have been gone?'

'No. I've been waiting for you.'

'All right, I believe you. But I think if anybody should be seeing him today, and maybe they should not, it ought to be me. Besides, they won't let you in the attorneys' visiting room, Al. There's no chance you could get any time alone with him. I don't know what you'd be trying to accomplish.'

'I wouldn't be seeing him as his lawyer, if that's what you're worried about.'

'That's not it. I don't know how you can say that. Besides which, you couldn't see him as his lawyer, since you're not.'

'Oh, that's right. Rub that in.'

'I'm not rubbing anything in, Al. It's the simple truth. I just don't know why it's so important that you go see him.'

'You don't see that? Really?'

'Really.'

'Beck, it's because this Utlee thing is so devastating. It could have been – should be – all over, and now where's

Greg going to get another chance like that? He needs to know that somebody's with him on this.'

'What do you think I've been doing for the past six weeks, Allie? I'm with him on this.'

'Okay, I know you are as his attorney. But I mean personally, not as his lawyer. I think he needs somebody to hold his hand.'

Since she'd brought it up, Rebecca considered telling her that she'd noticed maybe a little too much of that between Allie and Greg yesterday in the courtroom. But that would only escalate things, and she didn't want that. In her frustration, she let out a heavy sigh. 'Look,' she said, 'of course you can go and visit him. Of course I believe he's innocent. He's in a terrible position. But what are you going to accomplish by going in there and figuratively holding his hand? You'd just be underscoring a setback, and that's going to make him feel like he's snakebit, that things aren't working out the way they should, when really I think the trial's going pretty well. Omar Abdullah isn't what I'd call the Platonic ideal of the great witness. And that's essentially all Braden's got.

'Even if they think Greg had sex with Anlya,' Rebecca continued, 'that doesn't remotely prove he killed her. Plus, with Liam Goodman's peanut gallery pulling out . . .' She sighed again. 'Given all that, Allie, the best thing for Greg – and I'm talking personally, not as his lawyer – is to try to stay optimistic. There's no way he can construe a surprise visit from you, talking about Royce Utlee, no less, as anything but a sign that his defense team thinks that we're screwed. And how's that going to help him in any way? You tell me.'

Allie pulled around a kitchen chair and sat down on it. 'I see what you're saying.'

Rebecca spoke gently. 'It's really not a good idea, Al. It's not going to help.'

Allie nodded. 'It's just that he's such a good guy, Beck. I

couldn't sleep all of last night thinking about it. My heart's breaking for him.'

'Mine, too. But the best thing we can do is win this trial, not visit him in jail to get him worked up over something we can't do anything about. Don't you think?'

Allie drew in a breath and let it out in a sigh. 'I guess so. I guess you're right.'

Rebecca nodded. 'I'm pretty sure I am.'

By THE TIME Rebecca had finished her shower and gotten dressed, Allie had lit out for parts unknown. Rebecca could only persist in the hope that she'd taken their conversation to heart and wasn't on her way down to Bryant Street to pay a completely inappropriate call on Greg.

She didn't know what to do about Allie. It was more than bad luck to develop a crush on your client, and there was little doubt that this was what was happening to her room-mate. It made her uneasy, to say the least.

Meanwhile, being her father's daughter, she possessed an eight-inch but very heavy version of Hardy's famous black cast-iron frying pan, a gift from Dismas and Frannie when she graduated from college. It permanently resided over the front burner of her stove, and now she turned the heat up high under it, poured in a few drops of olive oil, and opened her refrigerator to scrounge.

Flour tortilla, cheddar cheese, mango chipotle salsa, refried beans, a small leftover bowl of already cooked baby shrimp – done, folded over, and plated in under three minutes, the hot pan wiped dry with a paper towel and shining as though it had never been used.

She grabbed the *Chronicle* and brought her breakfast over to the kitchen table.

The main headline, naturally, concerned the manhunt and death of Royce Utlee at the hands of the SWAT team. Rebecca skimmed over the customary San Francisco sidebar about the overzealous police response and noticed in the lead article that the name Anlya Paulson, and Utlee's possible connection to her murder and the trial of Greg Treadway, did not appear.

She took another bite of her burrito – the salsa was insanely great – and turned the page, glancing next as she always did at Jeff Elliott's *CityTalk* column, accompanied atypically by what looked like a mug shot. Noticing right away that her uncle Abe appeared in the lead paragraph, she pulled the paper a bit closer and stopped chewing.

'I THOUGHT WE had a rule about calls before nine o'clock on weekends,' Hardy growled.

Rebecca ignored him. 'Have you seen the paper?' she asked. '*CityTalk*?'

'I haven't seen anything today except the inside of my eyelids. What time is it?'

'Eight-thirty.'

'Too early. Call back in half an hour, by which time in a fair world I still shouldn't be up, though I might be.'

'Daddy, don't hang up.'

'Is *CityTalk* about me or you?'

'No. But Uncle Abe's in it.'

He blew into the receiver. 'All right,' he said. 'What?'

'You'll see. Read it and call me right back. This could be huge.'

IN THE WARM morning, Hardy, Rebecca, and Wyatt Hunt sat in the shade of an umbrella over the picnic table on Hardy's back deck. Of the five elopers named in the *CityTalk* column, one was identified as Leon Copes. According to the article, he had been found incompetent to stand trial on a murder charge about four years ago and had spent the next three years in Napa State Hospital. Last December, he'd come down to San Francisco for psychiatric reevaluation and once again been found incompetent, so he should have been ordered back to Napa under a Murphy Conservatorship, but due to a clerical error, he was assigned to a halfway house in the city, from which he apparently walked away sometime within the past several months.

No one at the picnic table needed to be reminded that Leon Copes had been the boyfriend of Sharla Paulson and, in all probability, sexually abused Anlya Paulson when she was fourteen. And all of the principals on the deck understood that his by no means definite, but very possible if not likely, presence in San Francisco might prove to be an extremely critical element in the murder trial of Greg Treadway.

'Although, first,' Hardy said, 'we've got to find him.'

'Which is, let me guess,' Hunt said, 'where I come in.'

Rebecca gave him a smile. 'We were hoping. Any ideas?'

'I do, actually. Although maybe you want to call your friend Glitsky, and I'll talk to Devin Juhle and see if between them, plus this column, they can get a fire lit under the regular cops out on the street, watching out for these guys. That'll spread the net wider than I could. I'm a little shocked Abe didn't mention this to you earlier, Diz.'

'What, exactly?'

'Leon Copes,' Hunt replied. 'How could he not have known about the connection to your client? Especially when he found out he was one of these elopers out on the street?'

'Good questions. But he didn't do any prep work for the trial. He stopped working the case as soon as they arrested Greg. I've got to believe he never heard Leon's name in connection with it. If he did, there's no way he wouldn't have told me. He certainly wouldn't have let this *CityTalk* thing run without giving me a pretty serious heads-up. So I've got to believe he flat-out didn't know. And he damn sure doesn't know where Leon is now.'

'He could be anywhere,' Hunt said. 'If I were him, I'd be long gone.'

'You, however,' Rebecca said, 'probably would not have been twice found incompetent to stand trial.'

He cocked his head in her direction, broke a grin. 'Thanks for that "probably." That's a real vote of confidence.'

'You're welcome,' Rebecca said.

'But really,' Hardy asked Hunt, 'what are you thinking?'

'I'm thinking what The Beck says is right. He's not going to do what my hypothetical self would do, so he's probably still in town. This is where he's from. He knows people here. He's probably got family, although that's the first place where the police ought to be looking, so I'll leave it to them. He's got to have a place to crash. It's not impossible that he's got some kind of job.'

'Incompetent to stand trial and he could still get work?' Rebecca asked.

'Are you kidding?' Hunt asked her. 'That's the job description for half the service jobs in town.'

'Except that he wouldn't have a need to get a job in this town,' Hardy said, referring – they all knew – to the hundreds of welfare agencies set up all over the city to accommodate the needs of the homeless, the destitute, the abandoned. San Francisco might be the most expensive city in the country in terms of lodging and food prices, but for the truly needy, the unskilled, the unlucky, and the downright crazy, it was a socialist heaven.

'Again,' Hunt said, 'that's for the real cops to check.'

'If that's the case,' Rebecca said, 'I have to say I'm a little concerned about their motivation to find him.'

'Whose motivation?'

'Well, Devin's and even Abe's. And by extension everybody else.'

Hunt frowned. 'I don't see that. Why wouldn't they want to find him?'

Hardy spoke up. 'Because the minute Leon Copes is found anyplace in the city, he becomes part of the mix in

Treadway. Think about it. This guy raped Anlya when he was living with her family. If nothing else, that automatically makes him a threat to her.'

'Also,' Rebecca added, 'it makes her a threat to him. If she sees him someplace, if he confronts her.'

Hardy picked up the thread. 'So what The Beck is thinking is that if we can get any small part of that into the trial, just get this whole mess in front of the jury, make Leon out to be the phantom mugger, I don't care, it's got to be a huge negative for Braden, and if you lump that in with the Honor Wilson statement, I don't know how the jury could not have a doubt, and that doesn't even count the judge.'

'Bakhtiari put Braden on notice last time,' Rebecca said. 'He hates how sloppy this investigation has been.' She was thinking, however, that this was an almost unbearable complication in her representation of her client.

On the one hand, Bakhtiari was unlikely to let her throw out a bunch of accusations about Copes raping Anlya and escaping from his halfway house. She would have to have witnesses, evidence, and some indication that Leon had a connection to the crime and was not, for example, working at a convenience store in Louisiana when it happened.

On the other hand – here it was again! – if she asked for a mistrial in order to investigate these things, Bakhtiari would have to give it to her, but her relationship with her client would likely become untenable. No competent attorney could fail to ask for time to investigate this turn of events, even if her client objected.

And she wasn't talking about a few weeks when Greg would have to cool his heels in jail while they prepared for the retrial. With all of the complications that had arisen since the trial began – the Utlee connection and now the Leon Copes development – the investigations could not fail to take less than a year and possibly longer, maybe substantially longer. If she thought that Greg had been adamant before about not spending any more time in jail than he absolutely had to, now – looking at a year minimum – she could not imagine he would consider the alternative.

Rebecca realized that she wasn't the one spending every night in a jail cell. Greg's state of mind, especially with this new information, was that her job was to get this stuff in front of the jury, after which they would have no choice but to acquit him. If she'd do her job competently, he'd be free again in a matter of days, this horrific ordeal behind him.

And if she couldn't do that . . .

She knew that if she got him a mistrial, it would be the last thing she would ever do in the case. Greg would fire her the moment the motion was granted.

It would be a hell of a way to end her representation of a client in her first major case.

AT ALMOST THE same moment, Phil Braden – who was as familiar with the name Leon Copes as anyone – was on the phone with his boss, Wes Farrell.

'Yes, sir,' he was saying. 'I realize that you're the one who got the whole ball rolling about these elopers . . . Of course I think . . . Yes, in general you're right. These people should not be on the street. They need to be locked back up. Yes. Be that as it may, there is not anything in the record of this case that justifies introducing Mr Copes into the proceedings at this stage. But if we allocate our limited police resources to a full-scale manhunt that locates him within the city limits, that's exactly what they'll try to do . . . Well, that's what I'll argue, but the judge has given every indication . . . All I'm saying is that a call to Devin Juhle or even to the chief . . . Of course if he's innocent I don't want to convict him, but he's not innocent, as we know . . . All right, I just think it's worth considering. Thank you . . . Pardon? The foot? Oh, fine. Getting better every day.'

• • •

ABE GLITSKY DID not like to mix up his professional and personal worlds. Only a very few of his colleagues and – when he had been head of Homicide – inspectors knew his address. Those favored few knew better than to drop by unannounced at his home unless on a matter of great import. Consequently, he never expected work to come calling at home. So when he checked the peephole and saw Rebecca Hardy standing there, he immediately realized that she was here on business – what else could it be? – and it took him half a beat to get his head around it.

He opened the door with a full and genuine smile – after all, he loved this young woman – and gave her a hug and a buss on the cheek. 'How's my favorite almost-niece?'

He invited her in, and they went out the back door to say hello to Treya, who was sitting with another woman while kids cavorted on the playground set. Rachel and Zachary needed their hugs and a quick catching-up, too, but five minutes later, they were back in the living room, Rebecca on the couch and Abe in his favorite reading chair. 'So to what,' he asked, 'do I owe this pleasure?'

She started to give him the short rundown and got as far as 'I don't know if you know, but before he got arrested for homicide, Leon Copes lived with Anlya Paulson's mother. And, not exactly by the way, he molested Anlya during that time.'

Abe, who'd been sitting back taking in the narrative, came forward, his head cocked with interest. 'Leon Copes? You're saying Leon lived with Anlya and molested her? You're kidding me.'

'I'm not. I saw the name in *CityTalk* this morning and—'

'This is huge.'

'That's what I thought, too. So you really didn't know?'

Glitsky frowned. 'How could I have known? This is the first time I've heard of Leon in connection with Anlya. Wes Farrell took me off that case as soon as your guy got arrested.

If I'd known about this, I would have told somebody, I promise. You, for example. Devin Juhle. Maybe your dad. Somebody.'

'I know you would have. More important right now, we don't know where Leon is, do we?'

'No.' He thought a moment. 'But I'm guessing you'd like to find out.'

She nodded. 'It might be helpful.'

Glitsky chuckled. 'Sounding almost too much like your father. "It might be helpful." Meaning that you would kill small children to find out where he is.'

'Only a few of the very worst ones. And painlessly. But yes, we'd like to find him. And my dad was thinking since you're the guy who's on record for trying to locate these elopers, you might have a lead or two.'

'I wish I did. But the paper's only been out a few hours, and it's the weekend. I don't see anybody jumping on this till Monday at the earliest.'

'Well, maybe. Wyatt's going to talk to Devin Juhle today, but we realized that . . .'

When she finished explaining, Abe was nodding in agreement. 'You're right. Why would Devin want to supply you with another possible suspect when you've got one on trial? If Leon just turns up, okay, they'll bring him in because they have to. Otherwise, these guys have been AWOL for years, some of 'em. What's another couple of weeks? In spite of *CityTalk*, I don't see any heat under it.'

'We didn't, either. That's why we thought we'd come to you.'

Glitsky's lips turned up in amusement. 'And why is that?'

'Because these guys are your babies. You've claimed them. So you've got a reason to be looking for each and every one of them. If Leon Copes happens to be the first one you focus on, who's going to know or care? Whereas, by contrast, if Juhle sends his troops out looking, and he might not, it wouldn't surprise me to hear the four other guys are out in front of Leon.'

Glitsky clucked. 'My, my,' he said. 'Whence this cynical streak?'

She smiled back at him. 'I'm thinking you can guess, Uncle Abe.'

'I'm thinking I can. That parental-influence thing has a long reach.'

'It does, yes. But in this case, I'm not being cynical. I know the prosecution side never believes this, but the evidence doesn't prove that Greg Treadway killed Anlya, and if that's true, it means somebody else did.'

'And out of the whole universe, with nothing like any new evidence, or nothing putting him anywhere near where it happened, you think that person was Leon Copes?'

'I think it's a pretty darn amazing coincidence that he gets out of jail, and within six months, the girl he molested is killed. I think that needs to be looked at carefully, that's all. And we can't even begin to do that until we find him.'

'So you want me to go behind the backs of my peeps?'

'You're not going behind anybody's back. If somebody thinks you're stepping on toes and calls you off, okay, you tried. But if you're just following up on where these five guys might have gotten to, you've already announced that to the whole world. Then, if you find Leon Copes first—'

Glitsky held up a hand. 'I get the concept.'

'So what do you say?'

'I say, and it won't surprise you, I'm going to do my job.'

She beamed across at him. 'That's all I ask. Thanks, Uncle Abe.'

36

Wyatt Hunt wasn't thrilled to be working on the most beautiful Saturday of the year. He and his wife, Tamara, already had their windsurfing gear all bundled up and ready to go when they'd gotten a little physically distracted over breakfast. And so they hadn't yet left their home when Rebecca called and told him they had an emergency and needed him right away and probably for the rest of the weekend. Since Hardy & Associates was the source of much of Hunt's income, he had no choice.

The meeting at Hardy's house had been informative and instructive, but Hunt's later phone call to his good pal Devin Juhle was not. Juhle had given every indication that he'd been thoroughly briefed about the Leon Copes matter. As head of Homicide, he had and would have no official interest in locating him. His inspectors, as always, were all working on active homicide investigations and had neither the time nor the inclination to pursue escaped or eloped inmates. He was surprised that Hunt would ask.

Now Hunt was knocking at a door on a block that made even this picture-book day seem tawdry and bleak. The benign sun on the Hardys' back deck had revealed a different side of its personality and now seemed to bake down remorselessly on desiccated or grassless front yards. Heavy iron bars covered each door and downstairs window in every dwelling.

Hunt had been to similar places many times. During his

CPS years, he had carried children from houses like these while a parent cried or cursed or threatened. He had never met Anlya Paulson, although he'd liked her brother on sight, but seeing that they had both come from this environment, he felt a surge of empathy and sadness.

And anger.

The metal door stayed shut after the woman opened the inner one. Inside, the house was all shuttered up, well beyond dim. Invisible. He could barely see her outline through the heavy black mesh that separated them.

'Sharla Paulson?' he said.

'Who's askin'?'

'My name is Wyatt Hunt, and I'm a private investigator trying to locate Leon Copes.'

'What you want him for?'

'I'm not supposed to say, although I'm authorized to tell you that he would probably consider it good news.'

'Money? Who's he know got money?'

'I'm really not at liberty to say. Or even if there is money involved. We'd just like to locate him.'

'You with the police?'

'No, ma'am. I'm a private investigator. If you'd like to see my license . . .' He took out his wallet, opened it, and held it up.

She opened the outer door enough to glimpse his identification. And for him to get a look at her. She was not an unattractive woman, although at the moment she was unkempt, with wild hair and no makeup – and perhaps a bruise under her left eye. She was barefoot, in black pants and a Harley-Davidson T-shirt.

'It would be worth Leon's while to get in contact with me. If I could leave a card . . .' He passed it through the crack in the door. 'So,' he said, 'Leon.'

'Leon ain't here no more.'

'I understand that. But this is the last regular address we

have for him, and we thought someone here would know where he might have gone.'

She didn't respond.

Hunt pressed on. 'I wondered if he tried to stay in touch with you at all.'

'He was no good to my baby, Anlya. Then he killed a man in a fight and they put him up at Napa.'

'Yes. But we have him coming back to the city after that.'

Again silence. Then, 'He got spells, that's all it was.'

'Spells?'

'You know. Something goes off inside his head. He don't mean nothing by it. That's why they wouldn't give him no trial and just locked him away. He ain't a bad man.'

'But you and he broke up?'

'That's because after Anlya . . . He couldn't be in the house with her no more. It wasn't really his fault, but she got so she couldn't be around him.'

'Are you saying it was her fault? What happened between them?'

'He didn't mean it, is all, like she thought. He woulda stopped. He did stop. But she couldn't get over the one time, and she needed him to go, so wasn't really nothin' I could do. Wasn't her fault. Wasn't his. Just happened. So what could I do?'

Hunt had to fight to keep himself from saying, 'You could have strangled the son of a bitch for raping your daughter.' Instead, he summoned calm from some deep reserve and said, 'We thought he might have come back to where he felt comfortable, to some people he knew.'

'He knows a lot of folks.'

'Do you think you'd be able to put me in contact with some of them?'

'I don't think he'd like that. But maybe, I see him, I can show him your card.'

'So you are seeing him?'

Hesitating, she finally answered, 'I didn't say that.'

'Do you think you might see him?'

'If he come around . . .'

'So he does come around? You think he might come around?'

'No. I don't say that. I don't know where he's at. He's moving around, most likely. Here and there.'

Hunt took a beat, gathered himself. 'I understand you're going to the trial of the man charged with killing Anlya.'

'My poor baby.'

'Yes, ma'am.'

'I don't know why he did that. That boy. Don't seem like there was any reason.'

'Do you know if Leon's following the trial, too?'

'I don't know why he would.'

'Maybe he saw Anlya after he got out of Napa.'

'No. He would have . . . He wouldn't have.'

'Would have what, Sharla? Wouldn't have what?'

'Talked to her. Went and looked for her.'

'Maybe he had another spell. Do you think that could have happened? Maybe he sought her out and she turned him down.'

'No. She would have told me, told the police.'

'Did she do that last time?'

'She told me.'

'What about the police?'

'No. The po-po don't help nobody.'

'But didn't she come over here just a short while before she was killed, to see if she could move back in with you?'

'Okay. She did that.'

'So why didn't that work out? Your son, Max, said you were all ready for her, all set up, and then something changed and at the last second you couldn't go through with it.'

'I wished I could have, but . . .'

'But?'

'But it wasn't going to work, because it just couldn't.'

'Why not? Was it because what else happened at almost that same time, or a few weeks before, was that Leon got out of custody and showed up here?'

'She wouldn't live with him again.'

'So he did come back here?'

'I didn't say that.'

Yes, you did, Hunt thought. Yes, you damn well did.

WHEN HE LEFT Sharla, Hunt went back to where he'd parked his Mini Cooper at the corner. Opening the driver's-side door, he let the heat that had built up dissipate for a few minutes, then gingerly slid into the seat, started the engine, put all the windows down, and turned on the air-conditioning.

He could see the front of the house clearly, which meant that anyone in the house could see him, too. And the Cooper stood out amid the junkers lining the curbs on both sides. Still, he sat watching nothing move on the street for close to fifteen minutes. The place was eerily silent, still, and deserted. Some instinct prompted him to stay where he was – Leon Copes might be in the house, he realized, hunkered down somewhere in the dim, shadowy interior rooms. Or he might show up at any minute. Hunt had five employees and considered calling in and having them start a rotating 24/7 stakeout here, but in reality, there was no telling when or if Leon would ever show up at Sharla's again. It would just be an expensive waste of time.

Getting out his cell phone, he punched some numbers. 'Well, I talked to her.'

'What did she say?' Rebecca asked.

'She said whatever happened, it wasn't Leon's fault. He has spells. He's not a bad man.'

'Wyatt, he raped her daughter.'

'I know. And if you want my opinion, if he's the one who killed her, Sharla's going to say that wasn't his fault, either.'

'Her own daughter? How could a mother ever forgive that?'

'I know,' he said. 'It's hard to imagine. But the important thing is that he's almost undoubtedly in town, maybe hanging around with her from time to time, when he's not having a spell or two.'

'*Almost* undoubtedly?'

Wyatt gave her the gist of the interview. 'At the very least,' he concluded, 'I got her to admit that he was the reason it didn't work out with Anlya moving back in. Anlya didn't want to live in the same house as Leon again.'

'No shit.'

'That's what I thought. So I guess where I'm at now is: What do you want me to do next, if anything? I'm pretty sure he's in town. And I did get one idea that isn't too ridiculous to consider.'

'I'm listening.'

'It occurred to me that maybe they're talking by phone – Sharla and Leon, I mean – and if we could get her phone records, recent calls, we could find out who she's talking to. If the cops got the phone company to triangulate some positions, they'd have a chance of pinning the guy down. But that's all going to take a warrant, which means you're stuck with the regular cops, who I gather are still not on board.'

'Not necessarily,' she said. 'There may be a way.'

THE WEEKEND MAGISTRATE judge, Oscar Thomasino, had retired from the active bench a few years before but liked to keep his hand in. When Glitsky knocked on the door to his chambers in the Hall of Justice at four o'clock, Thomasino looked over the top of his paperback, took his feet off his desk, stood up, and stuck out his hand over his desk. 'Abe Glitsky, as I live and breathe,' he said. 'Until this morning, I thought I'd heard you'd hung 'em up. Then here you are, all over *CityTalk*, big as life.'

'Not all that big, Your Honor. Wes Farrell felt sorry for me, and because he loves my wife, he threw me a bone. I've been doing scut work with some of his investigations, but I suppose it is keeping me off the streets, which is all in all a good thing.'

'I'm sure it is. So what can I do for you?'

'It's about one of the *CityTalk* guys, the elopers. Leon Copes.'

'You've located one of them already? That was fast.'

'We've almost located one. At least we're hoping to. Which is why I'm here.'

'I somehow guessed as much,' Thomasino said. 'What have you got?'

Armed with his affidavit outlining the discussion between Wyatt Hunt and Sharla Paulson, including her inadvertent admission that Leon was living with her as of a few months before, Glitsky made his case for a warrant to access the records of her cell phone number – a number her son, Max, had supplied at Hunt's request.

Judge Thomasino thought this was all reasonable. Leon Copes was clearly a dangerous and unstable man who had run away from the custody of law enforcement. There was currently a warrant out for his arrest. He was still the prime suspect in the outstanding homicide of the man he'd allegedly killed in the bar fight. If Sharla's telephone records could prove critical in locating this wanted felon, Glitsky should have access to them. Thomasino had no trouble at all signing the warrant and putting those events in motion.

Glitsky never had occasion to mention either Greg Treadway or Anlya Paulson.

37

THE REST OF the weekend had been agonizing for Rebecca. And just when she'd thought there was a decent chance that she could pull a rabbit out of her hat, salvage the trial, and save her client.

But the plain truth was that though Leon Copes may very well have been somewhere in the city a few months before, and might be there today, there was no way Sharla's phone records were going to provide that information. Reporting his failure to her, and not going to great pains to hide his own disappointment, Glitsky had opined that Sharla was possibly the least connected telephone user he'd ever run across. It had been over a week since she'd either sent or received a phone call, and the last one was from her son, Max. Her contacts list consisted of a whopping fourteen numbers, none of them identified as Leon or anything like it, and all of them demonstrably someone else's – Juney's, Max's, Anlya's (still), her mother, her manicurist, three girl-friends, and so on. There were very few received calls, and all of them, as it turned out, were from marketing companies.

A washout.

In the meantime, waiting for Abe or Wyatt to call with something definitive about Leon Copes, Rebecca had spent all day Sunday, despite her father's assurance that she was wasting her time, preparing another motion to submit to Bakhtiari about Copes's very existence, his likely presence in the city – including Wyatt Hunt's statement about his interview with Sharla to buttress her claim – and his possible motive to want Anlya dead. Rebecca didn't fool herself. She knew without a doubt that her father was right to tell her she was wasting her time and that this, too, would be inadmissible: Bakhtiari wouldn't allow any part of it without more concrete evidence directly connecting Leon Copes to the homicide.

But she felt that no matter how he ruled on her motion, the judge needed to be aware of this reality. It might affect other rulings. It was, she felt, worth presenting.

Complicating matters at home, she and Allie disagreed about telling Greg about Leon Copes. Rebecca believed that the judge needed to hear about Copes in the context of this trial – hence her motion – but she did not see any advantage in sharing any of that information with her client.

She didn't expect anyone to find Copes. She didn't think evidence concerning him would be admitted unless or until he was found. And she knew now, goddammit, that at that point she would have to move for a mistrial, which would irrevocably destroy her relationship with Greg. She didn't want to cross that bridge until she came to it.

As long as Leon remained off the radar, the fact that he may have been around when Anlya was thinking about moving in with Sharla was provocative but not admissible. The judge wouldn't let it in. And it didn't involve Leon, directly or not, in Anlya's death. All this new lead would accomplish was to get Rebecca kicked off the case. In the end, Rebecca had told Allie she needed her to promise that she wouldn't bring it up with Greg. And though her roommate had dutifully, finally, made that promise, the tension in the apartment was thick.

Now Rebecca sat in the courtroom at the defense table with Allie and Greg on Monday morning, waiting for court to be called into session, assailed by her doubts. And obviously not hiding them too well, since Greg leaned in to her and whispered, 'Are you okay?'

She shrugged. 'Just ready to get started. I'm fine.'

She spent the next forty minutes listening to Deion Johnson give his testimony about his walk up from Chinatown with his wife, Mercedes, on the night of the murder. Rebecca had read his original statement to the police, of course, and she knew that he was on the witness stand for one reason – to say that he'd heard a man and a woman arguing up the street where it crossed over the tunnel below, and then seen a man running down the street afterward. Since this was all he had to offer, she found it somewhat difficult to keep a concentrated and interested look on her face as Braden patiently and, with an almost breathless urgency, minute after minute, led him through his paces. In the end, she settled on admiring Braden's technique in creating a sense of import and drama when there was precious little.

When at last – at last – he gave her the witness, she rose swiftly and said, 'Thank you,' so heartily that it sent a little titter through the gallery and brought a smile to a juror or two. After an initial stab of embarrassment, she allowed a small, self-effacing smile. If her behavior elicited any kind of sympathetic response from the jury, she'd take it. Somehow, she realized, the tension in her had dissipated. She nodded at the witness and got a relaxed nod in return.

'Mr Johnson,' she began. 'You've estimated that you were about fifty yards from where Bush crosses over the Stockton tunnel when you first heard raised voices coming from that direction, is that right?'

'Give or take. Yes.'

'And you were downhill from there?'

'Yes.'

'Did you hear any specific words that you could identify?'

'No. As I said, it was more like the sound of a struggle.'

'So, not an argument, really, as it's been called here? Not a back-and-forth, like a heated conversation?'

He considered for a longish moment. 'Not like a conversation. No.'

'So what was it like?'

'Struggling, kind of. Grunting, like.'

'So a physical fight more than a verbal argument, would you say?'

'Yes.'

'And how long did this go on from the time you started hearing it?'

'Not long. Ten or fifteen seconds. Until the scream.'

'A series of grunts? Sounds of exertion?'

'Yes.'

'But no man's voice? And no specific words?'

Mr Johnson allowed himself a note of impatience. 'It sounded like a man and a woman, fighting.'

Rebecca knew that because Mr Johnson had shown some uncalled-for impatience, the jury would allow her a snarky question or two. 'And how do you distinguish the sounds of a man and woman fighting, as opposed to two men fighting or two women fighting, when you don't hear any voices?'

Mr Johnson didn't immediately reply.

'Would you like to change your previous statement? Wouldn't it be more fair to say that you heard two people struggling?'

The witness agreed that this could be so.

As Rebecca had hoped he might, Mr Johnson threw a frustrated glance at Braden that brought the prosecutor to his feet with an objection. 'Your Honor, irrelevant. Asked and answered,' he said. 'Counsel is badgering the witness, trying to have him draw a difference without a distinction.'

But to Rebecca there was a clear difference between an argument and a struggle, and in defending herself against Braden's objection, much to her delight, she would get to explain that difference to the jury. 'Your Honor,' she said, 'there is a true and important distinction here. An argument implies conversation, disagreement, interpersonal conflict; a struggle is more impersonal and perhaps transactional – as with a purse snatching and mugging, for example.'

Bakhtiari simply nodded. 'Objection overruled. Go ahead, Ms Hardy.'

'Thank you, Your Honor.' She came back to the witness. 'So to rephrase, Mr Johnson, you say that the sounds of struggle you heard above the tunnel just before the scream were a series of grunts and exertions that sounded like two people having a physical altercation. Is that right?'

'Yes. All right.'

'From what you heard, it was not then a verbal argument as such, was it?'

'No,' he said. 'I guess not.'

Rebecca allowed herself the briefest moment of satisfaction, hoping that her body language would convey it to the jury. She felt she had clearly made her point, and it was an important one: According to this witness, Anlya and her assailant had struggled; they had not argued.

'No further questions,' she said.

DISMAS HARDY HAD some business in the Hall of Justice on another matter, and he'd sneaked in to catch some of the action, so he was in the back of the courtroom while his daughter conducted her cross-examination of Mr Johnson.

In the recess that followed, he stopped first to share a few words with the Treadways, a few rows back as they always were, then came up to the bar rail and tapped Rebecca on the shoulder. 'Hey, you.'

She turned around, greeting him. 'Did you catch any of that?' she asked.

'I did. Nicely done,' Hardy said. 'It sounds to me like she got mugged.'

'Good. I hope the jury picked that up, too.'

Hardy glanced over at the panel. 'A couple of them must have. Anlya sure as shit didn't walk up there with her boyfriend and then get in a fight with him there. It was all quicker than that.'

'I'm glad you saw what I was getting at.'

'I did. I also liked how you got it in, answering Braden's objection. That was slick.'

She smiled. 'I wasn't sure it would work, but I had to try.'

'It flew on gilded wings.'

'Well, thank you. I think the idea might have come from your old playbook. But what are you doing here?'

'Just slumming.' He nodded at Greg and Allie. 'No offense and nothing personal. How are you two doing? Holding up?'

'Staying out of trouble,' Greg replied.

'And how about you?' Hardy asked Allie. 'You learning anything?'

'Every day,' she said, giving Rebecca a look that he couldn't interpret, some drama going on between them.

'Are you staying around?' Rebecca asked.

'No. I've got to get back to the office. It seems like you've got things under control here.'

She gave him a hopeful smile. 'Trying.'

'A little more than that, I think.'

EVER SINCE WYATT Hunt had come by over the weekend, wanting him to share Sharla's phone number because they needed to find out if she'd been in contact with Leon Copes, Max had been in a low level state of shock.

Leon out?

Not just now. Apparently, he'd been out for several months. And if Hunt was to be believed, he had come back to hook up with Sharla and, even more astoundingly after all he had done to harm them, she had taken him back in.

Lying in bed last night, after he'd tried to talk it through with Auntie Juney, with limited success, Max had wracked his brain for hours, trying to work out some of the permutations, to fit them somewhere in his rapidly changing view of what the world really was.

According to Hunt, the reason Anlya hadn't moved in

with Sharla wasn't because she'd gotten back into her dependence on drugs and alcohol but because his mother expected his sister to live in the same house with the man who'd raped her.

All right, there was that for starters.

Almost more upsetting than Sharla's skewed and unreasonable expectations was the fact that Anlya hadn't told him about any of this. Anlya, his confidante and twin with whom he shared all of his secrets, for some reason didn't want him to know that Leon Copes had somehow escaped captivity and was now living not just in San Francisco but, at least part of the time, in their mother's house.

How could she not have felt he needed to know this? How close had their relationship been after all?

This led, in the black of the night, back to Greg Treadway, his other confidant, his other betrayer, whom Max had truly and stupidly believed innocent in Anlya's murder until they announced the DNA evidence. Which, face it, even if it had nothing to do directly with the murder, eliminated any doubt that they'd been fucking, even as that lying bastard had mouthed all of his platitudes about his responsibilities, his commitment to his near-sacred role as a CASA, his respect for Anlya, her age, and her troubled history. Of course he would never take advantage of her. Of course he would never use his position and experience to unduly influence her.

And yet that was precisely what he'd done.

If Greg had lied time and again about his sexual relationship with Anlya, why wouldn't he lie about killing her? Or about anything else, including the connection he and Max had built up? Max now knew that had been a fabrication as well.

He had turned in bed, thrown off the covers, pulled them back over his head, moaned so loudly that Juney had come in. Was he all right? Could she get him anything? She had sat down and rubbed his head and told him that everything was going to be all right. Really, this was just a rough patch, and he'd been through many before, some worse than this. He had to be strong and carry on.

Try as he might, he could no longer believe her.

Now, in the morning sunshine, he still didn't believe her. He couldn't will the belief back. What little faith he had left was gone.

Not just his own mother and Anlya and Greg had betrayed him – the whole world had betrayed him.

Because he was weak, because he was stupid, he'd somehow convinced himself that the world was a place of decent people. But that was wrong. The world, he now knew, was a place of darkness and deception. Ever since he'd moved in with Auntie Juney, he'd brainwashed himself with the notion that he could better himself, better his life, turn everything around from his troubled childhood. Now he knew beyond all doubt that this was a cruel, false dream.

He wasn't ever going to fall for it again.

38

HARDY CAME OUT of the courtroom and, way down to his right in the hallway, saw a grim-faced Abe Glitsky, in a sport coat and tie, involved in an animated conversation with another man who, as Hardy walked toward them, became recognizable as Phil Braden. As soon as he made that identification, Hardy stopped, keeping his distance.

Whatever they were talking about, it wasn't pretty. Braden's voice occasionally got loud enough to echo in the hall. Twice the prosecuting attorney turned all the way around in an obvious show of pique, throwing his arms in the air. Glitsky kept his stone face on and did not raise his voice, but there was no question he was taking Braden and his problem very seriously indeed.

Finally, Braden turned a last time, threw a parting volley over his shoulder, and disappeared behind the door that Hardy knew led to the floor's internal hallway, used by the bailiffs, the shackled prisoners, and the judges on the way to their chambers.

Hardy watched as Glitsky's shoulders rose and fell, rose and fell. Shaking his head in apparent misery, Abe stared at the door through which Braden had just passed. He sucked in a huge lungful of air, blew it out through his mouth, started walking up the hall with a heavy tread, and saw Hardy.

Who fell in next to him. 'Well, that seemed to go pretty well,' he said with a stab at cheeriness.

Which Glitsky ignored. 'You saw?'

'Did you guys just break up or what?'

'I can't blame him. He's in real trouble now.'

'Why's that?'

Glitsky stopped walking and Hardy drew up next to him. 'Because his main eyewitness – you may remember Omar Abdullah – has apparently decided not to honor his subpoena to appear in court today.'

'When was he due up?'

'Before my turn, and if you're wondering, I was supposed to be going on directly after him, which is why I'm out here waiting in the hall for my summons when I could be doing something worthwhile with my life. When I went to the hotel we've been keeping him at, there was no sign of him. The guy has been a complete pain, trying to use more than his meal allowance, having his street friends stay with him in the room, and raising hell. We must have had four noise complaints since we put him up in the place. But we talked the manager into not throwing him out. I even talked to him last night, and I show up this morning to pick him up, and he's gonzo. He's got to be around here someplace close, and I know we'll find him. How far could he go? But Braden has completely nutted out.'

'So does he blame you for this? Braden?'

'Essentially, although he doesn't want me to remind him that he went along with it. I mean, we put the good Mr Abdullah up somewhere safe, where we could keep our hands on him. We gave him a meal allowance. And for a month I've been listening to him complain about not having pay-per-view movies in his room. He's our witness. We treat him better than right. So when we told him today looked like it would be the day, I thought he was all set. I don't see what else we could have done, short of putting a guard on him twenty-four/seven.'

Hardy clucked in sympathy. 'The best-laid plans,' he said.

Glitsky pointed at him, shutting him up. 'Don't start,' he said. 'Don't even start.'

'What are you going to do? What's Braden going to do?'

'You're the lawyer. You tell me. He told me to stick around, so I'm guessing he's still planning to put me on the stand while half the city police force is out looking for Omar.'

'That would be kind of weird, wouldn't it? Having you up as a witness to talk about Omar's ID on Treadway before Omar gets on the stand and points him out? As your personal attorney, I can tell you that your early-ID testimony isn't even admissible until the jury hears the guy himself ID Greg in court.'

Glitsky shrugged. 'That's Braden's call. He thinks he can get the judge to take me out of order.'

'What else are you going to testify about?'

'Essentially, just my hooking up with Omar, or Malibu. How he came to my attention and so on.'

'What's Malibu?'

'The name Omar goes by on the street. And it's the car, by the way, not the town.'

'Major distinction. You wouldn't want to mix them up.'

'Basically, I'm going to be the warm-up act, then Abdullah comes on and puts Treadway in the tunnel right after the scream. Positive ID. He's the whole case.'

Hardy checked over the hallway, as always teeming with life up here near the front of the building, where the stairs and elevators deposited their loads of humanity – jurors, witnesses, attorneys, cops, spectators, groupies, media types – all eventually heading for the courtrooms. 'He might still make it.'

'He might, but the smart money says he won't.'

'Says the professional handicapper.'

At that moment, a bailiff approached, hesitated for a second, then came up to them. 'Excuse me,' he said. 'Lieutenant Glitsky? You're up in Department Twenty-four.'

'Thank you,' Glitsky said. Then, to Hardy, 'Wish me luck.'

• • •

BRADEN HAD OBVIOUSLY made the decision to soldier on as
though everything were all right and the game plan for the
trial was intact – a miracle might happen and Abdullah would
appear out in the hallway, waiting to be called in to give his
testimony – so before he sent for Glitsky, he had called
another of the first-night witnesses, Zhang Jun, the cashier
at the Sutter-Stockton garage. Jun's testimony was straight-
forward, simple, and from the prosecution's standpoint, critical – it established the exact time of Anlya's death, a fact
that would play into Glitsky's testimony on the accuracy of
the surveillance video's timeline. Jun testified that he worked
in the tiny cashier's booth inside the garage, and his cigarette
breaks started exactly on the hour every two hours – he
literally counted down the seconds, so he was one hundred
percent certain. He'd gotten up and left his workstation at
precisely the click of eleven. He'd not yet lit his cigarette,
so it was less than one minute later when the scream had
punctured the still of the night.

Rebecca didn't have any problem with this testimony. It
was prosecutorial housekeeping, touching the technical bases,
and she let the witness pass without any cross.

As it happened, Bakhtiari did allow Glitsky to go out of
order. With Glitsky in the witness box, Braden started off
following Abe's efforts to locate a critical eyewitness with an
entertaining and even dramatic showing of the surveillance
video from the tunnel, the highlights of which were what
Glitsky knew to be the back of Omar Abdullah's head and the
appearance of a white male – his hands were visible and clearly
belonged to a Caucasian – wearing a coat and tie within,
arguably, minutes if not seconds of the scream and Anlya's
death. Braden stopped the playback at the moment of clearest
resolution of the man's head – maddeningly for the jury; several
of them groaned in frustration – though he had been looking
down at the steps the whole time and moving rather quickly,
flitting in and out of the picture in under two seconds from

the first glance until he was around the corner and going down the second half of the stairway into the tunnel.

All anyone could make out due to the light and the camera angle was a head of dark hair, a blur of movement. The face was absolutely unidentifiable.

Glitsky, on the stand, gave it another careful look to go with the dozens of times he'd studied the shot, hoping that he'd see something this last time that had eluded him, but that hope got dashed in the still photograph's unchanging reality. The picture was not going to convict Greg Treadway or anyone else. But it wasn't going to acquit him, either.

When the lights came back up, Braden started in again. 'By the way, Lieutenant Glitsky, did you have occasion to check the timeline that appears at the bottom of the video screen?'

'Yes, sir.' Glitsky had explained his procedure. He'd taken a picture of the video camera with his cell phone, then gone to maintenance and had them pull the CD, verifying that its timeline exactly matched when Glitsky had taken the picture. He'd asked maintenance to do a similar test randomly a few weeks later, and again its timeline was accurate.

The white male had shown up on the video at precisely 11:04, within seconds of the scream, and the same time registered on Zhang Jun's official clock. There didn't appear to be any question about the time of Anlya's death, nor the time of the white male's appearance on the surveillance video.

'All right,' Braden said. 'After you'd viewed this video, Lieutenant, what did you do next?'

'I decided to go to the tunnel myself.'

'To what end?'

'I hoped to identify a witness, an African-American homeless individual who'd been interviewed by another officer on the night of the crime. I thought it was possible, if not probable, that his was the back of the head we all just saw on the video. Before he had disappeared, his testimony indicated, and the video seemed to corroborate, that he might have had a good look at the person who came running down the stairs in the seconds after the scream.'

'Did you make any special preparations before going down to the tunnel?'

'I did.' Glitsky went on to describe the making of his six-pack of California driver's license head shots, one of which was Greg Treadway's. The six-pack was marked as an exhibit.

'And did you in fact locate someone who identified himself as the individual who had spoken to police that evening?'

'Yes. As I suspected, he is homeless. He goes by the street name Malibu, although apparently, his real name is Omar Abdullah. He admitted that he had been interviewed on the night of the crime. The night of the scream, he called it.'

'And did he say he saw anyone coming down the Bush Street steps in the immediate aftermath of the scream?'

'Yes. A white male in a coat and tie. He said he got a good look at him, face-to-face.'

'What did you do then?'

'I showed him the six-pack and read him the admonition on the back.' Glitsky dutifully read the admonition for the jury.

Braden asked, 'Did he tell you he understood that admonition?'

'Yes, he did. I told him to take his time and asked him if he could recognize any of those six white males as the one he'd seen on the night of the scream.'

'And did he recognize any of them?'

'He did. The bottom row, farthest left.'

Braden was ready with the exhibit. 'How, if at all, did you have him mark this exhibit to indicate the identification he was making?'

'He circled the photo and signed and dated it.'

'And is that signature and date present on this exhibit?'

'Yes, I see it here.'

'Is the lower-left photograph the one identified by your witness Omar Abdullah as the white male he saw on the landing in the tunnel on the night of the crime?'

'Yes, it is.'

'And it is a photograph of whom?'

'It's a picture of the defendant, Greg Treadway.'

'Thank you, Lieutenant. No further questions.' He turned to Rebecca. 'Your witness.'

Bakhtiari cleared his throat and spoke up. 'Ms Hardy. It's been a long morning of testimony. If you don't object, I suggest we break for lunch and continue with your cross-examination of Lieutenant Glitsky at one-thirty.'

REBECCA'S FACE SHOWED her surprise. 'I thought you were going back to the office.'

'Fate intervened,' Hardy said. He had come up through the bar rail and over to the defense table as soon as the judge called for the lunch recess, passing Glitsky with a curt nod and no words as his friend exited down the aisle of the gallery.

'Fate in what guise?' Greg asked.

Hardy looked around to make sure he wouldn't be overheard and said, 'In the guise of a missing witness.' He lowered his voice further. 'Abe went out to pick up Omar Abdullah this morning, and he wasn't there. It looks like he blew off testifying.'

'Can he just do that?' Allie asked.

'No,' Hardy told her. 'Which is not to say that it doesn't happen all the time.'

Rebecca's eyes shone with hopeful disbelief. 'They didn't have him stashed someplace over the weekend?'

'Yes, they did, but it didn't work,' Hardy said. 'Pretty amazing, huh?'

Rebecca nodded. 'Staggering.' She cast a prayerful glance

at the ceiling. 'Wow!' She put a hand on her client's arm. 'Okay,' she said to Greg, 'I've been touchy about it so far, but starting now, you're allowed to be optimistic. A little.'

Obviously happy with the news, Greg remained somewhat wary. 'I'll think about it,' he said. 'But is this really that big a deal? I mean, they've already got his testimony. Couldn't they just read it out and get it in the record that way?'

'Maybe, but not in this case.'

'Why not?'

Rebecca pointed to her roommate. 'Al? Quick quiz. You want to take it?'

The paralegal waded in. 'Because Omar testified in front of the grand jury before it indicted you. And in the grand jury, we know, there's no cross-examination, so until he gives his testimony at the trial in open court, where he is subject to cross, that testimony's not admissible. By contrast . . .' Allie looked for Rebecca's tacit permission to continue and got the nod she wanted. 'By contrast, if he'd given the testimony at a preliminary hearing, he would have been subject to cross, and just reading out what he said would be admissible if he was truly unavailable.'

'So once again,' Hardy said, 'they hurried it up by going for the grand jury indictment first, and it's come back to bite 'em on the ass. Which, I must say, doesn't break my heart.'

'Mine, either,' Greg said, warming to the situation. 'So what next? They lose a witness, do they ask for a mistrial? I'm telling you, I don't want a mistrial. I don't want to do this again.'

Rebecca shook her head. 'The prosecution can't get a mistrial. That would be double jeopardy. They can't try you twice for the same crime.' She looked at her client. 'I get it, Greg. You don't want one. And I think under these circumstances, we don't, either.' She marveled at how the calculus had changed even since this morning. 'No, we want them to run with what they've got, which, without Omar, doesn't have you anywhere near the tunnel at any time.'

'Great.'

'It is great. It's basically the whole ball game,' Rebecca said with real excitement. 'I think when they finish their case in chief, without Omar – and if you want the practice, Allie, you can start writing it up right now – we file an Eleven-eighteen.'

Technically, this was an 1118.1, named after its section of the California penal code. In this directed verdict of acquittal, the judge would have heard all the prosecution evidence and directed the jury to acquit because he'd deter-mined that the evidence was insufficient to sustain a conviction. This was nearly always a standard boilerplate motion that the defense filed when the prosecution rested, which the judge summarily rejected. But this time, under these circumstances, it might fly. Rebecca turned to her father for corroboration. 'Dad?'

'I would. Definitely. If they can't put Greg here in the tunnel, then there's no proof he was there. They got motive, maybe, and a damn thin one at that. Nothing more. I don't see how the judge lets this go to the jury.'

'That's because I wasn't there,' Treadway said. 'Not to get picky.'

Hardy gave him an appraising look. 'I admire a man who stands by his story,' he said. Then he brought in the others. 'Anybody here have plans for lunch?'

'We've got a room reserved in the back,' Rebecca said. 'Lucca sandwiches ought to have been delivered already.'

'Have I died and gone to heaven?' Hardy asked. 'Anybody mind if I tag along?' He broke the ghost of a grin at the client. 'Nonbillable.'

Treadway nodded. 'Join the party.'

GLITSKY DIDN'T EXACTLY skulk out of the courtroom, but he had no desire to run into Phil Braden or Wes Farrell or anybody else, not even his wife.

There was no way to put a kind spin on it – this Omar Abdullah thing had become far more dramatic and annoying than it ever had to be. Right from the very beginning, the night of the scream, when the dude had walked away from the first canvassing patrolman who interviewed him, and because of his critical importance to this ridiculous rush to indict somebody for Anlya's murder, the super-ambitious Braden and even the more laid-back Farrell had given the homeless man options and considerations and a sense of control that was completely unnecessary and unprecedented in Glitsky's thirty-plus years of law enforcement.

First had been the simple matter of his identification. The self-styled Malibu, always confident and even capable of charm, had laughed off Glitsky's veiled early threat that they could arrest him and hold him as a witness until the trial. He was obviously no novice in the ways of criminal procedure. He had a pretty good idea about habeas corpus. He knew that as a witness, he wouldn't and perhaps couldn't be held in jail until such time as he could testify. Wasn't he already a voluntary witness? Wasn't he the soul of cooperation?

In reply to Glitsky's demand that he provide some documentation for his ID, Malibu repeated that he was registered at Glide Cathedral under the name Omar Abdullah. Glitsky had gone to check and found both the name and an actual identification document, issued by Glide, signed but with no photograph, which was, he realized, as good as it would get. He then ran the name and found Omar's ten-year-old rap sheet (car theft, battery), which Glitsky eventually supplied to Rebecca Hardy, so that she could keep up with him if she needed to.

But seriously, new clothes? (Even if they were from Goodwill.) A hotel and meal allowance between the grand jury and the trial? Patrolmen driving him around town as though they were a taxi service? And when Glitsky had tried to insist on fingerprints . . .

Fingerprints? I do not think so.

And Braden and Farrell had put up with all of it.

So now, of course, this.

Glitsky had to give it to Omar, though. Until today, he hadn't appeared to be a flight risk, always appeared cooperative if arrogant, even happy to see Abe when he appeared. (Glitsky thought it also might have had something to do with the fresh, hot *char siu bao* that he'd started delivering with every visit.) The exceptions as to how they treated him and gave in to his demands went on, from Glitsky's perspective, to an unfathomable degree. By the time they'd set up the appointment for him to appear before the grand jury, Omar had come to understand his critical role in convicting the guy he'd identified as the killer. He could trade perks for that. Accordingly, for example, he wanted to be admitted to the grand jury room via the stairway in the back of the building, accompanied only by Glitsky. And Braden had agreed.

Absurd.

And today, when it counted the most, he'd bolted.

Abe had already put out the word to the several shelters and food banks that Omar frequented, and he intended to canvass the usual square mile or two where Omar wandered downtown, hopefully persuading the captain downstairs at Central Station to lend him some officers to help.

Unmolested on the walk from the courtroom to his office, Abe got to his desk and saw that the blinking light was on for his voicemail. A few seconds later, he was listening to a message that had been left at 8:05 by the AT&T supervisor with whom he'd worked on Sharla Paulson's cell phone over the weekend.

'Lieutenant,' the message began, 'this is Callie Lucente, and I wanted to let you know that I checked the activity on the warrant number first thing this morning, and she's made a phone call to an unknown number, but I went back and looked and it's one she called twice before in December. If you recall, that was long enough ago that we didn't use it in our sample of familiar calls, but it looks like it might be someone she knows or used to know. Triangulation puts the recipient just outside the Ferry Building at just a few minutes ago, seven-forty-two, to be exact. If you could get back to me quickly and get a pickup on the number, we might be able to nail him right down. I'll be waiting for your call.'

Glitsky hung up and stared at the phone as if it were a living thing about to bite him. He checked his watch and saw that it was 12:10, a full four *hours* since this call had been made. Why hadn't Callie Lucente called his cell phone? He had given her his business card with every single number he ever used right on it.

Although what would he have done with the news of this phone call, which may or may not have been placed to Leon Copes? Four hours ago, he'd discovered that his prime witness was a no-show. Just because Sharla Paulson had made a phone call to someone, he wasn't about to change direction and forget about Omar. Besides, for all Glitsky knew, Sharla could have been calling her sister, or her manicurist, or returning one of the marketing calls, or anything else. In any event, Leon Copes, one of five elopers, was so far down Glitsky's priority list compared to Omar that he might as well not exist.

He'd get back to Callie on Sharla's phone call when he got a minute, if that ever happened.

Meanwhile, and far more important, he desperately needed to get his hands on Omar Abdullah before the trial reconvened in an hour and twenty minutes.

39

IT WAS AS if Max's mind had turned into a black miasma. Impulses he'd never considered at first left him almost unable to move.

He needed to hurt somebody.

He needed to get himself armed.

He was done taking shit from people, believing in them. It was time he got himself laid, while he was at it.

He needed to steal something.

Break something, too.

He needed to get into it with his dead loser of a mother.

Leon fucking Copes in town and out of jail and nobody even told him!

Fuck this. Just completely fuck it.

Juney kept a stash of emergency money in an old coffee container under the kitchen sink, and he took it out and laid the $462 on the kitchen table. Counted the money, stuffed it into the front pocket of his hoodie.

He grabbed one of Juney's good knives, the boning knife. It also fit in the hoodie's pocket, horizontal across his belly.

He had to get out of this claustrophobic place, down the stairs, and into the street.

Outside, he had no real plan except to keep moving and do some damage. He went into Bezdekian's market at the corner and walked back into the narrow aisles. George and Ida had never been anything but nice to him, but he had no doubt anymore that this was all false, too. While he was standing there, Ida called out that she was just going upstairs. Would he watch things down here for a minute?

Yeah, he'd watch things, all right.

He watched the pint of Chivas Regal from behind the counter get tucked into his belt under his sweatshirt. He watched himself take a Häagen-Dazs ice cream bar, a Snickers, some beef jerky, and walk out the front door.

See ya, losers.

Half an hour later, he'd made it to Sharla's street. This time, pumped up and with three good slugs of Scotch giving him courage, he didn't hesitate at the corner but went up to the house, about to pound on the outer metal door. His mother didn't seem to be able to stop her men from hitting her. He thought he'd see how she liked getting pushed around by her son, give him some information about what was really going on with her life, with how it impacted his own.

But before he knocked, he heard a male voice bellow behind the door: 'Goddammit, woman! I said I need it *now*!'

It stopped Max dead. He knew that voice, unmistakably. It was the same voice, the same tone, much of the same language he'd lived in fear of for so long. Leon Copes.

What the hell was Leon doing here with his mother?

He stepped up closer and put his ear to the door. His mother said something back to Leon in the mealy way she had that seemed to make Leon want to smack her. Max could hear that it was starting to happen again.

'I don't give a shit about that,' Leon said. 'You listening to me?'

Sharla and Leon might get through this particular moment, but Max knew it wouldn't be long before it came to blows. He knew that dynamic. He'd heard it play out a hundred times.

Standing transfixed on the stoop, he remembered the knife in his hoodie. He reached in, and his fingers closed around the handle. He could bang on the door, and when

Sharla saw it was him and opened it, he could brush by her. He'd knock her down and out of his way if he had to, because naturally, she'd try to protect Leon, as she always did. Once he got by her, he'd simply attack the son of a bitch. Slash him to ribbons.

Then he remembered the size of Leon, his physicality. Back in the day, when they were living together, Max had swung at him once, and Leon had simply stepped back and then struck with the speed of a panther, grabbing his arm, bending it effortlessly back out of its socket, then dropping Max to the ground and kicking him into the corner like a load of garbage, after which, the lesson delivered, he'd just stopped.

Once Leon's rage kicked in, he was unstoppable.

But he was here. He was *right here*.

DISGUSTED WITH HIMSELF at the realization, Max nevertheless knew that on his own, he could never hurt Leon. The man was too big, too skilled at fighting, too vicious, too crazy. Max hated to admit it, but if he had any chance of bringing down the son of a bitch without getting himself killed in the process, he would have to depend on someone with experience in these matters. It galled him, but he saw no other option. The plain, obvious, pathetic fact was that Max would never be a badass, but maybe he could use his knowledge and his rage to do some damage where it might make a difference.

Now, having retreated back across the street between some parked cars where he could keep an eye on Sharla's house and/or follow if Leon decided to relocate, Max whispered into his cell phone, 'Wasn't that the whole point of me giving you Sharla's number over the weekend? So you could get your hands on Leon? I thought you needed him for the trial.'

'We do,' Wyatt Hunt said. 'That hasn't changed.'

'Well, I'm telling you where he's at. Right now. You get somebody down here, you can get him, I'm sure.'

'All right. I'll see what I can do. Are you in a safe place?'

'Across the street, laying low.'

'If he comes out, don't confront him. Dial nine-one-one.'

'I thought that was you.'

'I wish,' Hunt said. 'I'm not a cop. But hang tight. Let me make some calls.'

GLITSKY SAID, 'I believe you, Wyatt. Sharla called somebody before eight this morning. Somebody she knew, or maybe she herself, probably saw the paper and made the connection about Leon, so she called him.'

'And told him he could hide out with her?'

'That's my assumption. Something like that. If he's with her now.'

'And you've known this since eight o'clock?'

Glitsky's voice went harsh. 'Don't bust my chops, Wyatt. I've got bigger fish to fry.'

'Than Leon?'

'Absolutely. Trust me.'

'All right, but I had the strong impression Leon was a high-level target. At least as of yesterday, when I got you Sharla's phone number from her son and you got a warrant and all that. You and I seemed to be working together to bring Leon in. You remember any of that?'

'It's one of my favorite memories,' Glitsky said. 'And if you've really got Leon run to ground, I still say find a way to get him. He's important. I'll have somebody call Villanova. You might try Devin. Or even nine-one-one. But I can't take this myself right now. I'm way under the gun, chasing Omar Abdullah. Really.'

DEVIN JUHLE WAS eating lunch with Ken Yamashiro at Lou the Greek's when he looked over to see Hunt moving toward their table with a sense of urgency. His face drawn with frustration, Hunt said, 'It would be great if you could pick up your cell phone or at least check your messages once in a while. You know that?'

Juhle shrugged. 'I got it turned off for lunch. Otherwise I'd never get an uninterrupted bite. What can I do for you?'

'We've got a probable location on Leon Copes. One of the elopers? Anlya Paulson's rapist? Ring a bell?'

'Probable location?'

'Ninety-nine percent. Anlya's brother has run him down. He's getting a little nervous holding the fort.'

'A LITTLE NERVOUS' didn't quite cover Max's state of mind.

After Hunt called him back to say that finally he'd gotten the attention of the police, Max was a lot more than nervous in his role as point man for the arrest of the most dangerous guy he'd ever met. He had two more quick good swallows of Scotch and took a bite of the Snickers bar and settled himself across the street from Sharla's.

Ten minutes after Hunt had called him, his head was swimming. Everything he looked at seemed to be turning around some fixed point in tight circles. He thought this might be what they meant when they talked about being drunk – he didn't know it could come up on you so fast. He closed his eyes against the spin, but that didn't help. If anything, it made it worse. And then, without any warning, his stomach lurched up at him and he found himself leaning over, puking into the gutter between the cars.

Spitting a few times, shaking his head to clear it, he backed away from the stink, then moved a car's length closer to the house. He never saw the Domino's pizza delivery car until it stopped directly in front of Sharla's.

What the hell is that about? he wondered.

Apparently, it was about getting something to eat, as the delivery man got his flat carton out of the back and walked up to the metal door and knocked. Sharla opened the door – at least the spinning had stopped – and stuck her head all the way outside so that she could look up and down the street. For a terrifying moment, Max was sure that she'd seen him sitting on the curb between the cars. But then she evidently paid the man and the pizza was inside and her door was closed and the delivery man got back into his car and drove away.

Where was Hunt? Where were the police?

He grabbed at his stomach as it cramped again, but this time he kept things down. He wanted to close his eyes and lean back on something, but he had to keep his watch on the house. At least for the next few minutes, he could assume they'd be eating and wouldn't be going somewhere else.

He hoped.

But that, he realized, wasn't close to the end of his worries. He was carrying several hundred dollars he'd taken. He had a third of the bottle of Scotch left, tucked into his belt. The beef jerky. Would the Bezdekians have reported all that stolen stuff already? What if the cops asked him where he'd gotten all that? And what about the knife?

His cell phone chirped, Hunt getting back to him and saying he was around the corner. There wasn't going to be any police show of force on the street until Max was safely behind their perimeter. Max should get to his feet and, walking naturally, head back to where they could meet up.

Walking naturally, Max thought, was easier said than done.

A FURIOUS DEVIN Juhle stood next to Yamashiro's city-issue car, around the corner and out of sight from Sharla's house.

Hunt had convinced him that Max Paulson's intelligence was reliable and important. Leon Copes, who, up until today, hadn't featured prominently on Juhle's radar, was nevertheless an escaped prisoner. Though he'd been found incompetent to stand trial, he remained a suspect in a homicide. Considered armed and dangerous, he was an undeniable threat to the community at large, as well as any individuals with whom he might come into contact.

But Hunt's 'reliable' contact turned out to be a drunk teenager. Based on Max's information, and not having any clue that he was impaired in any way, Juhle had gotten into a little bit of a heated discussion with Steve Rutledge, the SWAT team captain, about calling out his guys for the second time in four days. Especially after the flak they had taken for the result of the Royce Utlee action. Rutledge wanted to be sure: Was the man's identity established? Was the location solid? Was it possibly a hostage situation?

Juhle had assured him on all counts and taken full responsibility. He would even go out to the scene with them, make sure it was all according to Hoyle. Leon Copes was a homicide suspect, and Juhle, the Homicide lieutenant, would be there to take him into custody.

But now Hunt was saying, 'He didn't sound drunk when I talked to him.'

'Oh, that's a big help. Thanks. He sure sounds drunk now.'

'He was nervous, waiting for us.'

Juhle shook his head and waved that off. 'I don't give a damn about his reasons, Wyatt. The point is, your ninety-nine-percent assurance that this is even Leon Copes in his mother's house is now down to about fifty-fifty best case, and we've got two streets cordoned off and twenty officers in five cars, plus a few more for luck, and this is squarely all on my head. If it's not Copes, I'm probably looking for work by next week.'

'It's Copes,' Hunt said. 'I believe Max.'

'I'm so glad for you.' Juhle saw Rutledge approaching from where he'd deployed his troops. He shook his head in quiet disgust, then pasted on a hopeful look. 'Okay, Steve,' he said. 'How do you want to do this?'

'I figured we're going on two people inside. We've got both their phone numbers.' Courtesy of Hunt calling Callie Lucente at AT&T and getting the number Sharla had called that morning. 'We start there. That doesn't work, we go to bullhorn. We've got the back covered. Whatever happens, he's not getting away.' Rutledge took out his phone. 'We rolling?'

Juhle nodded.

Rutledge punched in a number, waited, then said, 'This is Lieutenant Steve Rutledge, San Francisco Police. Sharla Paulson, we have your house surrounded by armed police officers. We are here to arrest Leon Copes for homicide and unlawful escape from authorities. Mr Copes, if you get this message, please show yourself at the front door with your hands raised, then come outside and surrender to officers.'

Rutledge pressed the off button, punched in the second number, and when no one answered, left essentially the same message, except this one direct to Leon. He didn't act like the nonresponse surprised him too much, although it did mean a greater interaction with the unknown and, hence, more uncertainty and more danger.

'Okay,' he said to himself. 'Showtime.'

Juhle, Yamashiro, and Hunt, beside a sullen and brooding Max, all walked to the corner and watched Rutledge, keeping his head ducked lower than the roofs of the cars, make his way down the fifty yards to where a brace of black-and-white police vehicles blocked the street. Here he got his hands on a bullhorn. 'Sharla Paulson and Leon Copes!' The electronic, almost disembodied sound bounced off the stuccoed buildings, unexpectedly loud against the otherwise dead silence of the street. 'Your house is surrounded. Please surrender yourselves by coming to the front door with your hands raised above your heads.'

On both sides of Rutledge, clustered behind police cars and holding armored barriers, police had weapons drawn and trained on the front of the house.

For a full minute, nothing happened, and then suddenly,

every policeman holding a gun of any kind went on full alert
– something had moved behind the metal door.

A woman's voice carried out to them. 'This is Sharla. I
be coming out first.'

'Oh, Mom,' Max said as he waited. 'Don't be dumb. Please
don't be dumb.'

Carefully, she pushed the metal door all the way open.
Facing all the police, she said in a strong voice, 'I'm just
going to unlock it so it stays open now.' She half-turned and
pushed the locking mechanism at the top of the door. Then,
her arms still high above her head, she came forward all the
way to the police cars, where an officer gently took her arms
down and put her behind one of the cars.

A male voice got everyone's attention again. 'Okay,' he
boomed, 'now me.' His silhouette appeared in the door. And
then, stepping out, he stopped. He was a very large man,
heavily bearded, a full head of hair down below his shoulders.
He looked nothing like the bald and clean-shaven man from
Villanova's mug shot of the clopers. His hands high over his
head, he widened the gap between them imploringly. 'But
hey! I ain't no Leon Copes.' He raised his voice even further,
so there could be no misunderstanding. 'I don't know any
Leon Copes,' he said. 'People call me Malibu. You know, like
the car, not the city.'

Malibu, aka Omar Abdullah, came forward slowly, step-
by-step, hands raised all the way up until he, too, made it
down to the cars and let them take him peacefully into
custody.

DOWN AT THE corner, Devin Juhle threw a withering glance
at Hunt. 'Jesus fucking Christ,' he said, 'it's not him! I'll deal
with you guys later.' Without another word, he started jogging
up the street toward the center of the action. Yamashiro hung
back for a long beat, shook his head dismissively at Hunt
and Max, then took off after his lieutenant.

Hunt brought his hands to his temples, brought them to his sides, and looked down at Max. 'What happened here, dude?'

The boy kept staring down the street, then off behind them, clearly on the edge of panic. 'This is bullshit.'

'What's bullshit, Max?'

'What he's talking about. Malibu? That's just shit.'

'It's what . . . ?' Hunt put a hand on his shoulder.

And then Max, with a kind of garbled scream, shook Hunt's hand off and broke away into a dead run. Not behind them and away, as Hunt would have suspected, but back toward Sharla's.

Hunt took off behind him but couldn't catch up.

Max might have made it all the way to the handcuffed suspects if one of the cops hadn't seen him coming and gotten in his way, holding him as he tried to break through. 'Mom!' he cried. 'Mom! What are you doing? What are you doing?'

She looked over and saw him, took a step in his direction. 'Baby?'

Max struggled with the man holding him. 'Tell 'em. You've got to tell 'em.'

'Babe.' She nearly moaned the word. 'Oh, babe.'

'Hey now, hey now.' Malibu getting into the act, moving in Max's direction before someone held him back.

Hunt pulled up behind Max, his hands on his shoulders. 'I've got him,' he told the man who'd been holding him. 'Max, easy,' Hunt said. 'It's all right.'

Max twisted away from Hunt's grip again. 'It's not all right.' Looking once more through the gathered crowd of cops, he yelled out, 'That's Leon, goddammit! Mom! Tell them!'

'I ain't likely no Leon,' Malibu said in a reasonable tone. 'Check my pockets. I got ID in my kitchen name. Omar Abdullah, sometime Malibu. I'm a big witness for you all in a murder case. Call Abe Glitsky. Check it out.'

'That doesn't matter,' Max shot back. 'Ask my mom. She'll tell you. That's Leon Copes.'

Sharla, in an agony of indecision, turned from one of her men to the other, unable to pick a side. Finally, meeting Max's eyes, she managed another rejection. 'I can't . . .'

At the same time, Steve Rutledge pulled a formal-looking certificate out of Malibu's inside pocket, opened it up – the Glide Cathedral soup kitchen form identifying him as Omar Abdullah – and gave a nod of rueful acknowledgment.

Seeing that, Max exploded again. 'Take his fingerprints. Get his fingerprints. That ID's a fake.'

'It ain't no fake,' Malibu said. 'Who is this boy?'

The general plea wasn't doing him any good, so Max made it specific. 'Mr Hunt, get his prints. I promise you, that's Leon.' Then to Juhle: 'Lieutenant? Please?'

Juhle realized that if Omar/Malibu was who he said he was – not Leon Copes but a homeless person who was the key witness in the Treadway murder trial – that would never justify the full SWAT team call-up he'd orchestrated. His career might be severely threatened. He had to know Malibu's identity for sure, so he turned to Rutledge, nodded, and said, 'I don't see how fingerprints could hurt.'

Omar shook his head, adamant. 'Malibu don't be giving no fingerprints. That be part of my deal.'

'Well,' Rutledge said, 'I don't know anything about any deal, sir, but we take your prints, and that's all there is to it.'

Malibu's voice toughened up. 'I said I ain't doing that.'

Rutledge did a double take at the new sound of things, the cooperative victim of a misidentification turning surly and threatening. He gave a nod to one of his troops. 'Ned,' he said, 'we can settle this pretty quick. Get out the kit.'

Malibu looked from one lieutenant to the other. His eyes fell on Sharla and he snarled. 'Bitch.' Then, kicking out, he caught the cop nearest him, knocked him to the ground, and jumped over him, taking off up the street. Handcuffed as he was, he hadn't made it more than ten steps when a couple of the officers giving chase brought him down, burning and rashing his arms and cheek on the pavement.

Sharla shivered with either relief or fear. She watched in disbelief as half a dozen more policemen descended on Leon, restraining him. Looking over at Max again, she gave him a pallid, broken smile and said, 'I'm sorry, baby. Wasn't nothing else I could do.' And then, to Rutledge, she said, 'My good boy over there ain't lying. That be Leon Copes, all right. He's a good man, too. He just needs to get hisself in a hospital.'

40

DISMAS HARDY GOT the urgent call about the remarkable events on Sharla's street from Wyatt Hunt after lunch, just before Glitsky was about to take the stand for Rebecca's cross-examination. Hardy had enough time to give Rebecca the broad outlines about what had just transpired. His daughter then conveyed these facts to the judge in a sidebar.

Now they were in Bakhtiari's chambers, the judge directing his sternest visage at a crestfallen and obviously shaken Phil Braden. 'Can this possibly be true, counselor?' he asked. 'After everything that's gone before at this trial, now this?'

'Apparently so, Your Honor. We're waiting for a final corroboration on the identity question, but I've spoken to Lieutenant Juhle, and there seems to be a general consensus.'

'For the record, you mean there seems to be a consensus that Leon Copes, the former common-law stepfather of the victim in this case, and a man ruled incompetent to stand trial, has successfully passed himself off to you and your inspectors as an entirely different person from who he actually is. Further, that this person, under the false identity of Omar Abdullah, was supposed to be the prime witness against Mr Treadway. While he himself has an excellent motive to have committed the very murder where he is testifying as a witness.' With noticeably rising anger, Bakhtiari went on, 'And none of this was known to any of you, much less revealed to the defense? Can this really be possible?'

Braden swallowed. 'There was no reason to doubt his identity, Your Honor. Many homeless people—'

Bakhtiari cut him off. 'Many homeless people have false IDs? Or IDs issued by the places they eat or sleep to keep track of who's where? Yes, they do. And do you know what those IDs are typically based on? I'll tell you. The fancy ones with photos attached are bought on the street for a few bucks. Alternatively, they're simply sworn to at the site. You self-identify as Bob Jones, and the shelter on Eddy gives you a piece of paper saying that, for their purposes, you are Bob Jones. Does any of this sound familiar?'

'Yes, Your Honor, but—'

'But!' The judge held up a finger. 'But then if one of these indigent citizens happens to get caught up somehow in the legal system – which I believe has occurred a little more often than, say, a thousand times – those IDs are typically verified against police records by the simple expedient of taking the subject's fingerprints, are they not?'

'They should be. Yes, Your Honor.'

'But they were not in this case?'

'Apparently not.'

'Apparently not.' The judge's cheeks puffed out as he blew through them. 'How could that not have happened in this case?'

'But Your Honor—'

'Mr Braden, are you seriously going to try and defend any small part of this? Unbelievable.'

Rebecca made bold to inject herself into the conversation. 'With respect, Your Honor, I believe counsel for the People knows exactly why Mr Copes's fingerprints were never taken. It was part of the deal to get his testimony as Omar Abdullah into the record.'

'There is no record of such a deal, Your Honor,' Braden said.

'I should hope not, Mr Braden, since any such deal would

be moronic. But now I'm asking you directly if you are aware of any arrangement about fingerprints between your office and Mr Copes or Mr Abdullah such as that contemplated by Ms Hardy. And be careful how you answer me, counsel, because either way, you're guilty of gross stupidity. So you take your pick.'

'The option was never overtly discussed, Your Honor.'

'Overtly. I like that.' The judge shook his head. 'So you just decided to believe that Mr Abdullah was who he said he was?'

'The question of his true identity never came up. We had a rap sheet on him, Your Honor.'

'You had a rap sheet on him as Mr Abdullah?'

'Yes, Your Honor. He appeared to have a history consistent with who he said he was, and we, perhaps naïvely, went with that.'

'Perhaps naïvely,' the judge said. 'Perhaps naïvely. Perhaps criminally negligent as well. And so what about the rap sheet?'

'It was a real rap sheet, Your Honor, but for a different Omar Abdullah. Black man, roughly the same age.'

Bakhtiari's mouth actually dropped open in stunned disbelief before he caught himself and closed it back up. 'Did I already say "criminally negligent"?'

'With respect, the People dispute the characterization of this oversight as criminal, Your Honor. But we do apologize for the admittedly egregious blunder.'

'Really? You apologize? I'm not sure that's going to cut it, Mr Braden. Did anyone in your office, or under your guidance, consider surreptitiously lifting Mr Copes's fingerprints from something he'd touched?'

'It appears not, Your Honor. If it would help us resolve this problem, the People would not object if you declared a mistrial.'

'Hah!'

Bakhtiari seemed to get a perverse kick out of that proposal.

'Of course you wouldn't object. You'd get another chance to start over without all these errors. Ms Hardy, I don't suppose that would be of much interest to you?'

'That would depend, Your Honor, on whether the People still plan to call Mr Abdullah. His public defender has told me that because he has his own murder charges pending, there is no way she'll let him testify without a grant of immunity. She also says if he does testify, then he will say that his name is Omar Abdullah and that anyone who says he is Leon Copes is, and I quote, gravely disabled. But I guess if Mr Braden does want to give immunity to a delusional, psychotic murderer who is a principal witness in his case, he can do it. Otherwise, Your Honor, unless the prosecution has other evidence of which I am not aware, then in light of these new facts and the polluted People's evidence, we would move at this time for a directed verdict of acquittal.'

'I don't blame you,' the judge said. 'That's an entirely reasonable position, though I will reserve judgment for the time being.'

'Your Honor, if I may,' Rebecca pressed. 'Without Mr Copes's testimony, there is simply no proof that Mr Treadway was at the crime scene on the night of the murder. Absent that proof, there is no case.'

'Lieutenant Glitsky's testimony puts him there,' Braden said.

'Not a chance,' Bakhtiari shot back. 'I let you call Glitsky out of order because you told me you'd have Omar Abdullah. No Abdullah, no courtroom ID. No courtroom ID, no previous ID from Lieutentant Glitsky. I'm going to strike it from the record. You've got nothing.'

Rebecca saw her opportunity and took it. 'Respectfully, Your Honor, it's time to end this farce. Keeping my client in jail even one more day is a travesty. There is now no remaining shred of evidence tying him to the crime for which he's charged. The only person we can positively place at the crime scene at the minute of Anlya's death is Leon Copes, who once raped her and has a far better motive to have killed her than Greg Treadway. Anlya's recognition of Leon at the scene could have sent him back into custody.'

Bakhtiari sat straight up, shock in his expression.

Braden jumped right in. 'Your Honor, I object. There is nothing in the record about this alleged rape, and to introduce it in this fashion is irresponsible and prejudicial.'

'Prejudicial to whom?' Rebecca shot back at him. 'Leon Copes?'

Bakhtiari slammed a palm against his desk. 'Counsel will direct their comments to me and me alone. Ms Hardy, without any foundation, this alleged rape has no place in this proceeding. If you can introduce it in your case in chief, if we get there, and it is deemed relevant at that time, I may allow it. In the interim, Mr Braden's point is well taken. We have enough irregularities to deal with as things stand. Let's not introduce new ones.'

Bakhtiari pondered for a moment, nodding all but imperceptibly. 'Mr Braden,' he said at last. 'Were you planning on calling anyone else on your witness list to address the issue Ms Hardy raises concerning proof of the defendant's presence at the crime scene? I assume that even your office would not be foolish enough to immunize and attempt to call Mr Abdullah under these circumstances. So? Will you be calling other witnesses?'

'No, Your Honor, the People will rest.'

'And you will be offering no further testimony as to the defendant's presence at the tunnel that night?'

'No, Your Honor. Even without Mr Abdullah's testimony, the People believe they have made their case.'

Bakhtiari gave him a deathless, incredulous stare for a few seconds. Finally, nodding brusquely, he said, 'I'll have a ruling on Ms Hardy's motion for a directed verdict of acquittal when court reconvenes in' – he checked his watch – 'twenty-five minutes. That'll be all for now.'

WORD MUST HAVE somehow leaked out to the world at large when they were in chambers, because when Rebecca stepped into the courtroom again, the place was jammed with reporters, other lawyers, courtroom groupies, and a decent smattering of the former Liam Goodman posse, who, perhaps no longer under Goodman's active sway, seemed to be spread in a less than organized fashion around the courtroom.

Allie and Greg had remained at the defense table the whole time – and were currently holding hands under the table, as Rebecca noted with a frisson of anger – and Greg's parents, Barry and Donna, had moved up to the front row of the gallery right behind them. Also in the front row, Dismas Hardy spoke on his cell phone and, unable or unwilling to cut his connection, raised a hand to his daughter when she caught his eye. On the other side of the gallery, Wes Farrell huddled with Abe Glitsky, and when Phil Braden joined them, they did not make a happy group. Somewhat to Rebecca's surprise, *CityTalk* writer Jeff Elliott had made it down from the Chronicle Building and sat near the back door in his wheelchair.

As she got to her place and sat down, Rebecca turned her chair away from the jury, facing Allie and Greg and his parents. Her color was high, and she didn't want to project the giddy confidence she felt. 'How'd it go?' Greg asked her.

'Decent,' she said. 'The judge didn't like it at all. Abdullah can't testify, or should I say Copes? He's got his own murder charges pending. Giving him immunity would look even worse than letting you go, and no one would believe him anyway. If he's incompetent to stand trial, he's an incompetent witness.'

'But,' Donna Treadway said uncertainly, 'isn't that all they had putting Greg at the tunnel?'

'Pretty much, yes.'

'So,' Greg's mother continued, barely trusting herself to hope, 'shouldn't that be it?'

'It's not impossible. It's going to depend on the judge.'

'So it's all true, then?' Allie asked. 'Abdullah is really Copes? How did that happen?'

'Braden doesn't seem to know . . .'

'Yeah, right,' Greg said.

'No, that makes sense,' Rebecca said. 'If he'd known, he'd have had to pull out. I think Copes just played everybody.'

'This is the incompetent guy?' Barry asked.

'Right.' Rebecca nodded. 'Except maybe not so much.'

Dismas, no longer on the phone, was leaning in to join them. 'Okay, breaking news. Wyatt says the ID is a hundred percent solid. They ran his prints from the field, and Copes is Malibu is Omar Abdullah.'

'It was that easy?' Allie asked. 'That was all they had to do?'

Rebecca shrugged. 'Evidently, nobody thought to check out Abdullah earlier.'

'You believe that?' Hardy raised an eyebrow. 'You want to get the truth about that out in the open, Beck, your cross of Abe is coming right up. I'll bet you a million dollars that without anybody saying anything, he got the message loud and clear.'

'What message?' Allie asked.

'Don't rock the Abdullah boat. Keep him on board, no matter who he is. 'Cause who's going to ask? And guess what? It almost worked. It would have if Abe hadn't gone randomly looking for his elopers and one of them hadn't turned out to be Leon. In the next hour, we'd have all been sitting here, listening to Abdullah say it was you, Greg, out in the tunnel.'

With a grimace, Rebecca said, 'You remember when you told me I'd have a chance to get back at Abe for some of that early stuff he tried with me, and I'd love it? Well, I

don't. Not that it's going to stop me if I have to, but still . . .
I hope it won't happen.'

'I've got another question,' Donna said. 'How did this
Abdullah – I mean, Copes – get a real rap sheet under
Abdullah's name if that wasn't him?'

'Because there is a real Omar Abdullah,' Hardy said.
'Probably Copes knew him, knew they were about the same
age, stole his name. When Braden runs the name, there he
is, just what they're expecting, and they stop there. Why look
any further?'

'So who killed Anlya?' Greg asked. 'Leon? Royce Utlee?'

Rebecca shrugged. 'Leon was definitely there at the right
time. He had a motive . . .'

'What was that?' Allie asked.

'He raped her when she was fourteen. If Anlya sees him
anywhere – her mother's place, out shopping, anywhere – she
calls the police and tells them, and he goes back into custody.'

'Except,' Hardy said, 'dollars to doughnuts, he's still incompetent and never goes to trial.'

'But he'd still believe she'd turn him in. And if he saw
her first . . . All I'm saying is it's a real motive, and a good
one. If he sees her at the top of the tunnel, just running into
her, he wouldn't have to think too much about it. One push
and the problem is solved forever.'

'We'll never really know, then,' Greg said.

'It'll probably never get proven at trial, if that's what you're
talking about,' Rebecca said, 'because there'll probably never
be one.'

'The main thing,' Barry said to his son, 'is everybody will
finally know it wasn't you.'

'Let's hope, Dad,' Greg said. 'Let's hope for that.'

WHEN MAX WALKED into Bezdekian's, the bell sounded, but
nobody was at the counter. George called from the back
room that he'd be right out, but Max didn't wait around.

He had the two wrinkled twenties from Juney's stash in his hand, and he tucked them in a corner of the blotter by the cash register and then walked out, tripping the bell again.

Wasting no time, Max slid into the passenger seat of Wyatt Hunt's Mini Cooper, closed the door, and said, 'Go!'

'Mission accomplished?' Hunt asked. 'That was fast.'

'Wasn't much to it.' After a minute, Max confessed, 'I stole the Scotch from them this morning. I just went back and paid for it, with a little extra for the candy and ice cream. I don't think I'm cut out to be a badass.'

'You want to be?'

'This morning I thought so. I wanted to have some power.' Max brought both of his hands to his head and squeezed. 'Jesus.'

Hunt looked over. 'Still hurting?'

'That's one way to put it. Anyway, the only person left who I could punish was my mom. That's why I went down there. To have it out with her. Beat her around a little.'

'Bad idea, but lucky you had it.'

'Yeah. Now I'm realizing that wasn't the way to do it. Get down to her level. Why'd I think it was?'

Hunt shrugged. 'Trying things out?'

Max was silent as Hunt turned a corner, came up on Max's apartment house. 'I also took all of my auntie's extra money. And a knife.'

'Why'd you do that?'

'I don't know. I wanted people to take me seriously. I'm going to put it all back. It makes me sick that I did it in the first place. I mean, really, what do I have to feel sorry for myself about?'

'Is that what you felt?'

'I felt abandoned.'

Hunt had to chuckle. 'Really, a foster kid feeling abandoned? There's a first.'

'You can laugh, but all of a sudden I felt like it was all too much. It didn't matter how good I tried to be, what did that get me? So I go off the rails, who does that hurt besides me?'

'Why would you want to hurt yourself?'

'I don't know. To show everybody? So they could feel as sorry for me as I felt for myself. And look, I had every excuse in the world – my background, my sister, my mom, you name it.'

'So you could do anything you want?'

'Not just could. Should. Show 'em all. I'd be some badass they'd have to reckon with.' Max blinked his eyes closed, squeezed them down. 'How'd I let that victim shit into my brain?'

'Give it a little opening, start feeling sorry for yourself,' Hunt said, 'and it flies right in.'

'It's the goddamn devil, though, isn't it? I'm putting all this stuff back where I found it and never letting him near me again.'

'Well, if that's the only thing you take home from what happened today,' Hunt said, 'waking up was well worth your while.'

OVER AN HOUR had passed – Bakhtiari no doubt getting multiple-source corroboration on the Leon Copes identification – before the judge ascended to the bench and looked out over the SRO courtroom, now silent and tense with anticipation. He cast a glance out and down at Rebecca's table, then brought it over to Braden, next to the jury, and finally, to the gallery. He took off his glasses and set them to one side. After hesitating one last moment, he began. 'Since almost the very instant of the death of the victim in this case, Anlya Paulson,' he intoned, 'both the San Francisco Police Department and the Office of the District Attorney were under extraordinary time pressure, first to identify and arrest a suspect in this homicide and then to prepare and try the prosecution case against that person.

'In the course of this trial so far, albeit in chambers, counsel for the defendant has introduced alternative scenarios and motivations. While some of these were technically inadmissible as evidence, they brought into high relief the apparent reality that the prosecution, in its haste and zeal to get to trial, may not have pursued aggressively enough every avenue open regarding details of the victim's life and possible motivations of others to do her harm. This is not, in itself, unheard of. Frequently, a homicide victim might have several antagonistic relationships, and it is the duty of law enforcement to identify one suspect who, by dint of the evidence assembled against that suspect, seems most likely to have committed the homicide.

'In this case, defense counsel argued in chambers that another theory about Ms Paulson's murder ought to be admitted as evidence for the jury's consideration. Up until now, I have reserved ruling on that evidence, and the trial against Mr Treadway went on.

'This morning, however, a much more egregious example of the prosecution's undue haste in the preparation of this case came to light. One of the People's critical witnesses, a homeless man known as Omar Abdullah, was taken into police custody on another matter, fingerprinted, and positively identified not as Omar Abdullah but as Leon Copes, a psychiatric patient and, not incidentally, someone with a motive to murder Anlya Paulson.'

At the verification of this news, which until then had been rumor, the gallery all but exploded. Bakhtiari lifted his gavel but let the reaction continue for nearly half a minute before it wound down on its own.

'Mr Copes,' Bakhtiari went on, 'was to testify about the presence of Mr Treadway at the scene of and at the time of the murder. However, Mr Copes is currently and technically in custody under what is called a Murphy Conservatorship because, even after three years of rehabilitation and psychiatric counseling, last December he was again found incompetent to stand trial. This renders his proposed testimony highly suspect. In addition, I have been advised that he will refuse to testify in this matter, citing his Fifth Amendment privilege against self-incrimination, because he has his own murder charges pending.'

At this, the courtoom erupted again. It took several minutes for the bailiffs to restore order. For these eruptions, Bakhtiari seemed to have developed a tolerance, perhaps reflective of his own pent-up fury. When the ruckus died down, he went on, 'Not surprisingly, the prosecution has declined to offer immunity to Mr Copes, so he will not be available as a witness.

'I asked counsel for the People if he had any other witness or witnesses coming forward to address the critical issue about which Mr Copes would have been testifying. Mr Braden told me that he did not.

'Absent Mr Copes's or any other proposed testimony on this point, there remains no physical, circumstantial, or eyewitness evidence that Mr Treadway was present at the Sutter-Stockton tunnel at the time of Anlya Paulson's death. Therefore, on motion of the defendant, I will direct the clerk to enter a directed verdict of acquittal, clearing Mr Treadway of these charges. Ladies and gentlemen of the jury, I thank you for your service, and you are free to leave.'

Bakhtiari brought his gavel down, and this time the courtroom erupted into chaos.

PART
THREE

41

IN MID-OCTOBER, THREE months after the Treadway trial had ended, Leon Copes – aka Omar Abdullah, aka Malibu – finally had his long-delayed competency hearing. Wes Farrell's office had argued, given the fact that Leon Copes had survived and even thrived on his own under at least a couple of aliases, that he was obviously competent to stand trial for the homicide he'd committed four years before. Nevertheless, the psychiatrists who'd examined him found otherwise and, much to the disgust of Farrell and his team, to say nothing of the Homicide detail, Leon had again been declared Incompetent to Stand Trial. He'd been returned to the Napa psychiatric facility.

Still living with his Auntie Juney, Max Paulson started college at San Francisco State University, where he had already joined the Debate Club. He continued his part-time work at the Ace Hardware in Cow Hollow. The three-year extension on his foster eligibility had come through, and for the first time in his life, he had a bit of spending money. He convinced Auntie Juney to accompany him to dinner at his mother's every Sunday, which gave Sharla a reason to keep the place reasonably clean and herself some degree of sober. He had almost worked up the nerve to say hello to a girl named Natalie in his psych class and ask her if she'd like to have some coffee with him.

Sergeant Eric Waverly lost a ton of blood and nearly died from the shoulder wound he'd gotten courtesy of Royce Utlee. Ken Yamashiro, who had sat by his bed around the clock for the first two days of Waverly's hospital stay, took all the credit he could claim for his partner's survival, saying it was a result of the abuse he'd heaped upon Waverly every time he regained consciousness: How could he have been dumb enough to get shot that way? Though he was in physical therapy to combat his frozen shoulder syndrome, Waverly was back on the job, pretending to be as limber as he'd ever been, although the careful observer could note differences in the way he moved.

Wes Farrell burnished his credentials as a stand-up guy when he took full responsibility for the fiasco in the Treadway trial. At a press conference in the aftermath of the directed verdict, he resisted the temptation to put the blame on Phil Braden, Abe Glitsky, or the police department. He was the district attorney, he said, and the buck stopped with him.

Meanwhile, Abe got assigned to other work. In one of those assignments, locating the so-called elopers, he had been spectacularly successful. Within two weeks of the *CityTalk* column, four of the five elopers were back in custody, and the fifth man turned up a month after that in Arkansas.

Allie Jensen passed the California state bar and came aboard as the latest full-time (and then some!) associate in Hardy's firm. She started going out with Greg Treadway over the Labor Day weekend, after being part of a group he'd put together to take a limo and go wine tasting in Sonoma County.

When Bakhtiari had announced his ruling on the directed verdict, the true believers in what had been the Liam Goodman group of protesters in the gallery of Department 24 had put on an impressive display of outrage. They were disgusted and appalled that yet another suspect in the murder of an African-American was being let off. A dozen courtroom bailiffs and several guards from the adjoining jail had to be called in to restore order. Four of the men were arrested, but the rest of the protesters overflowed out through the Hall of Justice, trying to take their message to the street. Over the next few days in the city at large, and in Oakland across the Bay, demonstrators managed to disrupt traffic in several locations and block entrance to a few public buildings, but basically the rage over the purported racial injustice in the Treadway case failed to gain national traction, possibly because the agitators' charismatic leader had stayed out of sight, under the radar.

With the mayoral election coming up in under a month, Liam Goodman, currently polling sixth in a field of nine, was no longer considered a factor in the race.

THE CASA HEADQUARTERS in San Francisco was upstairs over some graffiti-ridden retail shops on a block of Mission Street that had been perpetually under repair for at least two years, although to the locals it seemed like the improvements had been going on for a decade or more. The offices formerly belonged to a chiropractor, and the haphazard arrangement of the inside rooms reflected a disorganized if entrepreneurial soul – whenever the business needed to grow, the past owner had knocked out a wall or erected a new one, with little thought for symmetry or scale. The new tenants had not removed all of the body and skeletal charts from the walls in the various offices, nor all of the outdated medical equipment, and all of these leftovers gave the space a weird and funky charm.

Adding to that charm (as well as to the general air of funkiness), a large and ancient library desk took up almost half the lobby, and on it, overflowing, were dozens of brochures explaining CASA's work, announcements about classes and self-improvement programs, volunteer guidelines, knick-knacks, craftsman bowls, several different magazines, and other specialty publications: the whole table a veritable smorgasbord of opportunity, commitment, and hope.

The executive director, Rachelle Garza, worked out of one of the smallest internal offices off the lobby at the head of the stairs. She was there in the dimness, closed off from the lobby, eating a healthy lunch of carrots, celery, and yogurt, when a knock made her look up. 'Yes. Come in.' The door swung open, and she felt a small twinge in her stomach but managed what she hoped was a believable smile. This visit was not completely unexpected, although the timing was. 'Greg,' she said. 'How nice to see you. I'm afraid, as you can tell, you caught me at lunch.'

'No worries,' he said. 'If you want, I could come back.'

'No. That's okay. You're here now. It's fine. Lunch will keep.'

He stood silhouetted in the doorway. 'Probably I should have made an appointment, but I was just in the neighbor-hood, and I've been meaning to come back and say hi for a while. How's everything going?'

She pushed her food to one side. 'About the same. Things don't seem to change that much. Come on in. Sit down.'

'Thank you.'

Easygoing, genial, polite, confident, and well groomed, Greg settled himself in the upholstered chair in the corner. 'Great chair,' he said. 'Has this always been here?'

'At least since I've been,' she said. She took a breath, openmouthed, trying to calm herself. 'So how have you been?'

'Pretty good, considering.' He made a face mixing equal parts chagrin and embarrassment. 'Still dealing with some of the fallout from the trial, actually. You'd think once you got acquitted, people would just accept that you weren't guilty, but I'm finding that's not always the case.'

'That would be hard, I imagine.'

He shrugged. 'I guess it's just what it is. You just try to keep moving ahead.'

'I hear a "but." '

'Good call. But, not to burden you with my problems, the job thing is turning out to be a bit of an issue.'

'You're not teaching?'

A bitter chuckle. 'There's a good example. It's safe to say I won't be teaching anymore. Anywhere. Two years experience, every district supposedly dying for good teachers, and I haven't even gotten a callback.'

'I'm sorry.'

He shrugged again. 'As I say, it is what it is. Something will turn up, though probably not in the teaching field.' He crossed a leg, ankle on knee, casual and relaxed. 'In any event,' he said, 'the few friends I've got left are unanimous that I should try to get back to what used to be my regular life. Let some time go by, let things shake out a little. Meanwhile, I'm doing something, keeping busy, maybe making some kind of contribution instead of just sending out résumés all day.'

'Probably a good plan.'

'I thought so. Which is I guess what really brings me down here.'

Rachelle let out a sigh and broke a tepid and, she hoped, kind smile. 'I was afraid you might say something like that.'

'And you're afraid,' he said softly, 'you're not going to be able to help me.'

'I'm really sorry, Greg. You know it's nothing personal. I've always thought you were a good guy and an excellent CASA, but now . . .'

'With me being a murderer and all . . .'

'That's not it.'

'No? Then what is it?'

'I guess the best word would be "perception." '

'So the actual facts don't matter?'

'Well, no, of course they matter. They matter a lot.'

'But?'

Someone was coming up the stairs, and Rachelle hoped that whoever it was would stop in and interrupt the conversation, but that didn't happen, so she had to come back to Greg and his very difficult questions. 'Like I said, it's about perception as much as anything. You know we depend so much if not entirely on donations, Greg. And frankly, we got huge negative feedback from many, if not most, of our donors when you were arrested. They were all like, "How could we have let this happen? What kind of show were we running? Didn't anybody supervise the volunteers?" I mean it, it was a giant problem and still is.'

'But I didn't do it, Rachelle. You know me. You know the kind of person I am. I am not capable of killing anybody. And that's what the trial found. Why can't people see that?'

Without a real response to give him, Rachelle inhaled and pursed her lips.

'What?' Greg asked.

Buying more time, Rachelle cleared her throat, inhaled again, finally found her voice. 'I'm so very sorry.'

Greg, sitting back in his comfortable chair, shook his head. 'You realize how hard it is to accept this when all I'm trying to do is get some normalcy back in my life, and when I didn't do anything except get caught in the system.'

'I do. It must be terrible.'

'But you can't help me?'

She kept hoping he would let it drop, thank her for her time, leave her office. But nothing in his body language spoke to that inclination. If she were going to get him to understand, if not accept, the basic problem, she would have to bring up the topic she'd been hoping to avoid, because the very idea scared her. 'As you probably guessed, Greg, this has come up with the board, and it's really not in my power to overrule them. They've made up their minds.'

'How about if I came in and talked to them personally?'

'That's not a viable possibility. I think you just have to accept this, Greg. They've made their decision, and they're going to stick to it. And you know, if I may say so, under these circumstances, I don't know why you'd even want to come back. There have to be other jobs out there, and I'm not talking volunteer work—'

He cut her off. 'I've got to start someplace, Rachelle. I've got to have somebody be the first to trust me, to give me a chance, to get around the stigma. I don't care about money. I need to be doing something and get my credibility back. I don't understand how you can't even let me talk to your board. You know me. I'm good at what I do. And you always need volunteers. I could help some of the kids, I know I could.'

'Helping is not the issue, Greg. Again, perception is the issue.'

'But I didn't—'

She held up her hand, stopping him. As she'd half expected and feared, he was going to make her tell him. 'You didn't kill her. All right. Maybe that's the truth and—'

'It is the truth.'

'All right, Greg.' Her patience at an end, she came forward in her chair, elbows on her desk. Her voice took on an edge. 'Even granting that you didn't kill her, let me ask you this: How do you explain the DNA evidence? Because let me tell you, the perception, and the very strong presumption, of everyone I've talked to on the board is that you took advantage of Anlya sexually. Did you do that? Did you have sex with her?'

His head snapped back as though she'd slapped him. He looked to the room's corners as though he were trapped and seeking a way out. When he came back to her after a few seconds, he sat up straight. 'The DNA was flawed.'

'That's not what I'm asking,' Rachelle said. 'I'm asking if you had sex with her. Because the perception is that you did, and there doesn't seem to be much arguing against that, is there?'

He met her gaze. 'So that's how it is.'

'It's a simple enough question,' she said. 'Your DNA was on her underwear. Nobody remembers that being in dispute. So the question again: Did you have sex with her, yes or no?'

'What's the point? I'll never convince you or any of them, will I?'

'You might. You might have some explanation that makes sense. And a simple no would be a good start.'

He stared at her for another long beat before he got to his feet. 'You're mixing me up with a different kind of person,' he said. He strode to the doorway and out into the lobby.

Rachelle brought her shaking hands up to her eyes and leaned back in her chair, nearly overcome with relief.

That relief was short-lived, as almost immediately, she heard a guttural groan and then a sound that struck her as almost as violent as an explosion. The floor actually shook underneath her feet, and for the next second or two she thought it was an earthquake, but there was a different quality to what she'd felt, more like something had been dropped from a great height and shaken the floor to the building's foundation.

She jumped up, coming around her desk. When she got to her door, all three of her current staffers were appearing in the hallway from their rooms, the question clear on everyone's shocked faces: *What the hell was that?*

The answer was an insult hurled directly in front of her. The huge wooden library table lay on its side, all of its brochures and magazines and knickknacks covering nearly every square inch of the lobby floor.

Down the stairs, a door slammed with another ungodly crash, and without seeing any part of it, Rachelle knew what the latest noise was – it was Greg Treadway letting himself out.

At seven-thirty Allie and Greg were sitting down to dinner at Verbena on Polk Street, a favorite place only a moderate walking distance from Allie and Beck's apartment. She had come straight from work, hopeful that her new boyfriend would have something good to report on the job front, which otherwise was not progressing very well.

'So how'd it go?' Allie asked after she'd kissed him hello and they'd taken their seats.

'Not great. Much to my surprise and regret, Rachelle seems to hang with the "he still did it" crowd.'

'How can she think that? I mean, after the trial? I thought you said she was your friend.'

'I did. She was, too. I didn't know she was so afraid of the board. I guess it's just easier for her not to have me come back in any capacity where she'd have to defend me.'

A waiter came over and they ordered – white wine for Allie and a second or possibly third bourbon drink for Greg. 'Well,' Allie said, 'you thought it was a long shot, and it wasn't like it was going to pay you anything.'

'No. But I thought if they let me go back to volunteering, I'd at least have some leverage talking to other people. If CASA could trust me, it might be someplace to start.' He tipped up his glass. 'But they can't, and they were pretty much my last resort.'

'Don't say that.'

'Why not? It's the truth. I don't see how this is ever going to end. I don't know what I'm going to do next.'

'Maybe try for some other kind of job, Greg. Forget about teaching. Forget about kids.'

He made a face. 'Starbucks?'

She nodded. 'If you have to. Or anyplace else. It wouldn't matter to me.'

'You say that now. But a few more months of this . . .'

'I'll say the same thing.'

He let out a small breath. 'You're great. Thank you.' Their round of drinks arrived, and they clinked their glasses. 'Here's to us,' Greg said, 'and getting through this.'

'Deal.'

He drank and put his glass down. 'Can I ask your opinion about something?' he asked.

'Anything. Shoot.'

'Do you think it might be worthwhile to ask Rebecca to go talk to Jeff Elliott?'

'About what?'

'That night.'

'What about it?'

'About what really happened.'

Allie considered. 'And what do you think that was?'

'Allie. We know what it was. We've got a witness and a deathbed confession.'

'Royce Utlee.'

'Right. And okay, I know it was ruled inadmissible in court, but that doesn't mean it didn't happen and doesn't matter. It matters a ton. As it stands now, people like Rachelle and the CASA board and the school district all think that since I'm the only suspect they've heard of, it must have been me, in spite of all the evidence problems. Whereas if *CityTalk* comes out with the real story . . . I don't know. It's just an idea. But it might convince some people that, hey, not only was I acquitted, I was acquitted because the judge actually knew who did it, although that wasn't allowed to get into the trial record. And that the guy who did it was not me. Don't you think that might be worth a try?'

CityTalk

by JEFFREY ELLIOTT

This is a small tale of social injustice.

Last May, most readers will recall that a young African-American woman named Anlya Paulson died at the hands of an assailant who threw her over the side of the Sutter-Stockton tunnel and into the path of an oncoming car. At the time, Supervisor Liam Goodman was in the middle of his vociferous and politically charged campaign calling for more aggressive police investigation and prosecution of homicide suspects whose victims were African-American. In that environment, Devin Juhle's Homicide Detail, and separately, District Attorney Wes Farrell's prosecution staff, faced a great deal of pressure to identify, arrest, and swiftly bring to trial a viable suspect in Anlya's murder, preferably somebody white.

That suspect turned out to be Greg Treadway, a 27-year-old Teach for America instructor at Everett Middle School and a volunteer as a court-appointed special advocate (CASA) for children in the foster system. Mr Treadway had no criminal record of any kind prior to his arrest for murder.

Soon after Mr Treadway's trial began, Honor Wilson, one of the group home roommates of Anlya Paulson, was beaten and run over by a car in the Fillmore District. Near death, she was transported to County General Hospital and admitted to the emergency room. Accompanying her was a San Francisco patrol officer named Janine McDougal, armed with a tape recorder. Unexpectedly, and in spite of being in critical condition, Ms Wilson regained consciousness long enough to talk into Officer McDougal's tape recorder and to say who had beaten and – as it would turn out – killed her.

But she was not finished with her statement. After identifying her assailant as her boyfriend, a pimp named Royce Utlee, she added a postscript: 'Royce killed Anlya, too.' I have heard a copy of this tape, and it is unambiguous. Within minutes of this statement, Ms Wilson died of her injuries.

Because of an anomaly in California law, the statement that Mr Utlee was the actual murderer of Anlya Paulson would likely not have been admitted in evidence. As a matter of fact, because the trial ended so abruptly, neither the jury nor, more important, the public ever heard it. Within a day, Mr Utlee was dead, too, the victim in a gunfight between himself and the SWAT team. His death, of course, eliminated any possibility of questioning him about the murder of Anlya Paulson.

Several days later, the prosecution's main witness turned out to have been misidentified. He was the former boyfriend of Anlya Paulson's mother. He was also an escaped psychiatric patient with a murder charge pending, who had an excellent motive to kill Ms Paulson himself. Judge Bakhtiari dismissed all charges against Mr Treadway due to lack of evidence.

End of story, you might say – justice is done. The good guy walks away, the man who was positively identified by his dying girlfriend as the bad guy is dead.

But it is not the end of this story.

In the three-odd months since his acquittal, Mr Treadway has been unable to find work, even as a volunteer. The specter of the murder charge against him remains, he believes, because Mr Utlee's alleged role in Ms Paulson's death has never become part of the narrative of the trial. In spite of his acquittal, that fact leaves Mr Treadway struggling under the weight of suspicion against him as the only viable suspect in the murder, when Ms Wilson's deathbed statement should at the very least – one would think – prompt a Homicide investigation into Mr Utlee's relationship with Anlya Paulson and the likelihood of his involvement in her death. Not surprisingly, the authorities cannot close quickly enough the book on the series of blunders that brought about this sordid miscarriage of justice.

Meanwhile, Greg Treadway needs a job.

42

Dᴉsᴍᴀs Hᴀʀᴅʏ ᴘᴜᴛ down his coffee cup, moved his section of the newspaper to one side, waited a moment, then pulled it back in front of him. He lifted his cup, stopped midway to his mouth, put it back down in the saucer.

'What?' Frannie sat across the breakfast table.

'What what?'

'What are you reading that's so upsetting?'

'Jeff Elliott. If The Beck is any part of this, I'm going to have to flay her.'

'Any part of what?'

He pushed the paper over to her. 'Check it out.'

After a minute, Frannie looked back up at him. 'What's so troubling about this, Diz? He makes a good point. If they knew about another suspect, that should have made it to the trial, don't you think?'

'No, I don't think. That kind of evidence is inadmissible for a reason, and the reason is because it's unreliable. The Wilson girl might have accused Utlee for any number of reasons, just to pile on more bad shit that her boyfriend did being one of them. Nobody's talking about it because the verdict went our way, but I never heard any evidence that put Royce anywhere near the crime. There's just Wilson's accusations, nothing else.

'As far as I know, nobody's even looked into what he was doing that night. What if they look and find out he wasn't anywhere near downtown? Then what? Then our Mr Treadway is back on the hot seat, even though, thankfully, he can't be tried again. He could still have a really damn bad couple of years, if not the rest of his life, forget whether he's got a job or not. And that doesn't take into consideration how the wonderful Mr Treadway, a twenty-seven-year-old teacher, was having sex with the seventeen-year-old sister of one of his charges. I think everybody on the defense would be well served by leaving this whole thing alone.' He jabbed a finger in the direction of the paper. 'It's just dumb,' he said. 'It's bad for the firm. It's a bad idea, period. I swear to God, if this is The Beck—'

Hardy's cell phone rang and he snapped it out of its holster. 'Speak of the devil,' he said into the phone. 'I'm hoping no part of *CityTalk* is you.'

'No part at all. I told Allie it would just be opening another can of worms. But she wanted to help Greg.'

'We're done helping him, Beck. The firm is, anyway. He got off. We won. We broke out the champagne, and that should have been the end of it.'

'I agree with you. Talk to Allie.'

'I wish I had. And I wish you'd told me she was doing this.'

'I didn't know she was. I thought I'd persuaded her not to.'

'So what's it about?'

'You won't like it.'

'Probably not. I don't like anything I've heard up to now.'

'They're going out. Allie and Greg.'

Hardy went silent.

'Dad?'

'I'm here. I'm just swearing to myself.' He paused. 'Are they serious?'

'I would say so. Or at least moving in that direction pretty fast.'

'I'd be lying if I said that didn't worry me.'

'Me, too. I'm a little afraid that she's confusing "acquitted" with "innocent." '

'A little?'

'Okay, maybe mostly afraid. But I've got some residual reasonable doubt. Don't you?'

'Perhaps a drop. Basically, I don't want it to be our issue anymore. The trial, as you might have noticed, is over. And so, in theory, should be our relationship with the client, unless he gets accused of killing somebody else.'

'Don't even kid.'

'You think I'm kidding?'

'I don't believe Greg's a cold-blooded killer, Dad. I really don't.'

'Okay. But we haven't talked about whether he's a hot-blooded killer.'

'It's just that I worry about Allie. This Jeff Elliott thing . . .'

'And yet you just said you were mostly afraid that Allie has confused "acquitted" with "innocent." Which means you don't think he's innocent, either, somewhere deep inside.'

He heard her sigh into the phone. 'I don't know what to think.'

'You want to know what I think?'

'Sure.'

'I think he's a classic heavyweight narcissist. He was involved in all this do-gooder activity because it fit his image of what a special guy he is, but woe betide anybody who gets in his way. That's what I think. You notice he kept saying that he wasn't the kind of person who would do this or do that. Just like OJ wasn't the kind of person who would have killed his wife – I mean, he was a football player, he was a TV star, and he was charming to boot. To the point where I think at the end he might have believed it himself that he didn't kill Nicole. Hell, he might still believe it. It was only one minute out of his whole life. One little slip. How could the whole world hold that against him forever?'

'And you think that's Greg?'

'I don't know. He wasn't my client, and I never got to know him that well. But if I'm trying to imagine the scenario where he's involved in Anlya's death – I'm not saying he planned it. It's possible it even shocked him. They're having an argument and it gets heated and he gives her a push and they're at the parapet and she goes over. Holy shit! What happened?'

' "Holy shit! What happened?" That's it?'

'Exactly,' Hardy said. 'That's what I'm talking about.'

'And you're saying he can live with that?'

'Didn't seem to be a problem for OJ, did it?'

'Trevor Ames here.'

'Mr Ames, this is Greg Treadway. Jeff Elliott gave me your number and said you'd like to speak with me.'

'Yeah, thanks for getting back to me. I read that *CityTalk* column this morning, and though I don't often find myself agreeing with Elliott and all the liberal madness that makes it into his column every day, he's a pretty good writer. Anyway, I thought the story about what's going on with you was pretty goddamn appalling, if you know what I mean.'

'I appreciate that.'

Ames went on, 'I'm having trouble believing the mess this country's in, where these legal shenanigans keep the truth out of the picture, bunch of lawyers scratching each other's backs, deciding what's allowed into a courtroom and what's got to stay out. When, in your case, correct me if I'm wrong, they had this guy's girlfriend who knew what really happened, and they flat wouldn't let it in. It's the last goddamn words she ever spoke. You think she's about to die and she knows it and she's telling a lie?'

'No, sir. I never thought that. She knew it, and I believe what she said is exactly what happened. Royce killed Anlya, and that's all there was to it.'

'And Royce Utlee. Let me ask you something. That sounds like a black name to me. I'm betting he was black, wasn't he?'

'Yes.'

'All these people, they were black?'

'Right.'

'And this man Royce, he was a pimp, too?'

'Apparently so.'

Ames's voice boomed. 'Isn't that just too perfect? They're trying to protect the reputation of some black pimp lowlife who's already shot a cop and got himself killed for his troubles. All I can say is it's an act of God that you managed to get yourself acquitted when the whole might of the government already decided it was taking you down, even if it was going to ignore obvious evidence that you were innocent. And I mean that literally, a goddamn act of God.'

'Well, thank you.'

'It's a goddamn miracle you got Elliott to write up the story.'

'Yes. He seems like a good guy. And I had a really pretty advocate, which probably didn't hurt.'

A chuckle. 'It never does. So, anyway, why I left my number. You still looking for work?'

Greg forced a small laugh. 'Not to sound hungry, but I'm close to desperate. It's been four months since my last paycheck, and I think my mom and dad are just about tapped out.'

'Standing by you, though.'

'Always.'

'Good families. Strong families. That's what makes this country great. The part of it that still is, I mean.'

'I hear you.'

'Point is, I run a little company here in the city, cleverly named Trevor Ames. Financial analysis, logistics consulting, good clean work. Kind of like a smaller version of Deloitte. And maybe we're number two now, but in spite of all the goddamn regulations we've got to deal with at every turn, we got our heads way above water. And we're always looking for young, smart, hardworking talent. I Googled you and saw you went to both Berkeley and Stanford. Is that true?'

'It is.'

'That's about as good a pedigree as it gets in this neck of the woods, wouldn't you say?'

'I've been fortunate, I'll admit.'

'And modest to boot. How about we set up a meet in the next day or two and you come on downtown, see if we might be a fit, if you're at all interested in this kind of work.'

'That would be outstanding. It sounds interesting, and I'd love to talk about it. Thank you.'

'Don't thank me yet, boy. You come aboard, you'll work your ass off, I promise. But I got a feeling that before too long, I'll be the one thanking you.'

PROBABLY IT WOULD have been better if Rebecca hadn't suggested that she and Allie have a glass of wine before they started to make dinner or ordered some food in. After all, both had worked a very long day – it was now close to nine-thirty, and they'd just gotten home after driving in together and being at their desks by eight that morning. So the one glass of chardonnay each had turned to two each, and then the bottle was gone, and they still had no food on the horizon, and they opened the second bottle and had put a good dent in it – already 10:22, by the digital clock on the decorative-only fireplace mantel – when Allie carefully set her glass down on the living room's coffee table. 'I can't believe I'm hearing this from you,' she said. 'How long have you been feeling that?'

'Actually, since early on.'

'Really?' Snotty and sarcastic, the tone alone might have warned Rebecca to stop if she didn't want things to get ugly. But she was not at her most sensitive and observant. 'When early on?'

'Right at the beginning, Al. When he told all those lies to Waverly.'

'It wasn't "all those lies." It was like a couple of things that had nothing to do with anything, and he didn't want to muddy the waters.'

'Except it turned out they did have something to do with everything.'

'He didn't know that,' Allie protested. 'And he stayed while your dad called the police. I mean, why even admit he knew her?'

'Because he knew it would come out, and the best thing would be if he just owned up. Of course he knew her. Of course it was a shock, seeing her there on TV. What else was he going to do? Run out the door? No, he had to stay. You know that's exactly the argument I made, Allie, so I get what you're talking about.'

'And you still think there's a chance he did it? He actually did it?'

Rebecca inclined her head affirmatively. 'I'm not going to go over that again. I'm just worried about you, that's all.'

'You don't need to worry about me.'

'Of course I worry about you. You're my best friend. And now I see you're just getting back on your feet after the whole bar thing . . .'

'Oh, good, bring that up again.'

'I'm just saying—'

'I know what you're saying, Beck. That if you hadn't worried about me and hadn't pulled the strings that you did with your dad, I wouldn't even be here. That no one else would have taken me.'

'I never felt that.'

'Never just a little tiny bit superior?'

'God! No. Not even a little bit. You were my friend, and I was trying to help you out.'

'As long as I'm second.'

'That is so not true.'

'And now – don't think I don't see it clear as a bell, Beck – Greg likes me and you're jealous.'

'Of you and Greg? Are you kidding me?'

'I think it's pretty damned obvious. Not wanting me to help him get a job and – oh, look at this! – as soon as I finally do something over your very strong objections, guess what? Greg is back with a great opportunity, and you know who he's got to thank for that? Me. That's who. On my own, without having to do any part of it through you and your father.'

'My father? How is he even part of this conversation?'

'Because it's no secret how he feels. I know the only reason he's keeping me on is because of you. You don't think I feel that all the time?'

'That just isn't true. I don't know how you can say that.'

'The other thing is that he thinks Greg is guilty, too. His own lawyers, and everybody thinks he's guilty. The saddest thing is that you're all wrong, and you just keep feeding yourselves these lies to keep believing what you already think you know. It's horrible, you know that? Completely horrible.' Allie reached for her wineglass and drained it, then banged it down on the table and, unsteady, rose to her feet. 'I don't have to deal with this anymore, with being Miss Second Class, going out with the wrong guy whom you wish you could have and whom I happen to be in love with. Me. Who doesn't get the first choice. Well, I got it now, and I'm keeping it, and that's all there is to it.'

'Al. Come on. We're not—'

'We're not anything!' Allie yelled. 'We're not anything anymore. You want him and you can't have him, and that's what this is all about.' She cast an almost frantic gaze around the room. 'I'm done with all of this! All of it!'

She ran from the room and down the hallway, slamming her door hard enough that the windows rattled.

43

REBECCA ALMOST TURNED down her new roommate without an interview, because, really, how seriously was anybody going to take you if you hung out with a person named Bunny Schreckinger?

But the young woman was exactly Rebecca's age. She had a good job as a corporate recruiter, no crazy boyfriend, and probably wouldn't have any trouble making the rent. Another plus, she wasn't a lawyer. Rebecca had enough lawyers in her life every day, all day, and maybe having a regular workingwoman for a roommate would be a nice change of pace.

What clinched the arrangement was Bunny's bubbly personality and her enthusiasm over the idea that the two of them could conquer the city if they teamed up as the dynamic duo Beck and Shrek.

Deal.

OUTSIDE REBECCA'S OFFICE window, the blessed, perhaps drought-breaking rain was coming down in nearly horizontal sheets. It had started around noon and only increased over the past eight hours as the dark, dark night had fallen. Now, alone in her office, she was catching up on some nonbillable administrative work that she'd let slide during the week she'd been up at Lake Tahoe with her mom and dad and brother between Christmas and New Year's.

When the phone rang, she gave it the evil eye, then

automatically saved the document she'd been working on and picked up. 'Rebecca Hardy.'

'Hey, it's me.' Shrek, in a nervous whisper.

'You sound funny. Is everything all right?'

'Not really. Your ex-roommate – Allie? – she's here. She says her boyfriend hit her.'

'God, that asshole.' Rebecca hadn't laid eyes on Allie since her former roommate had gone to work at another firm within two weeks of moving out of their apartment and in with Greg Treadway. Tonight's news didn't shock her to her roots, but it was very disconcerting. 'How bad is she?' she asked.

'Bad enough. Her jaw's swollen and her lip is cut. I think it's a nine-one-one moment, but she's begging me not to make that call.'

'Oh, sure, let's protect that jerk.'

'You know him?'

'He was my client last summer, and I've been afraid of something like this. Shit. Where is she now?'

'I've got her covered up on the couch. I told her I was calling you. Wait, just a second. Here she is.'

Allie's voice came through fragile and raspy. 'Hey, Beck. I'm so sorry to bother you, but I just had to get away and didn't know where else I could go.'

'Don't worry about that. Are you all right? That's the main thing.'

'Mostly. I don't know what happened. We were having this argument, about nothing, really, and all of a sudden he just—'

'Don't worry about that. You're all right now. Do you want to call the police from there, or should I do it from here?'

'No! I mean neither, you know.'

'No, I don't know. If Greg hit you, you've got to report it.'

'Beck, please. You know the history, what it would look like. That can't happen.'

'That's especially why it has to happen, Al.'

'Can we please not talk about that right now?'

'Okay, but we're going to have to talk about it sometime, and sooner rather than later. I can be home in twenty minutes, maybe a half hour. Are you okay till then?'

'I should be.'

'Okay. Just wait. I'll be right there.'

'THE POINT IS, Dad, I don't know what to do.'

'I think you have to call the police and get this on the record, even if I don't think there's much you'll be able to do, sweetie. If she's adamant that she won't talk to the police, you're stuck. When they show up, she'll just lie. If they've already patched things up, which you can pretty much bet on, then the DV' – domestic violence – 'guys ring their bell and Greg and Allie tell them they haven't been fighting. And you, you're not even a neighbor who filed a noise complaint. It's a dead end, but I'd say probably still worth doing.'

'I can't believe Allie would let this happen to her.'

'I'm afraid it happens every day.'

'I feel like I should do something more.'

Hardy's sigh came through the line. 'I hate to say "Get involved" because of all the bad overtones, Beck, but my best advice to you is to get at least a little bit involved. Make her feel better tonight if you can. In terms of Greg, you can't live her life for her, but maybe you can get her to think about things with him. If she wants to put up with this, there's very little you can do. It'll just have to run its course one way or the other.'

'That's what I'm afraid of. Run its course like it did with Anlya.'

'Hopefully not like that.'

'He did that, didn't he?'

'It's looking more like that now than it did yesterday, I'll give you that. And even yesterday, to me, it looked pretty good.'

'And I got him off.'

'That was your job, and you did it.'

'Okay, I'll grant you that. But you see why I might feel just a teeny bit responsible for what's happening now with him and Allie?'

'That's between him and Allie, Beck. You didn't put them together. If memory serves, and it always does, you went out of your way to talk her out of seeing him after the trial.'

'Only because I wanted him for myself,' she said with heavy irony. 'Don't forget that.'

'I never would. Bottom line, she can be your friend, but this isn't your business.'

'She came to my apartment, Dad. Doesn't that make it my business a little?'

'As far as that goes, be her friend, sure. Tonight. And speaking as your father, let's not forget that from now on, we ought to be considering Greg a very dangerous guy. If you can think of a way to get some cops involved in how he's treating Allie, that might not be a bad idea. As to you yourself doing anything that might get his attention, I'd keep my distance. Really. You think you can do that for your old man's sake?'

Rebecca sighed. 'I'll try, Daddy,' she said. 'I'll really try. Meanwhile, they're waiting for me at my apartment, and I really should be going by now.'

'Then by all means go,' her father said. 'Ride like the wind, but carefully, okay? The roads are a mess.'

'I'll be careful,' she said, thinking, Jesus.

REBECCA, OUT OF breath, hair dripping onto her already soaked raincoat, came in through her building's front entrance and half ran down the hallway to her apartment. Her hands were shaking with the cold or nerves, and it took her a couple of stabs to get the key in and turn it. Finally, it caught and she pushed at the door, which opened directly into the living room.

When she stepped in, the light was a little unnaturally

dim, but she saw Shrek on the couch and Allie, wrapped in a blanket, sitting on the facing chair, their expressions tense and furtive. 'Hi, guys,' she began. 'Sorry that took so long. It's just crazy—'

Before she could go any further, and before it could dawn on her that the two women were each sitting in a strained and unnatural position, their faces painted with fear, someone kicked at the door and it slammed closed behind her.

Startled, she whirled. Greg Treadway stood a couple of feet behind her, his hand outstretched, holding a gun pointing directly at her face, the O at the end of the barrel drawing all of her attention. 'That really wasn't too long, Rebecca,' he said. 'I'd say it was just about perfect. I only beat you here by about ten minutes. I'm afraid it took me a while to figure out where Allie must have gone. I know, now that we're all here, it's so obvious. That was a little slow of me, but no worries. You were a little slower. Now get away from the door. Easy. Sit on the couch with your roommate, here, and put your purse on the floor by your feet. Now.'

Rebecca obeyed, stealing a glance at the other two women, both of whom sat straight up, terrified, meek, and submissive, hands folded in their laps. It was immediately clear to Rebecca that if any of them had a chance – even if only to buy a few more precious moments of life for all of them – it would be her.

She started to speak, but nothing came out. Clearing her throat, she leveled her gaze at him. 'Greg,' she said, 'what are you doing?'

Out of the shadows now, he stood – the gun for the moment at his side – under the wide arch that delineated the living room's entrance. 'I would think that would be obvious, wouldn't you?'

'Not really, no. I see the gun, but that makes no sense. What are you going to do with a gun? Since when do you even have a gun?'

This brought a small acknowledging nod. 'Since that great patriot Trevor Ames hired me. He believes in every American's God-given right to bear arms, and I must say that, after a lot of reflection, I don't think he's all wrong. When he brings new people on board, the first thing he does is cut a bonus check that we're supposed to use to buy the weapon of our choice, if we don't already have one.'

She pointed. 'And that's the gun you bought?'

'No. No, no, no, Beck. If it were my gun, registered to me, then I really couldn't use it the way I need to tonight. A guy learns a few things if he spends some time in jail, believe me. This' – he held it up – 'is a gun I bought on the street in Oakland last month when I first started to think that things with me and Allie were going to end badly. Eventually. I thought it would be a good idea to be prepared for when the day came.'

'For what, exactly?'

He tsked. 'Rebecca, you're not that slow. You're not slow at all.'

'You're going to kill the three of us? In cold blood?' She shook her head. 'There's just no way, Greg. No fucking way.' She started to get up.

Stepping forward, he raised the gun, pointing it at her face. 'Sit back down, or I swear to God I will shoot you dead right now.'

She hesitated for a second, cast a frustrated glance at Shrek and at Allie, then sighed and lowered herself back down. 'Do you mind telling us why? And while we're at it, why Anlya?'

He was standing five feet or so from her, in front of the faux mantel. 'That was a mistake. I never meant for that to happen. I'm not the kind of person who would . . . or I wasn't. I'm still not. This is not going to continue, after tonight, I mean. This is not how I wanted anything to turn out. I just wanted her to move out. It wasn't working between us, and she just kept fighting me on it.'

'You're talking Allie now?'

'Of course. What did it sound like?'

Allie found her voice. 'I'll move out, Greg. I'm sorry. I didn't understand. I'll never talk about any of this. I'll never tell anybody you hit me.'

'You made me hit you! You could have just left.'

'I did. I did. I'm sorry. It's not too late, though. I've forgotten it already. I mean it. I'll just let it go and leave forever, and you'll never have to think about me again.'

'No. You can't now.'

'I can.'

'No. Because now you've told her.' Pointing at Rebecca. 'And she would never let it go. Would you, Beck?'

'The two of you could talk me into it, I'm sure.'

Greg barked out a quick laugh. 'Hah. Not after Allie came here tonight. That's what settled it.'

'All right,' Rebecca said. She threw out another gambit to keep him distracted. 'But you started talking about Anlya.'

'Anlya.' He shook his head with what appeared to be real sadness. 'I shouldn't have done what we did. The sex, I mean. I didn't plan that. I—'

Rebecca shot back at him. 'You used a condom, Greg. Of course you planned it.'

'*I didn't plan it!*' The thought, or maybe Rebecca's disregard of his excuse, clearly enraged him. And still he gathered himself to explain it all away. 'This just in, Beck. Smart guys carry condoms on the off chance. It wasn't about the condom.'

'No? What was it about, then? Love?'

For the third time, he raised the gun at her. 'You think this is a joke? You're making fun of me?'

'No. I think it's pathetic, not funny.'

Lowering the gun, he shook his head. 'You weren't there. We got to the car, and she just wouldn't stop crying. I was trying to tell her it would be all right. Maybe I loved her in some way, okay, but we couldn't do anything about it. It wasn't right. She was too young. If nothing else, no matter what I wanted, maybe what we both wanted, it would be illegal. If anybody found out, it would be the end of my job, my career. I might even go to jail. But she just wouldn't hear about it.'

'And one thing led to another?'

'I'm human, goddammit! How much am I supposed to be able to take? It got to a certain point and I gave in. All right? I fell.'

'And so you had to kill her?'

'I told you. That was a mistake. I never meant . . . I mean after, we went for a walk to talk things out. I couldn't make her understand that it couldn't happen again. We had to put it behind us and go on from there. Maybe in a year, when she was . . . in a different situation. But she wouldn't hear of that. And then we're getting back near the garage, and she became like a different person and out of nowhere started threatening me. If we weren't going to be together, then that meant I had used her, didn't it? I didn't really love her at all. If I did, I'd want to be with her, wouldn't I?'

'What could she threaten you with, Greg? This teenager?'

'She said she would claim I raped her, that I forced her. That if I really tried to leave her, if I went ahead and dumped her, then it would get bad for me. She would tell whoever she needed to, to get me punished. If I thought I was in trouble now, I should just wait. I mean, she just went crazy. You have to understand that. That's the main thing. She wasn't like I'd ever seen her before, holding on to me, grabbing me, not letting me go, begging me not to leave her, just crying out. "Please please please." That was when it went so wrong. All the noise in the world, right there out on the street, where any minute somebody could come up on us. She kept begging and wouldn't let me go.'

'So you pushed her?'

'Just to get her off me.'

'And over the wall.'

Greg grabbed a staggering breath. 'I never even saw the wall. I didn't know it was that low. I wasn't even aware of it.'

'And she went over.'

For a second or two, all was dead silence.

'I never meant to hurt her,' he whispered. 'I never meant to hurt anybody. I'm a good person. It was just one second of weakness.'

'That's not what killing us would be, Greg,' Rebecca said. 'Killing us would make you a real murderer, not an accidental one.'

'No. That wouldn't be my fault. This – what's happening here – isn't my fault. You've both pushed me to this. You and Allie.'

'And what about me?' Shrek said in a small voice. 'Why am I part of this?'

He shrugged as though truly apologizing. 'I'm sorry, I really am, but I'm afraid you're going to have to be collateral damage.'

He looked down at the gun in his hand, drew a breath, and started to raise it.

Three sharp raps on the front door, Dismas Hardy's voice behind it. 'Beck! Are you in there? Open up!'

Whirling halfway around, since he'd been facing Shrek, Greg extended the gun and fired twice in rapid succession into the upper center of the door. Without any hesitation, he started to turn back toward his three captives, but while he still mostly faced the door, he'd barely squeezed off the second shot when Rebecca saw her only chance and threw herself off the couch, headfirst into Greg's body, slamming him up against the mantel.

The gun went off again.

Swinging wildly, Greg was all elbows as he went down under Rebecca. She slammed the hand that held the gun into the wall behind him once, twice, a third time.

But Greg was stronger than she was, and she couldn't knock it loose.

With a screaming grunt, he managed to throw her off him, bringing the gun around to bear . . .

The front door exploded open and Abe Glitsky followed it in. 'Drop it! Don't move! Drop it!' He had a gun leveled at Treadway, who was sitting halfway up on the floor, frozen as though in a tableau before he locked his gaze on Glitsky, registered the gun pointed at his heart, and in one swift move brought his own gun up to his right temple.

'Put it down!' Glitsky said. 'Just let it go.'

'I can't. I'm sorry. I never meant for any of this to happen.'

'That doesn't matter. Let go of the gun. Now.'

Treadway directed a flat gaze at Abe. 'This is not who I am,' he said. His gun still pressed up against his head, he cast a glance at Rebecca, the other women, and finally, back at Glitsky. 'I am so so sorry. This has all gone so wrong.'

He pulled the trigger.

In the crowded room, all became stillness and shock.

His gun now at his side, Glitsky stared at the scene for a beat as Treadway slumped down and Rebecca scrambled around and struggled unsteadily to her feet.

'Anybody else hurt?' Glitsky stepped over closer to Treadway to make sure he wasn't moving, then turned to The Beck. 'Call nine-one-one,' he said. 'Your dad's down out here in the hallway.'

44

THE DOCTOR EMERGED from the operating room a little after one-thirty A.M. To Rebecca's eyes, her light blue scrubs sported a disconcerting amount of bloodstains. Her face was drawn with tension and fatigue. Neither, Rebecca thought, was a good sign.

Frannie let go of Rebecca's hand, and both of them stood up from the couch they'd been sharing. Glitsky, who'd arrived only ten minutes before, and Vincent, who'd made it up from Menlo Park in just over a half hour, got to their feet as well.

Her hand to her mouth, Frannie took a tentative step toward the doctor, who held up a calming hand, and some of the lines around her eyes seemed to soften. For an instant, Rebecca let herself entertain a flutter of hope.

'Let's start with the good stuff,' the doctor said. 'Your husband is going to live.'

The hand that had been over Frannie's mouth went down to cover her heart. 'Oh, thank God,' she said as tears began to overflow onto her cheeks. Her two children came up to flank her in a tangle of arms.

Off to the side, ignoring the relieved relatives, Glitsky said, 'What's the bad stuff?'

'Well, it's not all that bad. He'll have some recovering to do. He's weak from blood loss. Otherwise, he's got a broken rib that's going to hurt for a while but which stopped one of the bullets before it hit his heart. The wound itself isn't deep, and neither is the one where the slug bounced off his skull.'

Frannie, allowing a pulse of laughter through her steady tears, said, 'He's always had a really hard head.'

'His rib stopped a bullet?' Vincent asked. 'How does that happen?'

'They were twenty-twos,' Glitsky explained, 'and they went through a hollow-core door first, which tends to slow things down. Still, pretty lucky.'

'If you've got to get shot in the first place,' Vincent said.

'Well, yeah,' Glitsky said. 'That.'

THE FOLLOWING SATURDAY, Wyatt Hunt sat in the sand at Fort Point. It was a miserably cold and rainy day, but he was in his wet suit, and that didn't matter too much. Next to him, in Hunt's wife's borrowed wet suit, Max Paulson jumped to his feet, wanting to get back to the windboards and give it another try. He hadn't had a lot of luck staying up, with the near gale and the accompanying deep swells running in under the Golden Gate, but he was stoked by the entire experience.

That day the previous summer when Leon Copes had been arrested outside Sharla's house, after they'd stopped by the Bezdekian grocery to return the goods Max had stolen, Hunt had laid some good-natured grief on Max for having made him miss his planned day of windboarding. Max had told Hunt that he'd love to try it sometime, and though neither of them had followed up, obviously, Max had meant it, because when Hunt called to tell him about the end of Greg Treadway and his confession that he'd killed Anlya, Max had brought up the topic again: How about if Hunt took him down and gave him a lesson?

And now here they were.

'Let's give it another five,' Hunt said. 'Catch a little more breath. It'll beat you up out there if you're not careful.'

'Okay, but I'm good to go,' Max said, 'just so you know.'

'I'm sure you are, and I am, too,' Hunt replied. 'But I

need a couple more minutes. That last ride wore me out. Up as long as I was and all.'

'Rubbing it in, now,' Max said, showing the trace of a smile.

'Just sayin',' Hunt replied.

With obvious reluctance, Max lowered himself to a squat. 'All right.' He sifted some sand through his hands. 'So do you mind if I ask how much all of this cost?'

'All what?'

'You know. The wet suits, the boards, the gear?'

'The car to pack it in?'

Another smile. 'That, too, I suppose.'

'A lot. But you don't need to worry about it,' Hunt said. 'Give me some warning, and we can come out together again. Make it a regular thing.'

'I don't want to be a pest.'

'You get close to pestiness, I'll let you know. Meanwhile, bringing up the elephant in the living room – or on the beach, in this case – how are you holding up with the Treadway news?'

Max shrugged. 'I don't feel much of anything. He's gone. The world's a better place for that, I suppose. But nothing's going to bring Anlya back, and that's the only thing I'd care about that might make any difference. I guess it was good to find out for sure it was Greg who did it. Which didn't surprise me, though for a while there I was pretty sure it was Leon.'

'The elusive Leon.'

'You got it.'

Hunt clucked in frustration. 'That's the one thing I didn't get about that night, that just didn't make any sense. I mean, why was Leon there? In the private-eye business, there's a rule that there's no such thing as coincidence. And in this case, it's like, really? He just happened to be in that tunnel at that moment? Are you shitting me?'

Max glanced at him sideways. 'That wasn't it,' he said.

'What do you mean?'

'I mean it wasn't a coincidence. Leon went down there looking for her.'

'He did? How did he know where—'

'Because he was staying with Sharla that day when Anlya called her.'

'The day she was killed?'

'Yeah. And she told Sharla about her date with Greg, all excited about it. They were going to Chinatown, her favorite. And right after Leon finds out about that . . .'

'How's he do that? Find out, I mean.'

'Sharla just tells him. And as soon as she does, Leon lights out on Anlya's trail.'

'But why?'

'With Leon, you can never be sure, but Sharla told us – me and Auntie Juney – that he thought Anlya was a threat to him. She knew he was back with Sharla, she might tell somebody about him raping her, and that could get him back in jail.'

'So he went down there looking for her?'

Max nodded. 'Pretty obviously. He knew where she was going, and he wanted to talk to her. At least talk to her, maybe shut her up. So there it is, no coincidence at all. Just Sharla being Sharla. But when I told her about Greg, that he'd admitted he was guilty to three witnesses, I could tell it put her mind a bit at ease. Sharla might have told Leon where Anlya would be, but at least he didn't kill her, which means she didn't actually help her daughter's murderer, albeit inadvertently.'

'Albeit inadvertently?'

Max broke into a sheepish grin. 'Sorry. Debate Club words.'

'It's okay,' Hunt said, 'I can handle them. Hang out with lawyers like I do, and you get a lot of that, albeit inadvertently.'

•   •   •

ON THAT SAME Saturday, Rebecca finished her lunch at the family home on Thirty-Fourth Avenue, then went into the living room to check up on her pajama-clad father, who'd been asleep in his reading chair when she arrived.

Apparently, he still was.

She stood in front of him for a minute or two, then came closer and went down on one knee. He looked fairly old and battered, with several days of gray stubble and his head wrapped in gauze. Maybe he felt the weight of her gaze on him, maybe he became subliminally aware of her breathing, but suddenly, he opened his eyes. His expression softened before he closed his eyes for another second or two, then he reached out and touched her shoulder.

'How's my girl?' he asked.

'I'm good. A little freaked out about humanity but holding on. The question is, how are you?'

'I'd kind of forgotten how much fun it is to get shot, but otherwise peachy.'

'Peachy?'

'Relatively speaking. Everything still hurts more than I think it should, but that's probably me just being a wimp.'

'Probably. That's what Uncle Abe would say, anyway.'

'Then it must be true.'

'So' – she hesitated – 'I've got a question.'

'Wait,' he said. 'I've got an answer. Kevin Costner and Susan Sarandon.'

'That's not it. It's nothing about *Bull Durham*.'

'Darn. Best movie ever made, in my opinion.'

'Undoubtedly. But unfortunately not what my question is about.'

'Okay, then. What?'

Rebecca sat down on the corner of his ottoman. 'Why in the world did you show up at my place, and with Uncle Abe, no less?'

'Ah, that.'

'That,' she said.

'Well, remember when you called me to ask my opinion about what you should do with Allie and Greg just before you left to go home and meet up with her?'

'Sure.'

'And then as you were driving home, I'm afraid I called you again, didn't I? Just to make sure that you were driving carefully and the roads weren't too bad?'

'Yep.'

'When I got the very distinct impression that you thought I was being paranoid and a little overboard in the parental area.'

'Slightly.'

'And I asked you to call me after you got home and made sure everything was okay. And I made you promise you would, in spite of the fact that I knew you thought I was being ridiculous.'

'Okay.'

'Well, I was even more paranoid than you thought. It turns out I've had a little more experience with domestic violence than most people, and it struck me not as likely, exactly, but certainly not impossible that Greg would figure out where Allie had run to and would follow her there to try and get her back. That kind of stuff happens all the time. Not that I thought he'd have a gun with him – that never occurred to me – but it might get ugly. And the more I thought about it, given the fact that I always believed the guy was a killer, the more worried I got about it.'

'You should have called me back a third time.'

'Perhaps, but since you obviously already thought I was insane if not downright ridiculous around the topic, I called Abe instead and ran it down for him. And, God bless him, because he's a paranoid parent, too, he thought I might have a point. At least enough of one to be worth going by your place and the two of us meeting up, and if you called me and told me everything was cool, we'd just go back to our respective homes. But you never did. So when we got worried enough, I sneaked up and listened at the door and heard a male voice. I knocked, with Abe there beside me, backing me up. And the rest, as they say, is history.'

'No,' she said. 'History is a reasoned account of all the facts that have proved important in explaining human progress.'

'That, too.' Hardy leaned his head back against the chair, a grin tickling at the corner of his lips. 'And you, my darling daughter, are turning into just a little bit of a wiseass.'

'Gee,' she said. 'I wonder where I would have gotten that.'

Acknowledgments

This book got its start when I made a visit to Executive Director Renee Espinoza at the office of Court Appointed Special Advocates (CASA) on Mission Street in San Francisco. Renee showed me around the office and the neighborhood and was extremely generous with her time and expertise.

About midway through this story, I found myself stymied by the motivations of some of my main characters. Fortuitously, at a dinner party, I got into a discussion with Cora Stryker, a wonderful writer and winner of the UC Davis Maurice Prize in long-form fiction, and she effortlessly turned the key in what had been a locked door, and the motivations all clicked into place. Thanks, Cora, you saved me on this one.

My brother-in-law, Mark Detzer, Ph.D., was extremely helpful in clarifying some important psychological issues that arose as the story progressed. Also within my family, I've been inspired by the next generation and some of the details of their education, lives, and work – my daughter and (brand-new) son-in-law, Justine and Josh Kastan, my son, Jack, and my niece, Robyn Shaffer.

On a day-to-day basis, I remain forever grateful to the diligence, sparkling personality, and total efficiency of my assistant, Anita Boone, a mind reader and organizer extraordinaire without whom not only would these books of mine not appear in anything like a timely manner, but also the plants in my office would die. Also, here's a general thank-you to some folks who have kept life fun and interesting this past year: my partners in the Guys' Book Club – Max Byrd, Geoff Owen, Herb Berkoff, Tom Hedtke, and Andy Wallace; Alan Heit (Abe Glitsky's prototype); my brothers, Mike and Emmett; Frank Seidl, Bob Zaro, Chuck Krouse, and Glenn Nedwin.

As with all of my other legal books, this one owes much of its verisimilitude and flavor to the brilliant Alfred F. Giannini, Esq. Al missed his true calling as a book editor, but he made up for it with forty or so years of prosecuting homicides in San Francisco and San Mateo counties, and I have been blessed to be a recipient of some of his vast store of legal (and all sorts of other arcane) knowledge.

Several people have generously contributed to charitable organizations by purchasing the right to name a character in this book. These people and their respective organizations are: Karl Bakhtiari and Steve Rutledge (Serra Fund A Dream); Neal Schreckinger and Maureen Barrett (Brenda Novak's Online Auction for Diabetes Research); Richard and Connie Adams (San Francisco Court Appointed Special Advocates); and Kathy Pelz (Napa County Library Literacy Center/ Charitybuzz.com).

Taking great care of the entire social media package, including my Web page (www.johnlescroart.com), blog, Facebook, Twitter (www.twitter.com/johnlescroart), is the inimitable Dr Andy Jones (poet laureate of the city of Davis, CA). I'd also like to thank Doug Kelly and Peggy Nauts, who have been giving a last editing pass on my books for most of the past decade. Hopefully, by the time they're done, we've caught the last of all the typos and grammatical and factual errors that seem to want to show up in the finished book.

I am proud to be published by Atria Books, so thank you very much to my publisher, Judith Curr, and my editor, Peter Borland, for giving me the opportunity to work with one of the best imprints in the world. Thanks also to the efforts of the publicity and marketing departments at Atria, especially the indefatigable David Brown.

Finally, I truly love to hear from my readers, and I invite one and all to stop by any of the sites mentioned above and join the party.

The Hunter

John Lescroart

It started with an anonymous text:

How did your mother die?

Private Investigator Wyatt Hunt has never been interested in finding his birth parents, but the discovery that his mother was murdered and the main suspect was his father leaves him with no choice but to take on a case he never knew existed.

With the trail of the forty-year-old case long gone cold, Hunt's first priority is to find out who the mysterious texter is and that person's connection to him. But in confronting his past, could Hunt find himself up against a killer who's still very much alive and very dangerous?

From the dark streets of San Francisco to the Jonestown massacre in the remote jungles of Guyana, thrillermaster John Lescroart weaves a shocking tale about the skeletons inside family closets and the mortal danger outside the front door.

Praise for John Lescroart:

'This book succeeds on every level' *Publishers Weekly*

978 0 7553 9316 9

headline

The Ophelia Cut

John Lescroart

When Moses McGuire's daughter is raped by her ex-boyfriend, Rick Jessup, he vows to get his revenge. So when Rick is found dead the next day, Moses is arrested for murder.

Dismas Hardy has no hesitation in defending his old friend but as the evidence against him starts piling up Hardy can't help wondering, what if he's actually guilty? And to make matters even more complicated, the case threatens to bring to light an old secret that could destroy Hardy's career.

With the trial going against him, Hardy must draw on all his legal ingenuity until he sees a new way forward that might just save them all. But at what price?

Praise for John Lescroart:

'The best of the best' Lee Child

'John Lescroart is a terrific writer' Jonathan Kellerman

'Breathtaking' LA Times

978 0 7553 9322 0

headline

The Keeper

John Lescroart

When Hal Chase's wife, Katie, goes missing and he becomes the prime suspect for her murder, he wants Dismas Hardy as his lawyer.

Hardy calls on former homicide detective Abe Glitsky to look into the case. Chase certainly had strong motives but as Glitsky delves deeper, he identifies other possible suspects and he also uncovers an incident that might be related - the death of an inmate in the jail where Chase used to work.

When Katie's body is discovered, Chase is arrested and finds himself in his old jail, a place full of secrets he knows all too well.

Against a backdrop of conspiracy and corruption, an obsessed Glitsky closes in on the elusive truth. But as other deaths begin to pile up he realises that the next victim might be himself.

Praise for John Lescroart:

'Lescroart satisfies with every bite, and the finale is delicious' Jeff Ayers

978 0 7553 9324 4

headline

THRILLINGLY GOOD BOOKS
FROM CRIMINALLY
GOOD WRITERS

CRIME FILES BRINGS YOU THE LATEST RELEASES FROM TOP CRIME AND THRILLER AUTHORS.

SIGN UP ONLINE FOR OUR MONTHLY NEWSLETTER AND BE THE FIRST TO KNOW ABOUT OUR COMPETITIONS, NEW BOOKS AND MORE.